I0647825

Will of the Alpha 3

Edited by Rechan and Lafitte

Will of the Alpha 3

Copyright © 2015 by Rechan and Lafitte

Cover artwork by Sabretoothed Ermine (furaffinity. net/user/sabretoothedermine)

Published by FurPlanet Productions
Dallas, Texas
www.furplanet.com

Print ISBN 978-1-61450-293-7
eBook ISBN 978-1-61450-294-4

Printed in the United States of America
First Edition Trade Paperback 2015

TABLE OF CONTENTS

Plow Mare

Patrick "Bahumat" Rochefort

The sound of steel grating on asphalt shouldn't have struck anyone as sexy. But for the reindeer buck standing in lycra and leather in the doorway of the gym's loading dock, it was a sound he wouldn't miss for the world. The source of that sound was Holly, a big brown Clydesdale mare in the sledge harness.

She had her head down and eyes forward, fingertips brushing the asphalt of the service road behind the gym. Sweat ran off of her in streams, her powerful lungs pumping like bellows, nostrils flared wide in the Los Angeles summer heat. Her lycra gym suit bled moisture and air away from her fur, leather straining around her shoulders and hips as she leaned into the traces. The sledge behind her weighed sixty-five pounds alone, and she'd loaded on eleven plates atop it. Four hundred and ninety-five pounds of free weights rattled atop the sledge as steel grated on asphalt underneath, reverberating against cinder-block walls and the cement of the loading dock.

Like a titan, she struggled and surged against the weight behind her, the great muscles in her thighs and buttocks driving her explosively forward, lunge after lunge. Across the alley, and then back the other way, forty yards each time. She stank of sweat and exercise, of mare and leather and burnt adrenaline. It was a smell that made Eric's cock twitch, as he absently thumbed an itch at the base of his antlers. Watching her and catching her in that moment sent a clear, pulsing line from his balls to his brain: *I would fuck her for days.*

Holly flashed him a look as she unhooked her pulling harness from the sledge, and then sank her hands slowly onto her knees, heaving long, deep breaths. She wasn't an idiot; lycra didn't hide much, and this was the third time the buck had shown up while she was pulling, waiting to take his turn on the sledge after her. But he was handsome enough and wasn't being a creep, and she had to admit, it made her a little less nervous about being out in a Los Angeles alleyway in clothes that might as well have been painted on. And maybe, just maybe, it made her work just a little bit harder, knowing someone was watching her.

She could out-pull any of the regulars in the gym, and she made sure they knew it.

When she could breathe well enough to form the words, she called: "What weight do you want it at?" gesturing to the sledge.

"Four-eighty," he called back. He dug into his gym bag, and produced a sports drink that was a virulent shade of electric blue. He walked over and offered it to her. "Here. You'll kill yourself pulling in this heat."

Another day, another person, she'd have turned it down. But it was ninety degrees outside, and the bottle sparkled with condensation. And as far as offers for buying a girl a drink went, it was the right time and place. She accepted it with a nod, ran her thumb along the security seal on the cap of the bottle just in case, and found it intact.

"Thanks," she said. She straightened upright, opened the bottle, and poured most of it down her throat in a long, glorious swallow.

The sun hit her lycra and mane just right, and sparkled off of her sweat, and it was enough to make Eric's mouth go dry. She was the picture of some Amazonian ideal; six foot six, heavyset with muscle but no less feminine for it, and she looked exactly like the sort of woman ready to haul a small car's worth of weight behind her with a grin.

"Are you done staring, yet?" she said when she lowered the bottle.

"Nah, go ahead and finish," said Eric with a good-natured grin.

It was a response that was candid and frank, and it was accompanied by a disarming smile. Holly couldn't help feeling a little creeping heat around her cheeks. She gave him a snort, but didn't bother to hide the smile as she downed the rest of the bottle. It tasted like blue chemicals and artificial sweeteners and glorious electrolytes. It was the best damn thing she'd tasted all day.

Holly crunched the plastic bottle up in her hands and passed it back. "Alright, what's your name?"

"Eric Haugen," he replied. He tossed the bottle into the dumpster, and walked back to help her unload the first plate off the sledge.

"Well Eric, I'm Holly. What're you training for?"

"Plowshares," he said, as he helped her walk the plate over to the rack, slotting the heavy steel carefully into place.

"Is that like a church event?" she asked.

Eric shook his head, a gesture that sent his antlers swinging emphatically. "No, though there's some overlap. It's a non-profit group. We volunteer to pull plow for community gardens. Help clear the land, pull stumps, plow earth, help plow up potatoes. That kind of thing."

Holly's ears perked. "Okay, that's kind of cool. So it's like old-timey farming, then?"

Eric smiled and hooked his harness into the tracers, then began the careful process of checking his harness and straps. It would be too easy to injure himself if any part of the rigging snapped under tension.

"Pretty much, yeah. It's a good workout and all, but mostly, it just feels great to be helping out the community. Put food on their table, make sure families that can't afford much can get good produce on their plates."

Despite herself, Holly smiled. "Well, that sounds like a hell of a thing, Eric."

"What do you pull for?" he asked her, his eyes meeting hers.

It should have been an innocuous question, but there was a weight to the words, a hungry search for meaning in Eric's tone, that brought Holly up short. It was a question that expected a serious response. She put her hand carefully on the sledge.

"Fine. For the drink, I'll tell you the real, politically incorrect answer," she said, tail flicking side to side behind her. "It's not 'PC' to say it, I know, what with all the post-Uplift politics and bullshit. But when I pull it still feels like what I was made for, you know? I lean into the harness, and I pull, and for a little while I can shut off my brain and be an animal again, and I like that. My world gets to be simple, for a few minutes at a time."

Eric gave a thoughtful smile. "Well if a sports drink gets me an answer that good, what kind of answer does dinner and a glass of wine get me?"

She snorted, and pointed at the alleyway. "Tell you what, cocky boy. When you can do four hundred yards with that, I'll let you find out."

The buck gave a groan. "You're a real slave driver. My regular is two-eighty," he said with a low laugh.

"You want a shot at something this good, buddy, you're getting off easy," she said with an imperious toss of her mane. The wet splat of her sweat-soaked hair hitting her shoulder ruined the effect, and they both cracked a little laugh simultaneously.

"Alright, no arguments there," he said, raising his chin, meeting her eye with a bold smile. "But you have to watch. Gotta keep me honest, right?"

Holly gave his lycra-covered ass a deliberate glance, pursing her lips in approval. "Fair's fair."

It was double his usual distance, at that weight; and he strained his weight forward against the sledge. The hot sun beat down, and the buck's pulse pounded in his ears, breath rising from deep, gulping breaths to animalistically hoarse panting. Four hundred yards, that was ten times from the loading dock across the alleyway and back again.

Holly found a patch of clean-ish concrete around the loading dock, and sat back. She turned her head up to the sun, enjoying the cool-down. Her thighs and ass ached, and Eric wasn't hard to look at; just as the lycra of her gym suit had glued itself to her, so it did for the buck straining on the sledge weight. Watching Eric's ass and shoulders flex under the sheer black lycra gave her a warm feeling in the pit of her belly. When he reached the end of the alley and turned around, the way he locked eyes with her gave her tail the right kind of twitch.

She kept herself in damn fine shape, and that didn't make it so hard to attract men, but few of them attracted her. Eric, she decided, had a good shot. He moved with strength and care, and the passion he talked about helping others out with his plowing was infectious.

"One down, nine to go," she told Eric. And then she called out: "Three."

"Three what?" he answered over his shoulder, shouting to be heard over the noise of the steel sledge grating along behind him.

Holly smiled. "Three's the first number of my phone number."

Eric barked a laugh, nodding, and kept pulling. The rest of the numbers he committed to memory as he earned them: One, zero, eight, four, four, six. But just after the seventh number of ten, his legs gave out. Wobbling like jelly, he fell to his knees. The buck panted hard in the harness, grateful for the tension holding him upright.

"Oooh. Good try, Eric," she said, rising up to her feet with a tail-swish and smile. "Better luck next week."

* * *

Stacey stirred her martini, the ewe eyeballing her salad in comparison to the big bowl of oats and lentils Holly was devouring.

"Damn, Holly. If I ate that much I'd die," Stacey said, nibbling around the strawberry on her fork. "How much do you have to eat, working out that hard?"

"Mmn. Four thousand calories, about," Holly said around a spoonful of lentil-oat mash.

"What *for*? I mean, you're way beyond jacked, now. You're built like a fucking linebacker, Holly."

Holly smiled. "I like feeling strong. I like being strong. It feels good, you know? I mean, come on. I'm never going to be little and cute like you are, Stacey. So I've got to own what I have, and the truth is, I love it."

Stacey smiled back over her martini. "You know my pilot friend, Samuel, he was asking about you again. I think he loves what you've got too."

The Clydesdale mare huffed out a sigh. "Yeah and he's a mouse and four foot nothing. He seemed like a nice guy at your barbecue, but you know, you put that guy next to me and it doesn't matter how sweet he is. At best we're going to be somebody's idea of a bad joke. I've given up hoping I'll snag a big stallion, but come on."

"That's a shame," said the ewe. "You can't tell me you couldn't swish your tail and have five good stallion's phone numbers by the end of the night?"

Holly shrugged her shoulders, and took a few more hungry bites of her meal before she replied. "You'd be surprised. Face it. Most guys want to be bigger than their girls, and they're chasing tail down by the aerobics room. And the guys who want a girl with my build? Most of them, they're working out some sort of Amazonian fantasy, you know?"

"Mare Imbrium, Giantess Mare of the Moon!" intoned Stacey, breaking into a fit of giggles at the end.

"Exactly!" exclaimed Holly, laughing. She stole the martini from Stacey's hand for a sip of it, before passing it back. "And you know, end of the day, I'm strong in everything else in my life. Body and mind. And those little guys, the ones who can't stop staring? They'd want me to be strong for them too and it's just—when can a girl have a break, you know? Someone come be strong with me, or for me. Not because I'm weak. Just because I deserve it."

"You do deserve it," echoed Stacey. "You do."

Holly emptied her bowl, huffing a content sigh. This was her fifth meal of the day. Her legs throbbed as her body worked frantically to repair the wear and tear of the day's training. "You should come pull with me sometime, Stacey."

The ewe shook her head with a mock-horrified expression. "No thank you! I'm a lean, mean cuddling machine, and I keep it that way. Pilates and yoga, all the way. Besides, with this wool? You're crazy if you think I'm going exercising anywhere without air conditioning."

"You could always shear it shorter. Bet your husband would like that," teased Holly.

"Any shorter and I'll have some Uplift nutter throwing glue-soaked cotton balls at me," muttered Stacey. "Don't think I haven't thought of it. Dan would go nuts for it."

Then Stacey added with an impish smile: "He likes the bare parts of me just fine, anyway."

Holly grinned. "Uh-huh. I've seen him stare. Speaking of staring. Almost gave my number to a cute buck today."

"Almost, huh? Antler-buck or lucky-feet buck?" said Stacey over her martini glass.

"Reindeer buck. I'm making him work for it," said Holly with a gleeful smile. "You ever hear of Plowshares? Pulling plow for community gardens?"

Stacey nodded. "Yeah, my sister, she's got a plot where she does her gardening, she's big into that. She mentioned they have volunteers. Why do you ask?"

"Well, the buck? Eric's his name. He pulls plow for them, I guess. I just thought that sounded really interesting. He was really into it, like it was a big deal for him. Sounds like a better time than just dragging steel around an alleyway."

"If he's not a creep, you should ask him to take you out to that," offered Stacey.

Holly's ears pricked forward, and she smiled. "I think I'll do that."

* * *

"So how did you go about getting her number, but not all of her number?" asked Magnus.

The older, heavily-muscled reindeer took a pull of his beer. He held his plate perched on his knees. Three chicken breasts, marinated and grilled, dominated the plate. He'd made a point of carrying the barbecue out of the garage one-handed.

Eric grinned over his beer at his older brother. "Gave me a digit for every forty yards I pulled. Sounds like I get to try again next week."

Magnus pursed his lips. "You're going to be sore. You alright with that kind of hoop-jumping, though?"

Eric nodded. "Hey, if I thought it was gratuitous, I'd walk. But I don't think she's playing games with me. Not those sort of mind games, anyway. She sounded really into the Plowshares, and she's serious about taking care of herself. Big girl too. Six-six, fucking juggernaut, probably two-forty easy."

Magnus laughed. "Shit, man, She out-pull you?"

"Yeah, she does," said Eric, without a touch of remorse for that fact. "She pulls about five hundred. Throw another fifty pounds more on that and I'll bet she could go pro in the comps if she wanted to."

Magnus more or less inhaled the first chicken breast before he could carry on the conversation again. "What're you going to do with a girl that big?"

Eric flicked his ears. "Whatever she'll let me do," he growled, waggling his eyebrows with a grin.

Then, Eric continued in a more serious tone: "Honestly? After the way Janine was, it'd just be nice to get with someone who doesn't just foist all the hard work on me."

"And someone who doesn't bitch about us eating the way we do," pointed out Magnus.

Eric's ears pinned back as he grimaced. "Oh damn, I didn't even think of that. Yeah. Salad and water, water and salad. I mean, Janine had a lot of things going for her, but every meal was a minefield with her. Glaring at me every time she's on another diet. As if bodies like these happen without the food to fuel them."

"No chance of that with this new girl, you think?"

"Holly? No, no way. She's hauling like that, keeping her body up? No chance. She's chewing through four or five thousand calories a day for sure."

"Better watch where you take her for supper, then!" laughed Magnus.

"No kidding," Eric cracked a low laugh. "But hey, here's a happy thought. She's a horse, she probably likes beer."

Magnus touched his beer can to Eric's. "Amen to that. Don't know what you were thinking, going steady with Janine. Marsupial like that, you can't fit a life together. If you can't stick to your own, at least stick close."

Eric shook his head. "Let's leave the specists out in the woods where they belong, okay? Janine and I didn't work out because of what she was. Just who we were."

His elder brother held up an apologetic hand, yielding to Eric on the point.

The younger buck gave an itch on the velvet of his left horn a scratch, letting the subject drop. "Hey, if Holly decides she wants to do the Plowshares thing, you mind if I borrow your old tack?"

"Hell, take it," said Magnus. "After I blew my ankle I think I'm done with the heavy hauling. And you can only use the regulation harnesses for the strong-buck comps anyway. So it's just taking up space right now in the garage."

"Seriously? Awesome, thanks!"

Magnus inclined his head. "I'd rather see it on a pretty, young thing than on me, anyway."

"I hear you there!" said Eric.

"And hey, if you can make it work, awesome. Dating someone at your gym? That's convenience. I can't even start to count how many times I've wished some pretty thing would walk in the doors. Spend eight hours at work, four hours at the gym, doesn't leave much time for fun and games."

"Well, I think she's the sort of girl I should make time for," Eric said.

* * *

It took three more attempts for Eric to manage the four hundred yards under Holly's stern eye. The attempts became the highlight of their mutual weeks. On his second attempt, Holly slapped a sports drink bottle into Eric's hand.

"I decided it was my turn to buy," she said.

Eric's eyes met hers. "Thank you," he said. They shared a smile.

Eric drank it down while she checked his harness and ties. He didn't mind at all the way her hands would brush against him through the thin, sheer lycra. They had both worked hard for the bodies they'd earned. It felt even better to feel admired by someone else who knew the sacrifice and effort it took.

While Eric pulled the sledge, Holly asked more questions about the Plowshares program. Eric answered when he could afford to spare the breath. He told her how often he pulled, how many gardens, how many people there were in the program, and how many families it served.

"How do you know so much about this program, anyway?" asked Holly.

"I'm the volunteer communications director for them." he explained. "I write the pamphlets, sometimes, or help organize the fundraisers."

"Fundraisers? What, does Plowshares need that kind of money?"

Eric shook his head. "Plows are a few hundred dollars to buy, or to have made. The tack is the really expensive part. But if it's well made it can go for decades, so long as you keep on top of the maintenance. Tough to find a place willing to make custom tack for plowing, though."

"Post-uplift political correctness," guessed Holly with a sigh.

"On the nose," said Eric, grimacing. "Heaven forbid someone promote a bit of atavism."

Holly shook her head. "I've got some folks at work I can't even dare tell what I do for exercise," she said, gesturing at the sledge. "They'd be all up in my business about it, Uplift this and better purpose that. Like a grown mare can't make her own damn decisions."

On the second week she asked him to tighten up her harness and inspect it. Proximity and attraction lent the moment a crackling tension. Every brush of his hands along lycra and fur left Holly's skin tingling. Eric was dutiful in his inspection, as he ran his strong hands along the harness to check for cracks and fraying straps. Holly favored him with a small smile as he went about his business.

Up close, she smelled of healthy mare, of oats and hay and sunshine. He smelled of healthy buck. It was a gamy, wild smell that made Holly think of forests back in Tennessee. She wished she could ever fit into one of his shirts; she'd have borrowed it for certain.

While Holly pulled, they opened up about their families. Eric had a brother in the strong-buck competitions; Holly had two brothers and a sister who were all pro-am athletes outside of their careers. All their parents were still alive, but they were slowing down and nearing retirement.

"Hey, where do you go for your protein, anyway?" asked Holly, as Eric took his turn pulling sledge. "I'm using the Asian supermarket up on Sepulveda Boulevard. Cheap bulk chicken there."

"Asian markets are always the best for cheap meat," said Eric. "I use the one down on Cherry Avenue. They've got bulk lentils there, too. Dirt cheap."

Holly nodded. "Nice! I'm still paying way too much for my lentils. I found an organic brand that's just awesome, but if I tried to make that my bulk protein I might as well be eating steak for that price. So it's just boring supermarket bulk for me."

"I'm surprised you don't go for the wheat germ powders."

"Still more expensive than lentils, and doesn't taste any better."

Eric pulled hard on the harness, sweat prickling under the Los Angeles sun. "How about beer? Your diet plan allow for it?"

"I'm a lager girl," she said. "The old Germanic ones."

"Of course you are. Old Clydesdale brand loyalty," laughed Eric. Holly smirked and threw the empty bottle at him.

"Hey, hitch me to a beer wagon any day," she laughed. "Just don't blame me if I don't get far before I'm sampling the wares."

After their showers, they had a cup of bad coffee from the gym cafe. They commiserated on the life of an athlete; food costs, meal plans, training time. Most of all, friends who tried to be supportive but just couldn't understand.

On the third week, he accidentally over-tightened her chest harness. The kevlar straps pulled the lycra around her breasts tight enough to show the line of areola. Eric expected a sharp word from her for it, but Holly was staring off into space. Her mouth was agape, and her nipples were stiff under her sports bra and lycra.

"That's a little tight, I think?" offered Eric.

Absently, she nodded, and Eric backed the strap off a little, ducking behind her as he did so she wouldn't catch him smiling. There was no hiding the smell of her, though. Holly was flustered. Color creeped up her ears, and she gave a little prance in her step in place. She stepped into place in front of the sledge, waiting to have her harness hooked in.

She hauled like a champion, and Eric didn't bother to hide how he ogled her. His gaze was hungry, male, and eager to watch her move. The more he stared, the more she blushed, but the defiant glares she kept shooting him were moderated by her smile.

Show me you're worth it, her look said. *Prove it.*

He did. With his shoulders in the traces, and pouring sweat under another soupy-hot day, he pulled. Back and forth to the screech of the steel on asphalt and her cheers from the loading dock.

The last forty yards were cruel; his legs wobbling like jelly, his knees threatening to fail him at any time. With his pulse pounding in his head, he pulled blind. Eric didn't even know he'd made it until his chest bumped the loading dock. He sagged down with a beatific smile.

Holly was cheering, and her hand that settled on his cheek was bold and strong. "Alright, mister Haugen. You can pick me up at seven," she said, tilting his chin up so he could see her.

He responded to her haughty tone with a quick turn of his head and gentle nip of her thumb. She shrieked and laughed as she jerked her hand back. When they were done with their showers and met in the lobby of the gym, she slid her number into his hand with a lingering touch.

He gave her hand a squeeze, and smiled. Then he asked the all-important question: "Protein or pasta?"

"Yes!" she replied with a laugh, her hand returning the squeeze.

"Got to feed the beast," Eric said with a knowing smile.

* * *

Stepping into the restaurant with Holly on his arm was a delight for Eric. She'd looked Amazonian and glorious enough at the gym, but the dress she'd chosen for the night magnified the effect. It was a short, black affair with matte sequins sewn in a way that suggested armor as much as femininity. She'd done up her mane into fine swedish-crown braids. Holly carried herself like equal parts warrior and princess on Eric's arm, her chin high and proud. The way she smiled as she held Eric's arm left no doubt that her pride extended to her choice of company for the evening.

Eric, in turn, had put on one of his better suits. They had only seen one another before in their gym clothes and after-gym sweats. Putting on a better impression for each other was a priority for the night. Eric's charcoal gray wool suit was smartly striped across matte black, and with a pale blue shirt under the suit. On impulse, he'd put his buckskin brown tie on, the one that matched his fur tones. It managed to look smart while suggesting bare fur, and Holly hadn't been shy about admiring it in the cab.

They were seated graciously by the host, and their orders taken: A double order each of meatballs, spaghetti, and water to drink.

"So you were saying in the cab about this sleigh-ride you go on every winter?" asked Holly.

"Right. Well, my family's Norwegian by ancestry. I guess back during the Uplift they had this festival in Norway, called Julebukk," Eric explained. "So this is going way back. But the tradition was, you'd get nine reindeer together. Then you hook them all up to a sleigh, and the lead buck, the Julebukk, you had to get him drunk. And I mean, really drunk. And then the team had to follow him and drag that sleigh wherever he leads them."

"And I'm guessing the rest of the team isn't too sober to start with, either, right?" asked Holly, eyes sparkling in pleased laughter.

"You know it. So we load the sleigh with a cask and a brave volunteer to pour the drinks. Anytime anyone wants a break, they have to call out 'Roodolf! Roodolf!', and everyone has to drink a round before the Julebukk can make them go again. Along the way, if you pass anyone and they call out 'Roodolf!', you have to stop and pour them a drink. Sometimes we sang while we pulled, too."

"So, did you grow up in Europe?" she asked.

"No," replied Eric. "Northeastern Americas, not far from where they had the old border. Town called Skowhegan. Lots of snow there. Grew up pulling snowplow for the neighbourhood. Weighted sledge is almost easy by comparison."

Holly gave a wistful sigh. "Pulling in the cold, instead of the heat. That must be so nice. You could go for hours without overheating."

Eric laughed. "I wish it was that simple. But it was nice. A lot of old farm country and new; we still pull with the old-timey farm stuff up there. It's better built for it, really. Modern regulation pulling harnesses are good for competitions, but they're only built for strength, not for real work. Kevlar's great, but the nylon straps they use wouldn't live a season pulling plow back home."

"So why did you move to Los Angeles?" Holly asked.

"Me and my brother moved here. We were recruited for summer brush-cutting, they needed folks who could pull a saw-chain through the brush. Did it in summer for a few years while I took my veterinary degree. Cervine, of course."

"How long is that program, these days? Four years?"

"Four years general for Cervidae, and then another three years to add on Bovidae while I practiced medicine. We're not even close, medically, to where things used to be pre-Uplift. But that's what you get for going from one species to how many hundreds we've got."

Eric took a sip of water, and then continued: "And what about you, Holly? You know, I don't even know your last name."

"Gardner," she said, ears pricking up.

"Where's your family from?"

"The southeast, Old Tenasi. Moved to Los Angeles when I was a little filly, though. Lived here all my life, but I get to travel a lot."

"Oh yeah?" asked Eric. "What do you do that lets you travel so much?"

Holly gave Eric an impish smile. "I'm a tour scout. All those nice cruises and tours people go on to travel the world? Well, I put together those tours. I get to go scout, try out the hotels, see the sights and the sounds, try all the food. Then I get back into LA and put the tour together for the travel companies."

"That sounds like a lot of fun, when it isn't being a lot of work," said Eric. "You go all over the world? They ever send you anywhere sketchy?"

"All the time. Almost all the tour scouts are women, and there's parts of the world it gets pretty dicey. So they send me. Conceal and carry where I can, get by on size and being strong. Diciest place I've been to is the Branta Athabasca," Holly replied.

Eric grimaced and shook his head. "All those geese and ducks. Yeah, I can't imagine that was fun."

Holly nodded. "Yeah. Not to sound specist, but not my favorite folks to deal with. I went conceal-carry the whole time, and I couldn't go anywhere at night without three or four drakes following me around. All with bad intentions, no doubt. And they're all so damn mean. If the migratory market wasn't so lucrative, I'd never have gone. But it went alright. I've never had to do more than kick someone to get them to behave."

Eric smiled. "What about your family? They all in the city?"

"Everyone still lives around the city, except my sister. She married last year, she's up in Los Padres. She hauls timber for a living. She probably hauls out whatever the fires you used to fight didn't burn up, come to think of it."

Eric nodded thoughtfully. "Quite likely. No lack of forest-hauling work out there."

The topic exhausted, Holly glanced up at Eric's summer-felted antlers. "Can I touch your antlers? They look cute all fuzzy like that."

The buck nodded. "Sure thing, just touch gently. If I scrape up the velvet I can end up with a lopsided rack, or spent a year with them deformed. Hard on the neck if they're not balanced."

Holly's fingers ran carefully along the velvet. "Oh! They're sort of spongy right now. That doesn't hurt?"

"Not if you're gentle," said Eric. "They're pretty resilient, but there's a lot of nerves that grow in there. Autumn, all the velvet pretty much dries up and dies within a day. Then it's just dead bone until the next spring shed."

"Must take a lot of calcium," mused Holly. "You do powdered eggshells for that?"

"Right in the protein shakes," he replied. "Scary amounts of dairy involved."

Supper arrived as they talked, and the silences between them grew longer and more comfortable. The occasional brush of a leg against the other's went answered in kind. Each touch led to quickening hearts and long, knowing looks across the table. It was a pleasant change not to feel the need to justify the way they were eating, or how much. They stuffed themselves full of meatballs and carb loaded on the pasta as much as they dared. When the bill came, they split it and walked hand in hand out the door.

"Can I ask a personal question?" asked Holly, as they stepped out into the warm summer night. Their feet took them towards the ocean, reflecting the moonlight in the distance.

"I think we probably owe each other a few by now. Sure," said Eric.

"You're not into some kind of giantess fetish thing, are you?"

She'd expected him to laugh. Instead, he shook his head and answered the question seriously.

"No. You're strong for your own sake. That's what attracts me, I guess. You've got pride in yourself, but it's because you've worked hard to earn what you've got. You know you're worthwhile. That's attractive."

Holly pricked her ears and smiled. She leaned into his shoulder a little as she decided she liked his answer.

"I do have pride in myself. But it's nice to see someone willing to jump a hoop or two to show me they mean it."

Eric gave her arm a gentle squeeze. "I think you're worth it, and it didn't feel like you were playing games with me. So I honestly didn't mind. My quads and glutes did, maybe!" He tilted his head to look up at her, and smiled. "Having you cheering me on felt pretty awesome."

"And you liked strapping me in to that harness," said Holly, tail swishing.

"I do," he said agreeably. Once again, his tone turned serious: "Which, I guess, gets to tie into my personal question for you. Do you like bondage?"

Holly blushed, but her pride wouldn't let her play modest on the topic. "Yeah. You know what? *Fuck* yeah. I do. I like turning that kind of control over. If I decide I like you, maybe you'll get to cinch me in good sometime."

"On that note," said Eric with a gentle laugh. "I was thinking, second date, I should take you out for one of the Plowshares pulls. Next week I've got a plot of potatoes that needs a plowing. If you're interested, maybe you want to pull plow. Hell, if you're game, we can make it interesting."

Holly cast him a sidelong look. "Yes to the plowing, probably not to the 'interesting'. Which isn't a 'no' yet, either. But yes to a second date. As for the, um, interesting, I don't recall reindeer coming up in high school sex ed. What's the chromosome count on a reindeer?"

"Seventy," he said with a reassuring smile. "Six off. You're fine. No chance of you muling."

Holly nodded. "That's good to know. If things end up going that far, it's one less thing to worry about."

"You've got something you need to worry about, with me?" he teased her.

She gave him a playful shove. "You just watch it, buddy boy, or you'll find out how I keep the geese in line."

"You never minded my gander before!"

"Puns are a hard limit," snorted Holly.

"Fair enough!" laughed Eric.

They walked down to a pier, sharing stories of the various wildlife of Los Angeles. They stopped at the pier's end, and gave a friendly wave to a party of seals swimming around a floating boombox. Staccato pops of porpoise and whale song melded with the synthetic bassline.

"Hey, Eric," she said, as they stood watching the ocean. "Thanks, by the way. For what you said earlier, about being worth it."

He nodded slowly, and then turned and touched his nose to hers. Holly drew and shared a long breath, and then closed her eyes and pressed in to kiss his lips. Her ears pricked forward as she enjoyed the little electrical jolt it sent down her spine and hips. The kiss left a surge of heat in the pit of her belly. She lingered, sharing and exchanging breath in that timeless equine way.

"Mmn. What was that for?" he murmured to her, when the kiss broke.

"Because you're worth it," she said.

* * *

The community garden was lush under the late summer sun. Green potato plant leaves stood tall in the soil, and the field around them was quiet. Eric unlocked the padlock on the door of the equipment shed and ushered Holly in. The inside was lit by a single forty-watt bulb. He shut the door behind Holly and put the big canvas duffel bag down with a jingle.

"You're kidding me. Jingle bells?" she asked.

Eric laughed. "Only tack I had that would fit, sorry. But it's the real deal."

He unzipped the bag and pulled out a heavy, solid leather harness. The smell of the rich leather filled the shed. Holly pricked her ears, and resisted the urge to lean in to smell it.

Her nipples began to stiffen as she shrugged on the leather. Eric buckling her in was even better.

"Tighter?" he asked, voice warm and low and knowing, in her ear.

Holly frisked from foot to foot wishing she had better poker ears. She gave a fractional nod.

He pulled tighter on the girth strap, and the way it pushed a little bit of air out of her sent a flush of warmth through her chest.

"Hmnf. Yeah," she breathed in turn.

"You want to wear the whole rig?" he asked her, as he buckled in her shoulders. Then he strapped her in over the top of her breasts, leaving them emphasized by leather and lycra.

Holly licked her lips. "Maybe. What's left?"

"Yoke collar, bit and bridle," he said. He held up the heavy, padded wood of the yoke collar in one hand.

He watched as her eyes dilated, and her throat bobbed when she swallowed.

"Like livestock?" she said, the words hesitant and confused.

Eric stepped forward, and touched his nose to her ear. His voice was a low, hungry growl: "Like livestock," he agreed. "Just an animal, with a simple purpose."

Holly quivered, a half-hiss of breath escaping her closing throat. Her tail was climbing on her, and they both knew it. His voice held a promise, an understanding, that was making her breath and tail both hitch. "Eric…"

He turned his head, to meet her eyes. The buck reached into his pocket and produced a bag of apple slices. He fished one out to cup under her lips.

The smell of apple and leather filled Holly's senses, and the warmth of his hand along her lips and nose was its own private delight. She blushed brilliantly. A tremor ran through her as her eyes came up to meet his, searching for any sign she should back away, any reason she could come back to her senses and salvage her dignity. She found none.

Her lips hesitated, and then parted. She lipped in the apple slice, touching her nose to his hand with a warm, wet whicker. Eric smiled in approval, as her blush turned into a more general flush. Her nipples perked hard under the lycra, and his gaze caught her tail and hips arching. He settled the heavy, padded collar around and over her shoulders, and strapped it into place.

His hands were strong, and warm, and the way he stroked them over her face made them both smile. Each touch smoothing out the fur of her cheeks, or brushing the wet warmth of her mouth. Eric made her lip and suck the last hints of apple off of his fingertips. He fed her two more slices. Each piece was more embarrassing and more arousing than the last.

"That's a good plow mare," he said, and Holly felt her body give an involuntary, all-over writhe of delight.

He held up the bridle and bit to her nose, letting her smell it. Letting her appreciate the feel of leather sliding over her face. The bit was unfamiliar; a soft rubber snaffle bar. Holly had never had a bit in her mouth before, and balked at first.

"Tch, tch. There. It's fine," said Eric in a low murmur. "Open gentle, it won't hurt you. You'll still be able to talk. Unless you think livestock shouldn't talk?"

She tilted her mouth up to kiss him. Her lips and tongue hungry for his, caressing, curling, meeting over a moaned breath. Then she laughed softly. "Fine, bucko! Thumbs up is green, thumbs down is yellow, shaken fist is red. Deal?"

"Deal!" he agreed, and his hands curled around her muzzle. He stole another kiss, just as hungry as hers. His dull fingernails scratched a gentle line under her jaw. Holly nosed insistently at the bridle as the kiss broke off, and her lips and teeth parted to take in the rubber bit.

Eric's cock throbbed against his thigh, while his fingers brushed along her lips and wet, warm mouth. Both of them were already imagining what it would feel like with his cock and not his fingers. The bit slid into place in Holly's mouth. He buckled the leather bridle around her head, and adjusted her blinders inward.

Leather hugged and cinched around her, and stole much of her vision. Holly melted more and more into Eric's touch.

"There we go," he murmured, as he finished strapping her in, and his hands dutifully checked her harness contact points. "Such a pretty, strong plow mare I've got, today. If you pull really well, there's a sugar cube or two in my pocket for later."

His hands reached into the bag, and he produced two silicone plugs. They were new and sealed in their bags. Eric held them up in front of her nose, so she could see them, while his other hand traced up behind her hips, the buck's warm palm pressing flat to the rising heat of her cunt trapped under lycra. Holly gave an appreciative groan, her ears pricked in curiosity towards the bag in front of her nose.

"Plugs. Do you want them before you pull?"

Holly hesitated, but the warmth of Eric's hand around her pussy was the right kind of distracting, and he gave a knowing smile as he felt the twitch of her hips at the thought of stretching around them.

Eric doubled down, with a low, fond growl: "I wonder how much the lycra will hide. We wouldn't want them to figure out what a dirty secret my plow mare's keeping, would we? Plowing all plugged up."

The mare's head was swimming. Her blush was so intense it felt like her cheeks were cramping. Her heartbeat felt like a war drum, somewhere between her ears and her hips. Her ears tried to flag back, but she couldn't sustain the pretense. After a few heartbeats, they flagged forward hard. She gave a thumbs-up, trying to ignore the creeping heat wave growing between her thighs.

Eric's warm hand peeled her lycra pants down to find her flooded in need; heat and moisture steaming up from her hips. A full-body shudder of pleasure ran through her as Eric's warm hand cupped around her cunt, and spread her open. He kneaded fingers into her sex with firm pressure. A moan escaped her, her words lost to the gentle pressure of the bit on her tongue. Holly shuddered in urgent desire, longing to lose herself to the mental space his handling and the leather was sinking her into.

With a smile, he unwrapped the first plug, and slid it slowly into her hips. As he pushed, he gently twisted the plug to slicken it along her sopping wet cunt. The mare moaned again, harder. He planted his palm against the base of the plug, and kept up the pressure until the rounded silicone slid and nestled inside her.

"You're going to smell like sex, down every row," he growled in her ear.

Holly didn't try to stop the throaty, earnest laugh that bubbled up and escaped around the bit at the sides of her mouth. It was an intoxicating thought, a gloriously shameless thought.

"Oh, you already knew that," he teased her, and Holly nodded emphatically, while giving her hips a sinuous wiggle.

It was a reaction that drew a delighted laugh from Eric. "Well, let's see how that wiggle changes with this one," he said, holding up the second plug.

Holly trembled. The blinders kept her from seeing what Eric was doing, and her ears swiveled back sharply in anticipation. She listened for the sound of lube spluttering out from the bottle onto the plug, and clenched when she heard it. When the cold wet touch of the lubed plug met her asshole, she jumped. She gave an involuntary, surprised whinny.

"Whoa, girl. Whoa. Easy now. That's it. Nice and slow," said Eric, bracing his hand against her ass.

She pressed her ass back against the wet intrusion, her breath hitching as she met the flat of Eric's palm. The second plug was an aching, warming stretch inside her. Holly let out a second whinny at the feel of her ass starting to stretch and ache. Her eyes closed, and Eric's patient hands paused, watching for her slow nod before continuing.

When the nod came, so did she; a convulsion rolling up her thighs as the hot stretch of the plugs met her excitement and tension. The plug slid home, and she let out a hoarse, inarticulate cry. A splash of her cum flooded out from around the lower plug, and fell with a wet splat into the dirt.

"That," tutted Eric with a fond laugh, "was not slow."

Holly gave a slow grind back against his hand, and snorted. With a dutiful smile, Eric pulled her lycra leggings back up over her backside. The majestic curve of her ass helped to hide the flared bases of the plugs; but it wasn't perfect. Anyone staring as hard as he would be would surely notice the faint outline as she flexed and walked.

"Alright, plow mare, lets get you hitched," Eric said, and threw open the doors of the shed.

Squinting against the summer glare, Holly found herself grateful for the shade of her blinders. She followed obediently as the reindeer buck took her by the collar and walked her out into the sunshine.

The plow was waiting, a solid steel thing with long handles and a look that promised it had been hand-crafted, once upon a time. Every step shifted the plugs inside her pussy and ass. When they stopped, she squirmed in place, staring at the plow. Long rows of potato plants lay ahead of her waiting to be plowed.

They had the garden to themselves, and the climbing ivy and kudzu around the fence screened most of the crop from the sidewalks and road. But it sent another shiver through Holly's hips to know that someone could peek in, or just walk in. They would see her plugged and pulling, strapped into the plow traces like livestock.

Eric took his time in strapping her in, and held a water bottle to her mouth to get her well hydrated. A little knowing smile tugging at his lips.

"Don't want you getting dehydrated today, do we?" he murmured, before tucking the bottle into a loop on her harness.

Holly gave a willing huff, and strained into the harness. The plow skittered forward a foot before the blade bit and dug into the earth. It was much lighter than her hauling sledge, but the footing was crumbly earth, made dry by the Los Angeles heat.

"Nah-ah, we have to do this with rhythm," said Eric. "You step, I lift, you step, I lift. There we go. Step."

The plow bit deep into the earth as Holly strained forward. After the foreplay in the shed, her muscles were warm and eager to move.

"Lift," Eric said.

The reindeer buck pulled the plow up, breaking up the chunk of earth with the front of the plow.

They fell into the steady rhythm together. Holly's eyes lidded as the warmth of the sun combined with the constriction of the leather around her body. Her legs skidded, feet dug in to dirt. Every breath smelled of leather and good earth upturned. When her footing held, she pulled. Every step shifted the plugs inside her, keeping her awareness on the aching, warm stretch inside her.

Eric's voice became a warm, fuzzy metronome, and by the end of the second row she had stopped hearing his voice as words at all. The blinders kept her eyes focused straight ahead. Her entire world faded until all there was, was her own body, and the row that lay ahead. Sweat ran down her breasts and back, and every shifting step made her more and more aware of the plugs inside her.

With aching arms, Eric lifted the plow, overturning dirt and exposing potatoes. The aching in his arms couldn't draw his attention from the sight of Holly in front of him. Her steaming, sweaty body bent into the traces in front of him, her tail arched high.

His approving sounds as she shifted and worked were all pleasant noises to her. The stray thought of his eyes on her made her cunt clench in lusty joy. With dirt underfoot, and leather around her face, Holly pulled, losing herself to the simple joy of the exercise.

The buck couldn't tear his eyes off of that swaying mare ass, the plugs inside her showing their bases through the lycra. The smell of her was powerful and musky, a primal invitation. Every now and then her hips would hike her ass high in as blatant an invitation as her body could make. He couldn't do a thing about that provocation until they had finished the field, and she knew it. Eric had never been more determined to plow a row before.

On the sixth row, they snagged the plow-blade on an old root. Eric stepped off the plow and walked around beside Holly, using a gentle hand to guide her back a few feet. His other hand curled around behind her hips, and brushed against the base of her plugs. With a low, moaning whinny, Holly came again. Lycra stained a wide patch of darker black, as she squirmed in erotic humiliation. Eric's voice, of course, never missed a beat:

"You just came all over yourself, where anyone could have seen. Imagine that, all those eyes and ears out there, seeing what a filthy piece of livestock you're being for me."

Holly let out a gagging moan. The bases of the plugs briefly protruded against her lycra clothes as the next aftershock hit. By now, her nipples were fit to cut glass.

Eric circled around her, carefully lifting and clearing the plow. The glorious, curling stroke of his words came again: "Horny little plow mare, out in the fields. Just gagging for a fucking now. Craving cock. What's going to happen when you're tied up tighter, helpless, in that tool-shed?"

The mare let out a loud, flagrant groan. Her tail trembling as she hiked it higher at the all-encompassing thought. She wasn't even Holly in her own mind, at this point. Just a beast, a creature of need. The idea his voice fed her, the promise, and the encompassing grip of leather and role closed around her mind. Her last fleeting thought before words left her mind entirely was a fervent wish: *Don't stop.*

He didn't. On the last row of the field he seized her wrists, and she gave them up to him happily. He pulled her hands behind her back to just above her tail, where he lashed them in place using her own tail. From that moment on she pulled the plow untroubled by words or conscious thoughts. She was a creature given purpose, entirely in tune with the throb of her cunt and ass. Raw animal need roared inside her, and made her throb in eager desire.

Eric walked Holly back to the tool shed, pausing to water her as she swayed, hot and dizzy. As soon as the door banged shut behind them, Eric unhooked the plow and clipped her harness lines around the steel frame of the shed. With the mare anchored, his hands tugged down her leggings, and exposed the plugs.

The buck's left hand slid under Holly's hips, and his thumb rolled over her clit. Holly bellowed a groan as she squeezed the plug in her cunt. It popped right out in a wet splatter of cum.

"Do you want to get bareback-fucked like a proper broodmare?" growled Eric. Holly's response was an emphatic thrust of her ass backwards, hips and back arching in blatant, explicit offering.

"I can't hear you," he teased when he mounted her, lycra peeling down his legs as his cock sprung free, nestling his cocktip just inside her.

Her thumb shot up with a frustrated laugh, muffled by her own groan and the rubber bit in her mouth.

"Good plowmare," he growled behind her, and Holly shuddered to hear him speaking to her in that knowing, devilish tone.

Eric's warm hands wrapped around her ass, and spread her flagrantly. Just at the point Holly thought she'd lose the plug in her ass, Eric surged in behind her. His thrust pushed his upper hips against the flared base of the plug, and both cock and the plug sank hard into her. She was a molten furnace around his cock, drooling wet down his balls, just as hot from arousal as she was from the sun and exercise. His first thrust produced an incoherent sound of joy from the bound mare.

She began to struggle against the leather bindings. To Holly's delight, the leather held her fast no matter how she strained. Her muscles flexed, every motion futile, her predicament helpless.

"You're caught," Eric growled down to her. "A broodmare, all tied down, with nowhere to go. Helpless. Needful. And all mine."

Holly bucked back against him, and thrilled at the feeling of hands wrapping around her bound wrists. He pinned them to her back as he drove his powerful body into hers. His cock slid, slick and hot inside her, and her lips could no longer contain her moans. She was barely aware of the way her tongue hung blatantly from her mouth once he began to fuck her, and Holly was well past caring. Dignity, pride, those were the privilege of a woman. Not a plow mare.

In the moment, all that mattered to Holly was how it felt to be fucked so filthy. To strain and feel helpless, and earn that hard pounding cock inside her. Eric's big hands roamed her ass and hips like he owned every inch. When his teeth found her back half-way up her spine, her startled writhing hitched up two notches.

"This is what you're for," he growled in her ear. "This is where you belong. Bound. Helpless. Fucked, where anyone could come in, and discover what an animal you really are."

Eric's words strummed her like fingers that touched forbidden places nobody else had dared. The buck's lips caressed the words like filthy promises. Holly had always been the strong one, the proud one. Trusting it would all be returned when they were done, here, in secret, she could give it up in trust to him.

Eric's hips drove her hard against the bindings, and Holly gave up any pretense of resistance; her hips slamming back to meet each eager, hip-jarring thrust. His balls swung, bumping along her cunt. His cock drove inside her, sliding wet and slick and hot. Each thrust ached, hurt just a little. Each thrust hurt just right. And with every thrust bumping his body against the base of the plug in her ass, the aching heat just kept spreading through her.

The buck's hands slid up her body, and cupped under her breasts, kneading them hard through the lycra. Holly groaned, her wrists straining against her own tail, caught helplessly in the knot he'd made of her braid.

"Helpless," Eric repeated in her ear, and she shuddered in delight, adoring the way his hands gripped her like he owned her, like he had every right to roam and clasp and grip everything he pleased.

Their cries and the muffled slaps of their bodies together echoed out in the tin shed, reverberating back on them. Holly's shameless cries mingled with the filthy words pouring from Eric's mouth. Asking for him, begging for him. Urging each other on, demanding everything their hard-earned bodies could give one another. The shed smelled of dirt and leather and sex, the air hot and stifling and perfect.

If she had a use for words, Holly would have cried out for more. But she had no use for words now; a broodmare didn't need them. So instead, she came, a whole-body shuddering orgasm that forced her to her knees. Eric let her sink down, his hips following. Dominating her body, his strong hands pushed her down against the bindings. He finished with a shuddering roar, his hands clenching tight around her hips like a promise that he'd never let go.

His cock erupted in her, and they rocked together, breathless and silent. It was a moment past words, or even sounds, for them both. Eric's arms wrapped tight around her body, and Holly's bound hands reached back to grasp him as best her bindings would allow. Each of them were heaving long, heavy breaths, sweat trickling down their bodies. The salty scent of sweat and sex prickled in their noses.

They lingered in the stifling hot silence of the shed. Each listening to the other breathe, feeling their heartbeats slow from their frantic pounding. Eric's lips brushed against her neck, and Holly gave a soft nicker, turning her head. Craning enough for a shared kiss, sweet and slow.

"You've been a very good bit of livestock, today," he crooned in her ear, and she gave a slow wiggle back against his hips. "I think you deserve your treats, after all of that."

Holly's ears pricked, and Eric rose to his feet, circling around her to unhook the bit from her bridle. Delicately, he slipped the bit out of her mouth. Holly gave the tip of his cock a single, long lick of appreciation, and then straightened up on her knees. His hand tangled in her mane, and dragged her mouth back in for another, longer bobbing suckle, until he was clean from cocktip to balls. Her head was once more high and proud, her ears standing tall, as he drew out.

Eric's fingers along her lips were a thrill all over again. And they were made all the sweeter by the little sugar cube he slipped past her lips and onto her tongue. His eyes met hers, and his words came as earnest, admiring praise: "Good girl!"

He exhaled a little breath, as he hand-fed her another piece of apple. "You're worth this, too."

* * *

"Rooodolf!" came the slurring cry from the buck in the lead, and the reindeer team behind him echoed the cry. Skawhegan rooftops, thick with snow, peeked over the treeline a quarter-mile ahead.

Holly slapped her hand atop the wood of the sleigh, and called out with a laughing grin: "Come on boys! Are you rein-don't or reindeer?"

A chorus of groans and a few snowballs was her just desserts.

"Didn't you once tell me puns were a hard limit?" murmured Eric, when she stopped and refilled the little wooden cup chained to his harness.

Her hand slipped behind his ass, to press gently against the plug hidden under his snow suit. "Guess we're just good at opening each other's minds."

He kissed her twice, to the catcalls of the team around him. With cups refilled, and cask and mare safely returned to the sleigh, they drove away to the sound of merry bells and singing.

DOMINANT ROLES

Dark End

The Big, Bad Fox—that's what they all called Jun down at the Kennel, the local BDSM club. He had arrived in town a few years ago with a new job, a new life, and a chip on his shoulder, eager to prove himself in the scene despite being two inches shorter and fifteen pounds lighter than the next smallest dominant at the club. Some regulars thought they would humor the fox by letting him be in charge; Jun made sure they all left with a sore ass and a new attitude. After that they started calling him the Big, Bad Fox, and they meant it.

So how, after earning the respect of the entire Kennel, had Jun let himself fall so easily for a woman? A human woman, at that.

Rebecca was sprawled out asleep across Jun's bed, naked from the waist up, just as he had told her to be. The sunlight that trickled in through the branches outside and the shades inside moved over her brown skin like milk swirling in a cup of coffee. Most mornings she was his preferred jolt of java, one that woke up his loins first and his head second. Just watching her sleep was enough to make his jeans feel tighter.

He could take her right there if he wanted. She would let him. She always let him.

That was the problem, really.

She stirred in bed. He stirred, too, standing a little straighter in the doorway to his bedroom. There was no rest for the Big, Bad Fox.

Rebecca exhaled sharply and blew up a tress of chocolatey-brown hair. When that failed to move it enough, she used her hand instead. As soon as her hair was out of the way, her eyes immediately focused on

Jun and traveled down his body to the bulge tenting his pants. Unlike Jun, Rebecca was a morning person. She rolled over onto all fours facing Jun in a position every canine understood: arms stretched forward, chest almost touching the ground, rump held high and wiggling in excitement. The posture silently said, "Let's play." Rebecca may have been human, but under his training she made a good bitch too.

"Not now," he said and stifled a yawn. His head felt heavy from lack of sleep and the ever present thirst in his throat.

She pouted, although her smile never completely disappeared from the corners of her mouth and her eyes never completely left his bulge. "But you want it."

"Not now," he repeated. "It's been a year."

"What?"

"A year since we met. To the day."

Her head tilted in confusion. Then she burst out laughing. "Wow. Does that make it our anniversary then?" She sat up and rubbed at her chin in a very human fashion. "Can you really even have an anniversary for a date that only consisted of tying someone down to a bench and fucking them silly?"

He stayed in the doorway, staring down at her.

"Uh, happy anniversary?" She gave a small cheering motion with her hands.

He took a deep breath and steeled himself for the words that had to be said. "A year so far, and I'm uncertain. I'm uncertain if we are right for each other. We never get beyond being good friends who share a bed. We stay together more from inertia than anything else, and I want more than that. So I'm giving you one more day."

The remainder of her smile disappeared. "And what happens if you still aren't sure at the end of the day?"

"We stay good friends, I hope. Otherwise, we go our separate ways."

The two fell silent. They had long admitted that their relationship never quite clicked, but making the end of their relationship a distinct possibility in the next twenty-four hours shook them both.

Rebecca was the first to break the silence. She nodded to the nightstand nearby and asked, "Do you want me to put it on?"

Sitting on the nightstand was a plug attached to a faux foxtail, the toy Rebecca used whenever she wanted to impress Jun. Her first boyfriend had been an asshole who had insisted one night on having anal sex without lube because it felt better for him that way. She'd hated anal ever since, and yet she would still willingly take that tail for him (with a generous helping of lube, of course).

"No," he insisted. "No, I don't want that."

"Then what?"

He could ask for anything he wanted. He could fuck her. He could make her wear the tail, despite her distaste for it. He could tie her up in the tightest bondage and force her to deep throat his length. He knew she would submit willingly and without question.

The level of power he had over her had begun to frighten him. He (Big, Bad Fox though he was) had nightmares of losing his self-control in the heat of the moment; maybe hitting her to generate pain and not pleasure, or maybe biting hard enough to draw blood.

Two nights ago the nightmare had been set in a hospital. Rebecca was being swarmed by worried doctors. Jun was curled up in a corner, tongue burning with the far too familiar taste of alcohol and mind filled with the sense of dread that he was the reason she was there.

Last night, he chose not to sleep at all.

No, he did not want Rebecca, the perfect fantasy slave girl. He wanted Rebecca to be a woman who would stand up and protect herself, even if that meant protecting herself from Jun.

"It's rather dark in here," he said. "Go open some of the blinds."

"Yes, sir." She reached out for her shirt, left discarded from the previous night.

"I didn't say you could get dressed first."

"But—"

"Bitches don't talk back," he reminded her.

Rebecca's hand froze outstretched to the shirt. She realized the implications of what he was asking, and indecision flitted across her face.

Part of him wanted to reach out a hand and let her know that refusal was an acceptable response, but that was not the way of the Big, Bad Fox.

Just when Jun thought she was on the verge of saying "no," her smile returned and she nodded. "Yes, sir." She hopped to her feet, still topless, and marched dutifully out, making sure her naked breasts brushed against his arm on the way out.

Jun, confused by the sudden change in her attitude, turned in the doorway to watch.

Rebecca went around the back side of the house first, opening the blinds in the kitchen, office, and side hallway. All those windows looked out over the secluded back yard. That only left the big living room window at the front side of the house, in full view of the suburban side street Jun lived on. Rebecca took the cord in hand and, just before pulling, turned sharply to face him. Light burst through the opened blinds, forming a shimmering aura around her.

She was shaking slightly. A tremor ran along her shoulders. Anyone who was passing by on the street might be able to see that she was topless, even if they couldn't see her breasts directly, and she had to know that. She had obeyed, but her hesitation in obeying was some amount of progress at least.

Her curvaceous silhouette begged for Jun's touch, and her submission—irritating as it was for his ultimate goal—nonetheless got his blood pumping as strong as it always did. The fox came up and wrapped one arm around her. Warmth radiated from her body, unimpeded by fur or clothes, and sparked a similar warmth within him. Jun's jeans became entirely too constricting now as his shaft attempted to push out under his belt line. His body wanted nothing more than to fuck her right there, but he restrained himself.

"Not going to call me a good girl?" she whispered in his ear.

He did not want to reward continued quiet obedience, so he said, "I shouldn't need to say it, should I?"

Whatever answer she may have had was lost in the soft moan as his claws traced around her sensitive navel. From there his hand dipped down, slipped under the waistband of her pajamas, and ran a finger along the edge of her sex.

As he stroked her, her hips seemed to lose their connection to the rational centers of her mind. If they wanted something, they would move to get it, so it was not long before she was grinding against his solitary finger. Dew began to form against his pads.

"I thought you didn't want to play," she said, a touch breathless.

"I can change my mind, can't I?" He spoke with his shaft straining against his belt and his muzzle buried against the crook of her neck and shoulder. The urge to nip and bite her as he would a proper bitch returned. He bit his tongue instead. "Do you want me in you?" he asked.

"Mmmm, yeah."

"Do you crave me in you?"

"Yeah."

"Do you need me in you?"

"Yeah." There was a blissed-out tone to her as she fell into a submissive headspace.

"Then go get ready for your morning jog," he said, hand withdrawing.

The sudden shift jolted her back to attention. "Yes, sir," she said, and almost turned to obey, before she remembered the open living room window and her naked breasts. She covered herself with an arm and went back into the bedroom to change.

While she was gone, Jun set the next challenge in motion. He pulled an item from the toy chest they kept in the closet and hid himself in the privacy offered by the front door. When Rebecca returned, now in a sports bra and matching shorts, she gaped at the lubed dildo he held in his hands.

"You want me to go jogging with that in me? I can't."

Jun grinned. Finally, after all this time—

"I mean, there's no way I'll be able to hold that in me the whole time."

That was her excuse? Not that she didn't want to, but that she didn't think herself capable of doing it? He growled and pushed her up against the front door. His hand slid back underneath her waistband and shoved two fingers deep inside her. She was slick, but still shuddered at the sudden intrusion. "Clench," he commanded, and she did. "Good. Not as good as a vixen, but it'll do. You can hold it."

She gripped at Jun's fur as he pushed her shorts down a bit and slipped the dildo (far more gently now) inside of her, easing the knot in with a twisting motion. Her nails dug into Jun's fur as the dildo settled into place.

"Clench," he repeated and then gave the base of the dildo an experimental tug. It wasn't coming out. "Consider it good practice for the next time I tie you."

She gave a stifled grunt as she lifted her shorts back into place. "Fuck, I'm going to cum before I get back."

"That's the idea." He pressed in closer, pinning her tightly to the wall. "And every canine on the block is going to know it from the smell of you. You have a problem with that?"

She should have. Rebecca loved showing off for him in private, but insisted on more decorum in public. No collars at work (despite how accepting her artist friends were of alternative lifestyles). She wouldn't call him Sir in front of her friends. No fucking anyplace where someone might walk in on them. And so on.

Instead, Rebecca looked up into his eyes, smiled, and said, "Not at all."

Stymied again, and more than a little shocked, Jun jerked his head to the door. "Get going."

She left. The door shut. In the absence of other noises, the normally quiet background sounds became amplified. The lights hummed. The fridge whirred. The wind outside caused branches to tap against the walls. And in the midst of it all, Jun's heart pounded and thudded louder than a rock concert.

He collapsed onto the couch, head hung in his hands.

This was not how Jun had expected this morning to go. Her obedience came faster even though he was sure he was pushing her farther out of her comfort zone. This day had been planned for almost a week with a list of nearly a dozen activities planned, each pressing Rebecca harder than ever before to try and eke a refusal out of her. But now, as he considered each one, it disappeared into a void, replaced by an image of her smile.

* * *

A year earlier, Jun had been at the Kennel early, right after work had let out. The last week had been a bust, with not a single partner to warm his bed, and the frustration of unsatisfied lust was starting to affect his job performance. As he looked around the club for his next plaything, he saw a human woman seated in one of the club's leather armchairs, dressed in a fish-net shirt and half-torn jeans like she had been expecting dancers, not kinksters. As the city had a large canine majority, the Kennel was themed around canine life in the city. On any given day in the club, you could find wolves, jackals, dogs, foxes, even hyenas, and maybe, once a month, a confused-looking cougar or rat in the corner. This human though seemed more fascinated than confused.

Jun bought her a drink and, without a single word spoken, handed it to her. Then he sat in an armchair across from her.

She took a sip. "That's…wow, that's actually pretty good," she said.

Jun's tailtip twitched as he contemplated the possibility of a successful conquest. "It has to be. Dungeon rules: you don't play while drunk. They'll let you have one small drink, and they'll make sure it's pretty damn good."

"It is pretty damn good," she confirmed. She took another swig, and this time held it in her mouth, savoring the taste a moment before swallowing. "But none for you?"

"Not a good idea."

"Oh? Lightweight, are you?" she teased.

"Recovering alcoholic."

Her jaw dropped in sudden horror. "Oh, oh god, I'm sorry. I didn't know." She looked down at her glass. "Should I put this away?"

"No," he said firmly. "It's fine. I gave it to you, didn't I?" Seeing that his words did not calm her down enough, he continued, "I've been sober for four years now. Seeing that glass, wanting a drink, but being able to say no every time, I find that rather empowering actually. It reminds me that I am still in control."

She nodded, but when she took another drink, her hand turned as if to hide the glass from view. " Anyway, I'm Rebecca," she said.

Jun ignored the hand she had reached out and leaned in, his muzzle against her face, nuzzling and licking. Never before had Jun been so close to a human; her scent had an alluring quality, familiarly feminine but exotically human. He masked his surprise with another lick to her cheek. "That's how we greet each other here. You may be human out there, but you get treated like a bitch in here. Got it?"

He was surprised again when her tongue reached out and touched his cheek. "I got the idea."

Jun sat upright in his chair. Although she intrigued him, he tried to hide his curiosity under the demeanor of the Big, Bad Fox, back straight, arms folded over his chest, ears forward. He could feel that position breathing power and confidence into him. "You're the first human I've seen here," he said. "What made you stop by?"

Rebecca gave a small shrug. "There's few enough humans in this town that the odds of me finding a guy interested in both me and kink is bad enough, I thought I'd try my luck here."

Not too surprising, Jun thought. While most people tried to find someone of their own species for a long-term relationship, cross-species flings were common, especially at the Kennel. And perhaps Rebecca, unlike the wolves and jackals so common to the club, did not have any preconceived notions about whether foxes could dominate or not. He leaned forward in his chair, closer to the woman. "And are you feeling lucky now that you're here?"

"That depends."

"On what?"

She turned in her seat and looked out over the club and the few couples already making use of the shared play space. "You said that I would get treated like a bitch in here. What all does that mean?"

"That means I do not treat you any differently than if you were a fox yourself, except in those ways that might injure you. So biting your scruff would be out, but shoving my knot in you would not."

She seemed to think about that for a while, finishing off the remainder of her drink. And when she turned back to him, that smile was on her face, a smile unlike any he had seen before in the Kennel, not a taunt or a tease or a dare, but a smile which simply said, "Show me more."

His relationship with Rebecca had not followed the arc all his other relationships had. Normally, there was hot, sweaty, passionate sex for a few days, then the cracks would start to show up. He wanted something steady; she wanted a weekend fling. He wanted quiet time at home; she wanted to go out to parties. He wanted seafood; she thought that lobster was revolting. He wanted caution; she wanted to be carefree.

He did not care how it looked for a fox to be in control; she did.

But it wasn't that way with Rebecca.

A week passed and Jun expected something to go wrong. Yet Rebecca remained just as eager as before. A month passed. They clearly had their differences, but outside of a few hard limits, she ultimately deferred to him in every way. She was happy to explore what it meant to be Jun's plaything.

It was not just Jun whom she had impressed. Two months into their relationship, they arrived together at Jun's parents for dinner, the first time in years Jun had brought someone home. Rebecca had walked right up to Jun's father, nuzzled his cheek, and complimented him on how good his whiskers looked. Jun's father was beaming all throughout dinner, and when it was over, he, not Jun's mother for once, took Jun aside to ask if he was planning to marry Rebecca. Jun was shocked that his staunchly traditional Japanese father would even consider the possibility.

A month after that, she invited Jun on a camping trip with friends from her work (a small marketing firm where she did graphic design). They had laughed and made s'mores and failed to be anything other than urbanites in high-quality tents with lots of bug spray, but she made it all worth it by insisting they share a single, extra-large sleeping bag together.

The one thing that Rebecca did not share with him was her own family. As best Jun understood, they were control freaks and had tried to force her to attend a local religious school and major in business. She ran away, put herself through an art degree at the most liberal-minded place she could find, and had barely talked with them since. They sent a Christmas card during the holidays, which Rebecca tore up and tossed in the trash without even reading. She had Jun, she had said, and that was enough for her.

* * *

Something gnawed and twisted inside of Jun's stomach as he seriously considered that this could be the last day they spent together. He could go back on his promise to give her only one more day, but the Big, Bad Fox did not go back on his promises.

He caught sight of Rebecca making a lap around the block. The dildo was having its desired effect: her mouth was open in an "O" and her jog had an odd gait to it.

Jun's head was still feeling so heavy, so he got up from the couch and paced the floor to clear it. The image of Rebecca's smile slipped out, but nothing came back to fill its place. There was an emptiness that consumed his mind as he kept thinking this could be the last day.

Feeling suddenly thirsty, he stopped in the kitchen and pulled a drink out of the fridge.

The cap was off and the liquid on his tongue before he realized what he was doing. He held up the bottle: Strong River IPA, Rebecca's favorite, the only alcohol he let into the house. A feeling like cold ice wormed into Jun's stomach. All the motions were just as he remembered them: open the fridge, take out the bottle, kick the fridge shut, pop off the cap, and take a quick swig. One long fluid dance that did not take an ounce of thought. Five years on, he could still do it easily.

Too easily.

His mouth watered at the partial taste it had received. Part of his mind whispered that it would be okay just this once to have some more, but the Big, Bad Fox did not—absolutely not—go back on his promises. Especially not the one to stay sober. His hackles raised and his muscles tense, Jun dumped the contents of the bottle down the sink and tossed the empty container into the recycling bin.

He had to get that damn taste out of his mouth. He snatched a glass off the counter and tried to take a quick drink of water, but his hand had started shaking so badly that it spilled over his muzzle.

The glass slipped through his fingers. The fragile material shattered on the edge of the sink. A dozen broken shards skittered across the metal basin and wooden countertop.

Jun stared down at the broken glass. His hands shaking, his head reeling from vertigo, broken glass everywhere. It felt just like five years ago.

Jun's stomach revolted. He didn't wait even a second before running for the bathroom, slamming the door shut and dry-heaving over the toilet. There was nothing in his stomach, but the urge was still there.

He had been so close to giving in, so close to reliving that nightmare all over again. His long-honed confidence started to flake away. Every mistake he had made all those years ago welled up to haunt him with the possibility of becoming real again.

When he stole from his parents for booze money.

The DUI.

The time he woke up in the bathroom of a bar with no memory of how he got there.

Screaming at his mother, telling her that he had it under control.

Getting fired from his job for showing up drunk. So scared of telling his father that he had spent ten long minutes on the sidewalk, crying his eyes out and wondering if he should just take a step off the bridge.

He took a deep breath and held it. The wave of nausea and painful memories passed, and Jun, feeling so very, very tired, let himself fall to the side, propped up against the bathtub.

"Jun? Jun, I'm back!"

The front door slammed. Rebecca must have seen the light from under the bathroom door because she came up, tried the knob, then knocked. "Jun, are you all right?"

"I'm not feeling well," Jun croaked. His throat refused to work properly. It kept trying to reverse a swallow. "I'll be out in a bit. I dropped something in the kitchen. Be careful."

She shuffled off after telling him to take care of himself. With his ears turned towards the bottom of the door, the fox could hear her moving about, cleaning up the glass in the kitchen, running a vacuum to pick up any remaining shards, and changing in the bedroom. Then she came out and set something down outside the door. After that, silence.

His back ached in a dozen places from the odd position he was in and the hard tile floor underneath him. It took him several minutes before he worked up the courage to crawl to the lip of the sink and turn it on. Hot steam wafted around his muzzle and flooded his sinuses. The heat woke him up, made his hands stop shaking, gave him peace.

Since he had run into the bathroom, Jun had avoided looking at himself in the mirror. But now, with his hands calm once again, he did. He looked like a mess. No longer the Big, Bad Fox, his fur was matted and his ears held flat against his head. He was small, weak, pitiful.

Then again, he had always been small, weak, and pitiful. Jun had never truly been the Big, Bad Fox. It was all just an act. When Jun had hit dead bottom, with only the promise of another bottle to blot out the pain of the previous one, he latched on to the idea of the Big, Bad Fox, someone successful and unshakable. He just played the part, like a method actor. Inside, he was weak; outside, he was the Big, Bad Fox.

It didn't matter that part of him wanted nothing more than to curl up around a six-pack and drink until he couldn't think straight. It didn't matter what he felt. It didn't matter if he hurt inside. He was the Big, Bad Fox now. That was enough to pull him through before. It would be enough to pull him through again.

Jun checked his posture: a deep breath to straighten his back, a roll of his shoulders to get rid of any slouch, a clear focused gaze. That was a start.

With a brush in one hand, he started straightening his fur again. He could feel the shakes inside, wanting to come out again, but so long as he went slow and steady, he could keep them at bay.

Jun gave himself one last check in the mirror, then turned and opened the door.

He had been wrong earlier. Rebecca hadn't left something outside the door. She'd left herself outside the door.

She lay curled up on her side, almost naked. Over her nose and mouth she wore a facsimile muzzle made out of rubber. Besides that, she had on only a collar and leash, harness, and her plug with the fox-tail curled around her hip.

She looked up at him and gave a shake of her hips in an imitation of wagging. It didn't look right at all. In fact, it looked silly enough that Jun, as awful as he had felt just a moment before, had to suppress a laugh. It was the thought that counted though. Unlike Jun, what Rebecca felt inside mattered. How she looked outside was unimportant.

"How did you get out here?" he asked. The front window was still wide open and she was naked, or mostly so.

Rebecca rolled over onto all fours and gave another wag of her hips. If she had crawled out like that, then the couch and chairs and the natural geometry of the house would have been enough to give her privacy. He grinned.

"Clever girl. Come on," he said and took hold of her leash. Seeing her like that, it was enough to lift his spirits. She truly was as good a bitch as a human could be, and probably a better one than most canines.

Jun led her into the kitchen, intent on cleaning up whatever remained of the mess he had made earlier, but Rebecca had done her job well. Nothing was left of the broken glass. She knelt beside him as he stopped, pressing her cheek and the rubber muzzle against his leg. In her motions and attempts to show herself off, Jun noticed the dildo tucked away inside of her.

Jun gave a light chuckle and reached down to tug it out, but it didn't move. She was clenching all right. They played a quick game of tug-of-war over the dildo, which she quickly let him win. It went into the sink, along with some water and soap to clean it off, but Jun did not get too far before he felt a prodding at his crotch. "Want the real thing back in its place?" he asked.

She didn't speak, but instead gave a bark (one that took every ounce of his self-control to keep from laughing at) and shook her rump excitedly.

"Beg for it."

Rebecca hopped up into a squatting position, bringing her hands up by her neck, looking like a dog begging for its treat.

"Good girl. Stay." He tapped her muzzle once.

Jun went to the living room and closed the front blinds before he allowed himself to undress. He came up behind her, naked. Her attempt to turn and face him was stopped with a quick growl and a command to "Stay."

Despite rubbing himself, he wasn't getting hard. The stress, the lack of sleep, the fear and nausea of a near relapse all combined to suppress his arousal, but more than anything else right then, he wanted to have one more great fuck with her. With a grunt, he just pushed his sheath down and gripped the base of his shaft tightly, forming a quick, temporary cockring with his fingers. That did the trick at last.

Jun unfastened her muzzle and tossed it aside, and Rebecca, already knowing what was expected, slipped the tapered tip of his shaft into her muzzle. It didn't matter how stressed he was at that point, he was staying hard.

Jun took hold of the back of her head and guided her down another inch along his length, but she had other ideas. She pulled off as soon as he let go and worked his shaft in a more canine fashion with licks and nuzzles. Incisors and canines added a sharp contrast to the soft warmth of her lips and tongue. Her touch heated his blood. It was not long before he gripped the back of her head and pushed her down his length once more, forcing her to take as much as she could.

Her mouth wasn't nearly as big as a canine's, so Jun quickly filled it with plenty of his shaft still wanting attention. He gripped his swelling knot and pressed in. All the tricks he knew about deep-throating Jun had taught her, but that was not enough for her to take in another inch of his shaft, and even then, only for a few short seconds. She gasped and gulped for air as he pulled out, but there was a fire and lust in her eyes.

Jun took a step back. His hand on his cock made it sway teasingly before her nose. As she fixated on it, he looked over her own body, still held like a begging puppy.

But a cold reality set back in on Jun when he caught sight of the faux tail coming out of her rump. He had not forgotten what he was trying to do today, and seeing it gave him another idea of how to finally push her over the edge and make her say "no." But could he do it? Could he do something that drastic?

Of course he could. He was the Big, Bad Fox after all.

"Get up," he said. "Bend over the counter."

She was happy to obey. Her naked hips swayed in the air before him, faux tail following the rhythm. The plug came out with a slick slurp and a mumbled thanks from Rebecca.

Jun nestled the tip of his length between her folds and ground back and forth, feeling the heat of her spilling out over his length. Rebecca turned her head to the side and shifted her hair out of the way to let him see: she was panting, mouth open, tongue lolling out. It was not something natural for her, but it was again something she did just for him, to let him know how much he was turning her on. His shaft gave a throb of desire.

Jun cringed inside at his next motion. He shifted his hips around, lifting the tip of his shaft up through the folds of her sex and then to the bud that lay behind them, resting his tip against her pucker. He may have cringed, but Rebecca shuddered. "Wait, Jun," she said, her panting completely stopped. "That's what you want?"

"It is," he lied.

"You didn't lube up."

"It's what I want," he insisted.

She shuddered again. Her hands clutched at the edges of the counter. She didn't look at him. She looked at the sink, at the fridge, out the window, anywhere but him. "Okay," she whispered.

"What?"

"I said okay. Just… go slow, okay."

"No," he said, pulling back away from her, nearly stumbling into the fridge. "No. This is all wrong."

"What? But you said you wanted this." She kept the position, her naked rear held out for him.

Jun found his fists balling up in anger, claws pressed against his pads. "What I want is for you to show me you can stand up for yourself. Say no to something for once! Why would you even think of letting me do that to you? You know how much that would hurt you."

Seeing that he was serious, she slowly turned to face him. She still didn't look at him though. "I thought… I thought you knew what you were doing."

"You should know better," Jun shouted.

"But you've never hurt me before, Jun, not ever. I trust you."

He clutched at the nape of his neck. He wanted to rip out his fur in frustration. "Trust me? Rebecca… I'm an alcoholic! I'm a drunk!" There. He had said it. It felt good to say it. To be completely honest, inside and out.

She finally looked at him. Her stare was cold. "You've been sober for years. You would never—"

"I almost downed a beer just this morning." He let that sink in. "I was stressed, I haven't slept, I've been having nightmares, and I'm not thinking straight. Next time, I might well finish it off. Even if I don't drink, what if I tie some ropes too tight and you don't complain because you think that's how it's supposed to feel?" He could feel the growl boiling in his throat. "You need to go."

Rebecca's expression remained unchanged. "No."

Jun rolled his eyes. "Rebecca…"

"No, I need to say this first. Then you can decide if I still need to go."

"Fine. What?"

She took a deep breath. Her weight shifted from foot to foot as she tried to put her thoughts into words. "It was a year ago, the night after we met. I went back to the Kennel. You have to understand, I didn't know you, Jun. You were some strange guy I met at a BDSM club, who I let tie me up and fuck me in public only minutes after meeting him. I had no idea if you were some creepy stalker or a genuinely nice guy or what. So I went back and I asked everyone about you. And you know what they all said?"

"Haven't the faintest."

"They all said that there was no one safer to be with than you."

Jun let his growl out. "No, they didn't."

"Yes, they did." She pushed off the counter and stepped closer to him. Naked though she was, she was as fierce as an Amazonian warrior when she wanted to be. "Think about it. The very first words you said to me were explaining the safety protocols at the Kennel. You weren't that way with me alone. You practically counted as an unofficial safety warden there."

Jun crossed his arms and looked away. "There's no way they would say that. They all know me. They know my past. They all know I could…"

She placed a finger on his lips and drew his gaze back to herself. "Yes, you could. You could have a drink and accidentally tie the ropes too tight. But you know what? So could anyone else. The difference between you and them is that you know your own limits far better and you know what will happen if you break them. That's why they trust you. That's why I trust you. But you need to trust me too."

"I do."

"No, you don't, Jun." She jabbed a finger at his chest. "You don't trust anyone else to get it right. You check the ropes every time you tie me up but you have not once helped me learn how to check them myself. Not once."

He swallowed. She was right. Deep down, the only thing he trusted was the Big, Bad Fox, a construct he knew he would never completely live up to.

"You don't think anyone else is as strong as you, do you?"

Jun's ears laid back and he shook his head. The Big, Bad Fox was cracking. "I think everyone is stronger than me, Rebecca."

"Then trust me."

"I do," he whined, even as he knew it was lie.

"I mean it, Jun."

Jun wrapped his arms around her and held her tight. The Big, Bad Fox wouldn't be emotional, but then again, the Big, Bad Fox also wouldn't care what anyone thought of him being emotional. "I do trust you, but please, Rebecca, try to understand. I don't know what I would do if I ever hurt you."

She pushed out of his grip, her face set and serious. Jun was sure she was going to march out of his life right then and there, but instead she opened the fridge. Jun watched, jaw hung wide, as she pulled out the IPAs, opened them one by one, and let them drain down the sink. "You don't get to have them, so neither do I. I'll give something else up that means as much to me as drinking does to you. I will show you I can be as strong as you."

It was silly, stupid even, but as Jun looked at her, he saw fire in her eyes—a momentary flicker of a Big, Bad Human. "You're really not going to leave, are you?" he asked.

"Not for a stupid fucking reason like that, no."

He grinned. "You know, a proper bitch would have obeyed when I ordered her to leave."

"Guess I need a lot more training then, what with all the safety rules you need to teach me too."

He pushed in and kissed her. A human kiss. She deserved that one. "Go get my crop then. You've got a lot to learn."

Mustard Maloto

Slip-Wolf

Ketchup, two harsh lines worth, olives, liberally sprinkled, and onions, glorious onions. Slide through your order please.

"Come here!" The voice was equal parts fierce and seductive, but the crop allowed for no uncertainty. It came down twice over a grey furred rump, leading to a plaintive moan and shiver. "Everyone here is as disgusted with your laziness as I am. Now you're going to suffer for it." Clamps on the nipples twisted slowly. The slave rose quickly, gasping.

* * *

She was mad again. But in the wrong way. Hélène kept her short grey muzzle level and glared, saying nothing over the glow of her laptop screen on the kitchenette table. Her striped tail, thick and bushy for a lemur, wrapped around her protectively.

Leonard sighed as he slumped against the wooden post at the end of their bed across the open plan condo he shared with his girlfriend. The raccoon didn't wear a stitch of clothing, his own thick striped tail twitching underneath him. He was forbidden to ask for what he wanted. He knew this. Hélène would know and bestow, or not. Rules were everything.

He fixed soft brown eyes on her and tried not to look like he was begging.

She didn't look up. The black mask around amber eyes made her tiredness look like some kind of restrained ferocity. "The proposal is due tomorrow," she said, traces of her French Madagascan accent showing through. She cursed under her breath as she deleted a line and frantically retyped it. "The MOMA has just two slots left for August and I need to secure funding for one of them now. Otherwise I'll be back to warehouse spaces in the sticks. Hell, I might as well be doing plastic bag sculpts in the park next to caricature doodlers and that rat Statue of Liberty who freaks out the cubs."

Leonard sighed, fingering the chain of the collar that sat unworn in his naked lap against his paunch. For a moment he fantasized about both of them penniless, kicked naked from their Soho apartment in the thick of summer and himself forced to give blow-jobs at a claw-shine stand in Grand Central to get by. With a small smile, Leonard felt his cock slipping free of its sheath and caressed himself with a hiss that was loud in the small space. He could see Hélène's long tail lash around to wrap her from the other side of the chair and sensed his game was distracting, getting her angry. He wanted her mad at him, just a little, but in the back of his aroused mind where he licked the excess polish off a cute leopard's toes, Leonard was confronted by the sober realization that Hélène faced extreme stress. She was frustrated and miserable in the moment and his needy games weren't helping.

His arousal fell and took his erection with it. He watched her pound keys and swear at her computer before he finally tossed the toy into the nightstand's lower drawer, wrestled on a pair of shorts and sat across from her at the small kitchenette table.

"So you're finally done playing," she said, tight-lipped. Her tail thrashing behind her.

We never started. It's been two frigging weeks, Leonard thought. "I'm sorry," he said. "I'm not being fair I know. It's been awhile since we played last and you know how I get." How he got was something that couldn't be described with words. He thought of the other day's meeting which he tuned out of because he was imagining himself tied spread-eagled on the table while the hot setter from the Irish-based sales team flogged him. He'd earned a stern look of rebuke in the real world when he failed to hear a question put to him by his manager two chairs over.

Hélène licked her small black nose. "This is important, Leonard. Artists fail and flounder all the time in this city because they never get more than a tiny space in some back-alley showroom nobody ever sees." She indicated the laptop screen as though it featured some sort of arcane idol. "This is the Museum of Modern Art, the center of the universe for me. An exhibit space there, even for just a few weeks, would make everything for us. I finally have a patron who might sponsor me. Those are extremely hard to get Leonard."

Leonard came around and looked at the proposal she was writing. As a part-time bass musician he had some exposure to arts and artists outside of his relationship with Hélène. But he started to read a passage of political dissention as a factor in the resurgence of Italian futurism and gave up. He just couldn't understand it. "So have you settled which ideas to choose from?"

She shoved the computer away with a force that startled him. "No! I can't settle on anything. I have the general concept, I know which elements I want to use for the sculpture but it's all static. It says what I want it to say with all the punch of a shitty subway ad, even if it will be objectively different from all sides." She threw a dismissive paw in the direction of the card-stock miniature diorama she'd put together, which sat next to their Florida vacation photos from a year ago. The sculpture featured the buildings of Wall Street, twisting in distorted angles skyward like architectural Godzillas looking to consume one another. A plasticine and wire mock-up of a dressed-for-business ferret cringed before it with a briefcase over his head full of broken masonry, seemingly caught between worship and existential terror. Leonard blinked at the display. "It's good, truly menacing. I get what it means. I think."

"Everybody will get what it means," Hélène moaned. "It'll be a curiosity that people gaze at for a moment and then move on. It's too static to stand out, even with the building motors having a hydra-like sway. I only have space in the exhibit for one piece. It needs to *start a conversation*." Hélène abruptly stopped talking and stared at the document on her computer like she was afraid of it.

Leonard put an arm around her shoulder and squeezed, ruffling her faded Yankee's shirt. She was punishing herself in that self-doubting way unique to artists for whom the spark hadn't hit yet, and who felt the fear it never would. "You'll think of something. I know you will."

Hélène didn't respond, lost in despair as she gazed from her proposal document back to the building sculpture mock-up and back again.

The night came with no satisfaction for Leonard and protracted grumbling from Hélène. In the uncomfortable silence, Leonard fought a torrent of emotions. He was annoyed that he couldn't satisfy his cravings with just a simple hand-job, yet felt guilty that he could be so wrapped up in his desires when Hélène was literally shedding with worry. It wasn't quite that Leonard was selfish, at least he didn't think so. His needs were a creature that needed him in a way, demanding things through his libido that he couldn't provide for himself. He could put the leash on, he could even apply most if not all of the toys in the nightstand on himself, but the results failed to satisfy. The arousal would subside after a few self-administered scoldings and applications of the rod on his sensitive parts because he couldn't apply the strokes properly and wasn't losing control in the way he needed. People just couldn't subjugate themselves.

Except to their day jobs of course. What kind of bullshit was that?

As he went to bed, staring at the ceiling and slowly succumbing to the pure exhaustion of his own deprivation, he heard Hélène curse aloud, pressing what had to be the delete key again and again, reducing another proposal to just a blank screen.

Morning came with a bloodshot vengeance. Leonard quietly and reluctantly jerked off in the bathroom, taking nearly half an hour to finish. When he left the bathroom, freshly showered for his meeting downtown, Hélène had risen and gone, her laptop taken with her. She left an ungodly mess of debris on the counter and Leonard felt a chill when he realized what it was. The mock-up of her proposed art piece had been shredded, mashed, and reduced to plastic, metal, and paper littering the Formica surface.

He hastily dialed her cell. *Stupid, useless piece of shit. She needed your support and you were too wrapped up in your whiny needs to see how you were failing her!* Almost immediately, Leonard's mind made a casting change. It was Hélène herself yelling that accusation at Leonard while he groveled before her, naked, black paws over his eyes. She yanked the chain that controlled him, raised her whip high—Leonard swore and swiped at Hélène's mess, scattering the broken mock-up remains. The phone rang and rang before going to voicemail. "Hélène, please… please call me. ASAP. I saw the mess and I'm worried about you." He hung up and cursed himself as he stomped over to grab the vacuum, plugged it in and nearly clogged it with the wire fragments among the mess. When he had the worst of it taken care of, he regained enough self-possession to text her. I'LL BE AT WORK FROM 9. PLEASE LET ME KNOW YOU'RE OK.

He put his clothes on after and was in the subway ten minutes later. Work didn't take long to become exactly what he feared.

His job almost exclusively dealt with overseas clients either in the office or teleconferenced and he spent the morning listening to the no-nonsense guttural tones of the German contractors talk about how they would position his company's web-commerce services in Germany. The stereotype of German businesspersons sounding angry wasn't quite true, but as Leonard listened to one woman explain about television adverts in Austria, he found himself wondering what species she was at first, then what she was wearing and finally, what she would do to him if she found him wondering these things.

Probably nothing. If only she knew he was imagining her topless, with only a tight pair of lace panties over her lupine sex—if she was German she had a reasonable chance of being a wolf—and a commandant's military cap crowning her head between her ears, along with leather gloves on her paws, creaking as she twisted the wrapped grip of a riding crop, then…

A slight growl crept into her voice as Leonard took notes and she went on. Definitely canine, an alpha type in his imagination, demanding of discipline. She would inflict pain where it was needed, particularly with snotty little New Yorker raccoons who lost focus in tele-conference meetings and would need to be sent downstairs to stand naked in stocks at the street corner where she could administer a proper punishment for the passing crowd.

A growing erection disturbed Leonard's slacks as he leaned back in his chair but he didn't fight it. Unlike other meetings where he could get a conference room, he was teleconferencing this one from his solitary cubicle. His cock began to push at the tight bulge of his slack fabric and he felt himself begin to heat up, covering himself with his paw but avoiding any stroking. A German wolf would know what to do with him, maybe fly over and give Hélène a few pointers in schooling filthy, slovenly raccoons who couldn't maintain workplace discipline. Hélène had been tight lipped on the subject of his playing with other people, stating directly that *she* would never betray *their* relationship. If she were to find her naked raccoon being punished on that street corner by a strange wolf, they would have a claws-out battle to—

No, that wasn't how it would go. That just didn't work. The German song of figures and projections over his headset rumbled along as he realized that Hélène would be furious at him, at his failures to her. She would snatch the whip from the German wolf's paw and go to work on him herself while the people passing that street corner would stop, point and laugh. The humiliation when he'd squirm, shout and beg for forgiveness would be unbearable. He could picture his own tail trying to curl underneath and the bob of his dark, vulnerable sac as the furiously employed crop sought it out.

There was a spread of warmth underneath and he lifted his paw to realize with shock he actually came in his slacks. The beige CK's had a dark spot, slightly discolored by foamy whiteness that had seeped through both layers. He blinked down at himself in disbelief. He hadn't ejaculated without a touch since he was fourteen years old. The chlorinic sweet smell of seminal fluid drifted upwards.

His ears pinned back, flushing with worry. At least ten other noses were at work in that room, all stuck in computer monitors, tablets or photocopier screens. Any second the scent would start to carry. He muted his line on the call, stood up to hurry to the supply closet and then immediately sat down again. The stain on his pants would be seen from outer space for fuck's sake.

His paper files were cleared away to the cabinet across the hall and all he had was post-it-notes. He had no water, but his coffee sat on the desk, grown cold with neglect. He weighed his options and finding none that could save him embarrassment, deliberately spilled a dollop of coffee right on his crotch.

He swore loud enough for Ned, the fox who handled customer complaints, to hear him. "Gotta get a stain remover from the closet," Leonard said clear and loud before clicking back on the call. "I'm very sorry, have a little situation here. Can I confirm the figures I've taken down and call you back shortly?" The affirmative sounded a little annoyed. Leonard thanked her profusely, cut the call and trotted to the closet, coming back with stain remover and scent-suppressor. He sprayed the aerosol to cover the seminal miasma before going to the men's room to fix the mess. His assistant manager averted his eyes as they crossed paths and Leonard panted over the men's room sink for nearly ten minutes.

A torrent of emotions flooded through him as he worked at the mess. He was ashamed of what had happened, but even in that moment, with release achieved, he felt titillated by the idea somebody could have caught him. It wasn't to the extent that he would have let that happen, he didn't want to risk losing his job, but the realization of what had nearly happened both thrilled and terrified him at the same time.

His phone buzzed in his pocket, Hélène's ID on the call display. He heard the worry in her voice right away. "Hey, you okay?"

"It's still not going well," she mumbled. "I've been wandering for hours, wracking my brain and nothing is coming. I think I'm going to lose this one." There was no sob in her voice. Hélène didn't do that. She was a strong person who had little time for sentimentality which was one of the many reasons why Leonard loved her. Regardless, he could hear the resignation in her voice.

"Come on, you can't give up on this. You've been at it for months. You'll come up with something I know you will. You always do."

"I don't think it's going to happen this time, Leo." He could imagine her head shake.

He went to a stall and whispered to keep their conversation private. "You've been hard at this for days. Get your mind off it for awhile. See a movie, read that Sapphic poetry you like, anything to clear your head. It'll help."

"Goddamit I've been trying to clear my head for days! It's impossible. This is everything and I can't *get* it. I promised a concept to a patron who can get me in. When I deliver nothing after all his patient waiting—" She broke off with exasperation. "Why the hell would I even expect you to understand?"

Her snappy comment stung Leonard, but even as dejection crept in, a familiar twinge at her barking put-down surfaced in his hindbrain and the next words left his mouth before his emotional intelligence kicked in. "Well there is something that will get your mind clear, sweetie," he breathed. "You could put on those high-heels in the closet and punish your anxieties. I'm sure we can flog our collective worries if we just let the goddess of Madagascar punish an unclean maloto who's broken the fady taboos."

Dead silence was broken by the honk of a car on Hélène's end. Leonard had one brief moment to realize what was coming before Hélène roared into the phone. "My whole fucking life is unravelling before your eyes and all you can think about is getting off with your fucking submissive boy-toy games? You shit!"

Leonard cringed.

"I have just six hours left to write a proposal that will define my whole career trajectory in the art world and it's just another excuse to feed your whining, pitiful sex drive!"

"But you love doing it! You said so," Leonard burst back without thinking.

"I *sometimes* love it. I *sometimes* find it liberating. Like when I'm *not* going through an emotional hell that just needs a little support from you, just the smallest acknowledgement of the misery I'm going through you feckless, selfish child! Hell you're probably getting off on this right now."

Leonard realized coldly that if he hadn't accidentally rubbed one out five minutes ago, she would likely have been right. He fought for his next words. "I'm sorry," he managed weakly.

"Bullshit," Hélène's voice crackled with fury. Leonard felt it like a stab. "Not to mention that I fucking told you not to bring my ancestral myths into it any more. Just because you don't have religion, it's so fucking like you to just grab whatever's lying around and drag it into your culturally insensitive cesspool of a mind."

"It was a bad idea. Please Hélène, I swear I was just trying to help you relax. I know I have a bad filter when it comes to my needs. Please understand I don't want to put them before yours, ever."

"But you do, Leonard," she responded flatly, a heavy weight in her voice. "You used to be sensitive and conscientious of my feelings, of allowing me my space when I needed it, but it's like you don't care anymore. Now you're just an animal who can't put your wants away. You play the submissive in your fantasies but you dominate everything in our relationship with it. You just take control."

"But I don't want to." Leonard nearly wailed. Everything was going so horribly. He was so lucky to have Hélène as a girlfriend and he didn't know what he could do to make her see that. "I just don't know what to say. I try so hard to please you, but I know I'm not perfect, any more than you are. You get so damn mad and standoffish when things don't go your way and I feel like only a sub, that is somebody like me, would even stick around to put up with it. But hey, we can't customize our relationships to have every single thing we want and there's bad with the good. I know I'm at fault right now—"

He got no farther. The line had already gone dead.

* * *

Brown mustard, hot peppers, dash of relish. Order wrestled into the waiting slot with sweaty, anxious paws.

The supplicant whistled with delight as his chest and caged cock was squirted with oil. A rough paw grabbed his sac and teased it for one relaxed moment before starting to squeeze. There were no words necessary as cold eyes gazed down like daggers. The Mistress moved round the slave's back after releasing the testes and squeezed the bulb on the end of the rubber tube that fed up into the invaded rectum. The hose pulsed snake-like beneath his tail and the slave drew ragged breath, delirious with excitement as the pressure within increased.

* * *

Hélène wandered through Little Italy, cellphone gripped with shivering knuckles. The cloying summer heat and the idiocy of the man-child on the phone's other end were conspiring to make her dizzy with the rage already swimming through her over her listless muse and impending failure.

The bastard was just using her dejection as an excuse to play his games. "I try so hard to please you, but I know I'm not perfect, any more than you are. We can't customize our relationships to have every single thing we want and there's bad with the—"

She broke the call, swearing out loud. New Yorkers passing by ignored her as she mimed throwing the phone through a pizzeria window. Hélène stalked west towards the water, heart hammering in her chest and long tail lashing behind her.

She had to come up with something. There would be no support from Leonard. She was coming to understand that now and had serious pangs of worry that she would likely be ending their relationship soon. Both their names were on the lease and they would both have their things in boxes if it all broke down.

How could anybody be so selfish? She did enjoy playing games with him in happier times, taking on the dominant role and making him cower before her, beg for her favor, service her by whatever means she wanted. It made her feel like a Goddess, the 'coon's whole world laying at her feet. But now all their best moments together seemed a million years ago, happier days played out with someone who was lately becoming a stranger to her. Right now, in the hour of her dire need, with everything on the line, he was just a cock puppeting a horny raccoon, lost in his own urges. *We can't customize our relationships to have every single thing we want.* True as that ultimately was, it sounded mocking in her mind and she just wanted to smack him if she were with him now.

She turned a corner and moved around a hot dog cart that was fully loaded but gave off no telltale scent of cooking street meat. It was unattended. Strange things being the norm for Manhattan, she ignored it until the ferret shouted. Out of the corner of her eye, up a ramp into a small loading dock, she saw a second cart thundering towards her. Reflexes honed by squash court follies and centuries of ancestral tree climbing took over and Hélène leapt out of the way as the second hot dog cart collided with the first, knocking condiments all over the place. The errant mercantile missile bounced and came to rest against a newspaper box, nearly bowling that over too. A ferret at the top of the ramp scurried down towards her

"Lady, lady, I'm so sorry!" the weasel shouted in a Brooklyn swagger. "It got away from me, dammit."

"You could have killed somebody," she hissed. "You're lucky all you have is a mess to clean up."

The ferret nearly stepped in a dab of hot sauce as he straightened the laden cart out and began closing the lids on the ketchup packet tubs. "Let me make it up to you. I'll fire this up, make you one on the house. Any way you like it. You vegetarian?"

It took Hélène a moment to register the question. Ordinarily she didn't eat hotdogs but on the cusp of her worst day ever, why the hell not. "Not completely. I'll… I'll have a beef one."

She looked at the rusty, empty cart that had nearly flattened her while the ferret navigated around the mess and started the burner on the laden one. "You use two carts at once?"

"No, that one's had it, falling apart. I'm scrapping it." The ferret sighed and put a frank on the grill. "It won't meet code anymore."

Hélène nodded distantly as she gazed at the loaded cart that cooked her next meal, sale signs flipped back and ranks of tubs and squirt bottles still askew like it was frozen in the midst of an explosion. So many options to choose from. Too bad poor Leonard couldn't customize himself a relationship with all the options laid out here. Probably weren't enough for him, nothing ever was. She avoided snickering so as to not have to explain to the ferret, who seemed grateful he wasn't getting an earful about her nearly being knocked into the street.

"Nothing like making one of these exactly how you want it," the ferret said amiably to break the silence. He rolled the tube of meat over on the grill and withdrew a bun to toast with it. "Not much in life that we can have that way, right?" The ferret's brows rose hopefully as his paw rubbed his fresh clean apron.

Hélène stared into the disordered maelstrom of mustard squeeze bottles, spoon-dipped bacon bits and white onion curls. There was a profound moment of calm when her mind clicked and a torrent flowed in right after. "How much is that cart you're scrapping?"

The ferret frowned as he put her meat in the bun. "Won't get more than a hundred for it. Hell, getting it there's gonna cost like—"

"I'll give you eighty."

There was a frantic three hours spent arranging for storage of her purchase, firing up her laptop down in the coffee shop and getting her stormy mind down on paper. She could barely write fast enough. By the time Leonard took the subway back from the office, Hélène had arrived at the apartment, gone into her closet, and was thoroughly prepared. A weight lifted off her even as a wicked fury remained.

She needed catharsis, which she intended to extract. A smile crept to her lips and her tail flowed like a slow-cracking whip when the raccoon unlocked the door and entered with his eyes down.

"Get in here," Hélène ordered, her voice rumbling dangerously. Leonard's ears went reflexively flat and he froze, his eyes rising slowly to meet hers like a drunkard's in a police cruiser's floodlights. What he saw made his face go slack.

Helene stood with clawed feet spread wide in an aggressive stance. Black mesh stockings followed her thighs up to where hooks hitched on skin-tight black leather underwear. Whitish fur gleamed around her bare midriff all the way up to a shiny grey PVC halter that covered her shoulders and the underside of her breasts, staying open between them, exposing the bare cream of her chest and neck fur. This was broken only by a choker around her neck, from which dangled a short chain with a single key.

The tiny apartment rang with a snap as her riding crop struck the table. "What did I just tell you?"

Leonard closed the door behind him with a shivering hand and took a hesitant step towards her, his shoulders already drooping, his muzzle dipping low and his eyes aiming at a point in space below hers. He fell into his role speedily and seamlessly, conditioned to react. "I'm coming," he muttered meekly, slouching further with each step. Hélène could almost smell the confusion coming off him, pushing back the arousal he would typically be feeling at this point. She knew he deserved to feel that way, and didn't pity him.

It might just ruin things for both of them if she did. "You were a total shit today."

There was a flutter of his nostrils and twitch of his ears when he realized that hadn't been forgotten. "I'm sor—"

"Shut up." The riding crop was up under his chin fast enough to snap it shut. His eyes found hers and Hélène felt proud of the fear she put in them. "You're going to earn my forgiveness tonight and it's not going to be easy. Get. Down." She didn't shout a word. She didn't need to.

Leonard's paws came up in supplication as he fell to his knees and started to unbutton his shirt. She stung his wrists with her crop. "No. Apologize with a kiss."

Her crop lay across his muzzle, instructing him not to get up and he clearly didn't know where his lips were to go. She pushed down,

down on the bridge of his nose until he was looking at her lacquered toe-claws. His breathing began to pick up in pace as he understood and lowered himself, until Hélène could feel his frantic excited breath on her knuckles with each of his kisses. "I want you to clean between them. Be thorough." His tongue tickled the blunt digits with each lick, moving the short fur in circular massages. The sensation between her toes was wonderful but what came with it was even better. The thrill of raw domination over him flowed through her. Still she kept stern and silent, her face a mask.

It was possible that Leonard had been right. Maybe, had she still been unable to complete her proposal, she would have been helped into relaxation by engaging in their game. She had her mind solidly on him and away from her dilemma when the clouds had parted.

Some might reward him for helping her arrive at the solution. Some might have punished him for the selfish way he had done that. It was like a fiery liquor burning through her to know that she could see it the way she wanted it, and treat him accordingly. He reached out to touch her toes and she stuck his slack-dressed rump with the crop. For Leonard, she could do both at once. "Pants off. We both know you didn't even feel that."

A curt nod. One foot on his shoulder kept him down to the parquet while he worked at his belt. He had to lay on his side to slide them away, underwear, slacks and everything. His wallet fell out and she kicked it away. Meek eyes awaited further instructions. His pinkish dick was already peeking out of his sheath, leaking itself shiny. "You're going to spend tonight in the cage," Hélène told him as she brought her foot-pad over to his face. He sniffed at it before licking away the pavement dust she'd walked on today, a sour look of supplication on his face. That got him a little harder. "But first you're going to take the punishment you deserve."

She stood in total silence, feeling him lap the sole of her foot in slow, long drags, his dress shirt disheveled and his lower half bare, with legs askew. She watched his thick tail shake in anticipation, unsure of whether to sway or tuck itself under. Somewhere in the middle of all that tail's indecision was Leonard's disposition, terrified, elated and uncertain. She was still mad at him after all. He needed to know that. "Bed, now." Her foot came away and he was fast crawling towards it, tongue lolling out one side, expecting the forced cunnilingus and backside thrashing that had become their preferred pattern, like the contents dumped on a favorite hotdog. He froze when he saw the handcuffs locked around each bedpost, their mated cuffs yawning open.

"Put the right one on." She didn't wait for him to comprehend her instructions before she struck him on the rump and he scurried to obey. She was needed to attach the second cuff and swore at him for that.

"I'm sorry, Goddess," Leonard whispered.

He was cuffed facing the bed, barely able to kneel with his arms spread-eagle and his muzzle on the mattresses' end. She left him there a few minutes, poised to accept a spank from her crop while she removed her underwear quietly and prepared her surprise.

When she strode on the bed and made the cowering raccoon look up, she sported her new toy, her long lemur tail curling languidly out behind her. The thick red dildo projecting from the harness she wore gleamed with a flaring silicone sheen, smelling chemically of its virginity. The toy Leonard favored was smaller, shorter and nowhere in sight. His eyes grew wide as he squirmed before the demon from Madagascar above him, a feral glint in her eyes. The artist laughed. "You thought this was going to be a pedestrian makeup play, didn't you, Worm?"

"No," he said weakly, afraid, nostrils spreading.

She couldn't see his dick but she knew it was boring into the baseboard. This was completely out of his control, just the way he needed it, but was frightened to have it. It was the very scenario he deserved, and the thrill of power that Hélène already felt grew to excited heights as she watched him cower, eyes wide. She let him see that she was enjoying it, her heart beating faster to see him squirming pathetically against what was coming to him. Hélène crouched, spreading her legs wide and dangling the synthetic member in front of his face as her long tail sinuously curved around her. "I'm going to let you choose the degree of your punishment."

His slack face told her he didn't understand.

She sat on the bed with the dildo touching his nose and held up a squirt bottle of lube for him to inspect. "Beef flavor, better than you deserve. I'm going to put this in your mouth, and then you've got one minute to wet as much of this as you can before I mount your pathetic, slavish ass. If there's nothing on there and I go in with this dry, that's your problem." She took a breath that heaved her breasts, making the PVC barely containing them crinkle. "Are you ready?"

He blinked several times, uncertain how to respond. Woe to him if the next thing out of his mouth was the safeword. She would respect its power, but not him, not after this. She felt empowered, but she was still angry and not afraid to show it.

"I'm ready, God—" he nearly gagged when the water-based lube splashed against his tongue.

"Don't swallow. You can spit after and have water if you need it, you pathetic asshole, now suck!" She pushed forward and her lips parted as he began to administer the lube, tongue frantically working. His eyes sought hers to gauge how serious she was about what was to come next. Her stone cold golden eyes confirmed she wasn't joking. "Forty seconds," she said smoothly. He began to suck on her ersatz member frantically, trying to cover as much space as he could. The handcuffs clicked against both bed posts and he fought to keep balance. His tail was so far underneath him she couldn't see it. "Ten left." He took it so deep in his throat that he nearly choked and she withdrew her hips back from the raccoon scabbard with a flourish, splashing a few drop-lets of spittle and lube across his muzzle. He coughed until she grabbed the waiting tumbler of water and let him swish it around before he spit it back into the cup. By then she was already behind him, yanking his tail up and smoothing the fur back from the pale star under Leonard's tail with the recovered riding crop.

"Ass up, slave!" She thwacked his buttock sharply and his ass raised so fast his shirt flipped forward on his back, leaving him naked from mid-spine down. "The longer it takes for this to get started, the dryer

I'm going to get. You don't want that to happen, do you?"

"No, Goddess," Leonard responded breathlessly.

Hélène lined up the strap-on with his anus, explored its tip with the wet, bright probe and entered slow but firm.

The toy was slick, but he wasn't and he grunted painfully with the first slow advance. She set the crop on the bed, took his cheeks in both paws and forcefully spread him on her second push, slow but insistent. He gasped as she buried the first couple inches, slid back to spread the lube and then pressed forward again a little deeper. Leonard hissed like a convict on a Victorian whipping post at the first lash, gritting his teeth against something much less painful, but a profound shock to his senses. Back and forward Hélène went again, burying the smooth member halfway inside him. Two more retractions then two more thrusts and she was all the way in. They held still a moment while their breathing slowed. Then Hélène started the race.

She withdrew slightly and then pushed all the way to the hilt, then again, each time eliciting a gasp from the raccoon that grew shallower and shallower as she picked up the pace. Leonard spoke something that wasn't the safeword and she struck him across the back. He shivered, holding himself up with paws braced against the ball joints on the posts and pushed back against her. Hélène brought the riding crop low, breasts pressing into his back, and massaged Leonard's chest under his askew shirt. Hélène pulled the crop downward, stripping the buttons binding the shirt closed, and threw it forward, flipping it inside out and covering his head with it. Leonard's back was left bare for Hélène to strike when he tried to control their pace. She drew the crop back to his cock and stroked it with the birch handle, cold lacquered wood dragging moisture back to his dangling sac.

Inside the leather harness that held the dildo, a pre-wet nub rubbed Hélène's clit furiously with each thrust. The power she held over the enslaved raccoon was aphrodisiac enough but the hot slide of the dildo's nub against her clit was getting her wetter than April as speed increased. She could see stars, serenaded by her slave's moan and was barely aware when he abruptly came, coating the baseboard in a white bliss. He would clean that up later.

Hélène came four bucks later with a high-pitched cry, burying the dildo inside him and shivering to her very core. They both became still and panted, allowing silence to fall.

"Did I gain your forgiveness?" Leonard croaked.

"Not yet." Hélène undid the clasps and let the kit fall away from her hips to leave the dildo dangling, buried deep in Leonard's ass. She brought him back a glass of water, finding him struggling. He was still cuffed and the toy was still rammed deep despite the hip harness dangling from it. It was a delightfully amusing sight.

"Goddess?"

"Two things left. First, you clean me. Then you do a little reading. When you are done, you'll get into your cage." She gave him more water to swig and drink. Then she turned on the television and sat at the end of the bed with her spent sex in Leonard's face and a cola in her paw. He cleaned her up with efficient licks while she watched the six o'clock news and relaxed in the post-play haze. Twenty minutes later, her vaginal lips still buzzing from the attention, she reluctantly rose. She set her laptop on the end of the bed and let him read her proposal while she gingerly removed the dildo with a satisfying pop.

After cleaning the toy she returned to where the still-bound raccoon knelt, reading intently. She was gratified to see his tail swinging.

"I'll have a mask?"

She nodded. "I know you work in the city. I won't risk your job, just take a week of your vacation time. Or you might say you'll take mine."

Leonard screwed up his face. "But hot dogs and… will this be enticing to people?"

"It will be challenging to people's perceptions. It will make them think. That's what's important." She put a paw between his ears and teased the fur there. "And it will satisfy both of us. Tell me I'm wrong."

Leonard nodded, tail darting left and right. Even sexually spent, his nervous reply was electric. "I'll do it. Whatever I have to sign, I'll do it."

"Sleep on it. Don't make this decision in the heat of the moment.

It's a big commitment."

He looked up at her, breaking away from the confines of his role for just a spare moment. "Honestly, I really wish I'd thought of it first."

Hélène allowed herself a thin smile, the only departure from character she would allow herself as she popped the catches on his cuffs. "Just the same slave, I won't let you tell me you're absolutely certain until the morning comes. There will be lots of things they'll make you sign, waivers and such. Lawyers in the art world have a million safewords." She pointed at the wire cage that she'd assembled in the bottom of their closet. "In the meantime, not a strip of clothing goes in there with you. Prepare yourself and move."

Leonard took a quick bathroom break, then hurried back, slipped out of his dress shirt like a sloughed skin and crawled on all fours to the cage, pulling his tail in after him. She closed it and sealed the latch.

Hélène sent the proposal. In the total quiet of that night, neither could sleep with their excitement.

* * *

Hélène Brouges, Madagascan born, 1983
"None with Everything," 2015 mixed medium,
interactive sculpture and live performance.
Patron sponsor, Barry Tanner

Bacon bits, sauerkraut, yellow mustard. Hot sauce was written down but then scratched out.

"Down! Time for you to worship." The dildo wedged inside the slave buzzed intermittently, an invasion that never abated. His shoulders were forced back by the harness that bound him. The Mistress yanked a rope, pulling his tail upwards exposing abused buttocks while the slave's leather-masked face buried itself into the dias he was displayed on. In delicate but fast flicks of the wrist the goddess' riding crop whipped his bare testicles, bringing bright gasps to his lips. Once the slave's latest punishment finished, he stood with shaky legs upon the treadmill and marched fruitlessly, trying to pull the hot dog cart he was yoked to forward with the red leather harness that bound him from shoulder to waist. The cart could not move, fixed in place and festooned with a combination of condiment bottles and assorted colorful sex toys that could be used on the slave as required. The mask that obscured most of the wretched raccoon's head gleamed in dull black. His hard-on was kept bent within a sculpted metal cage.

Short podiums placed at three points around the slave and Mistress featured tearaways for the taking of individual hot-dog orders. While most of the exhibition goers stood back and pondered at the spectacle, a few hastily filled in the sheets and watched as the Mistress came by to collect the orders for their individual ideal hot dog, the specific arrangement of condiments for tubes of street meat which most of those assembled would never actually choose to eat in their real lives if they could help it.

Nor would they here. These orders were translated by the pre-arranged system of associated punishments which the un-named Leonard, the anonymous subject at the exhibition's direct center, would willingly suffer for as long as he was willing to hold back the safe word. Ketchup lines equated to whippings, while mustard represented humiliating put-downs. Olives demanded teasing and violation of his exposed testicles and so on through a long list of more exotic toppings and punishments.

The controlled abuse accumulated as the Mistress, in her white leathers and tight smock, pulled slip after slip and carried out the orders taken with thin cruel smiles. Leonard bore a stream of insults with flattened ears before the pump-expandable dildo was pushed all the way in again, slowly but insistently. The toy's tightness inside of him drew a shiver as the dozens of eyes studied the bound creature with critical stares and more than a few amused snickers. The sheer sensation of all those gazes on him, those noses drinking in his musky discomfort, each reaction in his field of vision held something different. He sensed amusement, awe, pity, disdain, disgust and barely restrained arousal. The air was heavy with pheromones crowding in around his and Hélène's. She strutted assuredly, sternly keeping him in line and taking her orders. The slave knew from the way she carried herself, with that feminine bouquet wafting out past the smooth stink of her fresh leathers that she was enjoying every minute of her artistic, slavish masterpiece.

An unseen male whispering to his left drew the slave's ear. "Simply put, this installation encapsulates the core existential dilemma of all thinking animals in regards to the negotiation of menial working lives. We seek pleasure to alleviate our pain, while assuming pain as a means of gaining access to that pleasure. In the cyclic trade the two become indistinguishable and the rewards are as horrible for us as the punishment themselves."

"Um, doesn't it already say that in the pamphlet?"

"No, not exactly," came the defensive reply.

There was a moment of hushed curiosity as the slave was made to sniff the crop that abused him. Paws reluctantly shuffled on and a fresh group of viewers wandered fully into his view.

A painfully skinny vixen in a black dress worked black fingers that seemed to yearn for a cigarette. She gave the naked raccoon a cold once over that just barely restrained a sort of hunger as her tail swished slowly. "We are enslaved by the oppressive forces of free choice," she said to her turtle-necked cougar escort. "The hot-dog makes for a perfectly disgusting example. Notice how when you figure out what you actually tolerate on one of those things you are loathe to ever change that formula?"

The cougar nodded, studiously devoid of expression. The vulpine sighed. "Well the suffering of all free creatures stems from choice. Years of slavish calamity easily surrendered for the happiness of option-less conformity. The slavery that results thus begets a comfort." She coldly met the slave's eyes, for it was only in those terms that Leonard would think of himself, and a twinkle there was reinforced by her wink.

The cougar brightened at what she might be thinking. "Shall we go home?"

"Shut the fuck up." She watched the slave get his buttocks flogged for a moment, savoring the view. Her penetrating gaze made the slave's cock stiffen harder before she tightly stalked off to the next exhibit.

A caffeinated weasel in a leather jacket filled their void, his whiskers trying to dance off his face. His black-shirted nose-studded rat companion muttered a monosyllabic question.

"Yeah. Oh yeah, I totally got this. So this is about the enslaving of native peoples through the vicious weapons of exported culture. See how the leathers represent the hides of aboriginal dress, taken and commoditized into tools of bondage? We baste the natives with the red, white and blue of subjugation and shove our cultural manifest destiny up their asses. Then we sell them as consumable products.

"Um, I get the red ketchup and white onions in that basting bit, but what about the yellow mustard?" The Goth rat asked dubiously.

The weasel sniffed. "Well they had to go with yellow. What's blue that ever goes on a fuckin' ballpark frank?"

At that moment, a yank on his lead dragged the slave back to the here and now and the Mistress squirted water on his face, nose and chest. "Move again. Take the cart up a block." The crop stung his shoulders. The slave began to march. Three minutes of tread-mill marching in front of the motionless exhibit was equivalent to one city block. So far today, he'd gradually pulled the cart more than twelve.

Time passed quickly in the joys of his subjugation, attended by the supplicant eyes of hundreds of art loving New Yorkers. It was something out of a fantasy come true, and he enjoyed every minute of each two hour block during which he was displayed. The breaks in between were blissfully short, just time to relieve, hydrate and get into character, heart racing the whole time in anticipation of the next set. When the curtain was finally pulled back on the exhibit after the final set and the Mistress became Hélène again, he was at the verge of bursting. "May I cum? Oh please, may I?"

The crop touched his balls, massaging them menacingly as the cock-cage was slipped free and Hélène's paw took its place. She massaged it firmly and growled carnivorously into the raccoon's ear, sinking with him as he dropped to the slick treadmill surface. The whole exhibit smelled like him now. "I command you to," she whispered beatifically as she nibbled his ear and caressed his flushed member.

Leonard had spent hours on the brink, ready to tip into completion, and he came around fast, joy pearling on Hélène's paw and forearm. She watched him pant as they sat in the curtained-off null zone of the now vacant exhibit space, his breath deep and ragged in the muffled spot. She waited a minute for him to come down.

"We need to make something clear." Hélène had fully stepped away from her Mistress's role and met his eyes with a frankness that brought him out of his role. "This worked out for both of us, but it shouldn't have. You can't simply twist things to satisfy your desires, no matter how strong they are. That's not what our relationship is about. That's not what *any* healthy relationship is about. You seem to be trying to understand that, but I still don't know if you do."

"I do," Leonard said readily. "I truly do and I'm sorry."

The lemur gazed at the masked raccoon locked by leather and steel into her exhibit. His shoulders were hunched even as he sat on his haunches, arms still restrained behind him.

"Prove it." Helene said.

Leonard took a deep breath, his mouth opening and closing with nothing to say. Hélène waited for a long time before he finally spoke again. "I'll get help. I'll see a shrink."

"That might be a good idea. I enjoy my part in this, and you know that. How you handle yours is the problem." Hélène sighed. "It's a matter of self-control, Leonard. You can't spend your entire waking life in this state and you need to take steps to dealing with that, whether you involve someone else or not."

"I don't know how," he said, honestly.

"If you will let me, I will help you. We just need to take a few steps at a time, not move a whole block at once." She nodded to indicate the cart behind him. "Can you do that for me?"

Leonard's lips turned up to a smile and he nodded. "I will. If it will make you happy, I'd be honored to. I just ask for one thing in return."

Hélène canted her muzzle attentively.

"Even though I understand it when you get mad, please don't take your work stresses out on me. Most mates would walk out on somebody who snaps at somebody and talks down to them, deadline problems or not. It's just ironic that you doing that very thing triggers my arousal. Maybe we both have some work to do."

Hélène blinked and gazed at him and Leonard was relieved to see her expression soften. "Yes, of course you're right. I can be downright wicked when things aren't going my way. I'm sorry."

Leonard smiled. "The best thing about our relationship is that most of the time, you don't need to be."

Hélène put a dark paw under his muzzle and scratched his chin. Were he feline, he would have purred through the grinning muzzle under those closed eyes.

"I'm going to go clean up. You want me to untie you now?" Hélène asked.

"No rush. I can wait till you're cleaned up and have gotten a bite to eat." Leonard sighed, jangling the metallic locks and buckles on his outfit. "This is a truly great exhibit you put together."

Hélène laughed. "Shut up you filthy worm." She parted with a self-possessed smile that her raccoon beamed back at her, the curtain swinging in her wake.

THE DUCK QUACKS TWICE

Ocean Tigrox

My bill clamped down hard on the wet cigarette as I pulled my fedora further over my brow. Couldn't keep anything dry in this damn rain. Looking at my beat-up watch, all it told me was I wasn't getting any younger. No sounds of life echoed through the street, only the rain and a lone lamppost had my back. I glanced at the large house window but the drawn curtains blocked my view of any movement inside. What mallard could ask for a better night to confront a killer?

The case had been open for months. Someone was going around whacking males and taking more than their lives. The guy always went missing for days, maybe weeks depending if they were just some loner who kept to themselves. No signs of a fight or kidnapping—just gone without a trace. The only thing that tied them all together was the piece we'd kept from the papers: each mallard was missing their manhood. Made all the rookies back at the precinct lose their lunch or squeeze their legs together. Just made the chief angry. Seven dead ducks in a row and this case had to find its way into my lap.

I was left doing what I do best: sticking my bill in places it didn't belong. My scars eased me into the crack dens and gambling halls without much trouble. But it wasn't money or drugs that killed my victims. That left the deadliest option—a dame.

Took a while to waddle through some leads. Paid some off. Called in a favour or three. Eventually all the paths crossed here. I had accounts of locals seeing all my dead ducks passing through this door-way. Now I'd have to follow in their footsteps if I wanted to find out what happened to them.

Spitting my soggy cigarette butt onto the walkway, I knocked at the door with three sharp raps. When the silence inside was broken by footsteps, instinct had me wanting another smoke. Wasn't my first time undercover or going in alone. That's how I got these scars after all. Took a lot to scare me. Yet, when that knob began to turn, something told me this wouldn't be the same.

The door swung wide, and there stood a white, middle-aged dame silhouetted by the bright lights from inside. The duck wore a large, dark blue housecoat that sat like a murky pond on her shoulders. She took a step forward, her orange bill looking down, moss green eyes meeting mine. The cold frozen stare of an ice golem held me in place.

"Can I help you?" Her words cut the silence, snapping me out of my hypnotic gaze.

With a blink and a shake of my bill, I regained myself. I looked about to see if any prying eyes were watching. "I have an appointment?"

Her eyes drew up and down my body. "Mr. Dubois?"

"Yes." I swallowed. She had the same stance as the instructor in the academy who made you shut your yap and sit up straight. "We spoke on the phone."

This seemed to be enough to convince her of who I was. She turned and walked back in, her words trailing but concise. "Come in, quickly. Shut the door behind you. Don't keep me waiting."

I felt released. Her eyes no longer held me where I stood and I was free to move. I nodded, not sure why with her back turned, and entered the house.

Once inside I shut the door and removed my hat, scanning the foy-er. It looked as ordinary as any other place on the block: simple wood grain furniture; dull, fading carpet; the occasional painting adorning the otherwise boring eggshell white walls.

"Take off your coat and shoes, leave them here." That voice snapped me back to attention and reminded me who I was with.

"Yes, of course." I complied, not thinking twice about a simple request from a homeowner. I placed my soggy hat and coat on the stand next to the door, sliding my shoes from my webbed feet to the floor beside them. There was nary a spec of dirt or dust to be found in this place. The vase of flowers perfectly arranged on the side table, the mail stacked in a neat pile, the rotary phone with notepad and pen set next to one another—the whole residence spoke of strict organization, regulation and discipline.

I turned to her and took a step back. She stood in the archway to another room, hands on her hips. The face of a sculpture, reserved and patient, sternly waited for me to finish my task. Once she saw that I was focused on her again, she nodded. "Follow me."

We moved from the foyer to a large living room containing a tall bookcase filled with leather bound books and vinyl records, a large plush sofa and two smoking chairs with a record player between them. She marched over to one of the chairs and, with her back turned to me, removed her housecoat. As that murky blue fleece fell like a swampy waterfall from her pure white neck and naked shoulders, it revealed the cross-laced backing of a black leather corset. The inky garment clutched her mid-section, but left the soft down on the small of her back free and exposed to a light breeze brought in by the ceiling fan. My eyes continued to fall with the housecoat, watching as below the fluff of her tail, a matching black bikini line trailed around her waist and cupped her tight rump. Clipped on to the garters snug on her thighs, straps ran down the backs of her long pale legs. They reached the tops of stockings that stretched past her knees and all the way to her feet planted squarely on the floor. A drake like me never gets to gaze over a sexy dame like her; little to say I was mesmerized.

I stood in awe of the ebony and ivory figure before me. She was at first slender but had hidden a strong, athletic build underneath that house coat. The lady turned to face me, her stance perfect, straight, like that of a drill sergeant. The corset slimmed her build even further while exposing her small but perky chest. Her face still remained in that steely stoic stare, my body stiff as a board while my eyes roamed the curves of this lily pad, taking in the power and grace that radiated from the woman in front of me. From her head to her toes, she wasn't much taller than the average bird, but seemed to grow an extra foot when she stood at attention. Or at least she seemed to be growing. Maybe I was just shrinking as I felt my shoulders slump.

She crossed her arms behind her back and spread her webbed feet to shoulder width. Standing at ease but still alert. "Now, sit." Her bill pointed to the large ruby red rug sprawled across the floor.

Without hesitation, or even questioning, my body did as commanded. I took a few steps forward to the center of the mat and lowered myself to its rough sewn surface. What was going on here? I blinked down at the rug and then back at the woman who had been barking orders. Satisfied at my complacency, she stepped back and sat in the smoking chair behind her, leather creaking with delight at her touch. Crossing one leg over the other, she curled her hand up under her bill, allowing my eyes to linger on her lean, muscular thighs.

A moment of silence passed. I wasn't sure who watched who anymore as her eyes swept over me again. Like a standoff at gun point, we waited to see who would make the next move. Patience growing thin, my lips parted. Her chin rose, eyes widening, challenging me to speak up. An omen shivered across my neck and I shut my bill. This seemed to appease her as the corner of her mouth cracked its stoic demeanour, curling up into a sly grin, the first true emotion I had seen of her this night.

"Well done, Mr. Dubois, I'm impressed." She uncrossed her legs. Clasping her hands together, she placed her elbows on her knees, leaned forward and rested her chin on the backs of her hands. "And you said this was your first time, too?"

"Yes." I nodded and looked up to see that scowl on her face, staring me down again. I choked and sputtered, "Y-y-yes, Ma'am." Did I just say that?

"Excellent." She leaned back with a smile. "You're learning quickly. This meeting should go smoother than most. First, I will go over the ground rules. As you have already noticed, you will only speak when spoken to. Anytime you address me you will do it properly using either ma'am or mistress. You will do as commanded without hesitation. If you fail to obey any of these rules, you *will* be punished. Do you understand?"

My backside shivered at her dark tone. Wondering what I was getting myself into, I nodded. "Yes, Ma'am."

"As for the business aspects, each time you come over you must discard your shoes and jacket when you enter. After that you will come here and sit as you are now. Once you are sitting on the rug, all the rules I explained previously are in effect. We will discuss any concerns or issues that need to be brought up and then you will pay me. Payment will be made in cash, up front, before each session. No exceptions. Do I make myself clear?"

The stern tone she struck held my bill firm as I continued to nod in compliance.

She snapped her fingers. "Speak, Whelp!"

"Yes, Ma'am!" I sat straight up, barking my reply. Memories of being yelled at by the ex-wife prickled the back of the brain and my crotch started betraying me. The bunching in my pants made me shift my seating to grant some extra room.

Her sly grin returned. "Good. Once payment is received we will move upstairs. There is a bedroom up there that I will allow you to enter. In that room you will strip to your underwear and sit on the mat I have provided at the foot of the bed. You will find a small dresser which you may place your belongings in. I will proceed to enter the room and the session will begin. Each session will be an hour in length, and that begins when you enter this house, so be prompt but do not come early. Once the session is over, I will leave the room. You will put your clothing back on and leave the house without any further contact from me. I allow five minutes at the beginning and end of each session for you to dress and undress accordingly. Do not try my patience. Nod if this is acceptable, Whelp."

Caught off guard with my mouth open, ready to shout my agreement, I blinked and eagerly dipped my head.

"One last point: if for any reason you should need the session to end, the safe word is *slate*. Remember this. Speak this word loud and clear, and I will stop and release you. Be warned, once you have stopped the session, we are done for the *entire* session. I will remove myself and you will have five minutes to dress and leave this place. No refunds will be granted, and we will have *serious* discussions before beginning another session. If you have any questions about the rules or these procedures, ask now as they will not be repeated. You will be expected to understand and obey them without fault."

Her speech was intoxicating and well-rehearsed. Took me a moment to remember what I was doing here again. This woman was quite possibly a murderer; I had to find proof and get out. With so much to take in at once, my mind raced through it all, trying to think if there was anything that wasn't touched on. Her rules were structured and tight, little leeway for me to do any real snooping around. It sounded like the only time I would be alone were those five minutes to change, unless…

I raised my hand unconsciously, confused at the action since I was the only one in the room. She acknowledged me and I asked, "What if I need to use the washroom?"

Her eyes narrowed and she leaned in close, her voice returning with that steely blade's edge. "I would advise you, Little Whelp, to relieve yourself before coming to one of my sessions."

I swallowed hard, holding back a whimper and shaking my head. "Nothing further then, Mistress."

"Excellent." She steepled her fingers together, relaxing into the back of the chair. "Then we can move on to discuss your sessions. You revealed on the phone that you were interested in experimenting with bondage? Am I to assume you have not had any experience with this before? It's very common for new people to jump into the unknown and see what they like."

My thoughts reeled back to the telephone conversation we first had when I decided to take the plunge and see what her deal was. After finding out that all the dead ducks had been seen entering her house,

I had to get in there myself. Problem was I didn't have enough to get a warrant. Some victims were seen leaving too. Also didn't know what exactly I was looking for. High profile case like this, chief didn't want to take any chances on "just a hunch", his words. I was out of leads. There was only one way in. I set up an appointment with the mistress.

Wasn't too sure what went on at these places. I found out it was somewhere for people to appease weird sexual desires. On the phone she asked what I was interested in, catching me off guard. I was left to rely on what the last poor sod who fell to her was interested in: ropes, chains, gags, collars and cuffs. Apparently some people needed to lose control and be immobilized to get off. Been tied up enough times on this job. Wouldn't be too hard to fake enjoying that.

"No, Mistress, I have not." I played dumb. Hoped it wouldn't lead to too many questions. "A friend had recommended I might like it."

"Oh, a friend! You talk about your desires to others? I did not take you for one to be so open! And telling others before confronting your mistress first? Perhaps you are holding back on me. Who is this friend of yours; do I know them?"

I stammered and muttered, eyes darting about the room. Was I in trouble? Do I say one of the dead drake's names? No, quick, think up another name: a fake name, something, anything.

The icy tension shattered when she broke out laughing. "There, there, Little Whelp. I am merely playing. I keep all my clients names confidential so do not bother. Whoever they are, they sent you in the correct direction."

I tugged on my shirt collar and let out a heavy sigh muffled with a weary chuckle. Pulled my ass outta the reeds on that one.

She didn't seem to notice. "Now then, since this is your first session I will begin with the basics and go from there. I do need to know if you enjoy pain?"

The word 'pain' caused me to cringe. The scars under my feathers trembled. I shook my head with wide eyes. Not sure what she was asking but with a possible killer, staying away from pain sounded like the smart and safe choice.

"Fair enough." She chuckled again. "But I will warn you, I may use pain to punish you *should you stray.*" She shot me a pre-emptive glare, leaving me feeling guilty for something I hadn't done yet. "I think I have enough information. There is just one question left." Her eyes snatched on to my view and held me tight, that gorgon's gaze. "Do you trust me?"

Petrified to the core, I was left with no leeway or escape. The words formed in my mouth without thought, confused they were even mine. "Yes, Mistress, I am yours."

A smile spread her bill open. She stood back up, her hand raising, commanding me to stand. "If you are satisfied with everything we can proceed to our first session, assuming you have my payment."

Uncrossing my legs, I stood up and fished around in my pants pocket for the wad of cash I brought. My fingers flipped through the greenbacks as I counted out half a month's rent and handed it over. She nodded and walked out of the room, calling back to me, "Follow."

It was all or nothing now; I hurried to trail after her. She didn't look back, just continued to march back to the foyer and up a set of stairs. I looked about with my eyes wide but there wasn't much to see on the second floor. It was like any other hallway in a house: pictures of flowers on the walls and little else for decoration. All the doors were shut tight, denying my questioning stares as to what was held beyond their portals. I tried to pick up any muffled calls for help from would-be next victims but nothing perked my senses. Instead she led me to a door, opened it wide and waited for me to step inside.

I was expecting just another basic room but what she provided was extravagant. Against the back wall was a queen size bed with satin sheets and custom steel metalwork, rods twisting and twirling to form the scuffed silver bed frame. At the foot of the bed was another red rug, this one much smaller than the one from her living room. Behind the bed a heavy blood-red curtain cut off any light from what I imagined was a large window to the alley beyond. Instead the room was lit up by the large chandelier hanging from the middle of the ceiling. Bronzed, twisted rods formed a large hemisphere. Starting from the center and expanding and curling up to thick bases that tapered out, each rod held its own lit candle at the end. It must have been a custom ornament as the metallic pieces lacked symmetry between them as if handmade. I noticed a gap where a rod seemed to be missing; could be an indication of foul play, though it was too high for anyone to grab at without assistance.

"Here you are." She stepped behind me and stood in the door frame. "I will return in five minutes." Without waiting for a response, she closed the door and left me to prepare on my own.

Her commanding presence now gone, I was released and given free will again. Time was short; what do I do? Could I sneak out and look around? Was there even time for that? Dammit. That woman was a pro and ran a tight ship. I couldn't be sure she wasn't standing outside the door right now, a demon duck devouring my thoughts.

To the side of me stood a custom crafted oak dresser just as she had said there would be. A quick search of it turned up empty so I began to strip, unbuttoning my dress shirt while I glanced around the room. What was I looking for even? Hoping to find the victim's missing bits? A drake's lanky penis wasn't something you could store easily; just ask my briefs. Opening the top drawer, I removed my shirt and folded it, placing it inside, before continuing to undress.

Wrestling with my belt buckle, I heard a loud thump behind me. I jumped and stumbled, whirling around to see if she was behind me. On the floor gleamed the dark sheen of my revolver. Right, my exit strategy in case things went horribly wrong. The only friend I could trust. I had completely forgotten it. But what would I do with it now? Couldn't keep it on my person if I was stripping down to feathers and underwear. If I could place it somewhere for easy access should tables turn…

My eyes found the bed again, the lines between the mattress and the box-spring calling out to me. I waddled over and slid the gun between their folds, making sure that no lump showed and I could still reach for it if I needed a trump card tucked away for later.

I took a moment to check the window, pulling the curtains away.

The gleam of porch lights scraped at the glass and outlined the bars forming a lattice pattern beyond the pane. Escape wasn't looking good at this point. Tempted to open the window in case I'd need to call out for help, I decided against it. She could pick up the breeze and get suspicious.

My attention switched to the closet on the other side of the room. What was behind those wooden doors? A quick tug at the handles told me my question would not be answered. A lock on the closet held the doors in place. Maybe I could try to pick it?

A set of footsteps echoed behind the door. Crap, had it been five minutes already? Scampering back to the dresser, I ripped my belt from my pant loops. I slammed it into the drawer while shaking my hips back and forth to get my pants to fall from my waist. I thought I heard the doorknob jiggle as I tripped attempting to step out of my pants. My ass hit the ground with a loud thud, and I froze staring at the door, pants clinging to my ankles. To my disbelief, the door stayed shut.

Couldn't waste any more time. I removed my pants and slid them into the dresser with the rest of my clothes. I closed the drawer and stepped over to the red rug, not wanting to disappoint the mistress. My mistress now it seemed. This whole situation had my mind buzzing so much I hardly noticed when the door finally creaked open.

She marched in, still clothed in her contrasting feather-tight clothing. Her face had returned to the stoic void it first was when I met her and once again it stared me down. No words were spoken, no congratulations on being ready in time, no asking what those loud noises were, no questions about what I'd like to do, nothing. She walked past me instead, over to the closet, unlocking and opening its large wooden doors. From behind the sliding walls, all I could see were full shelves of leather devices, silver studded straps, different lengths of rope and cord, steel rods, hoods and masks, crops, whips, flails, and other pieces of equipment that my imagination failed to understand the purpose of.

I leaned over, wondering if perhaps something in that closet may have been used in the string of murders. Maybe she tied them down and beat them senseless. Could have covered their heads in a zip-up mask so they never saw it coming. That weird device on the third shelf, could it be used for—

Smack!

The stinging sensation burned on my bill and I quacked out in shock. The mistress sneered down at me, a brown leather paddle in her hands. I threw my arms up, "What was—" Another slap across the beak shut me back up.

"You were doing well, Whelp," she growled. "Has your juvenile memory already forgotten the rules?"

I rubbed my sore bill, trying to smooth the sting out. She held the paddle in front of my face, ready to swing should I make another noise or movement. I held firm and bit my tongue, breathing deeply. Once satisfied, she motioned with the paddle. "Bed, now."

Unsure her intentions with me and the bed, I rose and looked at it. I stepped forward, hoping to get a better glance into the gateway of the unknown, but the paddle returned to my field of view. With a change of mind, I turned, walked away from the closet to the other side of the bed and climbed on top.

"Stay," she commanded, turning back and rifling through her choice of tools. When she faced me again she held a leather strap with a shiny clasp and ring. With a flick of the paddle, she motioned I come forth, her eyes always boring down on me, never leaving my head.

I scooted closer, trying to look behind her but was unable to escape her gaze. Once I reached the edge, I swung my legs off the side of the bed. That sly grin returned to her bill as she tucked the paddle under an arm and brought her hands up to my neck.

Frozen between the terror of a possible killer reaching for my throat, but at the same time not wanting to disobey my mistress, I found myself unable to move. My eyes shut tight while pressure encircled my neck and squeezed.

"There," she cooed like a babbling brook.

I opened my eyes to find her hands on her hips, yet I still felt the soft squeeze around my neck. I raised my hand but stopped, not wanting another attack from her paddle. Looking up at her, she nodded and I proceeded to feel the smooth leather surface hugging my neck.

"This is your collar, Whelp." She reached up and hooked her finger around the silver ring attached to the strap. "Enjoy it." With a fierce tug, she jarred my body towards her. My eyes shot open wide. A jolt of electricity shot down my spine, shivers raced through my limbs and my back straightened out.

A playful whimper escaped my throat. My morality started losing ground; dark desires and instinct seeping in. Before I could stop myself my lips were already moving, "Thank you for this gift, Mistress."

That pleased her. Her bill curving wide in a smile, she tapped my nose with the tip of her paddle. "There's my obedient whelp. Now, lay down." She gestured to the bed.

Again, she wouldn't turn around until I was out of the way. Was she on to me? Was she keeping her weapon of choice hidden until the final moment? Either way I couldn't look into the closet with her in the way, watching my every move. There was little more I could do so I lay back in compliance, placing my head on one of the pillows like lounging on a lily pad. Once there I turned my gaze back to her, but her paddle was there to meet it. This time not in a quick swing, but instead she poked the side of my bill, forcing my view back to the ceiling.

"No peeking, Whelp. You'll ruin your surprise." She chuckled.

I listened for her footsteps and after two or three I started to tilt my head over closer back in her direction.

Whap! "Do I need to blindfold you to prevent your straying eyes?"

I fell right into her trap. The paddle had been waiting for me to make that exact move. I winced and clenched my fists, returning my eyes up and staying rigid as a corpse. I didn't dare look at the scowl plastered on her face. Inside my heart, I already knew I was disappointing my mistress. The noises of her rustling through the cabinetry of the closet tugged at my ears, clawing to drag my eyes over, but for all I know it was another trap, testing my obedience. No, I would be good. I would please my mistress for she is worthy of my trust. I shut my eyes tight, refraining from temptation.

Again, I questioned where these thoughts continued to come from. I had never seen other experienced detectives fold like a flimsy napkin while undercover. Sure, there was the point where you had to act the part but something about this was becoming too natural. Like bending the rules because I like it when the chief chews me out.

The bed creaked and my body dipped to the side. When I felt a touch on my arm, my eyes floated open to see her sitting next to me. She took my wrist in her hand and wrapped a length of rope around it. Fastening it into a tight knot, she doubled back and wound the cord again with another knot. I watched in slight confusion as to what was going on as she tested the knot and tugged it up. Pulling it back, she brought my hand back to the bedframe, tying the end of the rope to the intersection of the metal bars. When she leaned back to admire her work I yanked on the bindings, the metal frame chiming in with a clank. The rope dug into my arm the more I resisted their binds. Even rolling my wrists yielded no purchase. Satisfied, she moved to the other side of the bed and repeated the process with my other arm.

I'd been tied up and beaten too many times in the past. Run of the mill with my special style of detective work. Normally I'd be fighting anyone tooth and nail who'd come anywhere near me with a couple feet of rope. Yet this time…this time was different. I was in a daze, a hypnotic bliss, this dame of a duck could tie me up any day. She already had me wrapped around her finger.

Mistress returned to the closet; my desire to peer past her faded from my mind. My trust in her would not falter; I shut my eyes to withstand temptation. The mystery played into the enjoyment. I would allow her to choose what she felt best for me. Mistress knew best.

When a soft hand tickled the feathers of my chest I opened my eyes to see her standing over me. "My new whelp, you learn quickly from your mistakes." She climbed onto the bed, one hand squeezing my thigh for balance, the other hidden behind her. Sweeping her leg over my waist, she straddled my crotch and grinned down at me. "I will have to reward you for your obedience."

I looked up at her smiling face, unsure what she was up to. A shivering sensation slid past my lower feathers as something cold and metallic caressed along the skin underneath my down coat. The mystery object dragged along my inner thigh up to where my legs met. The tickling touch it gave my skin skittered to my crotch and up my body, releasing a gasp from my throat. My head tilted up to see her grinning at my reaction: a mixture of pleasure and confusion.

She placed her free hand on my rising and falling chest, pushing me into the bed. I couldn't tell what tool her hidden hand held, but something like sharpened sticks scratched at my soft skin, tracing along my hip down to my knees. Back and forth, a gaggle of knives that bristled my feathers. Their touch trailing heat and directing blood. The arousal came slowly but escalated with each trace through my feathers. My member expanded and unwound, bunching in the constraints of my underwear.

Mistress must have felt my growth underneath her since she started to shift upwards to give me room. "Mm yes, you're much more responsive than the last few slaves I had," she murmured, enjoying every twitch and whine from my bill. "They were not—" Her gaze fell down to the bed and she pushed her knee back into the mattress.

Her smile vanished to a scowl. She whipped forward, arm sweeping out from behind her. I made out flashes of blackened steel before a sharp prick pressed into the underside of my beak. She tilted my bill up and stared deeply into my eyes. The gorgon gaze held me tight. All I could do was gulp, unsure if I had displeased her or if the fear of my actual situation had risen above the pleasure.

With my bill held she leaned over and used her free hand to check between the mattress's folds. I saw her eyes widen. She sat back up, my gun now in her grip. Her eyes darted between the weapon and my troubled look.

She pulled back from my beak, allowing the equipment she wore to shimmer in the light. Adorned on her hand was a leather glove with sharp, studded claws imbedded in the fingers, the light catching their edges with a glimmer. A flick of her other hand and she tossed the gun to the floor with a loud clunk, causing my feathers to rustle.

94

"Who are you?" she sneered.

Frozen between the menacing glove and the uncertainty of the situation, I opened my mouth but no words came out.

This was not the answer she was looking for.

Her hand shot forward, the glove tightening around my throat, each sharpened claw pricking into my skin. "Tell me!" She squeezed and pushed me into the bed. "What are you here for?"

I coughed and sputtered, my arms flapping and flailing but the binds holding my wrists stayed firm. Struggling to give any response, I gasped and wheezed the only thought that came to my head, "Sla—te, sla—"

"There's no escape for you, deceiver," the mistress growled, her free hand pointing to the ceiling. "You'll just end up being the finishing touch on my latest work of art!"

My eyes rolled back up to follow her arm. Above hung the bronze-laden chandelier, the hole from the broken piece glaring back into my eyes. She reached back with her free hand and tugged my wriggling, extending member that pushed out from my briefs. The grasp caused me to cough, my eyes widening and focusing closer on the chandelier, its twisted rods of brass and their weird misshapen forms, none identical to the one beside it. The realization hit me. I struggled again, the reason for their asymmetry becoming clear. The shimmer of the bronze and the low lighting had played tricks on my eyes. They were not simple metalwork. No, they were trophies from her last seven victims. I was to fill the missing space and be her eighth.

Her sneer sucked the air from the room, and I gurgled for help. I watched the walls turn dark, matching the inky blackness of her leather corset, my view merging the two together. My consciousness grew weak. Life begin to flicker. The rush of blood pulsed heavily through my veins. My head throbbed, each beat thumping my sliding mind back to the edge of reality as it continued to slip further and further away.

Everything faded from view, save for her dark dagger-filled eyes, siphoning my life and draining every drop of my essence. Her grip on my throat grew ever tighter, cutting off the oxygen to my lungs and blood to my brain. I took one last look at her: my owner, my controller, my mistress. Her piercing gaze full of fury and death, yet in my last moment I saw deeper; I saw the joy behind her scowl, her hatred, her hurt. Her enjoyment of being in complete control matching my lifelong desire to put myself in danger.

I let the last bits of air in my lungs escape in a whimper, "All for you, my…mistress." My final thoughts were for her, to show how happy her slave was that he pleased her in the end. The excitement climaxed, and I felt my life spurt between my legs and drip down my thigh. My body shook and shuddered as my eyes rolled back and I went limp. Eternal darkness enveloped me, bringing my soul to peace.

A blow struck my chest. My eyes shot open. I gasped and gulped for air. The room phased back into view but remained hazy as I coughed, lungs heaving, my chest sore. My brain sloshed around, hammering away at my skull. Each pulse that ran through my temples was another beat of the drum. I tried to cup my head in my hands but found them unable to move.

"So you are still alive," a siren of a voice screeched through my distorted reality.

I winced and turned away, my eyes still blurry and unable to make out any of the moving shapes. One wrist fell limp against the bed, soon followed by the other. The itch to rub the agitated areas where my feathers had been ripped and rustled from the rope was not enough to overcome the sheer amount of energy it took to breathe with my weakened lungs, clinging to any life left within me. A few deep breaths and I could feel my heart rate finally begin to slow.

Her leather-wrapped chest and slim hips formed in my view once again. I could only blink and mutter at her, "Why am I?"

"I couldn't just rid myself of you now, could I?" She walked over to the dresser and placed a solid, metallic object on top. The clunk made me guess it could only be my gun. "You're much more devoted than the last slaves I had," she murmured, stepping back to the bed and caressing my panting bill, her creamy feathers smooth against my beak.

"They were not worthy of their mistress, they had to go. You…you are my prized whelp, the one I've been searching for."

"But—but I could take you in right now." I reached up and rubbed the points of pain pulsing from my neck. Pulling away, I looked down to see the fresh blood on my hands.

"Oh, but if you did that, we wouldn't get to play anymore." She smirked and leaned towards me. "The perfect slave requires the perfect master." Her fingers curled around the silver ring attached to my neck. "And you wouldn't want to lose your master now would you, Whelp?"

She gave a harsh tug, reigniting the fire inside me. My head shot up, back straightened, and eyes widened. "Never, Mistress."

HOME AT LAST

Laura "Munchkin" Lewis

Her world was darkness, leather, and musk. Invading that darkness, on the other side of the silk blindfold, she could feel the pressure of countless sets of eyes studying, admiring, molesting every inch of her nude form. Their phantom touch was just as clear as the soft voices whispering and commenting behind her, the illusory warmth of their breath drawing ripples through her marbled fur. Her cheeks heated with a flush and her body wriggled as awareness of their presence filled her senses. It made her feel dirty, so dirty, and she loved every moment of it.

She flexed her wrists and ankles, testing the restraints that suspended her from a hard metal frame. The silk rubbed smooth against her fur and sent a thrill through her body, drawing a soft purr through her chest. Bare feet arched and toes curled around the edge, causing her claws to expose themselves to the open air. Full access was granted to anyone who might be interested with how much her legs were forced apart, yet not so spread as to cause too much discomfort. Her wrists were held outward and raised a few inches over her head, with just enough bend to her elbows so she wouldn't grow stiff too soon. The one in control who had tied her up knew what they were doing.

The teasing scent of dark chocolate and nutmeg eased through the multitude of other smells, and she rolled her head back as a smile tugged on the corners of her muzzle. A slender hand caressed the bottom curve of her breast, the rough pad on the end of each fingertip scratching over the sensitive surface of her nipple. Her breath caught in her throat as the flesh prickled and hardened. The warmth she had felt in her cheeks seemed to spread through her body, through her out-stretched limbs and down her chest to pool within her belly. The hand moved to her other breast, this time a blunted claw teasing the tight-ened bare flesh around her nipple. The warmth of someone's breath tickled the tufts of fur in one ear and caused it to twitch. A voice just as warm and deep as the scent vibrated through her being, more of a growl than actual words.

"Are you ready to be made an example of?"

The sound sent a shiver through her body, causing her fur to raise from goosebumps forming beneath. Her long tail tried to lash out a few times before the pressure around the last few inches reminded her that the end was secured to the back of her leather collar, leaving her no possible way to cover her most private of areas. The tip flicked er-ratically behind her head, her words breathy as she answered.

"I'm ready, Sir."

Soft lips kissed the edge of her ear, causing it to twitch again. Her body hadn't stopped quivering, electrified by the anticipation his words had brought. The teasing fingers slid down her side and squeezed her hip. Its warmth left her body only to suddenly smack down hard across both of her rear cheeks, the fine fur there doing nothing to soften the blow. She gasped sharply as her body arched, a small mewl leaving her lips as the sting of the slap tingled through her flesh.

"What was that, slut?" the voice rumbled. "I don't think they could hear you."

She drew in a deep breath and forced words out harder, louder. "Sorry, Sir! I'm ready!"

"Mmm, better."

The hand caressed the delicious pulsations on her rear, drawing it into a glorious heat that she had been craving for far too long. Like a starving man so close to a meal, her lower back arched in, pushing her rear further into the calloused pads that covered the palm of the hand. Blunt claws teased at the bottom curve of each cheek as the palm mas-saged the firm muscles. The hand left her posterior, leaving a warmth behind, and her breathing deepened with the anticipation that continued to build. She knew what was coming.

Five more slaps rained down on her rear, the sting of each one landing alternatively on each cheek, coalescing into a tidal wave of pleasure and heat that pushed her closer and closer to the edge. The final slap landed across both cheeks, lingering there as if refusing to give her the chance to decide if what she felt was pleasure or pain or both. She sucked in her breath through clenched teeth, struggling to keep from crying out. The growl returned to her ear.

"Dirty little slut. They're all watching you. They should just line up now to have their turn with you. You'd like that, wouldn't you? To have that dirty little fuckhole of yours abused by all these males."

The last few words were punctuated by a sudden tug on her nipple. She gasped, squirming against the restraints. Embarrassment and shame heated her cheeks even as she felt a moistness seep through the fur on her inner thighs. Another mewl escaped her muzzle before she could stop it, and her nipple was pinched roughly in response.

"Beg for it slut. Beg for it like the needy little bitch you are."

Instead of words, it was a soft moan that answered his demands. She wanted this. She needed this. His hand left once more, no doubt to administer another harsh spanking. Maybe this time he would send her over the precipice she had been straddling. A hairline fracture ran through her subspace.

A peculiar scent tickled her nose for the first time that evening. It was cedarwood and oakmoss, with just a splash of vanilla tobacco. Even in her haze of drifting through submissive headspace, the familiarity of it was enough for her to latch onto. She closed her eyes beneath the blindfold and drew in a deep breath, before it struck her like a brick bashing right across her face. Her fingers curled around the silken bindings and her face flushed with sudden shame. Emotional scars she had been so certain had healed over ripped open, filling her eyes. Her mind felt sluggish as it struggled to work through the why and the how before it took a long jump to the worst possible conclusion. The safeword tumbled out of her lips before she could give it any thought, clear as a bell even as sobs threatened to choke it out.

"Edison."

Immediately the fantasy shattered into unyielding reality. There was the sound of something dropping to the ground, and the blindfold was up. Maria struggled to look around the male Doberman face, her bronze eyes wild. He filled her blurry vision though, the warm autumn browns in his eyes just as calm and steady as his deep, quiet voice.

"You're safe, Kitten. I've got you. You're safe."

His slender hands untied the ropes with practiced ease as he repeated the phrase over and over again, willing her to believe it. Once her wrists were free, her arms moved quickly to cling to him, trembling from her heart hammering against her chest.

"He's here, I know he's here. How can he be here?"

A blanket was wrapped around her shoulders, and one strong arm moved behind her knees while the other supported her behind her shoulders. The Doberman held her against his chest as he carried her away from the small crowd of on-lookers. Somewhere someone was using this as a good example for safewords and the responsibilities of a dom, but the feline didn't care. She kept struggling within her best friend's arms, her tail trying to curl between her legs as she struggled to peer around him at the group of confused faces. It was nearly impossible with the Doberman's bulky build, but she couldn't give up so easily. How could he possibly be here? He wasn't supposed to be here! The words threatened to erupt from her lips in a scream as they left the room through a back door, but the male cut through the panic coursing through her before her lips could release it.

"Kitten, what did I just tell you? You're safe. I won't let anyone harm you. Do you think I lie?"

Something about the words snapped Maria's molten eyes to the Doberman to find an arched brow and overly-exaggerated frown that bordered on a puppyish pout. Normally the expression would either melt her heart or have her batting at his chest with a smirk. Right then though, she felt herself slowly deflate within his arms until she finally shook her head and folded her ears back. "I...no, sorry."

The Doberman gave a single sharp nod as he carried her down

the hall, as if he had expected that reply. Some of the faces turned and there were a few worried murmurs from a couple of unfamiliar voices, but he ignored them all. "Alright Kitten, let's get you dressed. I think you could use some fresh air."

Maria nodded and relaxed in his embrace. She had hoped she could put off the explanation indefinitely, or at least enough years down the road that it wouldn't sting so much. She should have known Fate would flip the bird to those plans.

* * *

"So, what was that all about, Kitten?"

Maria's long whiskers twitched against her spotted muzzle at the name so few could get away with calling her, despite her genus and species. She held her latte between both hands, letting the warmth soak in through the thick pink pads on her palms and along her fingertips. The Margay stole a moment to study the fancy design on the top of her drink the baristas always insisted on making with the milk. Behind, her striped tail flicked with annoyance.

She finally glanced up at her best friend, her expression and the irritated flitting of her ears making her thoughts on the question quite clear. "He's just some guy from my past. Didn't expect him to be there. Small world and all that."

The Doberman leaned forward as he studied the feline across from him, making the chair built for smaller species groan in protest. His broad chest and powerful shoulders made him intimidating to most people. Each movement was enhanced by the gleaming black fur covering his bare arms, openly displaying his brute strength. The Margay knew Robbie as the gentle giant he was though, and it seemed emphasized by the delicate tea cup sitting in front of him. This was the same canine who had never budged on his declaration that the little chipmunk-ran cafe had the best hot drinks this side of the country, despite other cafes catering to larger species such as himself. It was nice to know some things never changed.

"You think I dumbed down over the years? When you said you wanted to volunteer for the demo, I asked if you really felt like you were ready. You said yes."

"And I was. Everyone botches a demo from time to time though."

"Not you. You were always the perfect little sub."

"No one's perfect—"

"—all the time. You were always perfect whenever you were in front of a new group, showing the perfect balance for following commands while making it clear you were giving yourself over to pleasure. You gave the perfect little display of what a good sub should be like for a good dom, just as I'm a perfect example of what a good dom should be like for a good sub. I wouldn't even call what had happened a botch. It was a complete meltdown. You've never reacted that strongly to anyone before—not even that time your brother walked in on us. So I'll ask again, what was that all about?"

Maria forced her long tail to curl around one of the legs of her chair before the lashing could trip anyone. She took a sip of her coffee, keeping at bay the snarl pushing against her lips. A few sips more had the calming heat spreading through her stomach and seemed to work through her chest. Her small frame wriggled a bit more into the coat she was wrapped in, trying to revel in the warmth despite the ice of the conversation that was threatening to freeze her. The cafe might have a decent heater, but all that warmth seemed to be escaping her at the moment. Finally she set the coffee down and replied with a quiet, "It's a painful story I'd rather not get into."

The canine arched a brow, the motion accentuated by the matching tan markings above each eye. His muscular arms folded across his chest—his typical 'I'm the boss' pose Maria knew all too well. His shoulders weren't rolled forward though and his hackles weren't raised—signs for when he was truly annoyed, but she could tell he was getting there rather quickly from the way he sat in his chair. "This from the kitten who preached the importance of openness in all relationships? Have you changed so much in the past few years?"

The Margay's coffee stopped just short of her lips, the words stinging in a way her rear never knew. Her rounded ears folded against her hair and her lips drew back slightly out of instinct, pupils dilating as if she had been slapped. She caught herself and forced her ears and lips to relax, taking a deep breath as she set the coffee back on the table.

A small group of customers leaving the cafe caught her attention as she tried to gather her thoughts, perhaps procrastinating a bit. She noted a bear wearing a t-shirt and shorts into the snow outside. Damn bears—she hoped he suffered for it during the summer. She shook her head at herself before her eyes closed partway and looked back to Robbie. His brows were furrowed with concern, yet he seemed so patient sitting there, waiting for her reply.

"That bad?" he breathed, one slender hand reaching out for hers. Maria pressed her lips together, but reached out to twine her fingers with his. Hot tears stung her eyes, but she refused to let them fall as she slowly nodded.

"I just… it feels so petty now, looking back." Her voice wavered, and she picked up her coffee before looking up at Robbie's dark eyes. She could get lost in the abyss she saw there, had been lost in them a few times in the past, snuggled up to him as he held her close.

Shaking her head at herself, she took another sip of her coffee before continuing on. "Don't laugh please?"

The canine frowned and tilted his head. His long ears were always perked up, but it was clear the request had him particularly curious. "Kitten, remember who you're speaking with, alright? It's your favorite pup. Your one and only Dopey Dobie. Of course I won't laugh at you." He leaned forward a little more with a small smirk tugging on his muzzle and lowered his voice to a conspiratorial tone. "It's not like you laughed when I first opened up about my interest in other males. And you were the first to get me to laugh about it and break the tension. You have any idea how much I treasure that about you? Least I can do is show you the same respect."

Damn mutt. She remembered that time. He had been acting so stressed and uptight after confiding in Maria and their friends that she was about to go nuts on him. Finally she quipped that he'd better learn to relax or he wouldn't get so much as a felid cock in him. It wasn't so much the joke as how Tom—their local felis domesticus—reacted. The poor guy never could take a joke and literally became hissing, spitting mad. It was all worth it to hear that laughter bubble up from Robbie though. It wasn't the polite smileless chuckle he had been doing, but the true, rich laughter from deep within his gut that they were used to from him. She just wanted to get him to laugh, yet he still treasured it to this day.

Damn Dopey Dobie. Maria's bottom lip wobbled, and her tail curled in close as her ears folded down once more. The tears she had been struggling with spilled over and dampened the fur that covered her cheeks. Robbie rose and scooted his chair over so he could sit at Maria's side. Those muscular arms wrapped around the small feline, and all at once her floodgates burst open. She hadn't even realized she had been struggling so hard to keep it all back this entire time. The safety of those strong arms picking her up and holding her close, the scent of chocolate and nutmeg and musk that was purely Robbie, the loud th-thump of his heartbeat that her sensitive ears picked up so easily—it was all too much. She buried her face in his chest and sobbed into his shirt, letting it all out.

It was a solid five or so minutes before a small voice in the back of the feline's head reminded her of all the people in the very public cafe. With a sniffle, she looked up at her best friend and blindly reached for a napkin from the table beside her. He produced one for her, but held her on his lap as she tidied up. After drying her cheeks and blowing her nose a few times, she finally pulled away from the canine to sit on the edge of her own seat.

"Sorry about that." There was still a waver to her voice, and only then did she notice a glass of water had been placed on their table, probably by one of the baristas on duty. She took a few swallows, letting the cool liquid strengthen her as Robbie shook his head. His expression was grim, yet softened with his concern for her.

"Don't worry about it Kitten. Looks like you've been holding onto this for quite some time. Just tell me, did he hurt you?"

Maria blinked at the question, and dabbed at the remnants of the tears still clinging to her lashes. "No, not at all. Most of this… I just… I'm ashamed of myself." Again her voice wavered, and she finished off the water

Robbie leaned back in his chair. "Alright then. Tell your Dopey Dobie all about it."

She reached back for her coffee, the warmth of her latte needed after the water had cooled her down. "There's honestly not much to share. Did I ever tell you about how we met back when I worked security?"

He shook his head before tilting it slightly, a smile tugging on his muzzle. "You'd already moved away then, and didn't really answer many texts or calls."

"That's because I was working double shifts and saving up. I told you that."

"I know, but still. Mmm, I struggle to imagine you being a very effective guard. Not all that intimidating with that small body of yours."

The Margay smirked and shook her head. "No, but I was approachable, and sometimes the most difficult of people just need someone who can empathize. Give them that, and most will continue on their way. Besides, you know how strong my lungs are. Turn on the stage voice, and most people are shocked so much volume can come from someone so small."

Robbie chuckled and parted his lips, but stopped himself and shook his head. "Alright, so you met at one of your company's sites."

"We started dating, things were melding pretty great, I made supervisor at another site. Chris and I got a small apartment together after about a year of that, and things were going well. I was even able to take fewer hours since we split a lot of the bills. It was so easy to talk to him. He already knew all the work jargon, so there was no translation needed. We even had similar tastes in movies and books and music and food. He could really cook well, too. It seemed so perfect, like we were made for each other. The only problem was the bedroom. I mean, he wasn't bad? He was just such a one trick pony."

"A stallion?"

Maria's nose wrinkled as she let out a small chuckle. "No way. I mean, he was very vanilla."

"Ah, I see." The twinkle in Robbie's eyes made it clear he had already known.

The feline's expression softened as she continued on. "He had maybe three positions he was interested in, and that was it. I tried easing him into new ones, but he just wasn't interested."

"Well, you know what they say: you can lead a horse to water, but you can't make them drink."

"Okay, that was just bad."

"Made you smile though."

Robbie was right, of course. Maria's grin was even accompanied by a few small chuckles, and her lips lingered in the upward tug, showing her canines. "You wanna hear my story or not?"

"Of course, but I also know laughter's good for the soul. I can have my sugarcube and eat it too, right?"

A small bout of giggles escaped from the Margay as she smacked his arm this time. "Okay, you gotta stop. I'm never going to finish saying what I need to if you keep this up, and, honestly, I need this out of my system. I didn't even realize it until today. It was so easy to believe I could handle it on my own because I didn't have anyone else. But now? Here, with you? I'm not alone anymore."

Her hand moved to his thigh and a few tears fell free. "I love you Robbie."

Instead of the million dollar smile he normally flashed when joking, he gave a more intimate smile that reached his eyes and gave her hand a squeeze. "Love you too Kitten. Always will, even when you run off with pony boys."

"Damn it, Robbie!"

He chuckled and held both hands up defensively. "Sorry, had to get at least one more in. Can't promise it'll stop there, but I'll try to show some restraint."

Maria sniffled lightly, though the smile kept tugging on one corner of her muzzle. "You know, I've laughed more in these past few minutes than I have in the past few years?"

Robbie's expression softened, and he leaned forward enough to wrap his arms around her once more. Resting against him, she drew in a deep breath and soldiered on.

"Every time I tried to bring it up with him, something else would interrupt or he'd just outright avoid it or give me such a sad and embarrassed look. You know I've dealt with people who had self-confidence issues in their sex life plenty of times before, but it was like he could sniff out the smallest mention of possible criticism no matter how thickly I coated on the compliments. Even suggesting we spice things up a bit drew a hurt look from him. I struggled to get him to open up, but he'd tighten up like a clam. I tried not to let it get to me. I figured he would open up in his own time, but it just never happened. Instead he asked me to marry him two years later, at the park where we had our first date, and I said yes. After all, relationships aren't all about the bedroom, right?"

The Doberman's lips quirked into a small smile. "Right. There's so much more to worry about, like stable maintenance." His arms shot up defensively as he quickly added, "Sorry, you made it too easy!"

Maria laughed and shook her head. "Anyway, I figured if I was patient, maybe he'd talk to me after we were married. We didn't get that far though. It ate at me. What was it he wasn't telling me? I tried getting him to talk several times, yet whenever it came to certain things about his past, or about what we did and didn't do in the bedroom, he'd steer the conversation to something else entirely or just shut down about it.

"I finally had a 'screw it' moment and looked up the local circle. After all, how often did we preach that BDSM wasn't just about sex? I could go there and try to fill the void with other things without having to cheat on Chris."

Robbie gave a thoughtful nod. "Like the McFees. It makes sense."

"Exactly. The circle was really small and only had so-so reviews, but it was better than nothing. So that week I told the man I loved I was going to the gym. I actually, flat-out lied to him, with a duffel bag acting as my goody bag and everything. My stomach still twists when I think about it, but I didn't know what else to do. How could I possibly explain it to him when he wasn't even willing to talk about our sex life!"

She paused and took a sip of her latte. She was starting to sound like she was trying to convince herself, even to her own ears. How could Robbie not feel the same way? One glance up to him though told her otherwise. There was no judgment in those warm depths, just genuine concern. She set her coffee down with a deep breath and continued on.

"Well, there's a reason the circle only got so-so reviews. There were only a handful of people there, and they weren't very welcoming of new-comers. Their equipment was old and worn, and everyone was already paired off. It was like crashing some elite club without any of the perks. I went home feeling empty, and that emptiness carried through when Chris tried to be intimate that night. I think he sensed it too, because he stopped after a few minutes of the same old routine and held me.

"The emptiness didn't go away. If anything, it just spread like an infectious disease. We talked less and less, and found reasons to spend less time around each other. Not even a year after that night, and we both sort of realized we had fallen out of love. We decided it was better to part on good terms, before we said our vows and made things that much more complicated. We were going to try to stay in touch, but you know how it is with most break-ups. He attempted one short text, I attempted one short email, and that was the end of that. The only problem was after the life we'd built in that town, everywhere I went was a reminder of him and how horribly I failed at our relationship. After a few months of that torture, I finally decided to move back home. And now, here we are."

Robbie tilted his muzzle down, his eyes closing partway as he processed all the information. Maria took the time to drink the rest of her latte, her eyes wandering to the cafe's walls. Instead of moderately decent pictures by local artists, the couple who owned the place opted for local vintage signs. It somehow gave the place less of the pretentious feel most cafes had these days—definitely a welcome change. Her eyes made it back to Robbie just as the Doberman shifted in his chair, eyes snapping open and his posture somehow straightening even further.

"Wait a sec. You said you met him after you moved away. So then what's he doing here?"

"Exactly!" Maria exploded, causing her knee to bang the table and her arms to fly up. The cups rattling as they bounced made her fur fluff, but she didn't seem to notice as she continued, "That's what I want to know. It's weird enough to see him at a BDSM circle, but here? Two hours from where we used to live? It doesn't make sense, unless he's doing the creepy stalker thing."

Robbie's frown deepened, though one large shoulder rose in a half shrug. "Well, we are the most reputable in the state. Maybe he's finally expanding his horizons and wants to make sure he does it with the best group within driving distance."

"That doesn't even make sense though. I'm telling you, this is as far outside of Chris' norm as it gets. The very thought of him going so far out of his way to even attend a demo just… it's not him!"

The canine arched a skeptical brow before he leaned forward again. His hands clasped together on the tabletop, his voice carefully calm and measured as if he were addressing a new client.

"Kitten, do you think he's stalking you? Is that why you panicked back there?"

Maria couldn't help herself—she shrank back slightly as her brows furrowed. "How else would you explain it? It's the only thing that makes sense."

Robbie sighed and touched her forearm as he continued in that calm voice. "Back up for a moment, Kitten. How can you be sure it was even him? There are people who have very similar scent combinations out there. What makes you so sure it was even this Chris guy to begin with?"

The Margay's expression drained from her face, leaving behind a deadpan look. He rolled his eyes and finally took a sip of his tea. Maria leaned forward as she pursed her lips and asked, "Tell me Robbie. Did you happen to notice a six-foot black-tailed jackrabbit with mottled coloring and an extra two-feet added to his height thanks to his ears?"

She watched his eyes close and his shoulders and face trembled slightly, fighting to control the cough with force of will. He exhaled sharply through his nose and put down the cup. Eyes still closed, he picked up a stray napkin and coughed into it. "Okay." His voice was slightly more rough than usual, drawing an amused grin from Maria.

"Okay? Now it's your turn to explain, my Dopey Dobie."

The canine cleared his throat a few times and shook his head. He let out a sigh and slumped back in the chair, his eyes closed as he gathered his thoughts. He shook his head again and grumbled, "Of all the things, your ex has to be fucking Lucky."

Maria felt her upper lip curl up as she growled, "Gee, thanks Robbie. Tell me how you really feel."

The Doberman tilted his head and furrowed his brows.

"Wait what? No!" His hands shot into the air and waved about a bit in defense. "No, I'm not saying he was lucky for leaving you. Damn, Kitten!"

Maria's ears lowered and her cheeks warmed with embarrassment. In a calmer voice she said, "Sorry. Then what did you mean?"

Robbie snorted a bit and shook his head again. "Your ex's name in the circle is—"

"Robbie! He's a part of the circle?" The feline's eyes widened, her lips drawing back.

"Take a breath, Kitten. Yes. He goes by Lucky. Y'know, the whole 'lucky rabbit's foot' thing?"

Maria sighed through her nose, before it crinkled. She answered, "Okay. Okay I got it. Can't believe he went for such a cliché."

"I was actually the one who came up with the name. Met him for the first time at last month's meeting. He told us about a collision he was barely able to avoid on the drive down, so I figured the name fit." He shrugged and tapped his claws against the tabletop. "Anyway, you remember I mentioned there was someone who might be the perfect match for you? Who's curious in a lot of things you already know you like? The new Dom in town I started schooling every Thursday?"

Maria nodded as Robbie motioned with a hand, as if serving her a tray. It was only then her pupils shrank to mere slits and her fur fluffed. Her heart jumped to her throat and she breathed, "No. No, Robbie. Not cool. So not cool. I thought you said he wasn't new to it all?"

The Doberman sighed and clasped his hands in front of him again, his voice growing calmer. "Kitten, he's not. From what he's told me, he had some really bad experiences with his first sub. She emotionally abused him, and took advantage of him. By the time she was done with him, he was a mess. Then he met this amazing woman."

Maria's ears sank, and she wrapped her arms around herself. "But… why didn't he ever tell me? I could have helped him, guided him, shown him what a healthy relationship between a Dom and sub is really about."

Robbie's smile softened, and he moved an arm around her shoulders. "He might not have wanted to risk going down that road again. I don't know, but I do know that you could be the one to teach him otherwise. Look, I'm not asking you to dive in head first. Just drop by my place next week. I can brew up some coffee and host negotiations. It'll be quiet, away from all the others, and I can be there as your safety net if things start to go south."

The Margay grabbed for her flicking tail and toyed with it in her lap—a good way to keep it from tripping anyone while giving her large hands something to do. Her voice was so small in her ears when she sighed, "I don't know about this. So much could go wrong."

Robbie's hand moved to hers, so much more slender than her oversized mitts. She looked up, and her heart melted at the sight of his sweet smile.

"So much could go right. I guess the one thing you need to ask yourself is if it's worth the risk."

* * *

Maria gazed up at the sprawling estate before her, the white marble and glistening snow difficult to tell apart. It had been way too long since she last visited the address, and the estate's size and wealth still amazed her.

She wrapped her coat a little tighter around herself and trekked up the shallow steps. Daphnes, Daphnes, Witch Hazel, and a few Christmas Roses were planted on either side. They added delightful splashes of color to the cold winter snow and drew a smile from the Margay. Her tail was in full sway by the time she caught the Doberman's scent, which seemed to meld well with the gentle fragrance of the flowers.

"Hey Kitten, glad you made it safe. Lucky's already waiting in the den."

Robbie offered his hand and escorted the feline in from the cold. The mudroom didn't offer much relief, but it gave her the opportunity to strip off her coat, revealing the silk blouse and simple pencil skirt beneath. They continued on past the side of the broad staircase, into the wide hallway that acted as the main vein of his home.

Maria stole peeks into some of the rooms, like his library with its floor-to-ceiling shelves crammed full of various books, or his solar with huge windows—curtained off for the winter, but every feline's dream during the sunnier months. Or his personal gym that had the best equipment money could buy, from free weights and benches to machines whose use she couldn't imagine. There always seemed to be something to marvel at in the Doberman's home.

The canine stopped in the middle of the hallway and lightly tugged on Maria's elbow, drawing the Margay's attention. "Kitten, before we go any further, last chance. I know I pressured you into this. I'm used to my role as a Dom, and part of a Dom's job is to push their sub to the limits and beyond, to find new pleasures they never even knew existed before."

Robbie moved in front of the feline and grasped both her shoulders as he went down to one knee, putting them closer to eye-level.

"I'm not your Dom anymore though—haven't been for the past few years now. But I'd like to think that I'm one of your closer friends."

"You're my closest friend, Robbie."

"Yeah, well, still. If you don't want to do this, just tell me. You won't even have to see him. You can leave now, and I can send him packing to an entirely different circle."

"He'd still know I'm here."

"No, he won't."

The feline mewled, confused, and Robbie offered an embarrassed lopsided smile.

"I wanted to be sure you were certain about this. I started training him in things steering your direction over the past week, but I never revealed it was for you in particular. If you said no, then he'd never be the wiser and simply be on his way."

Maria tilted her head, ears perked, then leaned forward and hugged her Dopey Dobie. "Thank you. I've given this a lot of thought though. I really want to give this a try. I just… I want to be owned again. I want to be used. I want to feel safe. I want to feel like I'm finally home."

She could practically feel the canine smile as he wrapped his arms around her and hugged her at a fraction of his strength.

"Y'know, if it's a matter of wanting to be owned, maybe you and I could work something out."

The Margay pulled back enough to look up at him with an arched brow. "I thought we agreed we make far better friends than anything else. Besides, wouldn't Fritz get all jealous?"

Robbie smirked and offered a half shrug. "He'd probably ask to join."

Maria chuckled and lightly shoved at the canine. "Seriously though, I told you on the phone, and I'll say it again. I gave this a lot of thought. I remember what it was like in Chris' arms, before we fell apart. If I don't at least try this, I'll always wonder, and I have enough regrets that I don't need to be adding to the pile."

She added a bat of her eyelashes as her voice suddenly grew flirtatious.

"Worse comes to worst, you'll be there to sweep me away, right?"

Robbie's smile reached his eyes. "Better believe it. Alright then, shall we?"

When the feline nodded, he regained his feet and walked to the door on their left, reaching for the knob. He would be the one to open it, but she would have to be the one to walk through. Her legs felt like jelly, but she somehow managed to keep her back straight and her head held high as she moved into the room.

The lagomorph made it halfway to his feet before collapsing back onto the edge of a large leather chair.

"M-Maria?"

The feline swallowed hard at the sound of the familiar voice, her heart jumping to her throat. The lean jackrabbit looked ready to bolt, both black-tipped ears perked up and forward with his surprise. Her nosepad flared with the draw of a breath, holding it a moment before replying in a carefully neutral tone, "Hello Chris. You're looking well."

It was an honest compliment at least. But then, the lagomorph always somehow made polo shirts and slacks work. She glanced up at Robbie with the unspoken question of 'now what?' Robbie rolled his shoulders back and motioned her inside further. Her eyes swept through the den as she walked, and found herself relaxing a little more from the familiarity of the room.

Flames danced in the large fireplace opposite Robbie's desk, adding to the warmth brought by the wood paneling on the walls and furniture. Chairs, couches, and even cushions of various sizes were strewn about to allow comfort for the numerous species that would join in the meets. Maria passed up her old favorite—a velvety cushion close to the fire—in exchange for a chair that would have her more on eye level with the hare. Robbie moved behind his desk but didn't bother settling into his chair yet. Instead he simply pressed a button and quipped, "Trinket, will you bring up that tray now? And a refill for Lucky please?"

"Yes sir."

"Thank you."

The Doberman grabbed a folder from the top drawer, then moved closer to the two and sat in the large armchair he normally reserved for the meets. Maria finally forced her eyes back to Chris, and her ears folded flat against her hair. His own long ears were lowered and turned to the side, and his body was turned slightly away from her—all signs he didn't handle her reaction all that well. She shook her head and rubbed her forehead with the back of a large hand, but stopped short. She had learned this action from Chris, as a way to tell him that what happened wasn't a big deal. Maybe this wasn't the right time or place. She ran her hands down the front of her skirt and looked the lagomorph square in his black eyes, determined to clear the air.

"So why are you here, two hours from home?"

Chris blinked owlishly at the Margay before his body turned a little more away from her. His voice was small as he looked into his coffee. "I… I thought a lot about what you used to tell me. About expanding horizons, and how things didn't have to be like in the past. If I was going to get back into the scene though, I needed to do it right, with a reputable circle. I honestly had no idea you were here."

Maria felt her fur fluff and snapped, "You couldn't think about all this while we were together? Why now?"

"Hold up, Kitten."

Robbie leaned forward in his chair, his hand up for silence. He glanced at each person in turn, as if daring them to speak over him. Seconds felt like hours as the silence stretched on, until it was finally broken by a light knock against wood. The Doberman nodded to the young brown bat at the open door, who carried in a silver tray with large mugs. Maria took the time to smooth out her fur before Rachel, er, Trinket offered her the mug of cafe con leche and murmured a small thank you. The girl moved on to Chris, who took his coffee black, then to Robbie, who gave his million-dollar smile and took his tea, thanking his sub with a squeeze to her rear.

"Be a dear and close the door behind you Rachel? We can talk over tomorrow's dinner menu later."

"Yes sir."

The bat stepped into a small curtsy before leaving the room, closing the door behind her. Robbie brought the tea to his lips and savored a few sips before setting the mug down on a side table. "Now then, if we are going to do this, we're going to do it right. From what you've both told me, you want a fresh start in your lives. A chance to begin anew."

"But I di—"

"Quiet, Lucky. I respect you as a budding Dom, but I have several years of experience over you, and this is my home. So you will respect me as the alpha male."

Chris' foot twitched as if he was going to thump it. Instead he nodded and took a sip of his coffee. The Doberman's smile returned and he continued on.

"I understand you didn't know the feline I was referring to would be your ex, just as she never expected the lagomorph I mentioned to be you. I also understand that this is an unusual case, with quite a bit of history between you two. However, from what I've seen and have been told, it's my belief you will fit together better than anyone else I could pair either of you with. So to make this work, let us wipe the slate clean, starting with how you address one another."

Robbie motioned to a couch near him as he began the formal introductions.

"Kitten, make yourself comfortable. I'd like to introduce you to Lucky, a new member who wishes to learn how to be a good Dom. He's had the misfortune of being in a relationship with an abusive submissive before, so I'm counting on you to show him just how a sub should be."

Maria hesitated, but only for a second before regaining her feet and moving to the end of the couch nearest Robbie. She set her coffee on the arm that doubled as a side table and stepped into a small curtsy.

"It is a pleasure to meet you, Sir."

Both of the jackrabbit's ears shot up as Maria busied herself with slipping off her winter scarf, revealing a black leather collar with an open d-ring. She had debated all week on whether or not to wear it with all that could be implied. Just before she left for this meeting, she had decided she was going to give Chris just as much of a chance as any other new Dom, which included playing all the parts of a good sub. She took a seat and crossed her legs at her knees as her eyes turned back to the Doberman.

"Lucky, this is Kitten. She's one of the best subs we have. Many of the things you said you're curious about are things she's not only learned in, but finds quite enjoyable."

The inside of Chris' ears turned a brighter pink than usual, but at least they were turned forward enough for the Margay to see them. Robbie cleared his throat, and Maria bit back a sigh as she motioned to the seat beside her with a small encouraging smile. If they were going to get through this, she had to at least try, right?

Chris moved to the other side of the couch, giving the Margay plenty of room. His body remained slightly turned from her, but both ears were still perfectly straight, giving him a height advantage that left Maria feeling even smaller than usual. Robbie leaned over and handed two pens and two small stacks of papers to the feline, who handed one set to the jackrabbit. Maria started to flip through the list of various kinks and fetishes and noticed quite a few categories were missing. Her tail flicked as she glanced up at Robbie, who shrugged with a lazy smile.

"There are a number of things you don't like and he's not interested in. I figured I'd save you both time and just take them out altogether. As for what's a definite interest and what's in the grey-zone, you two get to figure that out together."

The Margay sighed as she looked back down at the list, already noting a number of things she knew Chris wouldn't be up for. "So, no begging, no biting, no bli—"

"I, uh, actually was…"

Chris' voice trailed off as Maria glanced up at him. He shook his head and looked back down at his list, ears folded fully back. Robbie righted himself in the armchair and folded his hands on his lap.

"Kitten, remember, this is a fresh start. Don't assume you know why he's here."

It was Maria's turn to fold her ears back. "Sorry Sir. Perhaps we should start with a safeword, first and foremost?"

One of the lagomorph's ears drew up as a frown crossed his muzzle. "Don't you trust me?"

The Margay's ears shot up. He'd been a Dom before, yet he didn't understand the use of a safeword? Just who in the hell trained him?

She shook her head quickly as she recalled the mention of the bad sub, her tail curling close to her. That could have led to a range of painful experiences, from the physical to the emotional, not to mention any lawsuits. She was going to need patience to undo the damage his old sub might have formed.

"We'll be going into ground we've never ventured together before."

She heard the slightest tremble in her own voice, and paused to take a deep breath and push forward. "There are some things I do enjoy, like being spanked and clamps in certain places. Things that sit right on the line between pleasure and pain. There's also the risk of triggers. The safeword is just as much to keep you safe as it is me though. This way, there's no guessing game. No matter what I say, the fantasy we weave together can be kept intact, unless this one word comes out."

"Like during the demo. Maria—"

"Kitten. Just Kitten. Let's keep on track here. My safeword is Edison."

Both of Chris' ears swung up as he eyed the feline. Maria smirked with mischief, her tail picking up an easy sway.

"Think about it. Edison was such a dirty asshole, he's enough to kill any boner."

"Heh, you always were more of a Tesla fan."

"Always will be. So if you ever hear me say Edison…"

"I stop what I'm doing and make sure you're okay."

"Yes Sir. Now, shall we continue the list?"

Chris fidgeted slightly, his ears wavering as he looked back down at the sheets and chewed his bottom lip. She looked back at the list as well and drew in a deep breath, waiting for him to say something. After several seconds, the light clicking of claws came from the armchair. It seemed the hare was going to need a little more help.

How did she used to draw out someone who was shy during negotiations? How did Robbie draw her out her first time with him? A smile tugged on the corner of her muzzle as memories played through her mind. Her eyes moved to the jackrabbit, from his powerful legs, along his flat stomach, up over his slender shoulders that hid his upper body strength, to the long expressive ears. She always loved how small he made her feel, despite him being a prey species.

The Margay shifted to kneel on the couch and unfastened the first couple of her blouse's buttons. She slipped onto all fours and slinked across the cushions, her tail taking up a quick rhythm behind her. Chris must have felt the shift of weight, but he didn't expect to see her crawling over—that much was clear by the way one ear flopped haphazardly to the side.

She nuzzled into his shoulder before peering up at him through loose blonde locks. His mouth opened, then closed, then opened again as she nipped his sleeve and gave it a small tug. One hand played over his chest, and her voice was as deep and sensual as her velveteen purrs.

"I've been a bad kitty. What do you want to do to me? Do you want to tie me up? Spank me? Tell me what a dirty little slut I've been?"

The jackrabbit's eyes were perfectly round, and his ears all but glowed red. He nodded slowly to each question, though he didn't dare move a hand to touch her. It was like he was afraid he might tear apart whatever fragile dream this was. She continued on, her hand moving to his, guiding it to her cheek, down her neck, over the open blouse.

"Do you want to tear off my clothes? Use my breasts as a cock sleeve? Take a steaming big shit—"

"What the fuck!"

Chris yanked his hand free and nearly jumped off the couch. The Margay sat back on her knees, relief clear on her face as she murmured, "Oh thank goodness you're not one of those."

Robbie tried and failed to bite back a bark of laughter. He shook his head and took a sip of his tea before settling back into his chair, laughter still shining within his eyes. The lagomorph glared at him before looking at Maria, brows furrowed. She offered a half shrug and a small smile.

"Sorry, one of us had to ask it, and you weren't talking."

She leaned forward again and caressed his cheek. "Besides, it let me make sure that you weren't just agreeing for the sake of agreeing. That can be dangerous in a Dom/sub relationship. Now that I know you're going to respond if I suggest something you wouldn't be interested in, we can continue on with what we were doing."

Chris frowned for a moment before asking in a quiet voice, "Are you sure you're okay with this? I mean, with us, being here, like this? I don't want you doing anything you don't want to be doing."

A soft smile touched Maria's lips as she stroked his cheek again. "I'm sure, Lucky. I want to be here."

"But I mean, are you okay with me dominating you? Man-handling you, and things like that?"

Maria hesitated, then asked, "Why didn't you open up when we were together? I mean, about what had happened. Why didn't you give me the chance to show you how good it could be? Didn't I make it clear I'm interested in those things?"

Chris' ears folded back and his head ducked slightly. "I… I was worried I was the reason things went south the last time. I was sure of it, even. And the last thing I wanted to do was screw things up with you. You were like, this impossible girl from my dreams. I'd have given anything to keep from losing you. I didn't realize my silence was doing more damage than anything else until it was too late, and you were gone. I'm so—"

Maria placed two fingers on his lips and nuzzled into his cheek. The lagomorph's black eyes glanced to Robbie, who she could see give the slightest nod out of the corner of her own eyes. She sighed and brushed Chris' cheek. "I wouldn't be here if I didn't want to at least try this with you. Now, where were we?"

Before she could start with the list though, Chris grabbed her hips and pulled her onto his lap. Her ears perked with surprise, but her legs shifted and she tugged her skirt up enough to better straddle his hips. There was such hunger in his eyes, though he didn't dare move any more than he already had. He was already rock hard through his slacks, and she couldn't quite keep her hips from wriggling, her body aching to feel that familiar hardness within her once more. Quick to react, he took the motion as permission. His hips jerked up to meet hers as he buried his face in her cleavage, trying to stifle his moan.

She drew in a sharp gasp, but a soft clicking of claws drew her back to her senses. Leaning close, she lightly nibbled on the edge of the Jackrabbit's ear, her voice a mere whisper as she tried to get things back on the right path.

"Use your words Bunny Boy. Tell me what you want to do to me."

A small groan rumbled into her cleavage before he looked up into her eyes. His voice was deep and husky—she had never heard him so wanting before. Her fur fluffed as a thrill ran through her body, and she had to fight to keep from grinding her hips into his again. Large buck teeth caught the top of her blouse, and he gave it a hard enough tug to threaten a few of the buttons. Nuzzling into the base of his ear, she whispered again, "Words, Sir, please. What do you want?"

She ran her rough tongue over the outer edge of his ear, from base to as far up as she could reach without leaving his lap. His hands gripped her hips harder, little sharp claws threatening to tear right through her skirt, yet he managed to keep from grinding up into her again. Instead he tilted his head back and growled—something she had never heard him do before.

"I want to see you—all of you. Strip for me."

The Margay blinked a few times and drew back enough to look him in the eyes as her cheeks warmed.

"Whoa there Bunny Boy, slow down a bit. We're still negotiating, right?"

Something changed within Chris' black eyes. She couldn't put her finger on what, but a shiver shot up and down her spine to settle between her legs, making her fur ripple. His body straightened beneath her and an arm laid across the back of the couch.

"You asked me what I want. I told you, and you tell me no? Is that how this works?"

Maria's breath caught within her throat as her hips wriggled before she could control them. Her stomach twisted slightly, as if she had just been called a bad kitty by her Dom, and her ears folded back. Self-confidence radiated from him, joining the oak moss and cedar and desire. She slipped off of his lap as she answered, her whiskers flared even though her ears lowered. "N-no Sir, I'm sorry. I'll be a good kitty."

She heard Robbie draw in a breath, but ignored it as her hands slid over her body. Her blouse was first, her fingers drawing the bottom of it up so she could pull it over her head. Maria had barely started when another command stopped her.

"Slowly. I want to savor this."

"Yes Sir."

The silk cloth slipped back down her body before she unfastened the rest of her buttons and revealed the red lace bra beneath. The blouse slid down her arms and dropped to the floor with a soft whisper of unspoken promises. She reached to the side of her skirt, but her fingers hesitated as she recalled what she was wearing beneath. Instead, her hands moved behind her back to unfasten her bra, but the lagomorph's words were enough to stop her.

"Skirt first. I told you, Kitten, I want to savor this."

"Yes Sir."

Swallowing hard, her fingers moved back to the side of her skirt and unfastened the small catch. She drew down the zipper and caught the cloth before it fell, inching it down until she let it run through her fingers to fall to the floor. Nothing but bare fur was revealed, the scents of vanilla yogurt, honeysuckle and desire wafting from the feline. A soft chewing sound of approval came from Chris' muzzle as his nose-pad twitched.

His question threw her for a loop though. "Do you always go around without underwear these days?"

There was so much more he could have added to it, like insinuating she was just waiting for a random stranger to bend her over and give her a good hard fuck. It was something Robbie would have said. Yet coming from Chris, such blunt words were enough to jerk her tail forward to cover herself before she could stop it. She quickly pushed it aside and reached back to unfasten her bra, whispering her answer.

"I… I like to feel dirty during negotiations. It gets me in a mood to focus on things I'm actually interested in."

The jackrabbit arched an eyebrow and leaned forward a bit. "Hmm, really now? And what would that be?"

The bra joined her shirt on the floor, revealing Maria in nothing but her collar and fur. Her slender body shifted slightly as she fought the urge to wrap her arms around herself. Clasping her hands behind her lower back instead, she pushed her flat stomach and chest out a bit. Chris had seen her exposed nearly every night, yet somehow this was so different. Her tail wrapped around one leg as her tongue poked out to wet her suddenly dry lips. With her heart racing in her chest, she realized he had so easily turned the tables on her.

"I'm interested in feeling used, Sir. In feeling exposed and re-strained. I love being restrained, Sir, be it by silk ties or pure muscle. I like control being taken from me, and to be spanked by bare hand or paddle. Dirty talk is a guilty pleasure, and humiliation is embarrassing and a turn-on. Being over-powered tends to tie in with having control stripped away in a more physical way, and sensation play is a thrill, especially with silks or feathers or claws. The smell of leather makes me drool, and—"

She stopped short when the lagomorph raised his hand.

"Come closer, tramp."

Her heart jumped to her throat, but she swallowed hard and took a step forward before he shook his head.

"You can do better than that. I know you can... skank."

Her ears perked and she glanced at Robbie. The Doberman was carefully holding a calm expression, though his eyes betrayed him as he watched things unfold. He gave Maria the slightest nod, and growled his words softly under his breath. "He knows the safeword, as do you."

Chris snapped his fingers in front of his legs, and the Margay found herself quickly falling to her hands and knees onto the plush carpet. She crawled to the jackrabbit, her head down and ears lowered in submission until her nose lightly brushed his fingers. He ran his claws through her hair as the soft chewing of approval came from his muzzle once more.

There was something so mortifying acting like this in the nude when he was still fully clothed, and she couldn't help the way her blush spread down to her chest and up to her ears. She nuzzled into his knee, but he pulled her head back by her hair, sending sweet stings of pain through her scalp.

"Good little skank. Why did you come here today?"

Maria felt the muscles between her legs clench as her ears burned. "I… I came for negotiations, Sir."

The grip on her hair tightened, and he gave a little shake of her head. "Without panties? Tell me the truth." He leaned down and churred into her ear, "Why did you really come here?"

Her eyes grew perfectly round, and she whispered, "To be used, Sir."

"What was that," he growled, his warm breath ruffling the bit of fur within her ear.

She drew in a deep breath and forced the words out. "T-to be used, Sir!"

The grip on her hair turned into a gentle caress. "Such a greedy little beast. Show me what it is you want."

A velvety tongue ran across the edge of her ear, sending more shivers through the feline's body. Maria moved between his long feet and sat back on her legs, her eyes closing partway as she unfastened his slacks and drew the zipper down. The strong smell of musk hit her nose and invaded her sinuses before she could think to prepare herself for it. She shifted the fabric from his trapped length and watched it spring upright from its sheath.

Her slim tongue darted out and lapped the beads of pre that were glistening on his tip, the salty taste almost overwhelming. She could practically feel Robbie's eyes on her back, and she began to turn her head to glance to the Doberman when Chris' hand returned to the back of her head. This time he pushed her down as his hips eased up.

"Such an eager little skank. Would you be up for anything to keep those tight little holes of yours plugged?"

The small whisper of, "Yes Sir," barely left her lips before she was forced to tilt her head back to avoid a mouthful of pink bunny cock. Instead, her tongue trailed down from tip to sheath, the roughness of the appendage causing his length to twitch as a small moan escaped his lips. Her narrow tongue ran back up the underside of his member and she wrapped her lips around the tip, suckling hard while her tongue moved circles around him.

The strong meaty taste of musk mixed with the salt of pre, and a soft purr rumbled from her body and through his length. He shoved her head down harder, forcing her to kiss his sheath as his tip prodded the back of her throat. Maria's claws curled into his slacks, and he pulled her head back and pulled her up to her feet. He gave her a second to cough away from him before tugging her hair hard enough to grab her attention.

"Fucking skank. Do you think we're done already?"

Her breathing deepened as she stuttered out, "N-no Sir. I don't."

"Then present that hungry little cunt to me."

The Margay dropped down and crawled across the floor before slinking onto the couch. She bent over the wooden arm, tail sweeping upward and lower back arching down. Her eyes met Robbie, who managed to keep just as expressionless as before. There was a loud thump behind her and she managed to look back just in time for the jackrabbit to make his move. He grabbed her by the collar and pulled her fully upright, drawing a sharp noise of surprise from her throat.

Robbie jumped to his feet, his shoulders drawn up and hackles raised. His muscles were bunched like a spring coil, ready to jump should Maria say one word. Just one word.

The feline's ears folded flat as her long tail whipped about, smacking against the lagomorph's side. Chris grabbed her tail and wrenched it hard enough to send shots of pain through the base and right up her spine, causing her eyes to nearly bug out as a thin growl vibrated through her throat. Her safeword pressed against the back of her clenched teeth, trying to push loose. The jackrabbit leaned close, his fingers loosening just enough to let the appendage slip through his hand inch by slow inch. Her ear was given a rough nip before he growled in a voice that made her chest tighten.

"I don't care whose you were; whose you have been. In this moment, in this place, who do you belong to?"

"You, Sir."

Her own reply took her by surprise, but she didn't correct herself. She watched Robbie slowly lower himself back into his armchair, his body rigid with tension. His eyes were intense, watching every motion the two made, ready to react at the slightest drop of her safeword.

Chris' hand reached the last few inches of her tail and strung it into a loop attached to the back of her collar. He tightened the loop, securing it with surprising ease. She looked back at him when he released her tail, his hand moving instead to run his claws through her hair. His soft tongue licked her from earbase to the corner of her muzzle, and Chris' voice was husky as he gave her hair a rough tug that sent more tingles of pain through her scalp.

"Who does your body belong to right now?"

"Y-you, Sir."

"Then let that fucking bitch watch as I take you, knowing he'll never be able to so much as touch you again."

A soft growl rose from the doberman before it was quickly stifled. The Margay's breath caught within her throat, though whether it was from the words or the way he tugged her head hard enough to fully expose the side of her neck, it was hard to say. She squirmed when Chris dragged his teeth through the fur along the arch of her shoulder, sending a thrilling ripple in every part of her body.

His other hand left her collar to travel slowly over her breasts, brushing the pads on his fingers over each nipple and teasing them enough to make them pucker. Blunt claws grazed over the mounds and down her belly to squeeze her hip, pulling her closer against him. She bit hard into her bottom lip from the gentle caresses, but a small wanting mewl still managed to escape her muzzle.

The tickle of his gentle nibbles was suddenly replaced with a sharp pain as he bit into the crook of her neck, drawing a cry from her lips as her body arched and writhed against his. His other hand wrapped around her belly, pulling her hard to press her lower lips against his length. Spots formed in front of her eyes as pain pushed pleasure through her system in wave after delicious wave.

Her hips jerked and her tail struggled to rise even higher between their bodies. One hand flew back behind his head and the other to his hip, struggling to press him even closer to her. The words fluttered from her lips as the intoxicating cocktail of pain and pleasure set her very blood on fire.

"Yours! I'm yours Sir. All yours. Ah!"

The feline's body arched as Chris bit down a little harder and shook his head. It was just enough to shoot more tendrils of pain and pleasure through her body, blurring the line between the two. It settled deep within her belly and turned her into a single nerve. Her legs spread wide and her hips jerked again, encouraged by a hand that wasn't there. A sharp cry of ecstasy escaped her and the world suddenly fell away. All that existed was the two of them and the crashing force of pure unadulterated pleasure.

Her neck was only released from between his teeth when her cries weakened into a feeble mewling, but the feather-light licks he gave the swollen flesh was almost more than she could handle. The warmth and softness of his tongue contrasted so starkly against the claim bite from just moments ago that it left her trembling. Her feet still tingled from the power of her release when he growled into her ear once more.

"Did I say you could cum yet, you greedy little skank? This is about my pleasure. Or did you really think that's all I'm capable of? I'm far from done with you."

He pulled back just enough to angle the tip of his length, hot and throbbing, against her slick opening. Her body held no resistance as he slid between her folds, filling her fully as if their bodies had been made for each other.

* * *

Maria lounged on the couch, her tail taking on a slow, lax sway. She nuzzled into Chris' lap as her broken purrs vibrated through her body. The night had come and gone, and the first rays of light were piercing through the window. There was still so much they had to talk about, so much they had to relearn of each other. If last night was any indication though… The Margay began to doze when she felt a small tug around her neck, soon followed by a very distinct clink. She reached up to her collar and felt the flat circle of metal he had added; she was finally home.

INTERFACE

Ava Herries

Vertical lights flickered from the walls to either side of Lukia as she led the way down the corridor. Every few yards angular bulkheads jutted out from all sides to give the impression they were on a spaceship. The Aphellion Hotel went all out when it came to their theme; the staff even wore flight suits, for fuck's sake. The raccoon traded a hesitant smile with her canid companion Tav once they reached the door of their assigned room, a trapezoidal gunmetal slab cut deep in the wall. The key was themed too, not just a card with a magstrip but a tiny over-complicated tablet device with pulsing lights that turned green when aimed at the panel where a doorknob would be. Her misgivings fell away piece by piece with every detail, and when the door automatically slid into the wall and revealed their room she grinned in triumph.

Tav looked over her shoulder—his being a Pyrenees and well over six feet tall making it an easy task—and she could feel the displaced air on the backs of her knees when his tail wagged. Her own ringed tail bristled at the sight.

"Oh, this is credits well spent," he said.

"Couldn't agree more."

"The Alliance ships, *real* ships, aren't half this stylish. They can't afford it. Maybe a pleasure cruiser."

The room continued the theme even better than the lobby, which was good because for the next few days this space was theirs. More studded bulkheads framed the space, coming together over the bed where the neural interceptor hung, an apparatus of several robotic arms nestled in a bundle of cords. The datapad that controlled it stuck out to the side of the bed. Slick black tiles cut to resemble volcanic rock covered the floor, bisected in the middle by a narrow track in which ran a single chain lead. A faint smell of bleach assured her that the room had been recently cleaned.

Lukia bent over to retrieve the lead, then turned to Tav and held the end up to him. He lifted his head and presented the leather collar nestled in his thick fur. The black stood out nicely against his platinum coloring. She touched it to the magnetic plate, locking it in place, and taking it in one paw she led him inside. The door *whooshed* closed behind them as they moved away from it and the base of the cable rattled in the track as he moved.

"Clothes. Off."

He stripped off pants and shirt, revealing leather cuffs around wrists, ankles, and thighs that could all hook together if desired. A metal chastity cage wrapped his limp member up from tip to base. He'd been wearing it for two weeks now, and if it hadn't still been on him he'd already be hard from the simple knowledge that it would probably come off tonight. Probably.

A stirring in her gut from her new passenger said *yes, definitely*.

"Hello!" chirped a robotic voice. Lukia and Tav both started at the sound and looked around for the source. A datapad set in the wall beside the door came to life and a small animated character—a cat-o-nine tails with big googly eyes—hopped into view. "Welcome *Lukia* and *Tav*," it said, their names not quite working into its own voice. "I am Croppy, your digital assistant for the evening. If you have any questions just ask aloud or tap on any one of the screens you see in this room. If you wish me dismissed, tap again. Thank you, and enjoy your stay!"

Lukia stared at the cartoon for a moment, watching it hover and blink stupidly. Her elbow-length gloves had a cap on her right index finger that could fold back, precisely for operating touch screens like this. Lukia flicked it none too gently and the image blinked off without comment. She rubbed the bridge of her nose and groaned. Okay, one point deducted for Aphellion.

Tav smirked at her, and just for that Lukia left him standing where he was to look around on her own. "Stay," she told him. Tav froze save for the gentle sway of his tail.

Floor-to-ceiling windows dominated the walls in the main room, giving them an enormous view of the city. She would be concerned about voyeurs from neighboring towers, especially since everyone knew what Aphellion was, but the staff had promised them that the coating on the outside of the glass was impenetrable by any eye or cyberoptic. Lukia walked over to it and looked out at the city, appreciating how the metallic structures reflected the streetlights, how skywalks crisscrossed the air between buildings. Hovering billboards advertised various clubs and lawyers in garish neon. The twinkling lights of the Spires marked the edge of civilization in each cardinal direction for the colony. She could just make them out in the distance.

Lukia tapped on the glass and the image wavered and cut out, replaced by a scene from deep space. A swirling multicolored nebula churned toward them, like their space-hotel was careening through it. Fake as the image was, it succeeded in grabbing her attention and reminding her how very small they were.

Tav rolled his eyes. "We never actually see this stuff when we're out there, you know."

"Is that so, Private?" Lukia said.

"Yeah, mostly it's just a lot of nothing. Even the wormholes aren't much to look at, just a whole lot of black."

"How boring."

That was all he had to say on the subject, though he craned his neck to see the fictional view from his spot. Tav didn't like to talk about his work very much, and most of the interesting stuff was classified anyway. But the stress of it had been getting to him of late, and this excursion of theirs had not come too soon. They could afford it thanks to the new gig she'd managed to line up for herself. Lukia put a paw over her stomach, felt where the implant's attachments tugged gently at the organ walls. Her new passenger would appreciate tonight as well.

To the side a little hexagon table stuck out of the wall, on it several pamphlets, a legal pad with pencil, and a remote. She picked up the remote. With words like "ankle straps", she was confident this did not operate any TV.

Croppy chimed in from a screen by the table. "The remote provided controls the functions of several—"

"Thank you, got it," Lukia bit out and tapped the screen.

On one side the words "chain length" indicated a toggle that went up or down. Lukia pressed it down and looked up at a whirring sound. The lead attached to Tav's collar yanked and drew the startled boy down onto his knees as it retracted into the floor. She released the button and the retracting stopped just shy of Tav going prostrate, face reflected in the black stone. She eased it back up the other direction until he was on all fours.

Lukia grinned, ringtail twitching behind her. "Neat."

She stalked over to Tav and looked down on him, taking in the way his eyes were a touch wide and his tail, while still wagging, was now flush against his legs. Good. She removed the long coat from her body, revealing the black leather dress that hugged her curves and ended at the tops of her thighs. Red ribbon laced through eyelets ran back and forth over the wide gap down to her navel. Her steel-toed boots weren't anything special, scuffed and faded, but her favorites. Tav's eyes grew rounder and his pink tongue flicked out over his nose.

"Like what you see, boy?" she asked.

"Yes, Mistress."

The line of Lukia's dark gray mask arched high. He knew better than that. She was *Master*, never Mistress, never ma'am or madam either. Not that she had anything against feminine titles, she just didn't care for them in scene. They didn't have the right bite for her for some reason.

She sank her small leather-clad claws into his ruff and pulled his head up, deftly lengthening the lead with her other paw on the remote behind her back. Making it look like she was dictating the length of it with her will alone. He met her gaze and swallowed. She leaned in close enough to see the single fleck of brown that dotted the left of his baby blues.

Today called for a different title than the usual. "That's *Captain* to you, boy."

Tav's tail swished full force, giving him a vaguely innocent vibe that was at odds with his chain, the chastity cage, the whole setting.

Lukia couldn't help the small upturn in one corner of her muzzle. "And what are you? A stowaway? On *my* ship? Impossible."

"Yet here I am," Tav said.

"Yet here you are." Lukia measured out each word, warning dripping from them.

With the slack of the cord wrapped around her paw, she led him to the other room, turning right and bypassing the bed for the themed chair in the corner that looked like it belonged in a shuttle. Wide nylon belts protruded from one side and fastened on the other for the arms, legs, chest, and throat.

"I would ask how it is you found yourself way out here in the Castor system—" and really, how does one stow away on a spaceship anyway? "—but I am not the least interested. What I am interested in is what I'm going to do with you."

"Well, you certainly can't let this slide."

"No I cannot," she said, voice clipped.

"What would your crew think of you!"

"They'd think I was a pushover. But don't you worry about that. I know exactly how to make an example of you." Lukia pointed with the remote at the chair. Sit."

Tav made to obey and crawled over to the foot of the chair. He tried to climb into it but the cord wasn't long enough. Pausing, he looked at the lead, then back at the chair, then pulled harder against it. Lukia felt more movement deep in her gut as her passenger roused from sleep. With the remote she could decide if he failed to obey her on even this simplest of tasks, this first tiny order. She gripped it tight as her blood heated up, reveling for a moment, then pressed the up button. He took his seat with a flop, drew in a deep breath and sighed it out. Already getting tense, already desperate to please and lost in the fantasy that held all the threats of failure. Lukia held onto the rush of warmth in her chest for one last moment, then banished it. Here she was not warm. Here she was uncompromising and hard. A gunmetal slab herself.

She inspected the remote again, looking for more treasures. A blue button with the words "open shelf" looked promising. At the press, what had appeared to be an empty wall separated horizontally at the juncture of two panels, revealing a tall cabinet. A large collection of toys filled cubby holes from floor to ceiling. Whips, crops, ballgags, blindfolds, feather dusters, straps and cuffs and harnesses. Removing one glove, Lukia smiled and ran her fingerpads over them, feeling soft velvet, softer plumes, slick leather, polished wood. The leather items smelled fresh, new, suggesting that the hotel replaced the items for each new customer. Even knowing that, her passenger only gave her a few seconds to touch them before it pulled on a mental string, spiking her paranoia to put the glove back on. It was a little particular about germs. One of its defense mechanisms.

Another screen blinked on. "In addition to the latest technology, Aphellion offers a wide selection of classic gear for your enjoyment," Croppy explained, one of its black tails waving like an arm at the cabinet. "If there is something you don't see, call the front desk and it will be delivered via tube right away."

A blue light flashed on a bulkhead near the table to indicate a delivery tube that ran up into the ceiling. Presumably where their requests would show up. *Points for privacy*, she thought.

Lukia and Tav traded intrigued expressions. "Should we ask for something?" she said.

"I'm having trouble coming up with anything that's not there on the shelf."

She scratched at her chin, looking over the collection. Did she want to trade out anything for different versions? Maybe they could order food.

"Let's revisit that later. For now I think we can make do. Lashes are pretty standard punishment aboard ships, are they not?"

She withdrew a thin synthetic bamboo cane with a speed monitor in the base and held it delicately. She gave it a few practice swings in the air between the wall and where Tav sat waiting. It flared out at the end of its arc, cutting through the air. That last bit of motion, the extra flick at the end there, that was the key to making a light cane hurt like a bitch. After twirling it around her paw she pointed with it to the belt at his feet.

"Secure yourself, trespasser."

"And if I don't?"

"Then I guess I could just put you in the cargo hold and depressurize it." Lukia grinned, then cracked the crane against the base of the chair, making Tav jump. "That one first."

"Yessir," he said, words rushed as he bent to comply. He drew out the belt and fixed it into the buckle in a flash of motion. It lay against his ankles far too loosely. Lukia frowned and inspected the remote, finding a section of buttons reading "straps".

The first button succeeded in drawing the strap in with a slap against his skin. Tav buckled in the ones around his thighs, his belly, and his left arm, leaving the last three for her to do. She cued each one to pull tight then approached, looking for a place to set the items in her paws while she finished binding him.

"What is it you require, Mistress Lukia?" asked the damned cartoon. There was another screen set in the side of the chair she hadn't noticed before.

"It's *Master*," she growled at it and Tav bit his lip. "I don't know, Croppy, got an extra paw for me?"

The hexagon side table pulled away from the wall, a tripod of metal legs extending down to the floor. The thing actually crab-walked over and settled down beside her. Lukia stared at it with ears laid flat.

"Will this do for your needs?" Croppy asked.

"Yes, thank you!" she snapped and whacked the screen with her cane. Tav sucked in a breath at that, perhaps not happy with what was approaching vandalism, but she didn't care. She'd paid for this outing anyway. Being an incubator gave her a discount.

The screen froze for a second, then Croppy batted her long cartoon lashes. She said, "That's just how I like it, Master Lukia," before blinking back off.

Lukia snarled and waved clenched claws at the blank datapad. At that Tav lost the battle against his mirth and chuckled, before slapping a paw over his muzzle, but too late. She turned a disbelieving look on him, mouth a thin line, shutting him up instantly, but inside she was pleased. Here was an easy thing to punish him over.

"What was that, mutt?" she demanded, standing up straight and tilting her head like she was looking down on an insect. "You find me funny?"

Tav choked on a "no" but she interrupted him. "You don't seem to understand the seriousness of your current situation." Her voice rose, drowning him out. "You are a stowaway. That is a class D felony, punishable by death!" It probably wasn't. She didn't really know what a class D felony was either, but it sounded good. "Tell me, Tav, do they have keelhaulings in space?"

His eyes grew round. "They absolutely do," he said, his voice low.

"And how does that usually go?"

"Well, you have about a minute and a half before you die of exposure to vacuum. There's no barnacles, unless the ship's been to Aracreb and picked some up in the starwhale reefs. So if they pull you back inside within that time frame, you just have to survive the hypoxia and the worst bends imaginable. Some radiation burning. All in all, less deadly than regular keelhauling."

Lukia nodded. "And here I have you trussed up on a glorified dentist chair, completely at my mercy, while a wall full of *torture devices* waits at my disposal. Sounds like space-keelhauling would be preferable!"

"That it does, sir," he said, tone meek but his eyes sparkled, betraying his excitement. They said, *prove it.* So she would.

She snapped the belt over his other paw, then the one over his chest, then the last one around his throat. She tightened them with the remote, but left the last one slack. For now.

Lukia retrieved the cane and bowed it in her paws. Tav's tongue lolled out the side of his mouth as he watched her look him over. Honestly, this part was little more than foreplay to her, but the one he needed the most. This would leave the sensory info that would remain later, while the neural interceptor wouldn't leave a trace when they were done. And this part would get him to the right headspace for the things she wanted to do. They shared differing needs, her and Tav, but they met in the middle. He wanted pain, she wanted to use pleasure against him until it turned into pain, and normal pain worked to get them there.

Whack!

And then of course, there was what her passenger wanted. The Ormence larva was an opinionated creature, and she was sure it would let its feelings known as they went on.

She started with his feet, whipping across the pads with perfect accuracy and getting it just right on the arch. With a yelp, Tav's whole body jolted in the seat, head ducking forward and taking up the slack of the throat strap. She took her time and built up slowly, accumulated him to the pain before really wailing on him. The meter on the handle told her the speed of her strike and she tried to beat that with every successive hit.

Whack whack whack!

"Not laughing now, are you?"

He managed a "no sir" in between gasps. Tav bared his fangs but with his eyes pressed closed it looked adorably pathetic rather than threatening. She wondered how the things he fought felt about it, encountering that maw on the field of battle.

The stressors in their lives had piled up and up. Tav's job as a grunt for the Alliance's exploratory excursions took weeks at a time, and left him wrung out from the tension. Drones were sent out into the wormholes first so they had an idea what they were getting into, usually, but it was far from without risk.

Her own gig, as an incubator for the larva she had been placed with for the next twenty-three months, came with its own eccentricities. For example, it didn't tolerate synthetic food, and while they could afford the switch to purely natural now, it was proving a nightmare to stay on top of. The mere smell of synthetic food nauseated her now so no forcing it. Add to that their meal printer breaking and eating right was practically impossible.

Every little thing grated on her nerves to the point where she just wanted to lash out at the world or lay down and bawl. She'd like to blame her mental fragility of late on the implant, but enough of it had outside causes that the fault didn't lie entirely with it. And there hadn't been a real opportunity in months to wind down from it all. The anxiety was pressing in on her from all sides, this ineffectuality in the face of life's everyday bullshit, and she could push back in one direction but it would just collapse in another. Like being inside a deflated balloon.

But here she had the control over *something,* even though the part of her that hovered far off knew it was an illusion. With every strike, the suffocation eased up a little bit more and she could expand her lungs again. Using his pain and his pleas, she could climb rungs out of that pit of helplessness, back to the place where she was whole and real and not just a speck of dirt on the universe's boot heel.

Lukia wondered again how much of it was her, and how much of it the passenger. She'd been into this scene before, but now… The creature didn't crave just organic food.

She continued up his legs, aiming in between the straps at bared fur along the meat of his calves, his thighs, imagining the red lines each strike was leaving under his pelt. Lukia decided she needed to see them, right now, so took another look at the wall. In one cubby were prewaxed strips, and next to them an automatic heater to run them through. She stuck one in and it dinged in two seconds, releasing the smell of honey and lemon into the air. Tav looked up with eyes widened, and she gave him a wide grin. Holding the strip carefully by the paper edges, she placed it over the patch of fur on his bicep that had just received the last hit. She spread it over, patting it down gently, and ripped in one quick motion. The fur came right off, and Tav barked in pain.

"How's that for you?"

He whimpered at the next ding from the heater.

"Shall I keep going?"

Lukia did five more strips, getting curses out of him for the ones over his nipples. "You know what would be funny is if I did your whole body," she said, and he shuddered. "Or I could wax words into your fur!"

His gasped out a shocked laugh. "Puh, oh come on!"

"I could wax a little message on your forehead for the boys at the mission control."

He answered with a soft, unhappy whine that was mostly token protest.

"What do you think, Croppy? Think Tav here would make a good whitebaord?"

The datapad silently displayed several suggestions for what words to use. Tav shook his head to disagree, so she pulled tight on the throat strap to stop him. He made a strangled sound and his paws yanked at the arm restraints, trying to reach up and claw free.

"I'm sorry, do you think you get a vote here, Dog?"

Tav didn't respond, but his eyelids fluttered. Looking into what blue was still visible, Lukia could see he was floating, curled up inside his head and ready for her to do whatever she wanted with him. The dark thing in her gut turned over at the sight and she flicked her tongue over her small sharp teeth. *You're right, little passenger. He does look nice like this.*

Becoming an incubator to a young Ormence slug was regarded as one of the highest services a civilian could do for her country. Adults produced a substance that was used in space travel, some sort of fuel additive that made FTL possible at all. Thus they were extremely prized and protected by law. The problem was the larva required a very particular host. The only people authorized to receive the Ormence larva were asexual. Aromantic was also a desirable trait, but not necessary. What was more necessary was a strong willpower to resist the cravings the creature put into its host's mind. They didn't know why the creatures did this. Maybe to harvest something the body released into the bloodstream when the incubator indulged. The larva's homeworld was populated by many species higher on the food chain than the Ormence themselves, so it might have something to do with their incubators dominating other adults around them. Creating a pride of meatshields.

"For optimal enjoyment of both parties, it is recommended that you remove the chastity device soon!" Croppy said.

Tav sucked in a breath while Lukia narrowed her eyes at the helpful little twat.

"What makes you think I intend to take it off at all, Croppy?" She spared a glance at her companion and the distraught look on his face was so worth it. That right there, that was the kind of thing the larva responded to, couldn't get enough of. Which was what had made her consider the gig at all. It had taken their routine and transformed it into something a lot more interesting.

"Your activities at Aphellion are of course up to you! I am only here to provide you with guidance on how you can optimize your experience."

"And if we ignore your advice, are you going to get uppity?"

"Only if you desire me to." Croppy gave an exaggerated wink.

That chirpy little voice was going to get old fast. *But in this case, I believe Croppy knows best.* The chastity cage came off with only a little fiddling at the metal bits, and Tav grew half-hard in moments. Lukia ran her paw up his lower abdomen, upsetting the lay of fur there in brief but gentle reassurance.

Lukia pressed the button to draw the chest strap tighter until he huffed out air. Tav struggled in his bonds and she drew it tighter till he groaned. She grabbed his ear, digging her claws into the thin, delicate flesh and wrenching it toward her mouth.

"Let's move this to the Captain's quarters," Lukia said in a dark tone full of danger. "Get on the bed." He tried to nod and she released the throat strap, then the chest strap. Tav gasped in air, broad tongue lolling.

When all the straps were undone and hanging loose he slid from the chair, wisely predicting that the lead would retract and pull him down low. He crawled to the bed, lead clattering along the way, and she followed. Once flopped on top of the sheets, Lukia released the loop from his collar, then pulled each of his paws to the sides of the headboard. She fixed him by his cuffs to the magnetic plates bolted there. When she slid over to the side of the bed, the datapad that operated the neural interceptor swung out toward her automatically. Their little assistant returned to the screen.

"The Schedar Neural Interface is Aphellion's proprietary technology, taking neural play to the next level."

The apparatus whirred to life, little blue lights pulsing and gyros spinning as it disengaged from its dock in the ceiling. The metal head, shaped a bit like a whisk, lowered until it was in easy reach and the cable within could be extended toward Tav.

"Hook the connector into the spinal jack on the person who wishes to interface with Schedar."

Tav was the only one there with said jack. It was an ingenious device that allowed for countless agents to be sent into the field at once. Because while a team like Tav's would want to have, say, a field surgeon or special ops with them when they went exploring, there were only so many of such highly trained agents to go around. With all the teams sporting neural jacks, specialty personnel could be kept at mission control to remotely operate a body on any team that needed them at any time, over any distance. It also protected the more inexpendable types, while grunts like Tav took on all the risk.

Lukia couldn't imagine giving up that kind of control over her body, let alone undergoing a permanent cybernetic alteration to do it. Though there were other reasons to get one besides military, like medical scans and VR entertainment and schooling. The idea of remote full-body operation rubbed her fur the wrong way. One might say incubating a telepathic space-larva was similar, but it was different enough. At least she could overpower it with enough discipline. Tav did not have that option.

"Color?" she asked.

"Green," he breathed.

Lukia grinned and grabbed the whisk thingy.

She extracted a thin fiber-optic cable with tiny blue lights running up and down it, like a jellyfish tentacle. The double-pronged connector looked tiny and unassuming. Funny how this simple thing could hijack your entire nervous system. Lukia felt at the base of Tav's skull, finding the port hiding under the collar and fur there, slightly matted from sweat and the straps of the chair. She connected him and Croppy vanished from the screen, replaced by the spinning logo for Schedar. The words also blinked in lines mimicking bioluminescence. The logo blipped out and a simple menu slid in from the side with a tiny icon for Croppy in the bottom left corner.

"The menu is maximized for customer ease. You will find categories for many types of experiences and subcategories to personalize for you and your partner. When you have made your selection, take the stimwand and direct it to where you want the stimulation to take place. If you wish a category to be explained, drag me to it."

Croppy's icon kept to her corner and didn't animate further. Lukia was glad; this was starting to feel like a threeway.

One of the robotic arms separated from the mass, untangling itself and hanging low over the center of the bed, right at Tav's navel. The headpiece resembled a glowstick. *Well, that must be it.* Lukia guided it to one of the bare, bright red patches on his chest and ran the cold glass over it. The muscles there trembled at the contact.

Lukia flipped through the menu. There were four main categories: Pain, pleasure, bodily functions, and miscellaneous. Out of sheer curiosity but no interest in actually using them she looked under bodily functions. Lungs, stomach, bladder, and bowels were listed, as well as heart with a little "!" icon next to it. Hovering over it revealed the words "only used to speed up and mimic panic." That sounded reasonable, but she thought if you had to manufacture artificial panic then you weren't doing things right. One of the tabs in the Miscellaneous menu had options for the senses, dialing them up, fooling them, or shutting them off.

"You don't need your eyes, do you?" she said, then selected the option that shut them off.

Tav gasped. He jolted off the bed partway, eyes darting around unseeing. "Wha—holy shit!"

"Guess it works," she mused. His ears pricked up, cocking in her direction, already trying to take over for the loss of vision. His tail fluffed up to almost double its usual size.

"The Schedar Neural Interface works," Croppy piped up, "by intercepting signals from nerves at the brainstem and altering what reaches the brain."

"For fuck's sake, Croppy."

"In your case, options such as altering input from the eyes, ears, and tongue are available due to your specialized neural upgrades."

Yeah, there was a bonus for Alliance field agents everywhere. Their remote operators got the full sensory experience. Wouldn't want the grunts to have a moment's privacy, would we?

Croppy went on. "The device can intercept commands from the brain to the body and alter them as well. For example, if your brain tells you to pull away from a painful stimuli, the Interface can force you to lean into it."

Tav's fists opened and clenched several times, muscles in his forearms jumping.

"Okay, that's cool," Lukia chuckled. That must be under "responses" in the Misc tab. She flicked through to it and found a list that read "motion," "vocal," and "emotion."

At the bottom of the screen on the left side was a tiny heart icon with a plus sign on it. She tapped it and opened up a list of slots with dashed outlines and the words "drag favorite here." She pulled "lean into stimuli" from the "motion" tab into it, and when moving out of that menu the option remained in her favorites for easy retrieval. Lukia chuckled darkly and began adding more. Like an ingredients list for villainy.

Once her first list was complete she turned back to her waiting sub and rubbed her paws together. "Ready for this?"

"Yes, Captain."

She looked down his body, seeing that he was rock hard from anticipation alone. She eyed it, weighing her options about what to do with it. Neither her passenger or herself would want direct contact with that part of him, though both wanted the reactions they'd get. But that was a later concern. Lukia chose "ice cube" and guided the stim-wand to his left nipple, pressing the button on the side that activated the sensory input. He gasped, then giggled a little, shimmying away the few inches he could.

"Cold!"

"Is it?" She opened the electricity option and scrolled to the green side of the slider bar, where it would feel like little more than a static shock. He jolted, again trying to see what was touching him with blank eyes, not able to get past that instinct.

Handy, being able to take away his sight without having to cover up his eyes. She could still see them, the way they broadcasted his emotions, even worse than his ears or tail ever did.

Lukia dialed up the electricity and aimed it at his other nipple, leaving it there while he sighed and rattled his bonds, thinking how she was a little jealous. She wished she could know what this felt like, if it felt the same as the real thing when having your body played like a fiddle by a computer instead of gear or paws. But she could never trust anyone on the other side of it, anyone else's fingers on the buttons, *or* the real-life gear. She barely trusted her own with him, had to have the safety of the scene and the words 'yellow' and 'red' and built-in technological fail-safes to let her play out the fantasy of controlling the strings that operated this boy's biology.

She wanted the cold dawning horror that thrummed through her veins when she looked at what she did with power when she had her hands on it, but without that net to fall into she wouldn't be able to get there. Wouldn't be able to release the tight control over herself to play at controlling him. And now, when the larva was spurring her on at all times, demanding more violence, more of everything, those fail-safes were especially important.

Lukia slid the electricity up into the yellow range and he groaned through his teeth, legs kicking to deal with the pain. At the same time she brushed the thumb of her free paw over his other nipple, still sensitive from the treatment in the chair, but already having forgotten the false shocks. Starting with pain and mixing pleasure in gradually was the way to go with Tav, before switching over to erotic play. After a moment the nub hardened but he was still focused on the pain, thrashing his head from side to side, lost in subspace. With both hands occupied she couldn't reduce the electrical stimuli so she moved the wand down to his stomach above his belly button, an area that would handle the pain easier. Tav's leg and head movements relaxed and his brow furrowed, feeling the other sensations more clearly now. His breathing sped up.

She still had her gloves on, but the prolonged contact was pinging the passenger's anxiety, sure that it couldn't be good for it. She'd always been twitchy about touch, long before the implant, but now it was through the roof. She could barely stand self-touch anymore, even if she was simply cleaning herself in the shower. Couldn't even masturbate without cloth or some sort of buffer separating skin from skin, and even then she didn't care for it. That was going to prove an issue once they got further along, because eventually she would need to touch his cock. He'd been waiting too long for her not to. She could deal with that before, but with the new implant ramping up all her issues and adding new ones, she didn't know.

Lukia kept rubbing him at the same speed and force, moving the wand around languidly but staying in the same area. He let out a slight whimper and she continued on, keeping everything perfectly steady in a way that would turn maddening for him in a minute. Lukia was not interested in his sexual gratification. She was interested in his desperation. And she was the master at out-waiting him.

When he whimpered again and tried to pull away from her fingers, she moved the stimwand back to the overstimulated spot and restarted her ministrations on his other nipple. She knew that the sensations were sending bolts of pleasure to his groin, and it set off a thrill in her gut, not that she was turning him on, but because his sense of arousal was her favorite toy. His cock twitched, bright red and waiting for the abuse he willingly gave himself over to. Sweet, that he would and did so regularly.

Her brain instantly skipped over that fact, forgetting it in a moment that he was here by choice, because that wasn't the fantasy.

"Stop," he pleaded, struggling to pull away from both stimuli. His large ears flicked to lay flat against his skull.

Lukia withdrew her paw and went to the electricity bar, pulling it up into the red.

"Ouch! No, *stop!*"

With the tap of a button the neural interference forced him to arch up into the pain and he wailed.

She didn't need a computer program jacked into his brain to read when he was about to say Yellow. Lukia relented and switched it back to ice cube. Tav panted, relaxing back into the mattress.

In the pain menu, the temperature option also had heat, and there she had the choice of fire or acidic. Interesting. Things that would leave lasting damage in the real world were fair game in here. Though odd how 'electricity' wasn't in the same place. *What scatterbrained codemonkey designed this?*

She chose fire and dialed to a low yellow. Guiding the device over his belly-button, she tapped the button on the wand a few times, trying to recreate the feeling of drops of hot wax. His eyes snapped open and his middle pulled away.

Under the "responses" tab was an option that said "splay limbs". She selected it and was gratified to see Tav stick both legs out wide. Fever bright eyes looked down at her, skimming aimlessly over where he thought her face would be, wide and confused. She dribbled fire across his chest and he was helpless to get away, hissing in breath and grinding out pleas. Not that he really wanted to get away, she knew. Lukia increased the heat into orange, grinning at the string of curses he let out. The edge in his voice finally sounded like surrender.

She ran her fingerpads lightly up the length of his penis, and the passenger didn't seem to object, as long as she kept the gloves on. Tav didn't notice, so she kept at it for a while longer while the stimwand told the top of his thigh that it was on fire. She grew impatient at last—*how dare he ignore her*—and grabbed him in a firm grip. His intake of breath told her he had noticed that one. With one paw she turned the input back to electricity and set to red, stroking him firmly with the other until he was puffing breaths, then dragged the device down and aimed it at the base of his cock. He screamed for the single moment she left it there before pulling it off and letting the wand dangle in the air away from him.

"Oh my fucking God!" he rasped, then made a little whimpering giggle that was all barely leashed panic and zero mirth.

"We've got some interesting options, here," she said. "All sorts of pain. This one that says 'blade', I bet that would feel like I was cutting it off." Lukia was gratified to see the tremble that ran through his whole frame. "There's 'needle, frostbite', oh, and 'spurs'! Fun."

"You're *sick*," he hissed and flinched at the way she placed the tips of her claws on his thigh. But his fucking tail still wagged. Egging her on.

"Well, what do you expect from a space captain? I've been out here for so long, just doing the job, missing Earth. I never get to enjoy myself anymore and the crew is terrible company. But then you fell into my lap!"

Her fingers lazily toyed with him as she spoke. While Tav struggled to calm himself, she opened the menu for pleasure. "Stroking," "licking," "tickling," "sucking," "pressure," and "general" were the options, and Lukia thought that this was something she could get behind; a way to do these things without having to engage in the act herself. A way to preserve her distance. Because she wanted his responses, she just didn't want to physically be a part of them.

Tav's hips lifted, seeking out more friction from her gentle fingers. Lukia bit her lip and moved her paw with him, keeping out of his reach and feeling the coil of black inside her coming to life, rewarding her with jolts of warmth. She chose "licking" and guided it up to his nipples. Tav moaned at the sensation, moving his hips again without gaining anything.

A few minutes of this had him writhing on the bed, as much as the "splayed" command would let him. Finally he blurted, "Oh please, please, please!"

Back to fire. A cry caught in his throat and she snickered at him. Then turned it back to the pleasure stimuli and started over on the other nipple. Patiently waiting for him to erupt with more begging. Her passenger pressed her for less patience but she ignored it too.

Lukia changed the stimuli to generic pleasure and ratcheted it all the way up into red, directing the stimwand to a spot on his thigh. Tav gasped and his head shot up, trying to see what possible explanation there was for what he was feeling. Short grunts forced their way out of his throat until he flung himself back down and cried out, "Oh God, *yes!*" She aimed it to other places, turning any patch of skin into an erogenous zone that pleasured him as much as the head of his cock would. And really, it made as much sense to her.

Logically Lukia understood why some places felt amazing when touched the right way. Logically, she understood that normal people liked and sought out this attention, did not balk at the idea of another person inflicting sensations onto them that made them lose their grip on themselves. But she did, she balked hard. Maybe the idea of someone else playing with her body that way and eliciting responses against her will was too disturbing for her to contemplate, making her subconscious wrap the whole thing up tight into a box in her brain where it would never see the light of day. Maybe there was a deep-seated explanation for this distaste at the idea of her own sexuality. Whatever it was, it wasn't going away, so here she was.

Croppy hovered in her corner on the screen, perfectly happy with her role, no mental gears spinning away and ruining everything. No physiology complicating every aspect of life, no pesky needs or wants. Aside from being helpful, she seemed to be pretty keen on that. Must be a nice existence.

Lukia had aspired to be something like that, but choosing to be an incubator was her final admittance to herself that it wasn't possible.

And now, with the passenger piggybacking off her biology and pulling threads as it pleased, she was closer to experiencing things as a normal red-blooded animal than ever before.

Lukia teased him ruthlessly, hearing his sobs jangle in her ears and gripping the wand tight enough to drive her claws into her skin. Anger was one reaction the larva kicked up in her that she was perfectly comfortable with. She felt it surge seeing his reacting to this the way one was supposed to, this normal response that was beyond her, that made no sense and even creeped her out. *How dare he!* So she used it against him, made it something that was actively unpleasant, corrupted it for him like it was corrupted for her. She had that power, to take it away from him and warp it and decide if he ever got to have it the nice way again.

Also, maybe using that anger like a bludgeon would help her get past the passenger's aversion to touching him.

His erection looked painful now, a deep red that edged toward purple. "Do you want to come?" she asked. He agreed fervently. "Hmm. Maybe I'll let you."

Lukia tapped on the option that read "prevent orgasm," then paused. There was an arrow in the main navigation that popped up when she hovered over it. Tapping it brought up a new option. Automate. She eyed Croppy and the bouncy asshole was grinning, now that she had found this.

There were a few variations to choose from. One that let the apparatus take full control and ran through options based on what had been used up till then. One that randomly picked through everything available. And a voice commanded one. She would still have control over the screen, but the stimwand would guide itself where she told it. Lukia had to bite back the chuckle threatening in her throat. Perfect.

She chose it, and once again Croppy filled the screen. The stimwand pulled out of her paw and whirred in the air, readjusting its position as the mechanical arms took control. "Thank you for including me, Master Lukia!"

Tav's ears perked up. He could barely catch his breath enough to spit out the words, "*Whatdidshesay*?"

"My first mate here wants to be part of the action!" Lukia said. "I think she's earned it."

Tav had some protests but couldn't seem to find the words to voice them.

The animated crop's eyes took on a devious half-lidded tilt now that her role had changed. *So you're a switch, you little devil.*

"Shall I maintain previous settings?" Croppy asked. Meaning the 'prevent orgasm' option.

"Oh yes," Lukia said.

The apparatus turned over in midair, angling the bulk of its many arms upward so that it was all pointing down between Tav's legs.

Luki chose the 'tongue' option, sliding the bar into yellow. "Croppy, set up a slow rhythm if you would be so kind." The wand moved up and down in short strokes over Tav's erection, keeping its speed in perfect time like a metronome. His pants took on a panicked edge as he was still unable to move into it or affect the pace in any way.

"Shall we change it up a bit?" Lukia asked her digital partner in crime.

"I am happy to oblige, Master Lukia!"

Lukia watched closely, only taking her eyes away from the action to switch the sensations. The machine worked around his body to her directions, hitting all the important points, building up his need to a towering height before she ordered it back to his groin to set up camp. She played with the options on the screen like a DJ, swapping through various sensations, mostly keeping to the pleasure tab. He thrashed on the bed, frustrated beyond coherence.

"What, this not working for you?"

He replied in garbled words.

"How about this?"

The wand went back to a nipple at her command, settings dialed all the way up and she flipped it back and forth between pleasure and pain. Tav *screamed*.

If there ever was a time that she could enjoy something sexually, this was it. The passenger was hitting her with everything it had, activating sensations she barely recognized as indicating arousal. She could take advantage of the rare opportunity, even enjoy it perhaps, but it wasn't what she wanted, wasn't that weird unnamable thing she always got out of this. Directing the energy back out of herself and into him, punishing him for it, that satisfied both her and the beast inside, whereas her own orgasm would only frustrate her and make her suddenly lose interest in all of this. Anticlimactic. So she resisted the small physical calling, sending the momentary notion out of her mind, and focused on his.

"Hmm, you still aren't coming."

He writhed, tears leaking out of his eyes.

"You know, it doesn't look like you're having fun, maybe I should stop."

"*Nonono please!*" There was more, but she couldn't make it out, syllables strung together in a rush to change her mind.

"Tell you what," she said, the pinnacle of condescending helpfulness. *Eat your heart out, Croppy.* "I'm going to have my shipmate here stroke you ten times, and if you can come during that I'll allow it. Sound good?" Tav's ears laid flat against his head and he shook his head, knowing this game full well. Usually she only gave him to three. "Count for me, boy."

Lukia did not change the setting on his orgasm control, keeping the little muscles clamped tight. On the screen she adjusted the strength of the simulated grip to be painfully tight. The wand pulsed on the strokes and he forced out the numbers, getting all the way through them. At the end he made a sound that was half snarl, half sob.

"One more time," she said.

"One, two, three, four—" he wailed, then faltered on five and gave into wordless cries. With a click of her tongue she waved at Croppy to back away from him. He growled and tried to pound every limb against the mattress in sheer desperation.

Lukia chose the licking option again. "Put it on his balls, Croppy." His throaty moan set her veins on fire. "You think you deserve this?

You can't even fucking *count*, why should I let you come?"

His hips thrust against the phantom sensation, not making any difference in the strength of it. She chose "generic" and red and aimed the wand herself, directly at the tip. She leaned down close to look into his face. Tav screamed, whole body shuddering, beyond any ability to fight. She watched the tears trail through the short fur on his face, felt the thing in her gut swell and thrum with satisfaction at the beautiful sight.

"You must be pretty determined not to. We can go that route. How would another week without it feel?"

"Oh no no, oh please Captain!"

"Another month? Maybe I'll never give it to you, how does that sound?"

He knew she could do it, too. She got nothing out of it except the towering knowledge that it was hers to give or deny. Just like whatever gratification the passenger got was hers to give or deny.

But this whole thing was coming to a close. Her grip on the fantasy was failing, her head swimming back up out of the examination of her inner ugly depths. She felt light, pleased, relaxed, and the beast was satisfied too. As it returned to its slumber her interest was dying off in a hurry. Working quickly, Lukia removed the hold on his orgasm without telling him.

"On the count of three, boy."

He shook his head hard but obeyed all the same. "One! Tw—"

He screamed and thrust up off the bed, higher now that she had released the hold on his limbs as well. Thin ropes of seed spilled over his stomach. His orgasm wracked him, ran long and intense, and she watched it while sitting back on her heels, mildly interested but far away. Trying to figure out what made the act not feel like wasted energy for him. She only ever felt cold and unfulfilled after climax. Lost.

But she had given him permission to have his, which he clearly enjoyed—his whole body still shuddered every few seconds while he fought to get breath in—and she hadn't needed to let it happen. She was a good master, generous… or she was today. Tomorrow perhaps not. Lukia held the knowledge close to her heart, soothing the place inside that hurt endlessly, the pit that was there long before the larva had taken up residence.

"Thank you, Croppy, that will be all." The wand whirred and pulled up partway, waiting for her to disconnect Tav.

Lukia rose to her feet and went to each of his hands, removing the bonds. The little table brought a cloth over she used to clean him off. Then she reached under his sweat-damp head and pulled the cable from his spinal jack. It retracted on its own along with the stimwand into the main body of the apparatus and moved away, pulling back toward the ceiling and snapping into its dock. Tav blinked rapidly, trying to banish the tears as well as refocus his eyes. His pupils reduced to pinpoints, reacting to the sight he'd regained.

Lukia leaned over the bed and looked him straight in the eye to make certain she had his undivided attention. He needed to hear the words, because they were his favorites. "Good boy."

Tav sagged and curled up onto his side, hands latching onto her wrists. She climbed into the bed with him and lay down, drawing him close and letting him wrap around her, letting him sob into the short fur on her stomach. Lukia didn't care that much for cuddling, but he did and he needed it, and she wouldn't dare deny him, not until he was well and truly settled back down, and then probably not either.

As for herself, she was as the babbling brook. Rebalanced. Like there was nothing—job, budget, real cooking with actual pans, telepathic stomach bugs—not a thing that she couldn't handle. She wound fingers around one of his ears and stroked the fine fur, letting out a sigh.

"Good boy."

After a few minutes of gentle ear stroking, he asked, "How long do we have this room for?"

"You are scheduled to leave in three nights," Croppy answered.

Lukia looked at the screen in the headboard with an arched brow. Tav smiled then turned to hide it against her dress. But really, she couldn't even find it in her to be annoyed.

"Thank you, Croppy."

"Would you like to know your rating?"

She blinked. "Excuse me?"

"Would you like to know your rating?" the animation repeated in the exact same inflection, reusing the same damn voice file.

"As in… our rating for the *scene*? Are you serious?"

"I would like to know our rating," Tav said, trying to keep the grin off his face but failing when Lukia glared at him.

"Your rating for the previous scene was 7.4 out of 10."

Lukia scoffed aloud and Tav sputtered.

"Areas where the most improvement is recommended for a high score are 'variety' and 'timing.'"

"Timing?"

"Specifically, you showed hesitation when transitioning into erotic play," Croppy explained.

"Hesitation." Lukia attempted to stare down the stupid googly eyes for a minute while Tav struggled not to choke.

"The variety one I will give you," Lukia offered, "but like you said, we do have three more nights. I bet we could get through the whole menu."

"Don't forget all the stuff on the wall," Tav added.

"Right, because we don't need to sleep."

"Recommended sleep length for optimum performance is 7.5 hours," Croppy said.

Lukia swung her arm back and banged on the screen. "Then don't insult my 'performance', bitch!" Croppy giggled, unperturbed.

"I think you did great," Tav murmured, snuggling into her side and closing his eyes.

Lukia blinked down at him. Her eyes wandered over to the cabinet of toys. It wasn't too late to try out the heavier canes.

THE WERE-HUMAN

Chastity Chatterley

White Paws watched her mate lift his head from the felled dear. His muzzle was red with blood. The scent on the wind tantalized her. He touched his nose to hers and nodded to the exposed organs. She knew Blue Eyes wanted her to eat. He'd killed this deer for them, for her, but when she thought about keeping this tasty meal a secret from the rest of the pack, it felt wrong.

Pale moonlight glittered across the snow, casting the puddle of blood in dark shades of black and maroon. The nearby stream coursing past the banks below sang out a lilting lullaby.

Blue Eyes rubbed his muzzle against her. She resisted the urge to lick her chops. The fresh scent of meat called to her. Her mouth watered and hunger clawed at her insides. He stepped back from the body, allowing her a better view of their banquet.

Unable to hold back any longer, she dove forward and gorged on entrails. The juicy flavor of liver exploded on her tongue. She tore into muscle. She was so ravenous she hardly slowed to chew. The warmth of Blue Eyes' flank pressed against hers as he fed. He didn't push her out of the way like the other wolves would have. He was content to eat higher up on the deer body. She told herself it was because she was his mate that he wanted to ensure she ate, but she knew it was more than that. It was because Blue Eyes was different from the other wolves. Sometimes she thought he didn't act like a wolf at all.

If he'd been like the others in their pack, he would have hunted with them. He would have howled to them and they would have tracked the deer together. Instead he only called to White Paws with a soft woof to join him. He sniffed the snowy trails in the forest and found game, even when it was scarce, only he didn't chase it the same way others did. White Paws would have been too weak with hunger for a speedy chase anyway. He'd bid her to corral the deer to the stream where it had plummeted down the steep bank and floundered on injured legs, all the while making pathetic screeches that only made White Paws hungrier. She paced back and forth on the bank above in agitation. Her prey was so close, but out of reach.

Blue Eyes loped his way down a less steep slope further as if he knew the way well, and dived in for an easy kill. He dragged the deer back up to the snowy meadow, and shook off the frigid water.

He pranced around his kill. Triumph flashed across his haughty posture. He'd managed to hunt where the pack had failed. He lifted his chin, daring her to feast on his gift.

White Paws ate her fill. Blue Eyes tore out a sizable chunk and buried it under the snow. He tore off another and left it under an immense oak tree. He scrubbed his face against the snow, leaving red smears across the pristine surface. When White Paws backed away to indicate she had eaten her fill, he howled to the others.

They howled in response and came running.

Alpha glared with eyes half-slit in challenge upon seeing the kill. Blue Eyes bowed his head and tucked his tail under in a subservience that White Paws knew was a ruse. He licked Alpha's face to show respect, but as soon as the leader turned to feast, he pranced away. Every fiber of his being hinted at mischief. The others surged forward by rank. Granny Silverback lingered at the edge of trees, too arthritic and weak to fight for food despite her once respected station. She would die soon. When the others were occupied, Blue Eyes dropped the hunk of torn off meat at her feet. She touched her nose to his before gnawing at the deer flesh with her remaining teeth.

Blue Eyes rubbed his muzzle in the snow, cleaning himself in the odd way he was wont to do. His tail wagged and his tongue hung out, indicating he was quite pleased with his night's work. At times like this, White Paws loved him because he was different. Even so, she feared him because he wasn't like the rest of the pack.

Blue Eyes had joined the pack late into White Paws' childhood. Alpha would have driven him off, save for the giant turkey Blue Eyes had carried in his mouth that caused them all to drool. He'd dropped it and reverently bowed his head before anyone could fight him for it. Everything about Blue Eyes was exotic and foreign, from the vivid blue of his eyes that resembled a puppy's, so different to the pack's amber, to his mannerisms. Anytime a pack male had a bone to pick with him, he resorted to puppy-like antics that only made him more endearing.

She tried to ask him why he pretended, why he bowed down to a leader he had no intention of being led by. His responses were always silly and teasing, a woof to say, "It's rude to challenge your paw," or other such things he only half meant. She could never quite figure him out. He wasn't a lone wolf, but he didn't conform to what a pack member should be like.

Her hunger satiated by the kill, White Paws lay down as the others finished their meal. With her belly at last full after over a week of starvation, she could focus on other sensations in her body: the aching heat in her loins, the lingering excitement the kill had produced in her, and the hunger for something else.

Blue Eyes sauntered away from the other wolves, glancing back over his shoulder. White Paws eyed the nearly full moon, knowing her mate would be off to his secretive places again. He might return to her upon the morrow or in a week; she never knew when he would join her these days. He didn't stay with the pack like a normal wolf would have. Each time he returned, Alpha made him beg for his place in the pack again and once had even urinated on him.

She whined and lay her head on her feet, missing him already. When he returned, his fur would be laced with foreign scents. She wanted to know where he went but she knew better than following. Each time it was always the same. If she followed, he would chase her off or outrun her like last time. Still, she didn't want him to go.

He let out a gentle woof and she glanced up. His tail wagged in invitation. She trailed after him, and he waited for her to catch up, something he didn't ever do. Growl at her, yap, or chase her off she could handle. His bark was worse than his bite. In fact, he never bit. He let her leap back when he snapped at her. This new behavior was unexpected.

He ran circles around her, teasing her with nudges and licks to her muzzle. He woofed, his tone playful and light. Again, this wasn't the norm. She glanced up at the moon through spidery branches, wondering if she'd been mistaken. No, it was nearly full, the time of the month when he often disappeared for days at a time—sometimes weeks.

He tumbled into her and they rolled into the snow. His tongue wagged out of his mouth in pleasure. She offered a playful woof. Why couldn't he be like this more often? She rolled onto her back and offered him her neck in surrender. He nuzzled his face against the soft down of her belly and sniffed her genitals.

She groaned. Of course that was what he wanted. All dogs were the same. She pushed him away with her foot and planted her rear end in the snow. Black Coat, the alpha female, would never allow another female to mate. If White Paws was unfortunate enough to come to term with pups in their dog-eat-dog pack, those puppies would never be allowed to live.

Blue Eyes whined and bumped his side into hers. He whipped his tail in her face. She told herself she wasn't going to fall for this trick again, she wasn't going to be seduced by tail wagging … even if he had a nice tail. So fluffy and silver and the way it moved. . . .She turned her head away, but it was too late. She got excited and peed.

His lips drew back in a self-satisfied grin. He was always making playful jokes with his eyes and it was hard to not want him when she loved him so dearly.

White Paws moved farther off from the pack until she found a bed of warm pine needles under a shady tree. The drooping boughs offered them protection from wind—as well as prying eyes. Blue Eyes' tongue darted in and out as he sniffed at the air. She shifted her tail to the side to allow him to rub his face up against her. The world around her grew distant. All that remained was the two of them.

She panted with wanting. His licking only made her want him more. Already she was swollen and dripping in her heat. He climbed on her back and mounted her. It felt good to mate, good to feel this close. His front paws held her firmly in place against him as he thrust into her. Her insides tightened around the bulb of his shaft. He was hers now and she wouldn't let him go. They remained locked in place, panting while the moon crept across the sky. He filled her, satiated her craving for him. He grunted as he came, the sound somehow unlike other wolves.

Slowly his erection softened and slipped out of her. Exhausted, White Paws lay down in her alcove under the pine tree and he snuggled against her. His hot breath rushed against her face.

Her eyelids grew heavy. She'd nearly fallen into slumber when the warmth at her side slipped away. He'd distracted her into not following again. She forced herself not to give in to fatigue. She made herself get up to follow.

Tonight would be different. She would find out his secrets.

White Paws stole through the icicle-covered forest, careful not to make a noise. She watched him saunter into the open expanse of the snowy meadow. Silently she stalked her prey while her mate up ahead was seemingly unaware of her presence. She edged around the open meadow and stayed downwind, careful to remain invisible to his nose. She tracked his scent for miles. When she came upon the human crafted road before another lot of trees, she hesitated.

Why did the wolf cross the road?

A bark up ahead alerted her he was near. She didn't understand his reason for crossing the road, but hers was to get to him.

She raised her nose to sniff the air. Yes, he had crossed. Scent didn't lie. Warily, she made her way across the unnatural stone under her feet and found his scent in a deer trail. He had travelled this way many times. She had to be close to his secrets now.

He stood before an immense shadow. The stone and wood building was nearly invisible in the shadows of the trees. Blue Eyes stood out in the open like a daft young pup who had never seen the damage done by a hunter's bow.

His scent mingled in with the cedar and pines and slowly changed to something else—an alien scent he often carried to the packs.

He snarled and thrashed. White Paws leapt forward, afraid another wolf attacked. Instead she found him alone, rolling in a bed of pine needles. He whined and snapped at the air, in battle with himself. White Paws circled closer.

His breath came out in labored gasps. He whined, a long pathetic sound that wrenched at her heart. She returned his whine and nudged him. He snarled and sank his teeth into her leg. He'd never bit hard enough to break her skin before. His bite was definitely worse than his bark. She yelped and he released her.

She had known he would be angry if she followed, and this was her just reward. She bowed her head in apology. She expected a narrowing of the eyes to indicate fury. Yet, only sorrow flashed across his brilliant blue eyes before being replaced by pain. He threw his head back and his body contorted as though the bones inside him were breaking. He twisted and spasmed.

White Paw paced. This was too much. She didn't know what to do, how to help him. She howled in frustration.

After many minutes, he lay exhausted and spent, still save for the rise and fall of his ribs. Her gaze fixed on the small movement that meant he was alive. She observed the way his hair receded. His flanks elongated and grew. His face shortened and flattened.

She shivered and drew back in terror. What in all the moons was happening? Where was her mate?

Her nose twitched. Something was added to his scent, something human and dangerous. She padded closer. His skin was pale and hairless, soft and tempting like prey.

She edged closer and touched her nose to his. He didn't move. She sniffed at his neck and down his belly. His scent was her mate's. Still fresh against his genitals was her own scent.

Scent didn't lie.

The biting cold of the air closed in on White Paws. Her head spun and her knees wobbled underneath her as she retreated. She caught a whiff of her own blood. The wound in her leg left red droplets on white snow. She licked away the blood caked to her fur, but it tasted metallic and wrong.

She made it to the shelter of trees before collapsing into a heap. Fire throbbed in her limbs and her fur felt heavy and stifling. Every breath of frigid air burned in her lungs.

She stared up at the brilliance of the waxing moon. A lance of pain ripped up her leg and into her belly. She vomited the feast of deer meat from earlier. Her insides boiled. She howled out of pain but the sound she made was like no wolf's she had ever heard.

Eyes flashed and watched at her from the darkness. Familiar blue eyes stared out from an unfamiliar face.

* * *

White Paws's head throbbed and her mouth tasted like dried grass. Her eyes grew accustomed to the strange glow at the top of the cavern-like enclosure around her. It was as warm as summer but she felt oddly naked. When she moved her leg to scratch at her ear, she found her leg stiff and unable to reach as easily. Her leg was pale and hairless—like the affliction that had overcome her mate. Her paws were no longer white. She was all pink like a pig and she was wrapped in some kind of strange moss. She rolled on the soft bed of strangely smooth furs and clawed at the swaddling that covered her body until she'd torn it off. Exposed beneath was more of the horrible pink skin. She was no longer White Paws but Pink Flesh. Instead of looking like her family, she resembled every other human. She howled in defiance.

She leapt from the bed of furs and scratched at the walls of the enclosure. She toppled brittle stones from wide, branchless tree trunks and jumped back when they shattered. Water splattered across the floor from a bowl. She crouched to lap it up, finding she was thirsty, only to have the broken stone bite into her feet and palms. She thrashed against the walls, scrabbling for a way out, but could find none. Her nails were weak and left no claw marks. Her teeth were dull. She felt vulnerable and powerless in this form.

The only good thing at the moment was that the bite to her leg was healed. She didn't know how much time she had slept. Did her pack know she was gone and mourn her? She missed the sanctuary of their kinship and the strength of their number.

White Paws huddled in the darkest corner, whining in a voice that didn't resemble her own.

The muffled plodding of footsteps approached. Her heart thundered and she peed on the floor. A creak alerted her someone neared.

An opening parted from the wall and a human stood in the gap. His voice was rough like an animal's growl. "Easy girl. Don't panic. I know this is all new to you. It'll get easier, I promise." His voice was Blue Eyes' but not. She squinted and whined.

He crouched down, his eyes level with hers. Her nostrils flared. She knew that scent. Her mate was inside this human, but how could that be? Had he been eaten from the inside out? Had she? She couldn't believe it. None of this made sense.

Yes, a human had eaten her mate and now wore his eyes. Yet, that wasn't what she'd seen out in the snow.

"That's right. It's just me, you know me," he said in a soothing voice. She didn't understand the words, but she understood the placating tone she'd heard him use when he'd vexed her.

He sat on the floor, continuing to speak. She watched him take in the mess she'd created. His attention distracted, she pushed herself up and scrambled past him. Her new body was awkward and bumbling. She half-ran and half-crawled. It was no wonder he caught her as easily as he did.

A howl erupted from her throat, the grating cry so unlike the sound she was accustomed to. She clawed at the man's—her mate's—no, this horrible man's face who wasn't her mate's. She tried to bite his neck. He pinned her hands to her sides and held her far enough from him that she couldn't bite. More humans came running, though they halted upon seeing her. She snarled at them, but they warily drew closer.

The man who held her barked out words at them and they reluctantly retreated. He was the alpha here? How could that be? He was just another of the pack at home. He never challenged anyone. Why would Blue Eyes settle for anything less than being alpha in the pack when he had this here?

She stilled and whimpered, uncertain what was to become of her. He carried her back into her stone cage and held her on the soft platform in the middle of the room where she'd woke. She couldn't see the opening in the wall but she could hear the quick, light footsteps approach.

White Paws twisted her head to the side and snarled. A frightened female leapt back. In her hands she held a limp snake—or was it some kind of vine?

"Be still. No one is going to hurt you. Calm yourself." His voice was gentle, but in it he held the command of an alpha. "You've cut yourself and your wound needs cleaning. We're going to help you."

 She shook with exertion and fear, fighting him as he pushed her face down onto the soft cushions. He crouched on her back, pressing her deep into the unnatural furs. He looped the vine around her wrist, through the wooden board above her head and then around the other. Only then did she realize it was a trap. She yanked on the vine but it didn't give. He continued to sit on her as he tied each foot to a stump at each corner so that she couldn't move.

She howled.

He made his voice stony and low, the tone one that she couldn't ignore. "Put a leash on it. You aren't going anywhere." From the erect posture of his spine, she knew it was a command. She had the distinct impression his tail would have been lifted straight in the air to tell her who was in charge.

She cowed her head as best she could from her prostrate position.

"That's right. Who's your alpha?" he asked. His calm, confident demeanor pressed down on her like a weight. That command was far more effective in subduing her than his hands had been. He released her.

Her heart beat slowed and her fear withdrew. She didn't fight her alpha. He expected her to obey and she would.

Blue Eyes proceeded to torture her by plucking stone splinters from her hands and feet and pouring searing cold liquid over them. He wrapped up her arms and feet in stifling bindings and covered her naked pink flesh with human-crafted furs. He bid a youth to brush the broken bits of stone from the floor with a cluster of strangely gathered twigs and wiped down the puddles with chunks of stringy fur.

"I hate you. You never loved me," she tried to howl. "You tricked me." The words were neither human, nor wolf and made no sense to her ears.

The man's blue eyes gazed down at her with sorrow. She suspected he might understand her even if she didn't understand herself.

* * *

White Paws spent an hour shredding the fabric underneath her head. She might have bitten Blue Eyes the next time he sat on the bed next to her, but with him came the smell of fresh meat. Her mouth watered and she raised her head. He held out a large bone dripping with juices. She licked her lips and he laughed.

He set down the bone on the fluff next to her head. It was half as long as her arm and just as thick. Immediately she bit into a hunk of meat on the end.

"You're going to make a real mess of this place, aren't you?" he asked with a chuckle. "Good thing I pay the servants well, else I'd never hear the end of it."

The flesh on the bone was scorched with fire—like the time Blue Eyes had led the pack to the elk killed in the wild fire. The meat was tough and took effort to gnaw on, something she suspected he'd counted on to distract her. He unwrapped her hands and dabbed foul-smelling liquid on her palms. At least this time it didn't sting. Maybe he wasn't trying to torture her.

He crossed to the other side of the room and drew back a long curtain of lichen, or maybe it wasn't a plant. High up was an opening that showed the full moon glowing through the trees. She stopped gnawing at the meat to stare. She would be an anomaly like him now. With each full moon she would leave the pack to come to this secret place. If she was lucky, the wolf in her would break free and devour this human self. She didn't know how Blue Eyes could stand to go through such an ordeal each month.

He sat beside her and playfully tugged the bone out of her reach. She snapped at the air, trying to reach for it and he laughed. His humor was as ill-timed as always. She decided he was trying to torture her. She barked at him.

"You're a smart girl, aren't you? What's on top of a house?"

She could tell it was a question, but didn't know how to answer in this new body. She barked, "Roof!"

"That's right." He smiled, his blue eyes dancing the same way they did when he was a wolf. "How does sandpaper feel?"

"Ruff!" she said.

She knew he was teasing her about something, though what she didn't know. He placed a bowl of water near her face and showed her how to lap it up.

He smoothed a paw—a hand—over her long mane of hair, pushing dark locks out of her eyes. His scent was wild and tamed at the same time. It was familiar and comforting. He scratched her behind the ears and she melted under his touch just as she had when he nuzzled her in the snow.

"Stop that!" she tried to say. "I won't fall for your courtship distractions now." She nipped at his hand, not hard enough to draw blood, but enough to tell him she didn't want him grooming her. He never bit her hard enough for that—except for the last time.

He withdrew, sliding off the cushions underneath them. "They say a dog won't bite the hand that feeds them, but that doesn't apply to wolves, does it now?" Under the teasing, his tone was hurt.

The loss of his warmth against her was palpable as the loss of her fur had been. Immediately she was sorry she had driven him away. She whimpered, afraid to be alone in the strange cave and in this stranger body.

He stepped out the door and left her.

* * *

White Paws lay tangled in the covers. She'd managed to free one of her feet from its bindings and twist herself around so that she was facing the ceiling, though now she remained precariously close to the edge of the platform.

The door creaked open. Blue Eyes came in carrying a bowl of water. "Ah, I should have guessed you were up to mischief. You were too quiet." He set the bowl on the floor as he untangled the covers from her limbs.

Silently he untied her remaining foot and scooted her over so he could sit beside her. She wanted to tell him she was sorry for biting him earlier but she didn't know how. She tried to say it with her eyes like she did when she was a wolf, but he didn't acknowledge he understood.

He brought the bowl to his lips, tipped it up and drank. She wondered if that was the way humans did it. He lifted her head and touched the bowl to her lips. She slurped up the water, spilling some of it over her chin. He dabbed at it with a blanket.

Blue Eyes had always looked after her—and the others in the pack. He'd acted as a leader even though he hadn't been one. She wondered if it was his human alpha self that had shone through. Now that she was human, she could see he was no different.

He stroked her hair. "I'm sorry I did this to you. If it was up to me, we'd both be wolves all the time, but the moon calls to me. And now it's going to call to you and make you shift as well." He curled up next to her, draping an arm around her like he sometimes did when they cuddled. She smelled his hair and licked his forehead. He laughed and touched his lips to her cheek. It wasn't a lick. The gesture was foreign, yet she had a sense he meant it as affection. A bubble of noise erupted from her throat. She had just laughed like him?

He did it again, this time on her forehead and then her other cheek. She laughed and squirmed farther back. The chill of the air greeted her skin now that her coverings had shifted from her bare chest. She stared down at herself, noticing the way the hairless skin rose with tiny bumps. She only had two breasts and the tips wrinkled and puckered as her skin grew cold. It wasn't unpleasant. If anything, she almost liked it.

He watched her studying herself. "Being a human is still foreign for you, just like when I first became a wolf." He stroked her hair and she closed her eyes, melting into his touch. He'd always known how to win her favor with his caress.

Blue Eyes slid a hand over her ribs. The warmth of him felt cozy and intoxicating. Her nipples lengthened at his touch. He smiled and rolled one between his fingers. A noise like a growl sounded in the back of her throat but she wasn't displeased. She wanted more.

White Paws squirmed closer, pressing her body against his. She opened her eyes when he stopped. His nostrils flared and his lips parted, not so different than when he was testing to see if she wanted him.

And she did.

"Well, what do you know" he said. "Try not to get so excited you pee the bed."

She knew from the tone he'd made a joke. She hated that she couldn't understand him like she did when he'd been a wolf. All she knew was she smelled desire on him. His eyes were hungry as they feasted upon her naked skin.

She nuzzled her face against his and imitated the gesture of pressing a mouth to flesh. He pressed his lips to hers and bit her lip. A noise of surprise escaped her and when her lips parted, he darted his tongue inside her mouth. Her muscles tightened and she fought against the restraints holding her wrists. Of all the things he had to do to ruin the moment.

She only relaxed when he broke away.

"Too much? Too human for you?" The concern in his eyes told her she could trust him just as she did when he was a wolf.

She turned her head away in a huff to tell him how annoyed she was with him. "Bad alpha," she said with her eyes.

He returned to touching his lips to hers. She smiled. He brushed his mouth against her jaw and she moaned in contentment. The warmth of his hands stroking her body extinguished the prickle of cold on her skin. He kneaded her breasts until she ached between her legs. He surprised her doing things no wolf would have: plucking at her nipples with his fingers, nibbling at her belly and hips as though she were tastier than prey, dipping his tongue inside her mouth again. This time he did it more slowly. She decided she liked it and did it back to him.

"Well, it looks like you can teach an old dog new tricks," he said.

He dipped his face down between her legs and parted them. Just like when she was a wolf, he licked her to ready her body for him. Only this was far more intense than the times he'd done it before. She panted as pleasure mounted. The vine around her wrists dug into her flesh as she pulled against the restraint. Her limbs quivered with tension. She wanted to break free, to become a wild beast in his arms.

Perhaps it was best she remained tied up.

Keeping his mouth on her growing wetness, he reached one hand up and pinched a nipple. She gasped at the unexpected ecstasy this brought her. He sucked on her and she arched into his mouth, crying out as pleasure unlike anything she had ever experienced jolted through her body.

He lifted his face to hers. Her scent covered his face, something part wolf and part human. She shivered all over. He covered them both with the blanket. She couldn't see him stripping the human-crafted furs from his body but she could feel them slip away. His erection pressed against her, hard and insistent.

She lifted her chin and exposed her neck. She was his, whether human or wolf. A guttural growl escaped his lips. "Are you saying you'll be a good girl? Is this your way of promising not to scratch or bite or give me fleas?"

He nibbled at her neck to tell her who was alpha. She wanted to wrap her arms around him and bring him close. She tugged at her restraints but they remained.

He shook his head. "Leave them be." From the firmness of his tone, she knew he meant her to obey. Immediately she stopped.

He stroked her silky pink skin and scratched behind her ears just the way she liked.

He rewarded her with a smile. "You are a good girl. Now you get another treat."

He covered her breast with his mouth and suckled hard enough he made her want him all over again. She felt wet and slick between her legs. His penis slid against her, teasing her with the promise of more. She gasped and arched her hips to meet him. He thrust into her, moaning. She closed her eyes. The pleasure of it was so intense she could barely stand it. The guttural noises he made were more wolf-like than human. He enclosed her in his arms and panted into her ear. He pulled out and thrust back in. She clenched around him and didn't let him go. She could feel him swelling inside her. Her body throbbed in response.

For a moment she forgot where she was—what she was. In her mind she was a wolf again and they were tied together in passion. He mounted her in the sparkling snow and she felt content with her mate filling her with his seed. A wave of heat washed over her. She dug her nails into a soft pillow. She was wolf.

"Stay with me," he said. He smoothed a palm to her cheek. "This would be a very inconvenient moment for you to change back."

She opened her eyes to find his blue ones flashing in the light. The muscles of her body contracted. Her face felt like it wanted to grow longer. The teasing tension of hair waited just under her skin, about to burst forth. She cried out in a mixture of pleasure and pain. The throbbing between her legs built to new peaks, her orgasm spiking higher than it had before.

He tried to pull away, but he couldn't. Their bodies were joined just as when they were wolves. The change coursed through her and she welcomed it. She had enjoyed this brief affair as a human—at least the last few minutes of it, but she was ready to be herself again. Fur bristled over her flesh. The restraints holding her in place, taming her and tethering her, loosened and fell away.

Blue Eyes growled and his back arched. He clawed at the soft surface beside her and tore at the covers with his teeth. She howled in a mixture of satiation and terror at what was happening. The fire in her limbs throbbed like when she'd turned into a human and she could only hope it would soon be over. Her limbs stretched and lengthened, the sensation overwhelming.

He pulled out of her. She stared into his cool, blue eyes now set in the furry face she had fallen in love with. She rolled over and sat up. She howled and he joined in.

Feet came running and the door was thrown open.

Two wolves raced past. Free and wild…Until the next full moon.

The Importance of Trust

Tarl "Voice" Hoch

"Mind if I sit here?"

Holly blinked, breaking the spell that had been cast over her by the stoat seated before a baby grand piano. The jaguar scooted over in the booth and a woman sat down. Turning her gaze away from the glittering sea of electric candles, the feline got her first look at the voice's owner.

She was a hare, her body lean and taut with muscles that moved like velvet under her fur. A snug black dress sheathed her body, fitting well enough that Holly could tell the hare wasn't wearing any panties—or a bra for that matter. The jaguar knew from experience the dress would be uncomfortable to wear, being so tightly pressed against the hare's fur, but the resulting look was stunning. Holly said as much.

"Thank you," the hare flashed a smile, her front teeth shining in the candlelight. "You looked like you could use some company."

Holly motioned to the piano player who had paused in his playing to take a drink from a bowl of water. "The pianist has been doing a fine job so far, though I'm always glad to meet a new person."

"So he's good?"

"Very." Holly took a lap of her martini. The taste of jackfruit tickled her tongue and her ears splayed. Setting her glass down, the jaguar met the hare's brown eyes. The wiggle of the bunny's   nose was a mix of cute and sexy. Under the table Holly rubbed her thighs together, a light tingle running along her spine as she did. "I like your accent, where are you from?"

"Belgium." The hare's ears swiveled as she took a drink of her own beverage, something that smelled like grass and earth to Holly's nose. "My name is Enora."

"Holly, and Canadian."

The hare nodded and took another drink.

"I've seen you and your partner around. You and the panther make a good couple." The hare's eyes widened for a moment and a delicate paw rose to her muzzle. "You are a couple aren't you?"

Holly giggled. "That's Raven, my husband."

"The red panda and fox?"

"Very close friends." Holly smiled, careful not to flash any of her teeth. "In the time Raven and I have known them, we've gotten quite close."

Enora scratched a blunt claw across the table lightly. "I know that type of friend. I have a couple back home I am quite close with."

Holly's ears rose for a moment, unsure if what the hare had just said was innocent or some kind of innuendo. She tried to cover her surprise by taking another drink, only to find the glass empty. With a quick motion she flagged the waiter down and ordered a martini for herself and the hare.

"Did you come with anyone?" Holly asked while the waiter placed the new martinis on the table. Holly picked hers up and stirred the bright red coloring with the yellow that sat above it in the glass. Now that she thought about it, she had seen the hare around on deck. The woman had looked fantastic in a bikini and if Holly remembered correctly, even Raven had pointed her out once.

Enora shook her head, pulling the swizzle stick out of her drink and twirling it between her fingers. "I am, how shall I say, between partners right now. The last one was a bit too controlling for my tastes."

"I've dated a couple men like that."

The wooden swizzle stick snapped between Enora's fingers. "Cynthia was a bitch."

"That bad?"

The hare took a deep breath and set the broken stick onto the table before smoothing her dress. Holly swallowed as she watched Enora's paws run along the fabric. Her paws itched with the desire to caress the smaller woman's bare fur.

"Cynthia was good in bed." Enora's eyes took on a faraway look. "Okay, she was more than good. Ravenous, adventurous, and damned insatiable. We had an understanding, an open relationship. It worked, at least for the first six months while we were still figuring each other out. But then her demands in bed started to become…"

"Let me guess," Holly said. "Violent?"

Enora shook her head. "Oh no, I love a little violence in bed."

Holly's ears perked up. "Then, what?"

"She became more dominant. Extremely so." Enora picked up the broken pieces of her swizzle stick and started to snap them into smaller pieces.

The jaguar cocked her head to the side when Enora gathered the broken pieces into a small pile. "Dominant? You don't look like the type that would mind that, if you don't mind me saying."

The hare laughed; it sounded like sunshine. "No offense taken." Enora reached out and rested her paw on Holly's arm, her thumb tracing a circle on the rosette covered fur. "I may not look it, but I very much like to be in control in the bedroom. With the right partner of course." A tingle ran from where the hare's thumb brushed through Holly's fur and raced along the jaguar's skin. She wanted to lick the smaller woman's nose, it was so cute.

"That's rare for a herbivore."

Enora's smile broadened. "Tell me about it." She leaned closer to Holly, close enough the jaguar could smell the booze and blended grasses on Enora's breath. Their whiskers brushed. "But what really gets people is the fact that I love dominating… meat eaters."

The tingle became a line of warmth that curled in Holly's stomach before tracing downwards. Her whiskers trembled and she had to take a deep breath before she answered.

"Is that so?"

The hare answered with a low noise in her throat, an almost purr that tightened the jaguar's chest. Enora's paw moved over the top of Holly's leg, the flat of her palm warm through the jaguar's fur. The fingers slid down the other side, the hard nails preceding the pads of Enora's fingers and palm. Holly's breath caught in her throat. Turning her gaze to the hare she was rewarded with a soft kiss. The briefest contact of Enora's lips, the hardness of her front teeth while they pressed against Holly's lips before vanishing in a welter of gentle giggles.

"You taste like fruit." Enora's paw remained on the inside curve of Holly's upper thigh, her dress's hem brushing against the hare's fingers. It was all Holly could do to nod, her breathing heavy and deep. Her tail-tip flicked back and forth in a steady tempo matching her quickly beating heart. Enora scooted closer until her leg brushed the jaguar's. "I like it. So do you like a bit of violence in your play?"

"Depends on the person and the situation." Holly moved her paw to rest against the hare's thigh, enjoying the smooth texture of the woman's dress. Her claws pricked the fabric while they slid in and out of their sheaths. Enora's shoulder brushed Holly's and the hare's paw travelled up Holly's thigh, taking the hem of the dress with it until the fingers brushed the intimate cotton that was soaked with the feline's want.

"What do we have here?" Enora's voice was low in Holly's ear while she pushed against the tight, moist fabric. The jaguar's ears flicked up before dashing down and her claws dug into the hare's dress, puncturing through the fabric. "Seems as if my little pussy cat likes to be petted."

The hare's fingers danced across the dampness, the blunt claws teasing where the jaguar's outer lips pressed against the fabric. Holly's muzzle was open and she tried to cover it by pretending to take a drink from her martini glass. Enora watched the feline, blunt teeth catching the light, smile wide and knowing.

"Someone will see or smell…" Holly gasped.

"Possibly," Enora's fore-finger claw caught the thigh elastic of

Holly's thong, lifting it and moving it aside. Holly swallowed as she felt the air of the bar brush along her nether regions, cooling the moisture that had collected there. With a low chuckle, Enora moved her finger to glide along the moist slit. Holly gasped, almost dropping her glass as the hare's fine fur tickled along her naked flesh before caressing over her swollen clit. There was a low tear of cloth as Holly shredded five lines into the rabbit's dress, earning a teasing laugh.

"Naughty kitty," The hare whispered warmly into Holly's ear, making it flick. Enora's arousal reached the jaguar's nose when the hare shifted in her seat. "You've wrecked my dress. Now I have to change. Care to join me?"

Holly's ears shot up and she looked down wide-eyed at the torn fabric. "Oh no!" She slowly retracted her claws. "I'm so, so sorry!"

Enora rose, her fingers sliding from between Holly's legs. The sight of the dark, damp fur of the hare's fingers made Holly's tail dance. The hare traced a finger down Holly's arm and grabbed her paw. "Come."

The jaguar stood on shaky legs. She could feel a bead of moisture running down the inside of her thigh, tracing the edge of her thong where it dug uncomfortably into the soft flesh where her legs met her torso. Her first step sent another pulse through her body and only Enora's paw stopped her from sitting back down until the feeling faded. Instead the hare pulled, as if she was taking pleasure in the feline's discomfort. "Come this way my pet, I need a new dress and I think you need to get out of your underthings."

Together they walked out of the bar, the piano music dancing behind them. Down two flights of stairs they went until they turned into the thin hallway leading to the passenger cabins. The hallways had made Holly feel claustrophobic when they had first boarded, but now they reminded her of things tight inside her body. More than once she found her gaze drawn to the white underside of Enora's tail which flagged upwards. Unfortunately the woman's dress had a hole that the appendage could fit through, or it would be hiking up the woman's dress to show a very tempting slice of ass.

Still, the tightness of the outfit and the constant movement of the hare's rear made Holly bite her lower lip more than once. It was very, very distracting. More so than the cuteness of Enora's tiny nose, always in motion. The jaguar's own dress was starting to feel too tight, too confining, and she longed to tear it and her soaked panties off.

Enora looked around her. Holly followed her gaze. No one was in the hallway. The jaguar's back hit the wall and the hare's fingers were up her dress, palm pressed against the bare flesh between the feline's legs, fingers teasing around the moist entrance. Holly's gasp was loud, her eyes fluttering as she gripped the hare's shoulders.

"Such a pretty plaything," Enora cooed. "And so ready."

The touch of the hare's finger against the slick entrance of her cleft sent a shiver through Holly's body. Her tail bottle-brushed as the digit slid inwards. Holly growled, throwing her head back and hitting the wall hard enough to send stars across her vision.

Seemingly encouraged, Enora pushed her finger in deeper. She curved it, exploring Holly's inner-walls before slowly rocking it in and out of the jaguar's body. All the while the palm pad of her paw rubbed back and forth along Holly's clit, making the woman's body pulse in time with each thrust.

A cleaning cart clattered around the corner.

Enora was dragging Holly again, the jaguar stumbling after the hare more on instinct than anything else, chasing the sounds of the hare's giggles.

"We're here." The hare flashed a smile. Holly placed a palm on the wall as she caught her breath, her body still tingling but slowly coming back to itself. It had been far too long since she had been with a female who was so forceful with their own lust. Leah was a timid creature, always letting Holly take command. This… this was the other side of the scale.

"Open the door damn it," Holly managed to growl out. She longed to have the hare's finger in her again.

Enora reached out and traced a finger claw along the taller woman's cheek before slapping her gently. Holly's ears rose and she snarled. Enora chuckled. She grabbed a handful of Holly's curls and yanked the taller woman's head down to her level. "If we're going to play this game, we're going to play by my rules, pussy cat."

Holly blinked, ears flicking back. Slowly she nodded, clasping her paws in front of her when Enora released her hair.

"Banana."

"That's your safe-word?" Enora asked, her head cocking to the side as one ear drooped. "Interesting choice."

"Thank you."

"Now, enough talk." With a swipe of her keycard, Enora pushed the door open, dragging the jaguar into the room after her.

Much like Holly and Raven's room, Enora's room was economically small. A single queen dominated one side of the room, facing a mirrored wall. To the side a chair and small vanity was surrounded by elegant shell scones. What immediately caught Holly's eyes, however, was the large open suitcase taking up half the bed. Her practiced eyes immediately widened when they took in the plethora of items within. Enora slowly turned and pressed a paw against Holly's chest above her cleavage.

"You won't believe how hard it is to keep the concierge from going through that suitcase anytime he's in the room." The hare leaned closer, nose twitching. "I swear, it's like he wants me to catch him going through it just to see what I would do."

Enora traced her finger between Holly's cleavage. "Now, I have something I want you to wear." The hare turned and went to the suitcase, rummaging around to the sounds of metal jingling and the creak of leather before coming up with a rhinestone embedded collar. She walked over to Holly, eyes flashing, and fastened it around the feline's throat. The jaguar was pleased to find it snug without being too tight. Holly had played the role of the submissive before and surprised herself how quickly she slipped into the role as soon as the collar snapped shut.

"You are mine, my pretty kitty, until tomorrow morning. You are not some newbie to this, are you?"

"No ma'am." Holly's tail swayed slowly behind her. Taking advantage of the smaller woman being so close, the jaguar flicked her tail across the woman's nose. Enora's brow furrowed, her fingers slid under the collar and yanked Holly's head downwards, the sudden pressure against the feline's neck making her gasp.

"You better not try that again my pet. And I prefer Mistress."

"Yes Mistress," Holly wheezed.

The hare's fingers moved from under the collar to thread through the jaguar's curly hair. There they gripped, keeping Holly bent at the waist. "Very good," Enora winked before moving in and placing a chaste kiss on the feline's muzzle. "Continue to please me and I will continue to please you. But be warned, I am not a gentle Mistress, nor am I a gentle lover."

Holly's tail gave a stuttering lash behind her. Enora laughed.

"Is my pretty kitty worried she might not be able to handle me?"

"A little, Mistress."

"Good." Enora pressed her muzzle against Holly's, this time opening her mouth so that her tongue found the feline's. There they danced, the hare holding the jaguar's head against her own until she finally let go and Holly relaxed into the kiss. Enora tasted sweet yet earthy to Holly. She was also a practiced kisser, the gentle press and play of her tongue dexterous around the jaguar's own, broader tongue. When they broke, both panting while Holly blinked her eyes as if waking from a dream. The kiss had been amazing. Enora grinned.

Taking a step back, the hare reached up. With a small wiggle of her hips, she slowly peeled her dress down her body. Holly watched, the heat low in her building while the black dress inched downwards. Enora's small cleavage was first to be revealed, the twin mounds like halved oranges. They rose and fell with the hare's measured breath, the woman's nipples sharp in the light chill of the cabin.

Down the dress went, whispering across the fur of her sculpted stomach. The feline's gaze watched as the curve of the hare's hipbone was bared, then the tender shape of her navel. When the dress finally uncovered Enora's mons and her womanhood was fully revealed, the feline gave an appreciative growl of need.

Then the hare was completely naked before Holly.

"You're beautiful, Mistress," the jaguar whispered. The warmth from before had returned and she rubbed her thighs together. Things tightened low in her body and another bead of moisture escaped from between her nether lips.

Enora flicked her wrist and suddenly a dagger half the length of her forearm filled her paw. Holly's gasp sounded loud to her own ears as she took a step back. The knife had come out of nowhere, Holly hadn't seen the woman pick it up. Her back hit the wall of the cabin.

"Stay!" The hare's voice forced Holly's ears down and the jaguar froze while Enora advanced. The feline watched the shining blade as it came to rest on her naked shoulder. The look on Enora's face held a mix of lust and something darker. "As you have ruined my dress, I think it's only fair to ruin yours."

The blade hissed through Holly's fur as the hare moved it lower. The jaguar trembled when the point of the blade pricked along her skin until it came to rest against her dress. In one sudden movement the sound of cut fabric echoed in the room. Holly yelped, her tail thumping a frantic beat against the wall. It was all the jaguar could do to stay still as the knife slid down her body. She wanted to snarl, to hiss, to rend in her sudden panic.

Enora took a step back, her eyes moving along Holly's form as the dress fell from her. "You have a lovely frame my pretty kitty. Not like the waifs back home." Taking a step forward, the hare traced her free hand along Holly's bra, then lower, following the curve of the larger woman's hips. She cupped the feline's butt. "I especially love your hips and ass. So feminine, so full of dimension. You are so very beautiful."

Holly's ears warmed and her tail danced behind her. "Thank you, Mistress."

The hare's paw continued to travel through Holly's fur, tracing small valleys through it. Enora's claw parted rosettes and followed the planes of the jaguar's body. Holly remained against the wall, paws at her side. Her fingers were fists—though her frame shivered—and things low in her body longed for Enora's touch.

The dagger flashed like a dove in flight before Holly's face. She flinched away only to receive a slap from the smaller woman that knocked the jaguar's head against the wall. "No pet, do not fear the blade. The knife shall teach you the line between pleasure and pain." The hare wedged the blade between Holly's fur and her strapless bra. She swallowed as she felt the edge of the blade shave off a tuft of her fur. The fabric cut, Holly's ample breasts fell free, nipples instantly hardening at the touch of the air.

Enora cupped one of the heavy globes as if shopping for melons and made an appreciative sound in her throat. Holly whimpered as the hare tweaked a nipple. "I am jealous, such heft." Enora pulled away and traced the dagger's point around the underside of her own smaller chest. "Not like my tiny breasts."

"Your breasts are perfect, Mistress," Holly dared to state. "They are perfect handfuls. Your nipples are small and cute."

The hare paused in the tracing of her knife and her ears turned to face the jaguar. "They are a hair's breadth away from being a man's chest!"

"Try running with mine, Mistress."

Enora looked as if she was going to take a step forward. But she paused, instead tapping the tip of the dagger against her front teeth. After a moment of thought she waved the blade at Holly. "You have an excellent point. Well done my kitty cat. Now for your reward."

The hare stalked forward on her long legs. Holly swallowed, eyes darting between the shine of the blade and Enora's large eyes. The jaguar expected her to stop, so when Enora pressed herself against the line of the larger woman's body, Holly let out a sigh. The hare nibbled along the curve of the feline's throat. "I bet your panties are getting uncomfortable, aren't they my pet?"

Holly hadn't really been paying attention to her underwear. The dagger seemed to be a far more important element to the play. Now that Enora had mentioned it, however, Holly could feel the elastic cutting into her fur and skin alongside her mound.

After a moment Holly nodded, another shudder running through her as Enora nipped gently at the jaguar's throat.

"We must solve that then." The hare parted from the jaguar and slowly knelt before her. Reaching up, the smaller woman hooked the edge of the knife into Holly's panties and slowly pulled. The elastic stretched, then parted around the blade, falling down the feline's legs. Enora took a deep breath, ears sweeping back. "I can smell you, my pet."

Holly gazed down at the hare while she leaned in, caressing her cheek along the curve of Holly's hip. Just the sight of it made the jaguar's whiskers quiver, her tail swish hard behind her. Enora continued to run her cheek along the sensitive hipbone while her free paw rose to run along the feline's stomach and lower regions. The dagger—thankfully—remained resting with its blade along the back of Holly's leg.

"Does my kitty like her scritches?" Enora looked up at Holly, who met her gaze.

"Very much, Mistress."

"How is my pet feeling?"

"Very warm, Mistress."

"Good." Enora stood and clasped Holly's paw in her own, pulling her from the wall to the bed. There she beckoned the older woman to sit. Holly obeyed, paws clasped in her lap obediently. The hare separated the jaguar's paws and placed them on either side of the woman. Pushing Holly's thighs apart, the hare kneeled in the space between.

Holly watched as the hare lowered her head, small pink tongue brushing along the fur near Holly's knee. The feeling was unlike Raven's barbs; rather, this was very quick and delicate. In the large mirror behind the hare, Holly could see the gleam of Enora's own pleasure as her butt raised up.

The jaguar let out a soft whisper of a moan.

Enora moved higher and licked again, this time calling Holly's gaze with her own. Her licks deepened, brushing the fur. "Do you trust me my pet?"

Holly had to fight the tingling of her body to answer. "Yes."

The dagger came into view like the fin of a shark. "Do you?"

The jaguar bit her bottom lip, her ears lowered. Her voice was high. "Y…yes."

Enora grinned. Raising the dagger, she placed the point of the blade against Holly's inner thigh, tracing it gently through her fur. Holly's heart quickened in her chest, her breath fast and loud in her ears. She could feel the pricking of the point as it caught—but didn't cut—the skin under her fur. There was a flutter to her breaths, and Holly quickly considered using the safe-word.

Then the blade bit.

Holly threw her head back in a cry that quickly became a moan.

It was as if the pressure inside her released. A tremor shook her body. Her eyes closed. Her ears flattened. She could feel a small amount of warmth spilling onto her fur to be replaced by Enora's tongue a moment later. The flat warmth of the hare's tongue against the sharp sting of the cut made Holly cry out more. The jaguar's back bowed, claws digging into the bed as she rode the conflicting—yet similar—feelings that swept over her.

Enora raised her head and Holly's back hit the bed. Their gazes met along Holly's body.

"That was… that…" Holly swore.

The hare simply smiled back. Holly could see where the cut had been made. A shallow thing, the line of red no longer bleeding and almost hidden amongst the thigh fur, a slight red tint to the fur the only evidence. Enora lowered her head a moment later, her breath brushing along Holly's fur until it ghosted against her sex. The quick release Holly had moments before did nothing to stem the pulsing wetness that dwelt in the cleft there.

Enora's first lick had Holly's back off the bed again. It was quickly followed by another, then another, and another. The jaguar shook as her legs trembled, hips raising against the hare's muzzle, begging for more. Strings of vulgarity flew from the jaguar. Enora gripped Holly's thighs, her muzzle pushing deeper into the cleft. Her tongue slid along the outer folds of the older woman, tracing small lines of moisture there before plunging into the warm entrance.

Holly snarled and thrust her hips further up, fucking the hare's tongue with each of the smaller woman's tongue-thrusts. Enora dug her claws into Holly's thighs, pricking into the skin. The jaguar looked down her body, eyes half-lidded and pupils large.

"You fucking bitch." Any edge to the words were stolen by the feline's toothy grin.

Enora laughed, the sound loud and sharp as she rose to the bed. She sat with her knees folded, forcing Holly's thighs apart with her own. The jaguar watched as a heavy bead of moisture dripped from between the hare's inner lips to darken the sheets, thin strands trailing after it.

"Ready for more?" The hare asked, leaning over to place a dainty kiss on Holly's swollen nipple. A line of fire raced from her nipple to clit and back as the hare teased the wet moisture around the jaguar's areola. Holly answered with a rumbling purr. The hare's tongue circled around the nub of flesh, sucking it into her muzzle where she tugged on it between her blunt front teeth.

Enora reached over into the suitcase, which now hung half-suspended over the side of the bed. Her tongue never stopped its dance, not even when there was a jingle of metal and a pair of handcuffs swung into Holly's view. The hare leaned back, licking her lips, ears lowered behind her head.

"Hands above your head, now!"

Holly obeyed, her hands raising until they grazed the metal of the wall bracket where the cloth headboard hung. Enora snaked up Holly's body, her movements back-brushing the jaguar's fur until the smaller woman's petite breasts hung before the feline's muzzle. Holly's tongue flicked out, her barbs sliding along the puckered nubs. Enora moaned. There was the familiar sliding click as the steel encircled Holly's wrists. Nipple forgotten, Holly tugged experimentally against the restraints.

She could not move her arms.

Her skin goose-bumped under her fur.

Enora slid back down the feline's body. The wrongness of the back-brushing vanished in a wave of tactile sensation.

"Now where were we?" Enora's fingers brushed along the fur lining Holly's inner thighs, tracing random patterns while they moved upwards. Rumbles and gasps escaped Holly's muzzle as she glanced at the smaller woman. When Enora's fingers traced along the feline's swollen lips of her cleft, Holly threw back her head with a long moan.

The hare's fingers danced along the moist crevasse, teasing her entrance before finally brushing along the side of her clit. Holly was vibrating with need as the younger woman remained there, her blunt claws running along the gleaming hood. Enora's touch brushed not only the naked bulb, but also the nerves hidden from view within the fold of flesh.

"Your body has such interesting reactions." Enora half chuckled as Holly's tail lashed where it lay on the side of the bed. The feline squeezed her eyes shut when the hare sped up her affections on the woman's clit. Enora moved higher along Holly's body and the woman's breath brushed along her ear. "Open your eyes."

Holly did as she was told and screamed as the dagger cut along her chest between her breasts. The pain was sharp and blazing across her body. Blood welled up and Holly instantly knew the cut was deeper than the one on her upper thigh. She was about to say the safe-word when Enora slid a pair of fingers into Holly's entrance. They curved and pressed against the spongy tissue just inside her inner walls; the pain immediately washed away in a blaze of warmth and electricity. When the hare lowered her muzzle to run her tongue along the line of crimson, the warmth and biting sting twined with the building pressure low in Holly's body and threw her over the edge.

"There we go!" Enora crooned while Holly strained against her restraints, her inner walls sucking and pressing against the hare's soaked fingers. Small jets of fluid sprayed past the invading digits to soak the bed and Enora's own damp crotch.

When Holly's quivering had slowed she felt Enora shift. Opening her eyes, she had enough time to watch as something long and pink got pulled from the suitcase, which had shifted closer to the edge of the bed. A moment later something hard pressed along her slit and the jaguar wiggled her hips. Enora grinned and the object pressed against her entrance.

Slowly Holly felt herself open up to what she now realized was a double-headed dildo. Raising her head, she watched Enora work the crown of the false penis in and out of her. Each movement sent small sparks along her spine, each bump in the dildo teasing her already hyper-sensitive flesh. Bit by bit she felt her inner walls relax, letting the toy move deeper and deeper. The only thing stopping her from closing her eyes was the sight of Enora as she lifted herself up and pressed the other end of the dildo against her own slit.

"You are so sexy," Holly managed to whisper. The hare grinned while she moved the dildo against her own entrance, each movement creating a sympathetic shift along Holly's inner walls. Something about the mutual sharing made the touch inside her much more intimate for Holly.

Enora continued to move the dildo deeper and deeper into herself. Their sexes touched a moment later in the most fleeting of glancing brushes. The feel of the hare's clit against Holly's made the jaguar's ears splay and her muzzle opened in a moan that was more a rumbling purr. The smaller woman's paws came to rest on the feline's shoulders and the two stayed there for a moment, feeling their twinned pulses through the tiny heartbeats of their touching clits.

Then the hare started moving her hips, up and down, each movement slow and purposeful.

The previously released pressure inside Holly rekindled and she couldn't help herself from thrusting back, whimpers coming with each downward thrust of the hare, each brush of their clits. Holly could feel the wetness that escaped Enora's sex slide down the toy to soak her own already sopping slit. Each thrust became more need driven. The hare shifted her position until she was riding the toy like a cock, leaning over, her palms digging into Holly's shoulders.

The hitches in Enora's grunts as the woman lost herself to her pleasure made Holly's inner walls tighten and pulse around each thrust of the dildo. The jaguar wanted to reach out, to caress the hare's slim sides, to cup her hips, to drive her—and the dildo—deeper and faster into her. Her own voice was nothing but a series of grunts and growls, ears lowered and claws sliding in and out of their sheaths.

"By the gods you are a good fuck, my little pussy," Enora grunted. Biting her bottom lip, she bore down hard on the dildo, the tip hitting Holly at her deepest point. The feline threw back her head and roared as her body released. Her thighs shook and tightened against the sides of the hare who continued to push down on her. "Yes my pussy, three time's a charm. But now it's my turn."

Holly started to open her eyes when the hare's tiny paws wrapped around her throat.

The jaguar gasped as her windpipe closed tight.

Enora thrust herself up and down on the dildo like a madwoman, the strokes long and rough. Holly's body reacted even as the feline registered what was going on.

She started to struggle. The suitcase went crashing to the floor in a clatter of metal and leather. The claws on her feet tore long, ragged slashes into the sheets and the mattress beneath.

"Yes, oh fuck yes!" Enora cried.

The safe-word screamed in Holly's mind while she thrashed her head from side to side. Her body bucked and drove against the hare's only to move the dildo inside her into a frightening frenzy. Her lungs started to burn. One breath was all she would need to make the hare stop.

One small breath.

But the hare kept her hands tight while she rode the dildo, pushing against it with unrestrained thrusts. Grunts and groans escaped her shorter muzzle. Her ears splayed, eyes half closed while she watched Holly struggle. The feline's back arched as Holly threw her body back and forth, eyes wide while her inner walls grew tighter around the toy where it stroked her towards another climax.

"Can you feel it?" Enora's thrusts were rough and each one brought a brush of pain across Holly's womb. The feline writhed under the hare but Enora rode her like a pro. "So very close. Fuck. So close!"

Spots floated in Holly's eyes. She clawed at the handcuffs. She kicked against the bed. The sound of waves crashed against her ears and darkness edged her vision.

And still Enora's paws pressed against Holly's throat, thumbs crushing against her windpipe. Streams of swears echoed off the cabin walls in time to Enora's frenzied thrusts. The hare's gaze never left the struggling jaguar.

Holly realized she was going to die, never to see Raven again.

Tears streamed down her eyes even as her vision started to go black.

"Yes! Fuck yes!" Enora screamed while her thighs quaked against Holly's, her head thrown back, eyes wide.

The hare's paws left the jaguar's neck.

Holly's first breath was the sweetest she had ever tasted and her body released. The jaguar screamed through clenched teeth while her entire body tried to curl in on itself with the intensity of her orgasm. Stars danced across her vision and she squeezed her eyes shut at wave after wave of dizziness and pleasure washing over her.

Slowly Holly came back to herself to find Enora leaning over and stroking a paw along the feline's whiskers. She was whispering something soft and comforting.

"Why?" The feline managed to gasp, her throat raw. She fought the urge to turn away from the hare and cry.

"Would you have done it if I had asked?" Enora rose slowly. The feeling of the dildo sliding out of her left Holly feeling oddly empty. Small shivers ran over her body. Pulling the toy from herself, Enora walked a shaky path over to where a pitcher of water rested and poured it into a small bowl. She returned to Holly and offered it to the jaguar.

After a few licks Holly met the hare's gaze and snarled, "If you had asked, then yes. But this… this… fuck you!"

Enora's ears lowered and she bit her bottom lip. "I'm sorry I tricked you, hardly anyone ever says yes."

Holly let out a sigh, rolling her eyes. "I'm pretty open to things, you know. I'm not some new cub on the block—all wide eyed and innocent."

The hare reached over and unlocked the handcuffs.

Holly's fist came too fast for the hare to block and sent the smaller woman crashing against the wall. The jaguar rose to her feet—though she wavered a bit—as she rubbed her throat. "How could you know if you didn't ask first?"

Enora raised a paw to her head and groaned. "It's never the same."

"There are ways to deal with that." Holly moved forward and grabbed the hare's neck. Claws slid from her fingers to dimple the woman's skin, forcing the smaller woman to her toe tips. A shiver ran down the hare's naked body. "The knife bit was one thing Enora, but asphyxiation! I need some warning, some kind of trust!"

The hare raised her eyes to Holly. Moisture glinted in their corners. "I suppose I ruined things, haven't I?"

Holly shook her head, then coughed. The paw vanished from the hare's throat and she collapsed to the floor. The feline made it to the bed before the coughs forced her to sit. Enora rose and moved to the bed, rubbing the feline's back until the fit faded. She fetched Holly another bowl of water, the hare's ears lowered as she chewed on her lower lip. "I'm really sorry. I really fucked things up."

The feline held up a paw and shook her head.

"Enora." She pulled the hare into a hug, stroking her paw pads along the smaller woman's back. "You haven't ruined things, I just wish you would have trusted me and talked to me first. I would have liked to have Raven or Kai and Leah here." Holly ran her paw through her hair and chuckled. "Probably Kai. He would have totally gotten off being dominated by a slight little hare like yourself. If you just talked to me, I could have suggested someone better for you to play with."

"But you play the sub so well…"

Holly rubbed her throat, wincing as she did. "I don't mind it, but when it comes to women I generally prefer to be the one doing the commanding. Now come." She rose, grabbing the hare's paw. "Let's go see if we can't find Raven, Leah and Kai. Now that I know what you're into, I have some ideas I think we both can enjoy."

"You sure?" It was hard for Holly not to notice the straightening of the other woman's back and the way her ears rose. The jaguar's tail started to sway behind her.

"Very sure."

Enora moved forward and embraced Holly, their muzzles finding each other, the fur of their bodies sliding against each other.

"I should have trusted you, Holly."

The jaguar grinned, licking the woman's nose. "We have the rest of the cruise for you to show me just how sorry you are. Now, let's find the others!"

With nothing but towels wrapped around them, both women dashed out into the hall. Their giggles rose to laughter while they ran, paw in paw. Startled looks chased them as they shot past other guests, ever closer to the jaguar's room.

Holly couldn't help but think it was going to be a very fun cruise indeed.

THE LIGHT IN HIS EYES

StormKitty

"You came without a pet?"

Saskia glanced around the dimly-lit lounge at a couple of leather-clad bodies, then back at the grey rabbit. "You never know when you'll find the perfect cute subby boy looking for a mistress to put him in his place."

Fleur's nod was unconvincing. "So many boys here alone, and there's usually a good reason why."

The red wolf frowned. "Don't I know it. The old 'all the good ones are taken'. So call me an optimist, or desperate. It's been too long since my last pet and I broke it off."

Saskia's eyes settled on the chocolate brown marten kneeling beside the table. Coby had a yellow diamond-shaped patch that extended from his throat to the middle of his chest, interrupted by Fleur's collar. Besides the tight pair of red shorts that showed off his assets, he was adorned with wrist and ankle cuffs and a six-point harness. Saskia had met Coby when Fleur had him at leash's end the last time they were both here. His head was up with ears perked. He remained deferential and quiet as the two Dommes talked, but when Fleur reached out to rub him between the ears, he lifted his chin and smiled. Fleur looked back at Saskia. "So many wannabe pets just itching for a Domme like you to keep them in line. Maybe your standards are too high?"

Saskia snorted. "I refuse to lower my standards. A pet who can't handle me doesn't deserve to serve me." She wetted her mouth from her water glass. "I'd only end up with a pet I wouldn't be happy with for long. Better to stick to my guns until I find the right one."

"If you say so."

"I did the Goth thing for a while in high school. I learned not to let others decide what's right for me."

Fleur twitched her whiskers, glanced at Coby, then let out a giggle. "Hey, if your dry spell has left you hard up, you could have Coby for a few days." She batted her eyes at Saskia. "A chance to keep your knot and whip skills sharp while you're looking."

Saskia studied Coby. The marten was inscrutable, but that didn't mean much. A good pet doesn't question his mistress. She looked back at the rabbit. "You're serious?"

The rabbit made a dismissive gesture. "Nah, not really." She drank the last of her mai tai. The drinks were weak, in part to mitigate concerns about impairment in a BDSM setting where safety and consent were of the utmost importance. "It was an idle thought."

"Ah, for a minute there…"

"But you know," Fleur interrupted, "next month I have to fly off to a class in Virginia for a week."

Saskia steepled her fingers and took a longer look at Coby, who remained expressionless. "Pet or not, he's an adult. Can't he handle a week without you?" As the red wolf took a chug off her drink and sloshed it around her mouth, Fleur and Coby exchanged a look. The marten angled his muzzle lower.

Fleur looked back at Saskia. "What's your drink?"

"Rum and Coke."

Turning to her pet, Fleur spoke with a honeyed voice. "Coby dear, fetch us both refills."

"Yes, Mistress Fleur," he replied, rising to his feet. Nodding to Fleur, he turned toward the bar, and both Dommes watched his retreating rear end. The bartender would know to put the refills on his owner's tab.

Once he was out of earshot, Saskia looked back at Fleur. "You're not serious about this, are you?"

"Why not?" Fleur's claws tapped her glass. "You know, he's been sulky and ungrateful lately. It'd do him well to serve someone else that week instead of lounging about my place."

Saskia's ears perked. "I didn't realize he lived with you."

Fleur smirked. "Yep. Full time live-in pet."

The red wolf rubbed her muzzle, blowing out one side. "Lucky," she grumbled, then glanced toward Coby.

"Quite the looker, isn't he?" Saskia nodded and Fleur continued. "He loves serving, he's good with his tongue, and he's fun to tie up."

"Are you bragging, or trying to sell me on the idea?"

Fleur let out a melodramatic sigh. "You doubt my offer?" She shifted to a grin.

Saskia remained impassive. "He's sulky, you say? I don't want to deal with someone else's problems."

The rabbit folded her hands. "I will see to it he doesn't give you any."

"What kind of problems he giving you?"

"Well he... Oh, you're back already." Coby placed their drink refills in front of each of them. "Good boy." The marten gave her a smile and returned to his knees, looking up at her. "Mistress Saskia and I were discussing having you serve her when I'm at class next month. It would do you good to serve someone else."

"If it pleases you, Mistress," Coby replied.

Through his neutral expression, Saskia noticed a flicker of his eyes. She turned back to Fleur. "You were saying?"

The rabbit grinned back at her. "So, we have a deal?"

The red wolf studied Coby. "I meant is there anything I should be concerned about?"

Fleur's ears wiggled and a one-sided grimace made her whiskers twitch. "Let's see..." They both leaned closer. "Lately he doesn't handle being pushed very well."

Saskia nodded. "Go on."

"Like the other night, I had him bound and was edging him, asking if he needed to cum, and he got all whiny."

"Hmm, okay."

"He kind of shunned me afterwards. He still obeyed but acted sulky."

"When a pet shuns his mistress that's a problem," Saskia replied. Though Coby's eyes were averted he could obviously hear them talking. Was he ashamed? Saskia looked back at Fleur. "I can push my pets pretty hard. If he can't handle me…"

"He'll do it if he wants to please me." Fleur's voice was firmer, for his ears obviously. "If you're tougher maybe it'll make him appreciate *me* more."

"Can I talk to Coby?"

"Sure. Ask us anything you want."

"I meant privately."

Fleur rolled her eyes. "Oh, come on."

Saskia sighed. Fleur might not be following protocol but she had to when speaking with another's pet. Maybe she should have pushed harder or refused as a matter of principle, but something about the marten drew her in. Saskia turned to him. "Coby, are you willing to do this? Serve me for a week?"

He met her eyes and nodded. "Yes, Miss Saskia, I will serve you."

Her gaze was steel while she thought about what to say next. If her words were chosen well, his reaction would enable her to better gauge his feelings. She didn't get the chance.

"Then it's settled," cried Fleur, breaking the moment.

Saskia rubbed her forehead and let out a huff. "You have no appreciation for subtlety," she said to the rabbit.

When Fleur made a dismissive gesture and took a drink, Saskia nearly called off the arrangement, but then she saw Coby biting back a smile. Was he amused?

This might be worthwhile after all.

* * *

The first thing Saskia noticed when she answered the door was the luggage. Coby held a suit bag in one hand, pulled a large wheeled suitcase in the other, and wore a laptop backpack. "Welcome, pet."

Coby lowered his eyes. "Lovely to see you, Mistress Saskia. May I come in?"

Being deferential already, she noted. "Yes, do come in, and tell me what you brought."

"Clothes, mostly." He lifted the suitcase over the weather stripping and she closed the door.

Saskia reached out to run her fingers along the collar he wore. Fleur's collar. "You're aware you won't be wearing much here."

Coby draped the suit bag over the suitcase and shrugged off the backpack. "Most of it's for wearing to work, Miss Saskia. Did Mistress Fleur tell you I have a job? I'm scheduled four days this week."

Saskia nodded. "She did. Tell me your work schedule."

"My next shift is eleven to five Monday." It was Saturday. "I work the same hours Tuesday, Thursday and Friday. May I hang the suits before they wrinkle, Miss Saskia?"

She rubbed the underside of her muzzle. "Use the spare bedroom closet."

"Thank you," he replied, starting toward the doorway she was indicating.

"Before you get any ideas, you won't be sleeping there. Think of that room as a place to park your stuff."

"I understand, Miss Saskia."

"You have five minutes to put away your clothes. I want you naked and ready to show me what else you brought."

"Yes, ma'am."

As he disappeared into the room, Saskia smiled and licked her lips. She imagined Coby in her dungeon, struggling against his bonds on an X-frame as she teased him to her heart's content, or whimpering as she tanned his rear but good while he was bound to a spanking bench, or

squirming while she tested his pain threshold as he dangled by man-
acles from the ceiling. She imagined the look on his face the first time
she marched him into dungeon, whether it was to be rewarded for his
accomplishments, punished for his misdeeds, or simply savored for
being adorable and obedient.

Maybe in ten more years she would be living in her dream house
and would have all those things. There was no room for a dungeon in
her 1,300 square-foot two-bedroom two-bath condominium. Besides,
Coby was an unknown quantity who in any case was someone else's
pet on loan to her. But she could dream.

Saskia went into her room and studied herself in the mirror. Her
black shirt and jeans would have to do for now since she wasn't in the
mood to wear her leather dominatrix outfit. Dominance had everything to do with how you carried yourself; what you wore was icing on
the cake. She picked up her riding crop from her dresser and tapped
it against her palm, then picked up the collar she had fetched earlier
from among her supplies. She had debated buying him a collar but
had dismissed the idea for various reasons, the main one being that
she didn't know him well enough to feel comfortable choosing one for
him.

When the five minutes were up, she returned to the spare room,
tapping the doorframe with the riding crop as she entered. Coby, wearing only his collar, hurried to his knees. Saskia scrutinized him and
the room, glancing over the open suitcase and the items he had spread
out on the bed. Among them were the wrist and ankle cuffs and the
six-point harness he'd been wearing at the club, plus a ball gag, two
anal plugs, a blindfold, rope, a leather cock and ball harness, and some
articles of fetish clothing.

The end of her crop touched the underside of his muzzle, urging
his gaze upward. "I'm impressed so far." She caressed along his jaw and
down his neck with the crop. His eyes gave it a nervous glance but he
remained silent. The crop bumped into the collar. "Did Mistress Fleur
say to keep this on?"

"No, Miss Saskia."

"Take it off, then. For this week you shall wear my collar." She dropped to a casual tone. "You may address me as 'Miss Kia'. 'Miss Saskia' sounds too lispy."

Coby smiled as he unfastened the collar. "Okay, Miss Kia."

Saskia held out her collar so he could see the locking mechanism on it. She secured it around his neck, judging how tight it was by how many fingers she could fit beneath it. "Very nice," she said with a smile. She fetched his wrist and ankle cuffs from the bed. Coby extended his arms without being told to and she put on the wrist cuffs. She directed him to stand while she put on the ankle cuffs, and he knelt back down when she finished. This looked familiar and expected of him. "Now that you're mine, let's go over a few rules."

Coby nodded and perked his ears.

"While you are my pet, you will wear nothing except what I put on you or tell you to wear. You will obey all orders without question. Mostly. I don't expect you to abandon common sense and good judgment, but I do expect you to trust me. Fleur told me your safeword, and only you can be the judge of when to use it." He met her eyes briefly. "You will sleep in my bedroom, on the floor unless you earn the privilege of sleeping in my bed."

"Yes, Miss Kia." The marten had his chin up, not showing any fear or worry.

"On the whole I will be fair and reasonable, but that doesn't mean I'm going to be fair every minute. I have moods. Sometimes I'm unpredictable. I might do something you would consider a punishment just because I feel like it."

Coby's eyes barely flickered, and he nodded. "That is as I would expect, Miss Kia."

"Until it is time for you to return to Miss Fleur, you will wear my collar at all times. 24/7." She saw his eyebrow flinch, and she reiterated. "As long as you are my pet you will wear my collar."

Still Coby didn't respond. He glanced one way then the other, brow creasing, and finally downward. He closed his eyes and bit his lip, then reopened his eyes halfway. "Skittles." He winced as he said it.

Saskia sighed, and placed the crop on the bed. He hadn't been there half an hour and had already used his safeword. She reached out to lift his chin. "Okay, stand up. I need you to talk to me. What's the problem?"

Coby looked apologetic as he stood. "I can't wear a collar at work. Fleur and I went through this. She got me a collar, and the first time I wore it to work, my boss said take it off. It was locked on so I had to go home. I lost half a day's pay because of that."

"Where do you work?"

"I am a salesman at Hester's." Coby stood straight and gave her his best salesman smile. "We offer the finest in men's professional attire at affordable prices." Dropping the affectation, he gestured toward the closet. "I wear what we sell. We have to project a certain image to our customers and a collar doesn't fit that image."

"So you can't wear the collar at work?" Saskia's whiskers twitched. "I see people wearing accessories like that at my workplace. As long as it doesn't get in the way or present a safety issue, they don't care."

"Where do you work?"

"Metropolitan Food Processing. I'm a wholesale clerk."

Coby nodded. "You don't face the public?"

"No I don't, but you obviously do. Okay, good thing we cleared that up."

"I promise I'll wear your collar the rest of the time." His hand came up to feel it. "This one locks?"

"Yes. I'll show you where I keep the spare key in case I'm not around when you leave for work." She didn't think it necessary to explain there would be consequences if he removed the collar on his own without good reason. "While we're being straight, I have to ask, do you feel like Fleur put you up to this?"

"You mean being your pet this week?" Coby let out a heavy sigh. "She told you I'd do it before she even asked me what I thought of it."

Saskia tapped her lip. "That could be a problem."

"It made me think she doesn't want me staying at her apartment while she's gone."

Saskia tilted her head. "Did she say that?"

He looked down and shifted on his feet. "No, it's just a feeling I got."

"Why wouldn't she want you staying there?"

"I don't know. I come and go all the time when she's not home, so I don't see why it would be a problem." It was a non-committal answer. A good pet doesn't speak badly of his mistress in her absence.

"Are you locked out of her place?"

"No, I have a key."

That meant he could go back if the week didn't work out. "Whatever happened, Fleur's gone for the week so it's just you and me." Her gaze intensified. "Do you want to be my pet for the week?"

He met her gaze and nodded. "Yes, I want to be your pet, Mistress Kia."

She reached out to lift his muzzle. "You're sure about that? I don't want a pet who doesn't want to be here."

"I'm ready to try, Miss Kia."

Saskia nodded slowly. "All right. Anything else we need to discuss before we time in?"

"Not that I can think of, Miss Kia."

"Peachy. If you think of something, don't wait for me to ask." She picked up her crop and tapped his tail. "Keep your tail up." She surveyed the array of toys laid out on the bed, her eyes fixing on the anal plugs. "You've had your backside plugged before?"

"Yes, many times."

"You like having your butt filled?"

"Yes I do, Miss Kia."

"That's good to hear. I find a pet has an easier time remembering his place when his butt is stuffed." She picked up the larger of the two plugs, a red silicone toy. "Is this the biggest you've taken?"

"It is, Miss Kia."

She set it back on the bed. "I've got a bigger one to try in you. Go wait in the living room."

Saskia fetched the plug from her supply of toys along with some lube, and returned to find Coby kneeling in the living room. She held up the plug to gauge his reaction. The look of fear on his face brought to mind what Fleur had said about him and she wondered if he would safeword again, but the look passed. It was time to find out what he could handle. "This plug has ten ridges on it, each slightly bigger than the one before. Let's see how many you can take. Down on all fours and keep that tail up."

He obeyed while she gave the plug a liberal coating of lube. She applied more to his anus and rubbed it around, noting that he relaxed his sphincter without being told when she pushed her finger in. Saskia withdrew her finger and brought the tip of the toy to his opening, pressing inward. The first four ridges were small and went in easy. As she worked in the fifth, she heard the first groan from Coby. "Doing okay?"

"So far so good, Miss Kia."

Saskia twisted and pushed the sixth ridge in, stretching him more. He let out a sharp breath. "Still okay?"

Coby's tail twitched. "I think so."

She held the plug there for a pause. If this pushed new limits for him, she would have to pay close attention to his reactions. "You're on six. From here on out, each one is barely bigger but it can feel like a lot if you're not used to being stretched that much. Be truthful. Do you feel like trying for seven?"

"I'm ready, Miss Kia."

"All right, going for seven." The lube felt adequate as she wiggled and gently pushed the plug deeper into him. This time he grunted and hissed louder, and she could feel him struggling to relax as he squirmed his rump. "How is this?"

"It hurts." His voice was pained.

It was Saskia's first time pushing Coby and she didn't know his signals well. "Give me a color. Green, we go on. Yellow, we hold here. Red, we pull back."

"Yellow."

Saskia smiled. "Very well. If you change your mind, say red or green. Otherwise I'll keep it just like this for five minutes." His ears flicked. "Try to relax, get used to the feel of it."

Holding the plug in place, Saskia stroked his back and tailbase, noting that Coby had developed a partial erection. She could see and feel the tension from his discomfort, but he held his own and she felt some of it drain away as she continued rubbing. The minutes ticked by, probably much too slowly for him, until five minutes had passed. He could see the clock so as an experiment she left it in longer to see if he would say anything. Six minutes. Seven. Not a word about the time.

"Time's up." she announced at eight minutes. She eased out two ridges of the plug, hearing him release his breath, and the rest slipped out easily. "You did well, pet." She reached up to stroke his ears.

Coby glanced back and smiled. "I'm glad you are pleased, Miss Kia."

"Tomorrow we'll do this again."

"I'll be ready, Miss Kia." No fear, no hesitation, no complaints about the time.

She fetched his red plug from the spare bedroom, lubed it up, and slid it into place. "This should be comfortable compared to what you just took."

Coby gave his rear a wiggle. "It feels good, Miss Kia."

She noticed his erection had grown. "Now, over here on all fours in front of my chair."

He crawled to the indicated spot in front of the chair. Saskia sat and rested her feet on his back, using him as a footrest. "There you go. Keep still until I give you permission to move, or I might have to bind you."

Coby looked at her. "Sometimes I need to be tied up, Miss Kia."

The wolf's ears perked. "Do you, now? I'll have to remember that. Right now I'm not in the mood to do any tying up, so if you don't want to see me upset, keep still while I watch some TV." She watched Coby and thought she saw mischief in his eyes, making her wonder if he was about to test her.

He didn't. Through two sitcoms he stayed in place, and when the second ended, Saskia muted the television and got down beside Coby. She ran a hand from his shoulder, down his side to his hip, enjoying the feel of his fur. "Mmmm, I'm going to enjoy exploring you." Her fingers trailed across his lower back. "Fleur was all ready to tell me what you like most, where your soft spots are."

Coby turned his head. "What did she tell you?"

"I told her I like finding them myself," Saskia purred as she caressed his other side. "It's more fun to explore and discover a pet's soft spots on my own than be told where they are." Her fingers traced through the fur on the back of his neck, toward his ears.

An hour later, Saskia had learned that Coby loved being rubbed a certain way between the pads of his feet, and squeezing his tail near the base caused it to fluff. The insides of his arms were as sensitive as his inner thighs, and massaging the ends of his hipbone just the right way got him aroused. She briefly teased his nipples, and couldn't help grinning at his expectant look whenever her explorations came near his cock and balls. Those she was saving for later.

After reminding Coby to continue wearing the collar, cuffs, plug, and nothing else, she told him he was free to relax and do as he wished. The first thing he did was fetch his laptop. "May I request something, Miss Kia?"

"My router password?"

Coby chuckled. "I need that too, Miss Kia, but I wanted to ask, if I'm in the middle of a game and you wish me to come serve you, will you please allow me a few minutes to reach a save point?"

Saskia studied him a moment, then nodded. "All right, I'll keep that in mind. I play games too sometimes so that's understandable. Or maybe I'll tell you what time to be ready for me."

Coby nodded. "That works too."

Dinner was a simple affair. While Saskia debated whether to have him kneel on the floor, Coby set his silverware accordingly without her prompting.

Afterward, she noticed Coby giving her expectant looks. Was he hoping for something? She had not yet touched his penis, and for hours he had been virtually naked while she had been in her jeans and T-shirt. Saskia couldn't help smiling; she was Mistress and she wasn't going to be pushed. After receiving several such glances, Saskia responded. "You need something, pet?"

The marten tilted his head. "I wondered if you do, Miss Kia."

That was clever, making it about her desires instead of his own. "Go prepare the shower for me. I want the water nice and warm, fresh towels set out, and my bathrobe on the hook."

He started toward the bathroom, then paused. "I don't know where you keep your towels, Miss Kia."

"Do you think it would take you less than a minute to find them?"

Coby lowered his gaze. "Probably."

"Then you may ask me again after another minute." Watching him head back to her bathroom, she smiled, pleased that he got her meaning. A good pet shouldn't make his mistress explain things he could figure out on his own. Even so, she had to give him credit for asking before possibly sticking his muzzle places it didn't belong.

Two minutes later he returned. "Your shower is ready, Miss Kia." She found everything as she had told him, towels and robe waiting and the water running and warmed.

"Nice job, Coby," she replied. "Take it easy until I'm finished." Saskia waited until he left before she undressed, and she showered alone. She could have had him wash her, but to her thinking some ways of serving one's mistress were better thought of as privileges to be earned, and that was one of them. Saskia emerged from the bathroom wrapped in the robe. Coby was in the living room, so she slipped on a pair of lounge shorts before summoning him.

"Coby," she said once he reappeared, "tonight you will sleep on the floor. There is a pad underneath my bed which you may sleep on. You may fetch whatever sheets and blankets you need from the linen closet."

"Thank you, Miss Kia." If he was disappointed not to be invited to her bed, he didn't show it.

"Serve me well in the days ahead and you may earn the right to share my bed. Upset me enough and you'll have to sleep without the pad. Understood?"

Coby swallowed and nodded. "Yes, Miss Kia."

Saskia removed the cuffs and had him remove the butt plug and wash it. "You shouldn't wear your collar in the shower, but don't remove it yourself without checking with me if I'm around. We already discussed your job." She tapped the top of her jewelry box where a key sat among three figurines of kittens wearing top hats. "This time, I want you to remove it yourself so you know how. The lock can be a little tricky. Use the mirror if necessary. Don't forget to put the key back; I won't be responsible if you need to get it off without my assistance and can't find the key."

Coby didn't have much trouble with the lock as he removed the collar. He showered, and afterwards she put the collar and cuffs back on him before they settled into their beds. She never let him see her wearing less than the lounge shorts and a nightshirt before turning the lights out, though she slipped the shorts off beneath the covers before falling asleep.

* * *

Sunlight spilled around the curtains when Saskia awoke. Coby was asleep and oblivious to the morning wood he was sporting. Shifting to the edge of the bed she reached down to run her hand along his side down to his hip, enjoying the softness of his fur, wondering how much of this she'd get away with before he woke up.

Not much, as it turned out; he must have been on the verge of awakening. "Mmmf... G'mornin' Miss Kia," he uttered, blinking and twitching his nose as he came aware of his surroundings. "Ungh, sorry, I was…"

"You're not in any trouble… yet," she muttered, still coming awake herself. "Know how to make coffee?"

He sat up. "Sure. I don't know where…"

Saskia touched his nose with a fingertip. "One minute." He nodded, and she continued. "Use the Arabica dark roast. Half a pot plus whatever you'll drink. Be back here as soon as you've started it brewing. You may use the bathroom if you need to."

By the time Coby returned, she was seated with the covers off, revealing herself to him for the first time. Saskia grinned at the way he tried to steal glances without being obvious. Her state of undress made him act bashful, and the partial erection he was still showing wasn't helping matters any. "While we're waiting for the coffee, there's something else you can do to wake me up."

"Yes, Miss Kia?"

She slid down onto her back, pushing the covers lower, spreading her legs and planting her heels on the bed with knees raised. "I've heard good things about your tongue. Come, show me how well you can please your mistress."

Coby let out a murr of satisfaction as he crawled onto the bed, positioning himself between her legs and getting sight and scent of her sex up close for the first time. As Saskia reached down to stroke behind his ears, he caressed along her outer labia, and then eased her slit apart, bringing his muzzle closer and inhaling. When he took his first exploratory lick she felt his cool nose and his warm tongue. Saskia moaned and rubbed his ears some more, and he continued, working his tongue along her slit more confidently. Nice pacing, neither hesitating nor in a hurry. Saskia could feel herself moistening to his first teasing licks to her clit, and she shifted her hips and spread her legs wider.

The vibrations of Coby's soft murr felt good with his tongue exploring deeper, wriggling inside her while his nose rubbed against her clit. Saskia felt his warm breath more when he pulled her outer labia farther apart, alternating between her clit and her vagina with his tongue. Her breathing became ragged and she moaned in earnest, grabbing his ears to pull his muzzle against her as she thrust upward.

The red wolf guessed her buildup was slower than he was used to with his rabbit mistress, but that was partly because this was a test of sorts. As much as she despised any who would order a pet against his will, nothing satisfied her more than using a pet in a way she knew he wanted to be used. Having ordered him to perform this most intimate act, she was reading a hundred subtle signals he gave off. Allowing for his unfamiliarity with her, all indications were that he enjoyed pleasing her this way, which made it much easier for her to let go and enjoy what he was doing.

Coby was persistent and kept up the tongue work, and Saskia's moans soon escalated and her thrusts got wilder. The sounds of the coffee maker in the kitchen subsided by the time she approached her peak. A few more licks to her clit, a few tugs at her labia, and she arched her back and cried out, hips wriggling as she leaked an extra dose of her fluids, which he enjoyed lapping up.

Coby slowed his licks, grooming and cleaning her while she came down from her peak. Rubbing his head, she smiled at him. "Very nice, pet. You don't need any tongue lessons."

He beamed at her. "Thank you, Miss Kia."

"You are welcome. Now, go pour us some coffee."

He returned moments later with cups for both of them. Her teacups, Saskia noted as she took one, inhaled the aroma, and took a sip. She looked at Coby. "No cream or sugar?"

Coby looked crestfallen. "Sorry, Miss Kia, I'm used to drinking it black. I'll get them right away."

"I don't need sugar," she said as he hastened out the door. He was back in flash with her pint carton of half-and-half and a spoon. "I'll pour it myself," she said when he offered to do it for her.

For a few minutes, they discussed what to fix for breakfast. Their cups were getting low, but a refill could wait a few more minutes. "Up here on the bed," she said. "On your back, and hands over your head."

Coby was quick to obey, and she grinned at the look of anticipation and his erection that returned by the time he was in position. While she ran her fingers through his chest fur, Saskia smiled and murred, digging her claws in enough for him to feel them. She moved slowly downward, finding him fully hard by the time she teased circles around his navel, savoring his obvious anticipation as she took her time.

Finally she touched his cock for the first time, caressing along his shaft, and he let out a sigh. "You've been waiting for this, haven't you, pet?"

"Yes, I have, Miss Kia."

She gave him several light strokes, watching his cock twitch. "You know not to pleasure yourself without permission."

Coby moaned and squirmed. "Of course, Miss Kia."

It wouldn't take much to trigger an orgasm, so she moved to his balls, smiling at the control she had over his body. "So I've been thinking about whether you deserve to cum yet." Saskia didn't believe in following that up with 'What do you think?' when she had already made up her mind.

"Have you decided?"

Not begging yet. She returned to his cock, giving it more light, teasing strokes. Coby's hips wiggled more but he kept his arms up. "You did okay making coffee but had a couple of mistakes."

His ears flagged. "I forgot to ask about cream and sugar."

"Very good." She paused her strokes. "You also made it weaker than I like, and you served it in teacups I seldom use instead of my usual coffee mugs."

Coby's eyebrow quivered as his hoped-for orgasm slipped away. "If you show me how you like it and which mugs to use, I'll do better next time," he replied, voice tinged with desperation.

She teased him a few more strokes, then withdrew, knowing it would leave him frustrated, and stood, reaching into her dresser for a pair of panties. "All right, I'll tell you more while we make breakfast. Let's go."

She caught a whimper from him as he rolled off the bed, unsteady on his feet at first. Admittedly, she had told him to figure it out without giving him many details and he'd gotten some of them wrong, but sometimes in life you have to try different things to figure out the answers. Saskia could see the spark in his eyes that told her if he had to work harder for something, he would feel that much better when he achieved it.

Instead of going straight to the kitchen, she detoured him into the spare bedroom where she put his leather cock and ball harness on him. "How does this feel?"

"Not very tight, Miss Kia."

Saskia grinned at him. "It shouldn't be."

Coby groaned at the implication. If it was tight enough to keep him hard, he could safely wear it for half an hour at most. Less tight wouldn't keep him hard but he would still grow erect more easily and lose it more slowly, and he could wear it for hours. He shifted on his feet. "If it pleases you."

She gave his balls and shaft a caress. "I like how you look with it on."

It was tempting to think she was rewarding him by letting him see her in her underwear while they worked on breakfast, but in truth Saskia hadn't felt like getting dressed yet and was getting comfortable having Coby around. Reflecting on how he handled his first day, she recalled Fleur's comments about pushing his limits. Saskia was skeptical. When she had denied his climax, she hadn't seen disappointment or resentment, but determination to meet her challenge and earn his reward.

Whenever Coby was within reach, Saskia reached out to stroke his tail, squeeze his rear, or fondle his cock and balls, just because she could. When she noticed he was purposely giving her opportunities, she started ignoring him some of the time. Such was the game between mistress and pet, and Saskia enjoyed it. As the game escalated, he got feisty and gave her mischievous looks. After a reminder not to let his tail droop, he wasn't even subtle about brushing it against her when he could.

They settled into morning downtime. A couple of hours later, Coby was engrossed in a game on his computer when Saskia decided he'd had long enough. She peeked over his shoulder, ears perking at the sounds of him battling a horde of monsters. "Save your game in the next few minutes," she told him.

"Okay, there's a save point coming up." He never broke his concentration, and the fighting continued nonstop. As fingers flew on the keyboard, his life meter dropped steadily. He hadn't reached the save point when it hit zero and the screen went red. "Fuckin' gnolls," he growled, and then sighed. "I'll try again later from my last save point."

"Looks too tough for me," she said, watching him exit the game.

"I'm replaying this game on hard. You might like it more at normal difficulty."

Saskia tilted her head. "Really?"

He hibernated the laptop. "Do you like action games?"

"Sometimes. You'll have to show me more of this one."

Coby didn't wait to be told to present himself, kneeling before her, eyes downward. "How may I serve you, Miss Kia?"

"I want to see how you look in this." She held a leather armbinder.

He looked at it, his nose twitching at the smell of leather, and straightened up, holding his arms behind him. She slid it over his arms and began securing it. "This feels different," he remarked.

"Oh? Has Fleur never put one of these on you before?" She fastened the last buckle.

"She doesn't have one. She likes putting me in shibari ties." He took a breath as Saskia put a cuff on his tailbase and fastened the armbinder to it. "She's very good at shibari."

Coby's lunch was served on a plate on the floor. It impressed Saskia that he ate it all without spilling any or making a mess of his muzzle.

Afterward, she bent him over her couch and produced the same ridged plug from earlier. He hesitated to go to the eighth ridge but he was comfortable after a few minutes on the seventh, so she left it in place for what came next.

Coby's erection hadn't escaped her notice, so while wiggling the plug around to rub against his prostate, Saskia reached her other hand between his legs to trail her fingers over his hardness, caressing it lightly. She moved down to his balls, admiring how the harness straps made them stand out. He squirmed. "You ready for this, pet?"

"I've been ready, Miss Kia," he gasped.

She lightly stroked the ridge of his cock head a few more times, rubbing the sensitive underside, before unfastening the harness. He let out a sigh when she pulled it off. The teasing caresses resumed. Coby moaned and tried not to squirm as he leaked precum on her fingers. It reminded her how much she loved having a pet under her control. Did he have any idea she'd been anticipating this moment as much as he?

She curled her fingers around his cock to increase the friction and sped up the strokes, stopping only once when he started to hump her hand. After a pause of several seconds she resumed. "Cum for me, Coby. Show me how much you've built up."

Coby's panting and moaning escalated as he struggled to keep still through his final buildup. With a hearty groan he erupted, shooting several ropes of cum onto the front of the leather couch where they dribbled down. Saskia continued pumping until he twitched out his last drop.

While he recovered, she rubbed his back. "Feel better now?"

Coby regained his breath and smiled. "Much better. Thank you, Miss Kia!"

"You're welcome," she replied, removing the plug, followed by the armbinder. "Now you can clean up the mess. You remember where the towels are."

Saskia got comfortable on one end of her couch, and after Coby finished she gestured toward the other end. "Have a seat and look at me. Time for some straight talk."

Coby gave her a worried look as he settled into the proffered seat. "Is everything okay?"

Saskia leaned forward and lifted his chin. "You tell me. You're supposed to be here for a week that you weren't really consulted about. You've been here a day. How do you feel right now about the rest of the week?"

The marten glanced aside and swallowed. "Miss Fleur…"

She tugged his chin and his eyes snapped back. "Don't 'Miss Fleur' me. I want to know what *you* think. When he didn't answer right away, she continued. "If you've got anything to say, now would be a good time to say it."

"I don't know if Fleur wants me at her place while she's gone, and I don't have anywhere else to go."

"You're her pet." Saskia sighed. "How did you become Fleur's pet?"

Coby shifted on his seat. "About a year ago I lost my job. My employer at the time was cutting staff and I wasn't experienced enough to be worth keeping. I searched for another job but two months later, I was still unemployed and running out of money to pay rent. I cut expenses anywhere I could, and my car insurance lapsed. Then I got into a car accident and that made things a lot worse. My car was totaled and the other guy sued me, so just like that I'm over ten thousand in debt.

"I was being evicted from my apartment. My parents live several hundred miles away and I couldn't stand the thought of moving back with them, so I started calling friends asking if they would let me move in with them. God, I felt awful begging like that but when you're about to be homeless you'll do just about anything. I asked Fleur, we talked, and she agreed to let me come live with her if I'd be her pet."

Saskia twitched her whiskers and studied him. "When you asked, were you expecting her to make you her pet?"

"Well, I, um…"

Saskia lifted his chin again, forcing his eyes to meet hers. "Did Fleur force you into becoming her pet?"

Coby swallowed. "No, I don't think so." He sighed. "We scened a few times before all this happened and we both enjoyed it."

"So she didn't force you?"

Tentatively he shook his head. "I was running low on options but I could have kept looking. We discussed living arrangements. I told her it was important to me to get my finances back in order, which meant I had to get a job and needed a car. My parents helped out by giving me a twelve-year-old car they would have traded in, and I got on as a salesman at Hester's."

"So you're getting your life back on track."

"Trying to. My credit isn't any good until I get the judgment paid off. That'll take about another year if I can live rent-free."

Saskia nodded. "And you plan to live with Fleur that long?"

Coby shrugged. "Something like that."

"Except when she goes away for a week and gives you to someone like me."

Coby winced, and let out a sigh.

The red wolf finally filled the awkward silence. "Like I said, I don't want a pet who doesn't want to be here. If you need to go back to her place I will call Fleur myself."

Coby's tail lashed back and forth. He sat straighter and met her gaze. "Thank you, Miss Kia, I will stay and be your pet for the rest of the week."

She nearly followed up with, 'You're sure about that?' but one look at his eyes and she knew it wasn't necessary. "All right, go fetch your red plug." She watched him pad away toward the spare bedroom. "And keep your tail up."

* * *

That night Saskia almost invited him to her bed but decided against it. She was impressed that Coby didn't complain about sleeping on the floor again, rather looking even more determined to earn his way into her bed the next night.

The coffee was perfect the next morning. They both had to work, and she had to admit he looked sharp the way he was dressed when she unlocked and removed his collar. Later that evening he took the eighth ridge of the plug with little difficulty.

If he were hers to keep, she wouldn't allow him to share her bed for a week minimum, to further establish herself as the alpha. Since she only had him for the week and he was doing well, she decided not to postpone any longer. "On my bed, Coby," she told him. "I want you to sleep with me tonight."

The marten looked tentative as he crawled onto the bed, trying to figure out on what part of the bed to get comfortable, glancing her direction as if he was someplace he shouldn't be. "Thank you, Miss Kia."

Saskia smiled. "Keep it up and you'll get to sleep here the rest of the week. For now, on your back, hands over your head and keep 'em there while I explore."

After he got into the position, she ran her fingers over his chest and abdomen, luxuriating in his fur, using her claws just enough to remind him of her position. She continued downward, finding his cock at full attention by the time she reached it, and began to stroke. Coby let out soft moans and gasps as she caressed his maleness, sometimes venturing farther down to explore his balls, holding one between her thumb and fingers. A look at his face told her he knew she could squeeze, which told her she didn't need to. To have that kind of power over a pet was a narcotic like no other.

Saskia already knew he'd be fun to tease, but she had needs of her own and it had been too long since she'd last had a pet she could use for her own gratification. Slipping her panties off, she snuggled up to his side with her breasts pressed against him, slid her thigh over his, nibbled his ear and whispered, "I can have you any way I want." His breathing picked up as she used her whole body to explore him. "Now, pet, let's take this all the way."

She pulled herself on top of him, nuzzling his ear and muzzle, nibbling his neck, feeling his chest against hers. Hearing his breathing turn into moans turned her on more, making her growl as her pussy grew wetter. Coby squirmed when she rubbed her slit against his maleness, making her spine tingle in anticipation, and she lifted up to nestle his cock tip at her opening. She let out a hearty moan after sliding down, taking his cock inside her.

"Ahh, Miss Kia, you feel wonderful," Coby moaned, arching his hips upward.

"So do you." After a moment to adjust, she sat upright, pulled her knees up, and began riding him. "Use your hands on my breasts."

Coby obeyed. His hands felt luscious on her breasts, especially when he flicked his fingers across her nipples and ran his thumbs around them. He was being gentler than she preferred, perhaps erring on the side of caution rather than risking spoiling the moment. It was good enough; no need to interrupt a good fuck for a lesson when she had the rest of the week. Saskia lay back down against his chest and angled her hips lower to give her clit more friction. Her thrusts became more deliberate and her moans heartier as she got lost in the sensations of having his cock inside her.

Coby clutched at her back and groaned as he tried to ease his movements against her. *What is he doing*, she wondered. Then it hit her, and she stopped moving. "Trying to hold back?"

Coby caught his breath. "I shouldn't cum before you do."

Saskia hadn't told him anything of the sort; that he had assumed it gave her a warm feeling. "I don't cum easily from intercourse," she replied, nosing his ear. "Don't worry about it this time. Tomorrow I'll let you prep me better before I climb on."

"Uhn, all right," he sighed.

He sounded unconvinced, so Saskia sat back up. "Hold still," she told him and reached down to rub her clit. "Use your hands on me. I like nipple pinches."

Smiling, he reached up to roll and pinch both of them, setting off sparks within. His hands continued wandering over her breasts, sides, and around to her rear and tailbase. Meanwhile, Saskia teased herself, tugging the skin around her clit, building herself almost to climax while keeping her hips mostly still, periodically giving his cock a squeeze with her inner muscles. If she was going to help him hold off, she could enjoy teasing him a little while she was at it.

When she was on the edge of her climax and could keep still no longer, she leaned forward. "Fuck me, pet! Fuck me good!"

Coby grabbed her rear and began thrusting much harder than before. She matched his rhythm, and they devolved into a chorus of moans. Within half a minute, Saskia cried out and spasmed around his shaft just as he let out a loud groan and filled her with his seed.

They rubbed noses, smiling, panting hard. "Thank you, Coby. I'd forgotten how good it felt to cum with a cock inside me."

Coby's face was pure bliss. "Glad I could do that for you, Miss Kia." He gave her a lick.

They both slept well.

* * *

"You beat me home," Saskia remarked, closing the front door behind her.

Coby stopped typing and slipped off the chair, kneeling beside the dining table. "About ten minutes ago," he answered. "I was just catching up online."

"Take a few more minutes while I go get changed and cleaned up."

Upon entering the bedroom, Saskia discovered Coby had set out a change of clothes for her. Peering into the bathroom, she saw fresh towels and underwear. It gave her a warm feeling that he had taken the initiative.

She returned to the dining room, smiling at him. "You didn't turn on the water for me."

Coby looked up, eyes alight. "I didn't know how long you'd be and didn't want to waste a lot of hot water."

"I understand." She reached out to run her fingers through the fur on his head.

Fifteen minutes later, Saskia felt refreshed and ready to take on the evening. Even though the clothes Coby had selected might not be what she would have chosen, she liked his choices enough to wear them anyway.

When she returned to the dining room, Coby was just closing up the laptop. "Bring me your red plug."

"Yes, Miss Kia." He turned to put away the laptop.

He brought the lube too when he returned, and Saskia had him bend over as she prepared the plug and began to insert it. "Does this plug still feel as big as it did before?"

"No, Miss Kia, not since you've been using the other one on me."

Saskia grinned as the plug slipped into place. "Maybe you need a bigger one for regular wear."

"Oh, I can still feel it all right," said Coby and straightened up, tail shifting. "It doesn't hurt, but it's still very noticeable. I'm not going to forget it's there." His stance looked slightly awkward.

"I wouldn't want you to," Saskia replied, glancing at the wiggle of his hips. "Or to forget who put it there. Now, get some clothes on so we can go get some dinner."

The expression on his face was priceless.

* * *

Coby's walk looked normal when allowed to go slow enough, and for that reason Saskia couldn't resist making him go just a little faster. The whole world didn't need to know he was wearing a plug, but what fun was it if she didn't make him struggle with it a little? Ideally it should affect him enough that she could tell but no one else could.

The diner was one of her favorites. Without being told, Coby hurried ahead to hold the door for her, and when he did, Saskia noticed the slight arousal that he was likely struggling to keep under control. Inside, they approached the counter. "Have you been here before?" she asked.

"Never have." Coby looked at the overhead menu. "What do you recommend?"

Saskia licked her lips. "The gyros are wonderful. Their pitas are always fresh and I love the spice blend they put on their fries. Don't get a large order unless you're really hungry."

They placed their orders at the counter, took a number tent, and selected a booth. Saskia studied him as he settled gingerly into his seat and rubbed at his collar. Taking him out with a toy inside him stretched his comfort zone so she had to be especially attentive. So far, Coby had the spark that told her he enjoyed the challenge, but sometimes it could be hard to tell. "Are you doing okay, Coby?"

He quickly withdrew his hand and leaned forward. "Just a little nervous, Miss Kia. This is the first time I've done this."

Saskia leaned closer and spoke quietly. "When we're in public, you may leave off the 'Miss'. So Fleur never took you out like this before?"

"The collar, yes, but nothing like…" He gestured toward his lap.

Before Saskia could follow that up, her cell phone rang. She looked at the screen. "Speak of the devil," she muttered, punching the button and putting the phone to her ear. "Hello, this is Saskia."

"Hi, Saskie, this is Fleur."

Saskia briefly curled her lip at the nickname. "How is Virginia?"

"It's nice, I guess. I haven't seen much of it besides my hotel and the training center. I wanted to see how you're handling Coby."

There was a lot she would like to have discussed, but sitting in a diner waiting for their food wasn't the time or place for an in-depth discussion. "Coby and I are doing quite well. He's…"

"He's a fun pet, isn't he? At least when he behaves. Has he given you much trouble?"

"As I was trying to say, we're doing quite well. Yes, he is a good pet, and no, he hasn't. He's learned how to…" She stopped herself and glanced around. "We're doing just fine."

There was a pause at the other end before Fleur spoke again. "Well, I'm sure you can handle him when he gets difficult. Is he there?"

"Right in front of me. Want to talk to him?"

"Sure."

Saskia handed the phone to Coby. "Hi, Mistress Fleur." His eyes darted sideways at the word 'Mistress'.

For the next minute or so, she could only hear Coby's side of the conversation. "I am doing fine." A pause while Fleur spoke. "Yes, she's different from you, but I'm doing okay." "This afternoon I put out clothes for her like I do for you, and she loved it." There was a lengthy pause while Fleur rambled for a bit, and Coby's shoulders sagged. "No, I haven't whined at her." "I miss you too, Miss Fleur."

An attendant approached carrying a tray. He placed their meals on the table, exchanging smiles with Saskia, and took the number tent. Coby's nose twitched as he continued the conversation. "I know, Miss Fleur." The marten rubbed his forehead and closed his eyes for several seconds. "I promise I'll be good. Say, our food just arrived…" "Okay, I'll give you back to Kia." He handed the phone to her.

"Me again."

"So it sounds like Coby is learning some things from you," said the rabbit.

"We're finding a good dynamic," she replied.

"That's good," Fleur replied. "Just don't let him push you around."

"He's not," Saskia snapped, then calmed herself. "He knows who's in charge."

They ended the conversation, and Saskia picked up her gyros and peeled back the foil wrapper. She looked across at Coby, noticing that the light had faded from his eyes as he picked his up, but when he took a bite and saw her watching him, he smiled and sat up straighter. "Umm, this is really good. Thanks for showing me this place." His muzzle twitched and he shifted in his seat. "Sorry, for a minute there I'd forgotten about the… plug." The last word was whispered.

"Can't have that, now can we?" she replied, grinning. When Coby smiled back, she saw that the light had returned.

* * *

Saskia was not pleased about being let off work early. Upon stepping into her condominium she saw Coby on his laptop, wearing jeans and a T-shirt. His ears twitched at her entrance but his eyes remained on the screen as his fingers flew. Her hackles went up.

"Coby!"

Startled, he made a couple of keystrokes to pause whatever he was doing, and looked back at her. "Miss Kia."

"You're supposed to be undressed. On your knees, now!"

Though evidently caught off guard, he nodded and slid out of the chair to his knees, saying nothing.

"Out of your clothes."

Coby quickly obeyed while Saskia produced a flogger from a drawer on her end table and pointed to the couch. "Bend over, tail up, and count."

Swallowing, he did as instructed while she stood over him with her hand on her hip and her tail bottled. Once he was in position, she placed a hand just above his tail, and drew back. The first blow from the flogger got a flinch out of him, and he counted. No matter her mood she must be in control of the force of her blows, so she started easy and struck a little harder with each until the fourth felt just right. By then, Coby was lurching with each blow and panting. When he squirmed more, she pressed harder on his lower back.

The lashing continued with Saskia spreading the blows around his rear, and he counted out each one. After the tenth, she put the flogger down. "Put your clothes and your computer away. I need a foot massage."

Moments later, leaning back and breathing deep as he rubbed her feet, Saskia felt her mood improve. "Thank you, pet, that's good enough," she finally said. "Go make me some mint tea." As he stood to head to the kitchen she added, "You may make yourself some if you wish."

Warming her hands with the teacup, Saskia inhaled the minty aromatics, helping her relax further. After a few sips she studied Coby, who squatted on the floor with his own cup. "Do you think I was being unfair?"

Coby seemed reluctant to meet her eyes. "Miss Kia, you warned me that you have moods sometimes and aren't always fair."

Saskia nodded. "I did, but I still want to know if you think I was unfair."

Coby's tail gave a sweep across the carpet. "You told me what time you'd be home from work and I was going to be undressed and ready to serve you. You got home early, Miss Kia."

Saskia nodded again. "That's true."

"Were you were already in a bad mood before you saw me?"

She leaned her muzzle on her hand and studied the marten. "Could you tell?"

He reached back to rub his rear. "It was a hunch. I appreciate that you didn't flog me harder because of it."

That meant he was learning to read her moods. "You're right. They sent me home early."

"A lot of folks would enjoy the extra time off."

Saskia sighed. "Others might. I get an hourly wage and I'd rather have the money than the time off."

"What kind of work do you do, Miss Kia?"

"It's warehouse work, handling outgoing and incoming shipments."

Coby listened and nodded. "Are you hoping for a better job someday?"

The red wolf shifted forward. "I'm looking into some banking and accounting classes so I could maybe become a loan officer."

Coby's eyes wandered over her work shirt and cargo pants, and he smiled at her. "You'll have to dress nicer if you want a job like that."

She folded her arms and gazed back at him. "All right, mister clothing salesman, what do you suggest?"

"I don't know women's clothing as well as men's," Coby replied with a chuckle. "I suggest when you go to a bank, look at how the loan officers dress and plan to dress like them."

* * *

Dinner was in the oven and Saskia was playing an action game when the front door closed with a hollow thunk. Back from his shift, Coby leaned against the door. His snappy business attire couldn't hide the sag in his shoulders and the crease in his brow.

Saskia paused the game. "Rough day at work?"

"You have no idea," he began. "I spent two hours with a difficult customer. He tried on one suit after another, complaining about every one. *The stripes are wrong. It's too tight in the shoulders.*" He dropped the mocking tone. "I thought he looked great in some of them and I told him so, but he wouldn't believe me, and he had the most ridiculous questions, like whether they were moth-proof. Who worries about moths anymore! That's ancient. After all that he left without buying anything. Fred, the other salesman, meanwhile gets to help several customers and gets all the sales commissions."

She let out a sigh and gave him a hug. "I'm sorry you had a bad day." She held him for half a minute, listening to his breathing as he calmed.

They separated, and he reached for his collar on the foyer table. Saskia was quicker and got her hand on it first. Coby hesitated, then placed his hand on it. Their eyes met and held each other for a long pause, before he curled his fingers around the collar and pulled it from beneath her grasp.

As Coby stepped past her to go change clothes, she called after him. "You understand, once you put the collar on, you're my pet again."

"I understand, Miss Kia. Two more days."

That last bit caught her up short but he disappeared into the bedroom before she could reply. Did he mean two more days of serving her before he could return to Fleur? If being her pet was such a burden, why had he just passed up a chance for some time without the collar? Fleur had thought Coby couldn't handle a tougher mistress but she wasn't seeing it. Saskia had started off easy on Coby, as she would with any unfamiliar pet, but even when she pushed him harder he held up just fine.

It took Coby longer than usual to get undressed, but he soon appeared wearing only the collar, cuffs, and a red thong. She paused her game and made a show of looking him over, reaching out to cup his package through the thong, thinking. After a bad day at work, not only had he taken the collar, he had done something that might provoke her. "You're not naked."

"I thought you might like it, Miss Kia."

"Stay," she commanded, and went to fetch his red plug and the connector for the wrist cuffs. Standing behind him, she pulled his arms back and locked them together, then had him bend forward so she could insert the plug. "Very nice," she said. "The casserole needs about twenty more minutes. You can do whatever until dinner."

Coby wriggled his arms. "It'll be hard to get the thong off with my wrists bound."

Saskia smiled at him. "Keep it on. I like how you look in it," she said, running her hand over the front of his thong again.

"I can't help much with dinner either."

Saskia perked one ear. "Precocious, aren't we? Fine, I'll lock them together *after* dinner instead." Let him wonder if he would have spent less time with his wrists bound if he'd kept his mouth shut. She unlocked his wrists before returning to her game.

* * *

Saskia stroked his lower back above his upheld tail. Coby strained as she pushed, twisted, and tried to ease the plug into his back entrance. "Tenth ridge, pet."

The marten gasped. "Hurts, Miss Kia."

She rubbed around his tailbase, her voice soothing. "A little more, then it won't hurt as much."

His rear wiggled and he groaned, but held his place. "I know."

With a twist and a gentle push, it slid home. "There, you made it."

"Made it." His tail twitched and he continued squirming. "Still hurts."

"Five minutes. Think you'll last that long?"

Coby nodded. "I'll do my best."

Her hands caressed up his back to his shoulders and she scooted around in front of him. He wore a grimace and had tears in his eyes. "The longer you hold it, the less it will hurt next time."

"If there is a next time."

Saskia nodded. "True. I will tell Fleur when she comes by tomorrow. She will be so proud of you!"

His eyebrows twitched. "I hope she is."

The red wolf perked her ears. "I certainly am." She stroked behind his ears down to his neck. "I've enjoyed having you as my pet this week. I'm going to miss you."

Coby said nothing more. His face was still screwed up from holding the plug.

When five minutes were up, she worked the plug free, smiling proudly. "Achievement unlocked."

* * *

"So we have these new tools for testing web applications," Fleur explained. "But we can't use them with our existing applications because they have to be written a certain way to be testable with them."

Saskia didn't know much about web applications or software testing. "Why not just rewrite them?"

Fleur gave a snort. "You don't just rewrite a hundred fifty thousand lines of code when it mostly works now. If anything's not quite the same, somebody complains."

Coby wore only the collar and cuffs he had on when he greeted Fleur at the door fifteen minutes earlier. He placed the cup of tea on the table in front of the rabbit and a glass of sparkling raspberry water before Saskia, then knelt to await further instructions.

"Thank you, Coby." Saskia reached out to stroke his ears.

"Was he a good pet for you this week?" The question was for Saskia, but Fleur's eyes were on Coby.

"He certainly was," Saskia replied with a grin. "You're lucky to have him. I had forgotten what a joy it is to train a pet and be served by him."

Fleur leaned toward Coby and angled her ears forward. "I'll bet after a week as Saskia's pet, you're all ready to come back to me."

"I am ready to serve you, Mistress Fleur."

She reached to stroke the side of his muzzle. "Maybe once we're alone, you'll show me what you've learned?"

Coby nodded. "Of course, Mistress Fleur."

The rabbit ran a fingertip along the edge of his ear. "Saskia thinks she's a tougher mistress than me. Is that true?"

He nodded again. "She is."

"But you survived."

Saskia was watching the signals between them. "He did well, even taking a good-sized anal plug. Took a few days to work up to it."

"How many times did he safeword on you?"

"Only once, when I told him to wear the collar full time…"

"…and he couldn't wear it to work," Fleur finished for her. "I should've mentioned that."

"Otherwise, he met every challenge I threw at him. He learned and adapted. We got on well." Saskia sipped her drink. "He's got it where it counts."

"He certainly does," said Fleur, looking over his body with a smirk.

"That's not what I mean," Saskia replied, twitching her whiskers. "You know that look a pet gets in their eyes when they are determined to please you? He's got it."

Fleur's gaze turned uncertain. "You think you'll be a better pet for me now?" she asked him.

"I will do my best, Mistress Fleur."

Something felt off about Coby's answers. After a week, Saskia knew him well enough to notice that his responses were being stated flatly, as if he was parroting what he knew Fleur wanted to hear. "Is there something else, Coby?"

Coby bit his lip and his ears twitched, but before he could answer, Fleur spoke. "It's okay, we can talk more when we get home."

Saskia held up a hand. "Coby, you look like something's bothering you."

He glanced at her only briefly. "It's okay, Miss Kia. I'll be fine."

"See?" said Fleur, reaching for the collar on the table. Coby's brow twitched.

It might go against protocol, but her instincts told her he needed to be pushed. "He's still wearing my collar," she said to Fleur, then stood, towering over the marten. "To the couch, now." Apprehensively he stood and followed her over. Once he was there, she produced the flogger she had used earlier, holding it where he could see it. "I don't believe you."

Coby's eyes went wide at the sight of her hand on the grip. "Miss Kia… what do you want me to say?"

"I think you're holding out on us." She was all business now. "Bend over the couch."

He glanced at Fleur, still seated at the table, then got into the position. Saskia pressed on his back with one hand and gave the flogger a couple of experimental waves with her other before landing it across his rear. Coby flinched.

"Saskia, you don't have to do that," cried Fleur. "Whatever it is, I can get it out of him later."

Sparing only a brief glance at the rabbit, she delivered two more lashes to Coby's rear. The marten flinched, eyes squeezed shut and teeth gritted. "Something tells me he shouldn't leave here before I get it out of him." Another two lashes of the flogger landed.

Fleur bolted upright, hands on her hips. "Stop! He's my pet!"

Saskia stopped, looking at Fleur uncertainly until she noticed Coby holding a hand up. "What?" she said to the marten.

He beckoned her closer with his fingers, and she leaned in enough for him to whisper. "I wish I could stay with you."

Saskia tossed the flogger on the couch. She nearly ordered him to say it aloud but caught herself and thought it through.

Coby hadn't wanted to say it. He had no place to go home to except with Fleur and he knew the rabbit better than she did. If he said it aloud, would that damage their relationship? But if they didn't talk about things like this, what kind of mistress/pet relationship was that? Was Coby afraid Fleur would kick him out and he'd be homeless?

Saskia decided that whatever happened, Coby wouldn't be homeless, but first she had to try to get them talking.

Picking up the flogger, she stood. "Say that again, out loud."

Coby pushed himself up, looked fearfully at Fleur, and stared straight ahead with ears folded. "If I had the choice, I would rather stay with Miss Kia."

"What!" Fleur cried, ears angling back. "You said she was tougher than me."

"She is," Coby answered.

"But you couldn't handle *me*!"

"I could handle…" he started to say, but couldn't continue.

Saskia cut it. "Looks like you two have some misunderstandings. You need to talk this out."

Fleur glared at Coby. "I was pushing and you were whining. You couldn't take any more!"

Coby stood and glared at her. "I could've taken plenty more."

Fleur glared back. "That's not how you acted! You were groaning and whimpering…"

His voice went up a notch. "Just when it's getting good, just as I'm getting into my sub-space, you start in on me. 'Had too much already? Can't take any more?' And you say it like there's only one answer you want to hear!"

Saskia set the flogger on the end table. "Did you tell her this before?"

"He says stuff like that," Fleur started. "He's just trying to cover—"

"I tried to tell you to keep going, that you weren't pushing hard enough," Coby yelled. "You wouldn't listen to me. You wanted to believe that you were this hard Domme who could give me more than I could take!"

Fleur rolled her eyes. "I can't believe this. She's tougher and you like her better?"

Saskia interrupted, "You two—"

"Yes, Miss Kia was tougher on me," Coby continued, still looking at Fleur. "She pushed me harder, made me work more, and when I pleased her it felt like I had really accomplished something. I loved it!" Coby paused to catch his breath. "You didn't even want me staying in your apartment while you were gone. It makes me feel like you don't trust me."

Saskia glanced at Fleur. "Why didn't you want him staying alone?"

For an instant, Fleur looked defensive, but quickly recovered. "I told you, Coby needed to spend the week serving someone."

Saskia gave Fleur the same disbelieving look she had given Coby moments earlier. "What else?" When Fleur didn't answer right away, she continued. "Are you afraid he'll snoop around?"

The rabbit looked flustered for a moment, then frowned as if not wanting to answer that, and scoffed at Coby. "You want to stay with her? Fine, she can have you!"

Coby slumped to the couch, eyes closed and tearful. Saskia looked up at Fleur. "I'm not taking him away from you. You two have to decide where you're headed."

Dishes rattled as Fleur snatched the collar from the table. "I'm tired of dealing with him. You want him, you can have him."

Saskia placed a palm on Coby's shoulder when she heard him sob. "I won't let him be homeless."

"Fine," said Fleur, shouldering her purse and shoving her chair under the table. "You've got 24 hours to get your stuff out of my apartment." She turned and marched for the front door.

After Saskia saw her out, she found Coby still sobbing, head buried in the couch. She rubbed him from the shoulder blades to the neck. "Well, pet, it looks like you got your wish."

The marten whimpered. "I hated having to say it. I hated making her mad like that after she took me in when I needed somewhere to live."

"It needed to be said." Saskia returned to the table. "Come, have a seat. Need something to drink?"

"Just water."

She brought him a glass. "You know I can be tougher, push you even harder than I did this week."

Coby looked up at her, starting to crack a smile. "I know, Miss Kia."

"My most important rule is to be open and honest with each other at all times." She picked up the flogger and gave it a shake in his direction. "You know I'm not afraid to use this if I think you're holding out."

Coby glanced at the flogger. "I understand, Miss Kia."

She put it away. "For these conversations, just call me Kia. You sure you can handle me?"

He smiled bigger. The look in his eyes was all the answer she needed.

Saskia grinned back at him. "I'm going to pick out a collar just for you. Maybe I'll even learn shibari."

FOURTH AND LONG

Whyte Yoté

"I'm dying, Sheila. Dying, here." Harold Nehemeier panted into his forearm as he wiped sweat from his brow, his voice more than loud enough for his wife to hear. He did this on purpose. He did not like the dry African air and the hot African sun on his fur. He liked his double-wide back in Bismarck, complete with six inches of freshly-fallen snow just waiting for a shovel were he not currently aboard a canoe in the middle of a lake in Kenya. By the time they returned, that easily-moved fluff would likely have turned to a frozen crust, doing unspeakable things to the new concrete slab he'd poured just before the first frost.

Never mind that sun bears were meant to like hot climes. Harold, born and raised in North Dakota as the adopted son of arctic foxes, preferred a nice, brisk day in winter hovering around zero degrees to the God-awful arid heat of this place. Who the hell put a resort in the middle of a lake in Kenya?

Smart people. Savvy people. People who wanted to make a buck off poor American saps whose marriages wanted sorely for an overhaul. Saps like Harold and Sheila Nehemeier.

"Honey, please," Sheila said from beneath the purple sun hat that dwarfed—nay, *engulfed*—her stubby, chubby body. Over the years it had occurred to Harold that corgis shouldn't wear clothes that made them appear even smaller than normal. But, as Sheila had grown fond of saying since she'd joined her ladies' group, making it past middle-age had earned her the right to wear a big hat if she wanted to. Sheila was big into self-affirmation these days, the current focus of her attention instead of their lackluster love life.

Harold was big into staying put and ensuring a pension as fat as he was. As they both were. They should really go on a diet someday. Someday.

"I'm just sayin'," the sun bear clipped in his nasal Upper Plains accent. "If you wanted hot and dry we coulda gone to Palm Springs."

"They don't have Hakuna Mipaka in Palm Springs," Sheila said matter-of-factly in a tone that brooked no argument. Thirty-plus years of marriage had taught Harold not to challenge his wife when she used that tone. Sheila *hated* tones. At least the retreat promised something more than theme-park entertainment. Upon having the brochure shoved in his face, he saw the name and immediately thought of a meerkat and a warthog in hula skirts, beckoning them inside to put up their feet and fix their worries. Twenty years since that damned movie had come out, and its Broadway-show offspring still running strong.

But neither meerkats nor warthogs graced the pages, only well-shot vistas of Kenyan savanna and beaches and smiling muzzles gathered for the single purpose of repairing the cracks in their relationships. Which meant that Sheila thought their marriage needed fixing. Which it did, and badly at that. But Harold had long ago resigned himself to the role of "best husband but second-best sex partner", because when your wife's ex-boyfriend is a Clydesdale, not much else measures up. Paired with Sheila's insatiable craving for cock, Harold couldn't even see the bar, much less reach it. Menopause hadn't changed her appetite one bit.

It would be like a vacation, she'd said. Some time spent away from the hustle and bustle of Bismarck, which was a joke, really, but that wasn't the point. As the sun bear squinted over at his wife, who practically glowed despite the jet lag, he figured the middle of Kenya might be more effective than some sterile gray building back home.

Their native porter, a cheetah who appeared to have never eaten an ounce of fat in his entire life, paddled the canoe toward Central Island, his eyes narrowed in the bright sunlight. He wore only a loincloth, though whether or not it was for show Harold couldn't tell. Every inch of his spotted fur rippled with tight sinew from years of... well... being in Africa, and Harold felt genuinely ashamed of his very American waistline.

Against the far gunwale, less than four feet away but a million miles apart, his wife carefully unpeeled an orange she'd bought at the airport yesterday and popped a wedge into her mouth. Harold remembered the last blowjob he'd gotten from those lips and found himself envying that piece of fruit. If he tried hard enough, he could almost imagine his paw into her skilled mouth when he fisted his dick in the shower each morning. Almost.

Sheila finished the orange, folded the peel into the brown paper bag in which it had come, and tucked it back into her purse instead of tossing it over the side. Bless her, but she had a good soul. Deep down he really did want to try for her—for *them*—but he couldn't shake the cloud of dubious dread from his thoughts.

He wanted to get back to where they used to be, or at least as close. Anything was better than this purgatory.

For the rest of their journey across the water, Harold sat in silence and contemplated the retreat. He had bought the tickets, but Sheila had read the brochure and visited the website with its promises of panacea. Eventually he would have to get up to speed.

"Brace yourselves," the cheetah warned in friendly Swahili-tinged English, right before the canoe slid onto a sand bar, nearly sending the sun bear toppling overboard. "We are still a bit too far out." Their list to port placed blame squarely on Harold's fat ass, but the cheetah continued to smile broadly. "*Mfalme! Kunisaidia na viboko haya!*" Harold turned to see an equally thin young lion wading to the waist with a rope. After tying it to the cleat on the prow, he ran back to shore, where several more lions joined in, tugging until the boat was high and dry.

The cheetah leaped to the sand before bending to offer his paw to Sheila. "If Madame would…"

"Oh my, what manners," the corgi said, impressed by the un-savageness of it all. She stepped as delicately as her legs would allow to the ground. "*Asante.*" Her stub tried its best to wag, still her most endearing feature.

"*Karibu*, Madame. *Unazungumza Kiswahili?*"

Sheila demurred. "Uh, just enough to get me into trouble, as they say." Harold stepped out and stumbled onto the sand with minimal struggle. "What was your name again?" she asked as the cat bent to grab their backpacks—two each—and set them on the beach.

"My name is Kunta Kinte, but you may call me Toby," the cat bowed, almost to his toes.

Sheila's face froze, her usually ebullient nature clammed up. "Is... is that so?" she stammered. The cheetah exchanged glances with the lions and all burst out in a roaring chorus of laughter so piercing Harold wished he could fold his ears like a canine.

"No! No, nonono." The cheetah paused to catch his breath. "We love to watch your faces when we say it, though. We do a lot of laughing. I am Mwana."

"Thank you, Mwana," the corgi said, her paw trembling slightly. "Honey, could you pay the nice man?" Harold fumbled around for his wallet, but when he didn't immediately pull it out he heard a familiar sigh as she took out a 100-shilling note from her fanny pack. "Oh, never mind, I'll do it. Here you go," she smiled. Mwana eyed it hungrily from behind his veneer of polite patience.

"Oh, I can't possibly."

"Go ahead. You earned it!"

"You are very gracious, Madame. Enjoy your stay." Sheila may have been impressed by the obsequious hospitality, but Harold could tell the clever cat knew what he was doing, and probably went through those motions several times a day, every day. Not a bad way to make a living, on top of the wages Hakuna Mipaka paid him. A hundred shillings was a little under two dollars, and two dollars went very far in Kenya.

"Thank you," the sun bear repeated. As he shouldered his backpack and turned for one more wave, he noticed the cheetah had already pulled a cigarette from somewhere and lit it, using the butt to light those of his lion friends as well. He huffed so Sheila would hear. "I thought we left the riffraff back in Nairobi," he muttered under his breath.

"Five minutes in and you're already causing trouble." The corgi shot him a dagger of a glance. "I sure hope you plan on trying harder the rest of the week."

Harold forced a toothy smile. "Yes, dear." It was going to be a long week.

* * *

"Welcome to Hakuna Mipaka!" beamed the okapi from behind the front desk. "How may I help you?"

The main lodge turned out to be surprisingly modern, despite its ramshackle outside appearance. Gigantic fans and misters in the ceiling made it a blissful twenty degrees cooler.

"We're here for the therapy?" Harold said. He got an elbow in the side for his troubles. "Checking in. Nehemeier, for two?"

The okapi nodded and began sweeping her fingers over her iPad. "Yes, here we are. You are in the Kudanganya Suite. I am very happy for you." And she smiled wider, if that were even possible.

Harold thought this a very odd thing to say to a complete stranger. But hey, culture shock.

"Thank you," Sheila replied, undeterred by all the weirdness. The okapi beckoned over a zebra and a black-backed jackal, and after a short exchange in Swahili the young men took the backpacks away in impressively large strides. Harold tried to quash the dread that had been brewing in his gut since they touched down in the capital, and couldn't quite do it.

The sun bear leaned on the counter. "Is there anything else we need to do?" *Any guest books to sign? Any maps of the premises? Anything?* It couldn't possibly be that simple. Not that he was delaying the inevitable, but still.

"To your right, at the far end before you leave the building, you will find a map. Your suite will be marked, the second-farthest. Very private. No neighbors. Very *ionekane*."

Whatever that was, Harold hoped it was good. "Alrighty, thanks.

Come on, honeypot." How humiliating, since their very presence here practically reeked of dysfunction. He put his arm around her shoulder, because he was too tall to reach her waist. And felt nothing. Fondness, maybe, but little else.

Upon stepping back into the sun Harold immediately wanted to return to the main lodge. It felt like that hole in the ozone that had fried a bunch of Australians a couple decades back had centered itself over eastern Africa instead of closing up like the news had reported.

Why Sheila had thought Kenya would be anything close to a vacation was anyone's guess. Just one more thing to chalk up to her "flavor of the month," as he had come to term it. For a woman north of fifty, and a post-menopausal one at that, the corgi's sexual appetite was anything but subdued. Harold had seen her collection of toys, some as big around as his wrist, and the very sight had shamed him. While he had his alone time in the shower, she would have her own party in their marital bed. Houston might as well be living in their guestroom.

And since the sun bear had read that this type of pseudo-celibacy was common in marriages, he let himself be comforted by the solidity of those facts. He didn't think about the part right after, where it had said how many of those marriages ended up in affairs and divorce. That part didn't count because it made him feel bad.

Harold Nehemeier was very good at blocking out things that made him feel bad.

"I know you don't want to be here," said his wife, seemingly out of nowhere. "Could you at least *appear* to be invested?"

"Isn't that what I'm paying these people for, Sheila? To be invested in us? This was your idea."

"Don't give me that tone." Not the tone complaint again, anything but that. He might as well cut his balls off and stick them in her purse. She stopped, right in the middle of the trail, and turned to him. Sheila could barely look past the brim of her ridiculously large hat to meet his gaze, her twin deep azure pools (as the sun bear had called her eyes back when they were dating) shining with the suspicion of aborted tears. "At least pretend like you want to try. Open your mind. Live a little." Her lips formed the words, but her eyes said *I'm pretty desperate, Harold. I hope you are as well.*

"Okay, you win," Harold capitulated, but felt a half-smile at the end of his sentence. After year twelve or so, the sun bear had kind of called it quits on trying to win arguments, and this was not the hill he wanted to die on. His old passive-aggressive standbys wouldn't get them back into bed together.

They made their way to the Kudanganya Suite in stoic, stolid silence.

Halfway up a very shallow incline Harold ran out of breath. Hills just didn't exist where he lived, at least not where he walked. "God, I hope their water is purified," he gasped, realizing he hadn't had any since boarding the rickety bus that took them to the lakeshore. Even without the arid weather that was a bad idea.

"It's a five-star resort, Harold. I'm sure they've got that covered. It may not be Evian, so fair warning."

"Don't give me that tone. Ow!" Just because his hips had a protective layer of fat didn't make her fist hurt any less.

"You baby. Now get that rumpus up the hill." Sheila wasn't doing much better, having put on about the same percentage of extra weight since they tied the knot. But her cream-and-beige fur took heat a hell of a lot better than Harold's mostly-black pelt. "And tuck your tongue in."

I'd love to, baby, but you push my head away, the sun bear thought wryly. What woman in her right mind would want to refuse eighteen inches of skilled prehensile goodness? Well, besides Sheila.

"Nehemeiers!" came a powerful voice a dozen or so yards in front of them. "Harold and Sheila, I see you!" Harold looked up to see a vaguely canid thing waving its arms.

"I guess that's us," Sheila said, being obvious in her search for levity. A few choice phrases passed through the sun bear's head but he ultimately chose to stay smartly silent. They were almost there, and then he wouldn't have to think about anything for a while.

The canid thing approached them at a trot and eventually became discernable not as a canid at all, but a spotted hyena, lithe and nubile. "Welcome!" she bellowed in a voice with lungs behind it, half-kneeling to plant a European-style kiss on each of Sheila's cheeks. Then she stood and vigorously shook Harold's right paw in both of hers. Harold was starting to distrust all of these big smiles. They reminded him of shopping for a used Oldsmobile. "*Jambo?*"

"I'm sorry?" the sun bear said.

"*Jambo*. It is how we ask how are you doing. I believe the American term is, 'wassup.'"

"Oh, we're a few years too old for that, I'm afraid," Sheila smiled. "We're doing fine, fine. As well as can be expected, under the circumstances." Leaning in so she could whisper loudly behind her paw, she followed up, "Harold isn't used to the weather."

"Well now, Mister Harold, I can do a lot of things," said the hyena, turning to the sweating sun bear, "but I cannot change the weather. We have fans and spray, but the sun will always be there. My name is Jabari, one of your hosts and therapist for the week. If I do my job right, that is."

Harold bristled. "Well, you're welcome to it. Take your best shot."

"He usually takes a nap about now," Sheila said. "Plus the jet lag, you know… and we forgot our carpet square and apple juice."

Jabari looked from wife to husband, waiting for an explanation that never came.

"Kill me now," Harold moaned. "Lord, take me now." But the heavens only responded with more sun.

"Come," Jabari said after a considered pause, showing some impossibly white teeth. "I can see I have work to do."

* * *

The Kudanganya Suite turned out to be much more than a suite. It was a cottage of solid, modern construction with a faux-thatch roof. A large patio led into the main living area, with the Nehemeiers' bedroom off to one side and the hyenas' live-in suite opposite. To the rear, the kitchen's glass wall slid open so guests could eat *en plein air* if desired, which, according to Jabari, only really worked before sunset and its swarms of mosquitoes. In fact, the only things that marred the eclectic decor were the nets above the beds, resembling malaria tents.

Jabari led the short but thorough tour through the building with the effortlessness of someone who had done this hundreds of times before. Harold clutched a bottle of water he'd snagged from the kitchen as if it were the last one on earth, while Sheila oohed and aahed and squealed over such details as the open-air shower plumbed through a live acacia trunk and the closets already filled with their unpacked things. To the sun bear, the former looked dangerous and the latter felt like an invasion of privacy.

Finally the tour ended at the intimate backyard, fenced in by tall reeds and shaded almost fully by the thorny aegis of another acacia tree. Another hyena was arranging the lounge chairs there when Jabari led them out onto the grass.

"Complete privacy." She twirled around to present the space. The other hyena, a male, padded up. Harold noted that he barely came up to the female's chin. Everything about him was smaller. "This is my husband Mateka."

"Nice to meet you." The sun bear reached out but Mateka lunged for the opposite paw, shaking it (and the water bottle) in both of his. A cloud of starlings took flight at the sound.

"Apologies," he said, "but the left paw is a sign of impropriety for us. Always with the right."

Jabari added, "And if he clasps both paws over yours, it is a sign of great respect."

"We have lots to learn." For the first time, Sheila sounded reticent. "I hope we didn't offend."

Another belly-laugh from Jabari. "We host Westerners all the time. We can't afford to be offended!" After a few words of Swahili to her husband, she gestured inside. "I hope you brought your appetites."

Finally, something Harold excelled at.

The three sat down at the dining table and chatted about cultural differences while Mateka brought out each dish: *ugali*, a type of thick cornmeal; *githeri*, a bean-and-corn mix; spiced rice; steamed greens; and *nyama choma*, the pride of Kenya, a big platter of roasted meat. Every plate was wonderfully aromatic and filled the room with a combination of smells that rivaled the hyenas' musky scent. Not that it was unpleasant, as much as just plain strong.

Once set out, the food was passed around starting with Harold (the senior male, as per tradition) and conversation largely died, at Jabari's suggestion, until everyone had had their fill. Though Sheila didn't appear to notice, the sun bear sensed an odd dynamic between the two hyenas. Jabari didn't get up from the table to refill drinks or take back dirty dishes. Mateka did it all, often anticipating the table's needs and always acting with a smile. Not to say that Harold had never cleared a table before in his life, but he wouldn't want to make a habit of it.

Mateka opened up the dining area and the four relaxed over cups of decaf out of respect for Harold's travel-weariness. An early bedtime would not be unwelcome.

"You know," Sheila said, "I shouldn't feel weird drinking coffee that came from the same country I'm in, but I do. It was so exotic when they finally opened a Starbucks in Bismarck, and now I'm in the middle of where they grow it!"

"Those beans are local," Jabari replied. "Only an hour or so from here. We could take you there to see the fields."

The corgi lit up like an Autumnfest float from back home. "Oh, Harold! Wouldn't that just be a gasser?"

Harold adjusted his glasses and sipped from his mug. He wanted to say, *Shouldn't we be working on our marriage, dear? That's what we paid a few thousand dollars and flew a few thousand miles for after all, right?* But he held his tongue in front of their magnanimous hosts. "I'd be interested to see how they do it, yeah."

"I can arrange with Nyota and Mume for a tour later in the week," offered Mateka.

"Yes, that would be best. After some progress, maybe? Rekindling intimacy can take time." Jabari almost seemed to leer at the couple from behind the rim of her mug, her various bracelets and rings clinking as she moved. How did she know?

Harold shot his wife a withering stare but she merely shrugged.

"You told me to make the arrangements," she explained. "Part of registration was to give a description of the problems we were having. I was just being honest, otherwise we wouldn't get the help we needed."

"So you wrote a confessional on their site?"

Jabari stood and set down her mug. She carried an imposing presence, and Harold didn't like it. He didn't like the subtle change in her scent, either. "Several thousand words, actually. Your wife was very specific about what she thought was wrong. Very thorough. Very emotional. Most couples don't spend five minutes on that part of the application, and we spend the entire week breaking down the walls." Her grin returned. "I am hopeful we won't need the whole week."

"You didn't have to tell every—" But the sun bear cut himself off when he saw those tears starting up again. He knew they were in trouble, and he knew she knew. The part that felt betrayed backed down in favor of the part that really just wanted to make it all work out. And that made Harold massively uncomfortable. If the hyenas could smell it, they didn't let on.

Mateka spoke up but remained sitting. "Perhaps an early bedtime. Sleep works wonders for the soul."

"Agreed," Jabari said. "You two go ahead and prepare for bed. We will clean up out here."

Sheila pushed herself off her chair (she really didn't stand *up* as much as just stand *down*) and brushed her fingertips across her eyes before her muzzle got wet. "Thanks," she said. "We're probably just tired."

"*Hakuna matata*," the hyenas replied in unison.

"That sounded much more meaningful before 1994," said Jabari with a wistful cant to her ears. "But the sentiment stands. Off with you. We are just across the way if you need anything." She dismissed them with a flick of her paws.

As soon as the door closed, Harold slumped to the bed and sighed.

"This is going to be a long week." Sheila's petite espadrilles showed up between his bare bear feet. When he looked up they were muzzle to muzzle. She appeared to be vibrating. Or trembling.

"Harold Milhouse Nehemeier, you had better try as hard as I'm going to, or…or…I don't know what's gonna happen." She threw up her paws in frustration. "I'll…I'll run away with an oil-field worker, some…young stud who reminds me of Houston." Houston was the benchmark Clydesdale ex-boyfriend. This was Sheila's manipulation tone. "You'll be all alone." They'd traveled all this way and she was making threats?

So I can jerk off to lesbian porn without clearing my browser history? Good deal! Though he knew she didn't mean it literally, the dig still stung. He knew Houston would come up eventually, but couldn't she wait until the actual therapy started?

But the sun bear merely said, "Okay." And, having aired her grievance, the corgi padded to the bathroom, closing the door behind her because she had quit undressing in front of him years ago.

When he finally took his turn in the shower, he ended up jerking off to lesbian porn in his head, splattering the faux-rock wall with a strained, unsatisfied grunt.

* * *

The bedside alarm clock read a quarter past three in the morning when Harold started awake and rolled over to check. Again came the sound that had roused him, banging and cries of a barking sort. They reminded him of laughter.

Plucking his bifocals off the night stand and sliding out of bed as gently as he could, Harold tiptoed to the door and opened it, prepared for squeaks but relieved when none came. He had hardly pulled the door to before the sounds started up again.

"A week of this?" the sun bear mouthed to the dark living room. Sheila would have an absolute cow if she knew their hosts were having relations loud enough to wake others up. What rudeness. What inconsideration.

What a time for Harold to get a boner.

But there it was, a respectable (but still dissatisfactory) seven inches of pink shaft and blunt head poking out the front of his boxers, plain as day. No little blue pills needed. And it was *leaking*, dammit, the tip shining in the moonlight. Harold never leaked anymore.

"Ahh! Ahh! Eeeyah!" Mateka grunted from beyond the door. Jabari responded with gasps of her own. Someone slapped someone else, and the rhythm sped up dramatically.

Harold stroked himself and cupped an ear to the wood, the allure of sleep forgotten. He'd been away from any kind of sexual contact beyond his own paw and a screen for so long; just the knowledge that *real* people were having *real* sex anywhere close had him worked up.

"Give it to her good," he heard himself whisper. "Show her who's boss." One more glance back to the master bedroom to check for his wife and he shoved his boxers to his ankles. It wasn't cheating if you didn't touch anyone, was it?

For a tantalizing ten minutes Harold edged while listening to the two horny hyenas. Most of the time he couldn't tell who was doing what to whom, but the noises they made were more than enough to keep his motor running. Right around the time Mateka barked out his climax (it was hard to mistake that sound in any species, really) Harold arched his hips and painted his belly with his second load of the night. After a precious minute to cool down, he used his undies to wipe up the mess and made it back to the bed with no one the wiser.

Perhaps coming here wasn't a complete mistake after all.

* * *

Eavesdropping on the hyenas' sexual escapades turned out to be the sole highlight of Harold's next few days. In the morning they would share a breakfast with Jabari and Mateka (always cooked by the male) before heading out to their classes, where such riveting subjects as "Keeping the Spark Alive" and "Communicating Without Words" had him almost dozing while the rest of the couples sat in rapt attention. It all sounded like a load of feel-good psychobabble but his usual cynicism now fostered guilt instead of righteousness. Plus, Sheila's paw was warm in his as she took notes with the other.

Her pads were nice and soft, too. Sheila had started to add little touches throughout the days: a pat on the shoulder here, a rubbing of his ear there. He couldn't deny it was an improvement over their platonic marriage back home, but what guarantee did he have it would continue once they landed back in the Great White North?

Still, it was something, even if it did turn out to be temporary. If he'd been completely demoralized he never would have boarded the plane in the first place.

Lunch came in the form of a buffet line in the common dining area, followed by an hour of rest before afternoon classes. Harold felt like a kid back at the University of North Dakota, and just as bored. Afterwards came a field trip, usually a bus ride to some local attraction or bazaar. They then recounted the day's sessions at dinner with the hyenas and spent a quiet evening before sleep.

For three days Harold put up with it, and for three days he got his rocks off in the middle of the night, trying to mask his scent and keep Sheila's increasingly frustrated face out of his mind. She seemed to expect immediate progress but he just couldn't get out of his own way to step up to the plate.

On the fourth day, Jabari sent the couple to the Kahawa Coffee Company thirty kilometers away, nestled in the shadow of Mount Kulal. Nyota and Mume, a pair of zebras, gave them a personal tour of the fields and drying area, even going so far as to send them away with a pound of dried beans. Sheila bubbled over with glee, and even Harold had to admit he somewhat enjoyed the sights and smells. The coming evening, however, had already begun to command his attention. Tonight he planned to try to open the door a little and add some pictures and musk to his guilty aural pleasure.

Sheila, however, picked that very same time to start with the come-ons. A couple random touches during the tour, sitting extra close on the ride back, and even holding paws. While it felt nice, Harold wouldn't let her attempts sour his thoughts or plans. He was having too much fun without her.

"Oh, my feet," the corgi said, taking off one hiking boot. "We shoulda bought these much earlier. They haven't broken in yet and all the fur's rubbin' off my ankle!"

Howard didn't wear shoes. His pads were pretty sore, though. "Wish that bathroom had a hot tub or something," he said. "I could use a soak."

"Good idea! Maybe we could ask Jabari or Mateka if there's one nearby. That'd just hit the spot. And it'd be time spent together."

"Yes, it would," agreed the sun bear, imagining Jabari's sex spread open by Maketa's swollen knot, or whateer hyenas had between their legs. And he opened the door, allowing his wife to enter first. Chivalry wasn't completely dead, after all.

"Nehemeiers!" bombasted Jabari from the dining area. "Just in time for dinner! Come, join us."

Mateka spoke as they turned the corner. "We heard the tour went a little long, so we delayed cooking. It seems to have worked out." The hyena set a plate of cooked beans in the middle of the table and went back to the kitchen, wagging his short tail over his bare rump.

Sheila's paws grabbed the sleeve of Harold's shirt and pulled. "Harold!" she shout-whispered. "Why. Is. He. Naked."

"I don't know."

"Come!" Jabari repeated, emerging from around the corner in much the same state. She wore nothing aside from a pair of gold hoops that stretched from her ears nearly to her shoulders. Sheila put a paw to her face. Harold just stared at her tits. "Well, come on!"

The dining table sat full of delicious Kenyan food; like always, Mateka had outdone himself. But on either end stood a naked hyena, smiling, with no sense whatsoever of impropriety.

"Penny for your thoughts," Mateka said, arms crossed over his chest. "Aside from, 'Why are they unclothed'?"

Harold shrugged. "That's…about it." He noticed Sheila attached to his arm like a child on the first day of kindergarten.

Jabari came up to them. The closer her breasts got, the harder it was to avoid looking at them. Sheila trembled a little. "Your stay is half over. Now is the time for reflection and putting what you've learned to use."

Oh, shit, Harold thought. "Did you know this is part of the thing?" he asked his wife.

Sheila shook her head vigorously. "No, I swear!"

"Certainly you read about the mid-week consultation," Jabari said.

"It didn't say *naked*!"

"It didn't *not* say it, either. What kind of hosts would we be if we did not make it our business to see you got the most out of your vacation?" The hyena took each of their paws in hers. Harold noticed how perky her breasts appeared compared to the pictures in his *National Geographic*s. Hakuna Mipaka was all about defying expectations. "First, we eat."

If that dinner wasn't the very definition of awkward, Harold didn't know what qualified. Jabari and Mateka asked their questions and made small talk like each of the previous days, serving out food and cleaning up dishes without a single stitch on. The most maddening thing was the fact that neither hyena seemed the least bit uncomfortable, or concerned with the Nehemeiers' discomfort. As many times as he wanted to say something—*anything*—he kept silent out of respect for their, uh, culture.

At the end of the meal Jabari suggested sitting out on the patio with coffee, rather than inside at the dining table. Jabari led the couple out while Mateka prepared the drinks. When he had divvied out cups and saucers, cream and sugar, he returned to the kitchen and a pall of silence descended.

"So." Jabari sat with her paws on her outspread knees, giving Harold a direct view. Like her nipples, the flesh there was black, its lips much bigger than Sheila's, and with much more pubic fur. "What do you think has been the most helpful module so far?" She crossed her legs. *Fatal Attraction* happened to be one of Harold's favorite movies.

Harold crossed his own to mask any incriminating bulges.

"Well," Sheila said to the empty space a few feet above Jabari's head, "that one about making the little things count was okay. Makes you think about how you don't do the things anymore that you used to."

Jabari nodded. "Right. There is no such thing as growing apart. There is only you no longer nurturing the marriage."

Mateka came out with four steaming mugs and accessories on a silver platter. "I wish I could have used some of the coffee from your outing this afternoon, but they send that to the States for roasting." He bent to set everything on the table, giving the couple an eyeful of black balls and hyena hole before they could look away. Harold was dismayed to find his erection didn't suffer in the slightest.

Thereafter ensued likely one of the most awkward sips of coffee in the history of sipping and coffee. Harold glanced over at Sheila, who was studying her brew as if it contained the secret of life. He glanced at the hyenas, who were imbibing without the slightest hint of self-consciousness.

"Wonderful. So robust. It is a shame we have to buy it from stores in Nairobi instead of dealing directly with Kahawa." Jabari set down her empty mug. "Harold, what was your favorite module? Or do you even remember any of them?" she asked with tone and words so disparate that at first the sun bear didn't realize she had insulted him.

But her tone had been pleasant, and the smile she now wore matched it. After burying his nose in his coffee, faking a sip, and setting it down as slowly as possible, he managed to mumble something with the words "love" and "synergy".

"I thought so." Standing, Jabari padded over to Harold and put a paw on his shoulder. "None of our modules have the word 'love' in them. We took pains to avoid something so bold. And 'synergy' would work if this were a resort for middle management." While the sun bear tried not to tremble (and for someone his age to be trembling was preposterous), she continued. "Perhaps you were too busy pleasuring yourself outside our bedroom door to remember what you learned during the day?"

Harold wanted to die. If there were a sword to fall on, perhaps some tribal blade used as decoration, he would have grabbed it and run himself through.

Seconds ticked by. The more that ticked by, the more furious he knew Sheila would be. His exposure had been swift and complete. For one short moment he considered trying to backpedal but his resolve had withered along with both his erection and any anticipation of eavesdropping. His wife's eyes burned twin holes in the side of his skull.

Sheila put down her coffee with a palsy clatter. She smoothed down the front of her sun dress, though it needed no smoothing. She let out a long, loud sigh. And then she said, "Okay then," in a voice so calm he could practically taste the rage radiating from her. "Would you care to explain yourself, Harold?"

It occurred to Harold that this was worse than the time his mother had found his cum-stained poster of Farrah Fawcett and made him crumple it into a trash can and throw a match on it. The Lamborghini Countach that replaced the ferret bombshell just hadn't been the same.

Mercifully, Jabari stepped in on his behalf. "Mrs. Nehemeier, do not worry. If this were a bad thing, you would have heard it from us by now."

"How'd you know…" Harold began, deflated.

"It's quite difficult to mask the scent of bear semen right outside the door," Mateka said. "Also, our noses aren't so desensitized from pollutants, out here on the savanna."

"But we live in North Dakota."

Mateka smiled. "Oil fields." And that was the end of that.

"We smelled it the first night while we were making love," Jabari said, kneading both of Harold's shoulders from behind at the most inappropriate time in history for a shoulder massage. "It is very interesting, what goes on while couples are here for therapy."

Now Sheila directed her rage at the hyena. "You *let* this go on for most of a week? What kind of perverts are you?" Their laughter did not assuage her in the slightest. Big, booming African laughter.

"It is not just about the classes. As liaisons, we watch and listen to how you act together. For the first few days we observe, and on the fourth day we decide if intervention is needed."

"It's needed, all right." Mateka began gathering the drinkware and headed into the kitchen. Jabari nodded to the couple.

"He is right. Having Harold masturbating while listening to us, while flattering and quite arousing, does not help your marriage." As she spoke, her fingers traced along his throat and up the back of his head, ending up at his ears where they scratched and pressed. He let out a rumble he hadn't made in years. He had a breast on each side of his neck and he liked it.

Bristling, Sheila stood up to her full four-foot-two height. "How does fondling my husband help *our* marriage?" She was trying to be offended, but at the very most she was just disarmed. Jabari had a way of disarming people.

"I think it's time," Mateka said, having suddenly reappeared. "But you must trust us to know what is in your best interest."

Whatever gets me off the hook, thought Harold. "Jeez, well, we've tried everything else."

Without waiting for an answer from the corgi, Jabari said, "Then the clothes must go." This didn't surprise Harold as much as it did his wife, who sputtered and fumed and finally deflated, having run out of epithets. With a "when in Rome" shrug to Sheila, the sun bear started on the buttons of a tiki shirt that looked loud here in Kenya, never mind back home.

"I'm not getting naked in front of these people." Sheila clutched her sun hat tightly to her chest, looking on in horror as her husband shucked piece by piece until he was as naked as the hyenas. Jabari took each article and folded it neatly on the couch.

Despite his triphammering heart, the sun bear forced a wry smile anyway. "Now you're the odd one out, honey," he said, grateful to no longer be the center of attention.

"This was not in the brochure." Sheila was clearly running out of steam.

"We do not openly advertise, no," replied Jabari. "But we have yet to lose a guest on the fourth night. Hakuna Mipaka was founded in 1987. So…"

Mateka relieved the corgi of her sun hat and held out his paws. "If you would, please?" And Sheila finally gave in and slowly—reluctantly—started on the buttons of her dress. The hyenas' lithe bodies put their own abundant curves to shame, but the corgi carried hers better than Harold did.

Jabari took the sun bear's paw and led him further into the backyard, until they stood in the middle of the wooden patio under the acacia tree. Mateka and Sheila followed, and when the hyena reached up behind the trunk the branches lit up with strings of lights like little stars. Harold wondered how anyone could string up a thorny tree like that.

Then he looked down and noticed the way Sheila's dun fur seemed to glow under the soft white light. Without all the clothing in the way, he had no choice but to see her for her. And it was the first time he'd seen her—really *seen* her—in forever.

"I am glad you are looking," Jabari said, a paw gently pressed to the small of his back. "That means there is hope." Before he could inquire, the hyena continued. "Some must have their sight restored from the blindness of time, and a week in the wilds of Africa can only help so much."

"If you trust us," Mateka added, "we can make miracles happen."

"*That* I remember from the brochure," quipped Sheila, having gotten more used to her state of *deshabille*.

"And if you trust me," Jabari said, turning to face the sun bear, "you won't mind if I do this." And then Harold's paw was cupping the hyena's right breast.

His first impulse told him to withdraw, but Jabari's grip on his wrist wouldn't allow it. The second impulse was to turn to his wife and show her he had no choice. He did turn, but seeing Sheila's own paw on Mateka's sheath made up for any remaining impropriety. Harold wanted to feel lots of things—shame, rage, envy—but all felt inappropriate. Nothing about North Dakota could have prepared him for this moment. Nothing on earth, even. One thing was certain, though: that breast felt good on his pads.

He'd almost forgotten what a young, perky breast felt like. The flesh yielded in just the right way, the pert black nipple surrounded by a sea of creamy fur on one side and darker spotted fur on the other. He'd been staring for almost half a minute when he realized it and blinked away the mental cobwebs. Across the patio, his wife still held Mateka's sheath, giving it much the same treatment. An inch of shiny black flesh shone just enough in the light to make its presence known.

"Now, Nehemeiers, what do you feel?" asked Jabari. "You may feel betrayed. You may feel like a betrayer, but these are only barriers to distract you from what lies underneath. So, Harold: what *does* lie underneath?"

On instinct Harold took the question literally and focused his attention between his legs. And he felt a stirring as familiar as mounting a bicycle. "Besides all that other junk you mentioned, I feel kinda horny."

"Madame?" Mateka asked the corgi.

Looking quite stricken, Sheila still clung to the hyena. "I was going to say humiliated, and then embarrassed. But, now that I think about it, I guess I'm kinda horny too."

"Now why can't you feel that for each other?" Jabari guided Harold's other paw down until his fingertips entered slick wet heat. "What is so different about my body compared to hers?" Besides the obvious, the sun bear couldn't come up with anything to withstand scrutiny.

"What are you, blind?" Sheila blurted out, saying the words no one else dared say. "Look at you! You're perfect!"

"Perfect in your country, yes. America values very thin women for some reason. Here, I am a bit small. Certainly you know of the many cultures that appreciate a well-fed body as a sign of health and wealth."

"Yeah, but it's not the same." Sheila offered nothing beyond that, though. Harold became aware of Jabari's musky scent, brought his fingers to his nose and sniffed. He let out a chuff reminiscent of his halcyon days, perking up the corgi's ears. "Harold! You're being indecent!" Her discomfort had little effect on the other three.

Suddenly Jabari's fingers grasped him and skinned back his sheath a bit, exposing his half-erection. "I would say this is very decent, Mrs. Nehemeier. You are mistaken." Her constant smile was almost infuriating. Harold cared less about this than the warmth of the hyena's pads. "But this is not the way to Harold's heart, is it? Judging by the past few days, Harold likes to watch. Don't you, Harold?"

Fire rushed up the sun bear's neck and settled in his cheeks. His cock surged. "Fine, okay?" he admitted, his accent thickening slightly. "Jeez. I get up to grab something from the fridge and you two're moanin' around in there, and what am I supposed to do?"

"Go back to bed, maybe?" Sheila said, unperturbed by the penis in her fingers.

"Your husband was doing what felt good." Finally, some justification. "I am aware that you started advances toward Harold only today. What took so long?"

No answer was needed. The spark had left, plain and simple.

Jabari let go of the sun bear's various parts to address the corgi. "Harold watches…and you just want to be satisfied. I can see it in your eyes." Likewise, Mateka pulled away.

"You wanna know the real story?" Harold asked no one in particular, seething and brittle. He was shouting but he no longer cared. Nothing else had worked, and this probably wouldn't either. But god dammit if he wasn't going to fight to make his point. "Her ex-boyfriend, from *decades* ago, is a…a *fucking* horse, and how'm I supposed to compete with this?" He swung his junk around, flinging pre onto the ground.

"That didn't matter when we were dating, Harold!" One short, pudgy finger pointed up at him. "How many times did I wake you up in the middle of the night to play cowgirl?"

"A stud need not be a stallion," the hyena opined. "Size only matters if you don't know what you're doing."

Sheila blinked a couple tears onto her cheeks, speaking more softly. "I didn't need a horse because I had you."

"Oh, *now* you're just going for the sympathy play," Harold spat. "We've had this discussion before. No, no, it was a fight. It was always a fight."

Mateka held his arms out stiffly, eyes gleaming. "Yes! This is very, very good. Please, go on."

"You don't understand." The tears broke free and made parentheses around her muzzle. "It was never about size. You wouldn't listen."

Scoffing, Harold didn't budge. "Now that we're in therapy, of course you say that. You're just telling me what you want *them* to hear."

Sheila seemed to shrink into herself even more than usual, and the pit of Harold's stomach grew acidic.

"Not so good," Mateka muttered, re-crossing his arms with decidedly less-gleaming eyes.

Before any more barbs could be traded, Jabari barked something in Swahili that sent Mateka to the floor at her feet, kneeling obediently, where she proceeded to pet him between the ears.

Not yet ready to be defused, Harold balked at their hosts. "Oh look, Sheila, she's got her husband's balls in her apron too. Except she doesn't need an apron to do it." His wife gawped, aghast, across the otherwise romantic space.

Before she could respond, Jabari cut in. "This is normal, Mr. Nehemeier. In hyena culture, it is the females who outsize the males, and who command the mating game. We choose who and when, and how many times. Thousands of years it has been this way." She kept on smiling, and uttered a couple more words down to her husband, who didn't even pause before darting his tongue between her legs to feast.

Sheila clasped her paws over her face and moaned, but Harold merely looked on. If the commands and cultural differences weren't already enough, nothing could prepare him for the swelling tube of flesh that grew seemingly from within Jabari's lips, like a sock turning inside-out. As black as the rest of her flesh, it dropped—much like a horse's would—until it hung almost a foot along the side of Mateka's muzzle, and lifting rapidly as he licked along its length.

"You see," Jabari continued, "female hyenas have a very unique clitoris."

"That's a clitoris?" Sheila marveled, having peeked through her fingers.

Mateka paused in his ministrations. "Just don't go to Australia. Their kangaroos have three vaginas." He met with a swift smack to the side of his head, and cowered away until Jabari gave another command. Coming over to Harold, he led the sun bear to a low platform with eye bolts driven into the wood. He then went over to Sheila and led her to the female before returning to Harold.

"You can touch it, if you want," Jabari said. "In fact, it would be beneficial if you did."

"If you could please kneel, Mr. Nehemeier," said Mateka, a paw pressed to the sun bear's lower back just above his tail. Harold hardly noticed and went to his knees willingly. His wife was about to touch another woman sexually for (at least to his knowledge) the first time in her life, and he had absolutely no problem with this. Until the hyena moved his paw it would stay attached to his cock. "Spread to the edges?" Harold went prone.

No one could accuse Sheila of being a shrinking violet, but for a woman of size she sure could make herself appear small without really trying. She got her paw halfway to the odd appendage and drew it away twice, conflict knitting her brow. She even looked Harold's way, as if seeking approval. The sun bear made a "go on" gesture with his free paw and tried to seem like he wasn't champing at the bit to see his prude of a wife do something exciting for a change.

"It does not bite," Jabari said smoothly. "We are in Africa, but it does not bite." Mateka sniggered as he brought a rope around Harold's ankles and secured each one independently to a bolt. As long as no one brought out a blindfold he didn't much care what the hyena did to him.

"Okay then." Sheila's paw shook as she spanned the final inches and swiped the very edges of her pads over the tip of Jabari's clit, which didn't yet seem to have achieved full arousal but still dwarfed Harold's junk. He marveled at the similarities: narrow shaft, blunt tip, not quite straight. "It's warm," was all the corgi had to say.

"Pretend it is a penis," Jabari encouraged. "Ignore my gender and let your desires take over." It sounded like a bunch of psychological bullshit, but it got Sheila stroking, and suddenly Harold had his own personal peep show.

Mateka took Harold's free paw and tugged it toward another eye bolt, forcing him to abandon his dick to avoid bashing his chin on the platform. Only then did he really notice his restraints. He tore his eyes away from the females and asked, "How is this supposed to help me, again?"

"You'll see," Mateka offered cryptically. "Other paw, if you would?" Harold gave it and held himself steady while essentially becoming immobilized on all fours, his erection bobbing away against his belly.

"What do you feel?" Jabari asked the corgi. Sheila looked down dazedly at her paw gliding along the black length. Her other paw went between her legs, her fingers moving with absent purpose.

Harold had always enjoyed watching women pleasure themselves. This time he didn't have to squint at a computer screen. No skipping ahead to the juicy part, no clicking the full-screen icon to avoid ads. Just his wife, dropping to her knees to put the tip of the hyena's sex to her lips. And opening her mouth. And engulfing the head with a skill Harold had forgotten she possessed.

"Oh, my god," he murmured. "That's friggin' hot." His hips stabbed at air, and his belly fur provided a decent tingle. Perhaps the hyenas' idea was to force him to watch? Because that wasn't torture so much as eye candy. *I hope they're not teasing me. That's just cruel.*

For her part, Jabari appeared nonchalant about Sheila's lips and tongue working her over, but she did hold the corgi's head to keep it going. "I had a feeling about you the first time I saw you," she said. "I could smell it." Sheila was too occupied to respond in any meaningful way. "Let it go." And let it go Sheila did, grasping the base to aim the rest right down her throat. She made a sound Harold remembered from their dating days when Sheila would open right up, a technique she'd adopted while with Houston.

Man, he missed the sensation of a good blowjob. He didn't even mind when he felt Mateka's paw slide under his balls and give him a few pity strokes. It started him rumbling something fierce, though.

"You see, Harold likes to watch. I wonder, though, how he would have reacted if he'd opened our bedroom door last night to see me fucking my husband." Jabari showed her teeth again.

The image of Mateka on all fours below Jabari didn't do much for Harold, but when the sun bear replaced him with Sheila it sent him straining against the paw grasping his shaft.

"It would seem the idea is attractive. Mateka does have a very tight hole, Mr. Nehemeier. Perfect for fucking. You might like it if you try." Warmth settled over Harold's tip, Mateka's gender having absolutely no impact on his enjoyment whatsoever. All that mattered was keeping the spark alive, whatever it took. And that spark was very alive thanks to Mateka's tongue. The sun bear struggled within his bonds, not trying to get away but hoping for a better angle and deeper penetration.

However, the hyenas called the shots now, and Mateka would do what he felt like doing and Harold could do precious little about that. He wondered if he had enough room under his belly to squeeze in.

When he looked up again Sheila was standing and the two women had locked lips, north and south. Jabari had two fingers jammed up into his wife, and they looked very wet. Sheila had a breast in each paw, concentrating on turning the hyena's nipples to hard nubs. She made little whimpering sounds with each new penetration.

"You are very good at this," Jabari murmured once they'd parted to take a breather. "Are you sure you did not have any experiences at college?"

"Nothing, I swear…thank you," said Sheila while idly inspecting the pliability of the breast in her paw. "Never even thought about trying. Well, til now."

"Look over at your husband and tell me what you see."

Sheila looked, half-lidded, as Jabari continued to play around her bright pink labia. What she saw was an old fat sun bear with his dick in another guy's muzzle, a slack-jawed expression and no aversion to being tied up. What she said was, "I see more eagerness than I've seen in a long time. I thought we could fix it on our own. Maybe we couldn't."

Harold wondered what would happen once they boarded the plane back to the States. Would Sheila turn back into her old frigid self, or would she give him a chance?

Jabari nodded. "And what do you see, Harold?"

"I see," the sun bear began, grunting as Mateka bottomed out, "something I never thought I would see in a million years. And if she can do it here, I hope she can do it at home too."

"I don't see why not," Sheila admitted, the most positive opinion of the state of their sex life Harold had heard since he'd given up trying so long ago. It sure beat the hell out of all those mysterious headaches that had never been headaches to begin with.

"Then let us see how sexual we can be in front of each other," Jabari said. "If you erase vulnerability, confidence will fill the vacuum. Sheila, if you could go to all fours, please." She very gently pushed the corgi to her knees and Sheila turned slowly as if hypnotized. For having no tail to raise she sure could try.

As Harold watched the hyena pluck a small vial from an alcove carved into the acacia and pour its contents onto her fingers, Mateka withdrew from his cock with a wet slurp and came up for air. "What an interesting scent. I've not had the pleasure of a bear yet. I hope you are looking forward to this as much as I am." Harold wasn't sure what he should look forward to, but if it involved more of the same he certainly wouldn't complain.

Jabari squeezed a good amount onto her fingers and spread it before stroking that appendage she called a clitoris to a size half again as long as the sun bear's dick. Having had his share of penis envy, Harold felt a measure of relief that it was absent this time. He did, however, feel a surge of arousal watching the hyena toss the vial to Mateka and kneel behind Sheila. From her vantage point she had no idea what was about to happen, but Harold did.

Sheila jumped upon first contact, gasping when she realized what was entering her vagina and moaned something that sounded like a drawn-out vowel. Then she uttered, "Oh fuck, oh fuck, oh fuck!" and it didn't matter much anyway.

"Oh, fuck," Harold whispered, entranced. He wished it were him in those velvet folds, by God, and he hadn't even thought about that in years. The possibility that it *could* be him in the future, though…

Mateka came around in front of the sun bear's prone form and kneeled. Soon Harold's view was all balls and tail and hole. Slick hole. *Ready* hole. "What's the big idea?"

"No big idea," the hyena replied, lowering his hips while backing under Harold's chest. "Just a different perspective." Mateka's short stature allowed him to crawl almost completely under the sun bear's belly, his stubby ears flanking Harold's chin. He shifted until the blunt cockhead nestled in the cleft of his buttocks and held still, touching but not joined, their pulses in syncopation. "Ready?" Whether or not Harold was ready, Mateka moved anyway.

Harold sank in with no problem whatsoever, meeting minimal resistance until he felt the hyena's balls against his own. He made sounds unbecoming of a bear of any species, but then again his wife was groaning away while Jabari repeatedly filled her so he was by no means alone. He didn't have much of a say either.

"What's… going on?" Sheila asked between grunts.

"Nothing," Harold said.

"Your husband is deep inside my husband," Jabari informed her.

"Harold's… got his wiener in a tailhole?" The corgi sounded dubious, as if her own situation was acceptable but the sun bear's somehow flew in the face of convention. "I don't believe it."

"Believe it," Harold sighed. "We're going through this together, remember?" Mateka clenched and milked a bit more from the sun bear. "Okay, jeez, that legitimately felt good. God dammit." Encouraged, the hyena began a gentle undulation of the hips that Harold took over after just a few seconds. It felt too good not to.

Jabari pushed in until her hips touched Sheila's. "Tell him what you feel," she said before looking over her shoulder. Her face betrayed little emotion save for that ever-present smile, but they could be in the middle of a dust storm and Jabari would likely still be smiling.

Sheila tried to look over but couldn't quite make it, so she spoke to the empty space in front of her. "It feels good. I mean, real good... almost better than Houston. I didn't even know this was possible..."

"How'd'ya think I feel?"

"Harold, really." There went the Sheila voice again. Even when getting fucked, the woman had the ability to admonish. "Those two nice gentlemen down the street, with that pretty blue trailer? That ferret and the big black wolf? How do you think they do it?"

"Jesus, Sheila, yes. I know about them. You made me take a welcome basket over there, remember?" *Not like they needed any more baskets in that place.* "This doesn't mean anything," he said even as he worked to push deeper under Mateka's tail.

"Okay then." Sheila only took that tack when she figured further prodding was useless. If she let Harold "win" the argument she'd at least planted a seed in his brain and left it to either thrive or fester. Harold knew this, and he worked to push the thought of actually liking sodomy away from merely liking the sensations of sodomy. "God, just like that...no, harder!"

Jabari settled into a rhythm that set the corgi's breasts swinging. The resulting string of vulgarities from Sheila's muzzle told Harold he might want to try the same thing, since it turned his wife into a foul-mouthed whorish version of herself. Towering over her compact body, Jabari's solid curves undulated and rippled, and she looked like a male with boobs from this angle.

Focusing on the place of their joining, he muttered under his breath: "Fuck her."

Mateka rumbled and stiffened when the sun bear pulled on the restraints for a longer thrust. "You are a very good lover, Mr. Nehemeier. I wonder how you would be without the ropes." Harold considered asking that they be removed, but that would entail putting the fun on hold, which just wouldn't do. So instead of thanking the hyena he drove them both forward, finally eliciting a reaction. Mateka yelped but bore back just as hard, so Harold didn't bother asking if he'd caused pain.

Even if he had, he didn't intend on stopping. And to think, they could be in a dull office full of books, lying on couches and talking out their problems.

He wanted badly to crawl over to his wife, knock Jabari to the side and fuck the living daylights out of her. Since that wasn't an option, he started to think about the next time he'd be able to…perhaps later on or early tomorrow morning. The thought of creaming that hole for the first time in years made him drool over Mateka's neck and, since he couldn't think of anything better to do, he clamped down on the hyena's scruff and growled into the short, dusty fur. Mateka didn't mind in the slightest.

The end came swiftly and completely. Watching Jabari "deep-dicking" the stretchable contours of Sheila's sex, he pistoned until he felt the cum flowing up his shaft. He didn't even peak until the third shot, when he gave a thunderous bellow the hyena's fur hardly muffled.

"Oh Harold…" his wife muttered into the decking. "Let it go, honeypot…" Harold's whole body flushed. He sent his cock as deep as it would go and rode the waves, and when he stopped Mateka took over with his magical hips until the sun bear had nothing more to give and popped out, already soft. Perhaps he wouldn't be able to have a second go in one night after all.

Mateka crawled out and turned around to plant a big full-lip kiss on Harold's surprised face. No tongue, which would have been too much, but a solid gesture of gratitude all the same. "Thank you, Harold. You are more than capable. Now, go help your wife." A minute later the ropes were off and the sun bear was crawling across the deck, Sheila watching him with glassy eyes. Harold knew exactly what he wanted.

Without so much as a word he rolled onto his back and slid, mechanic-style, under the corgi. Between her breasts and his belly it was a tight fit, but when his snout brushed past Sheila's clitoris he got a nose full of musk, a hint of corgi overwhelmed by hyena. In the low light he could hardly discern any appreciable detail without his glasses, but he could still see enough to satisfy himself. Besides, he was back here to lick, not too look.

Up close, Jabari's extended clitoris did a pretty good job of mimicking a penis. In fact, it wasn't a mimicry as much as an impersonation. A good ten inches speared into his wife over and over again, slickened by their combined fluids and the lube, which had worked better than anything the sun bear had tried over the years.

His own drive had not diminished in the slightest, which excited him since on an average day he was a one-and-done kind of guy. But he was in a very un-average situation, and that situation kept him horny and on edge. He was unaware of his resurgent erection until Sheila's muzzle clamped down on it hungrily. Harold let out a surprised grunt, hoped Mateka possessed impeccable hygiene, and mashed his tongue up against the corgi's labia. Then he dragged it back over Jabari's shaft. Then he just went to town on both women. Mateka merely watched with a sly grin, while Jabari only hummed into the night air.

With a will of their own, Harold's paws went for Sheila's nipples and tweaked them like he remembered doing when they had honeymooned in Acapulco. She turned into a writhing, bucking, feral thing, mindless and starving for climax. Unimaginable heat poured from their coupling, and the sun bear felt the spasms even before his wife began to shudder all over. Starting as a low moan, it climbed to a fever pitch, turning her canine whine into something akin to a howler monkey on fire. For almost ten seconds it dominated the patio, the cottage, and who knew how much of the resort. All Harold cared about was flogging that nub and trying not to choke on the flood that came shortly thereafter. Even so, his face ended up soaked through to the skin.

"You might want to move," Jabari suggested airily, and he rolled to the side in time to avoid a gusher as she pulled out. If Sheila wanted a horse experience again, she'd sure as hell gotten one. Above him dangled a tube of black flesh whose end still dripped whatever it was Jabari had deposited inside his wife, and it certainly wasn't urine. He remembered reading somewhere that female ejaculation was considered one of life's greatest unsolved mysteries. Even if it were never solved, it was pretty darn hot.

"Sheila," Mateka whispered. "Mrs. Nehemeier?" The corgi fell onto her side, panting with a blank stare. Various parts of her twitched with aftershocks.

"Harold, I think you had better tend to your poor wife," Jabari said while still smiling. "She is a bit shaken up. We will bid you good night." And the hyenas padded into the cottage, holding paws and speaking in hushed tones.

By the time the sun bear found the energy to roll over and speak her name, Sheila had passed out cold, not even bothering to snore. Harold looked toward the cottage and considered trying to wake her, but convinced himself that the floor outside wasn't that uncomfortable after all.

* * *

He awoke not from the rising African sun but from a muzzle diligently coaxing him once more out of his sheath. Opening his eyes to a sea of acacia leaves, the first thing he remembered from the previous night was the warm fuzzy feeling that had preceded unconsciousness. Now that same feeling ushered him into the light of a new day. He looked down his belly to see his loving wife nursing on his cock, enough to surge him to full hardness without the benefit of a pisshard.

Sheila's eyes glimmered. "Morning," she said before deep-throating him a few times.

"Mo-ooornin," he groaned. "I feel hung over. Did those hyenas spike our coffee?"

"You're silly," replied the corgi in between licks.

Harold yawned, noticing he was tied down again at all four corners. "What did you do to my wife? And how did you move me back to the ropes?"

A sly grin crossed the corgi's face, giving it a sinister bent. "I moved them. There're lots more than just the four."

"You *what?*"

"I hope they don't mind. But I saw you sleeping there so sweetly and decided to risk it." This, from the most risk-averse person Harold knew. Hell, all she ever did at casinos was eat off the buffet. While his wife jerked him off in the middle of the deck, he looked toward the cottage but saw no one moving around.

"You know that was in someone's butt last night, right?"

Sheila licked him from sheath to tip, slowly. Agonizingly. He shuddered as much as he was able, finding that the harder he pulled the harder he stayed. What a way to discover a kink. "Butts are cleaner than you think, you know. Houston and I did this all the time." Harold waited for her to wince, to realize her mistake, but when all she did was keep looking at him with those smoldering corgi bedroom eyes his resentment evaporated into curiosity. "I already did it once, so I figured what's the harm in doing it again? Just for a little while."

The sun bear watched languidly as his wife gave his erection more attention than it frankly deserved, given his attitude so far. He decided to ask the obvious question. "How come you never told me about that? Not that ass-to-mouth gets me off, but still."

Sheila came off his dick with a pop. She'd regained some of the youthful glow that had attracted him to her in the first place. "First off, mister, you never asked. Second, since Houston was always the Voldemort of our marriage I didn't see any point in bringing it up."

"Volde-who now?"

"Sorry, it's from my book club. One of those he-who-shan't-be-named things."

Harold started to prepare a defensive snark in his head, but softened it up. "You wouldn't have had to mention him at all though."

"Yeah, but…I can't *erase* him, Harold. He's not this thing in my life that I regret. And when we found out it wouldn't work, we broke up. And then I met you. Who knows what woulda happened if I'd stayed for the horsecock and ignored his personality flaws." She wore a shit-eating grin that told him she was serious behind the levity, so he nodded to give her the deference she deserved. Not like he could move or do much of anything besides listen.

So he listened. "You have a point."

"I do?" The corgi looked incredulous.

"Yeah," Harold said. "I don't know when we grew apart."

"People don't grow apart. They just stop trying." Sheila toyed idly with the sun bear's flagging shaft. "One of us would bring up Houston, and it just broke down from there."

"I don't remember that part."

"I do. Eventually he stopped being the reason, but by then I thought you just weren't interested."

Harold grimaced. "And I thought I could never measure up." He leaned his head back; the leaves above him rustled just barely. Somewhere nearby a bird announced the morning. "And I got complacent."

"We both did, honey. Not anymore, I hope," Sheila said, turning her attention back to the flesh in her paw. It began to swell. She'd always had the magic touch. She emphasized her point by straddling Harold's groin and pressing his head up against her still-slick lips. "You wanna?"

Harold hesitated.

"It's not like you have a choice."

Harold capitulated. Sheila lowered herself slowly, biting her lip and looking twenty-five again, plus a few pounds. "Ohhhh, my god…" Acrimony had tightened her up something fierce. Not Mateka-tight, but pleasantly so. The sun bear fought the impulse to suggest she untie him so he could ravish her properly, but eventually settled back to enjoy the ride. Still, every time he "struggled" against the ropes he came closer to finishing.

"Tight enough?" asked his wife.

"You, or the ropes?"

"Either!" she giggled. When had Sheila *ever* giggled?

"Yes!" he giggled back, adding what little motion he could, which turned out to be just enough to hit her elusive G-spot. They writhed around for a few more minutes, feeding off each other's hormones, until Sheila had another of her seismic orgasms that milked the cum right out of Harold's balls. The release shook them both. Having his seed inside her again just…felt right. He could explain it no other way, and he didn't try to. He just let himself feel good. Because he was tied up and he couldn't do much else. And he was already looking forward to the next coupling.

The sound of soft applause made them both look toward the cottage, where Jabari and Mateka stood in the sliding doorway. "*Vizuri*," said the female. Both were still naked, though their raw sexuality had faded a bit in the light of day. That, plus two orgasms in less than eight hours. "I must say that is exactly what I hoped to see this morning."

Harold grinned, only slightly embarrassed. He had exceeded expectations, after all. "Oh jeez, how long have you been watching?"

"Long enough. To be honest I was expecting to smell you outside our door again sometime in the early hours, but I am pleasantly surprised."

"Yes, very well done," Mateka added. "The first step of many on the way to healing."

"This was nothing," Harold said. "You missed all the talk therapy before she sat on my cock."

Sheila climbed off the sun bear, trailing a stream of seed from Harold's lap across his legs. "Gosh, I hope so. This was fun! I never thought…never in my life did I think…well, *this*."

"Do we even need the rest of the days?" Harold ventured, secretly tugging at the ropes. No one seemed to notice the effort, or the small shudder that followed.

The hyenas came over and each took an end of him to untie. Jabari chuckled. "You can leave anytime you wish," she said, "but one night of lovemaking is not a singular solution. You would benefit from being present and mindful for the next three days. Besides, you are in the middle of Africa on vacation. You should enjoy it."

Wrestling with Harold's ankle-knots, Mateka added, "The rest of the modules shouldn't be as difficult now. I see a gleam in your eyes that wasn't there when you arrived. My heart swells with pride. How about a big Kenyan breakfast to celebrate?"

"I am a bit peckish," Sheila said, nodding.

"Seconded!" Harold chimed in, raising a paw now that it was free. "But I'll be damned if I'm gonna eat like this." He indicated his matted muzzle and groin, rapidly drying to a stiff mess in the warming air.

Jabari helped the sun bear to his feet, showing impressive strength for anyone, no matter the gender. Harold didn't even look at her boobs. They were old news compared to Sheila's impressive double-Cs. "You can find your way to the shower...together, maybe?" She waggled her eyebrows, making the couple laugh just as boisterously as the hyenas' signature hysterics.

"You think it's okay, hon?" Taking his paw in hers, Sheila looked up at him with her big, blue, *gleaming* eyes. Twin azure pools, even.

"You never have to ask permission to join me in the shower." His smile came easily and genuinely. When he crooked his arm his wife hooked herself on and joined him stride for stride.

With any luck, he'd never have to jerk off in the shower again.

Lucid Daydream

Lafitte

"Be careful in there, otter. We aren't responsible if you get into trouble." The bouncer, a gruff bear who could pass as a leather daddy in what he probably thought of as a "tough guy" outfit, handed Shell's ID back to him.

Shell decided against a catty remark and simply entered the club; Evolve, its name like a challenge in neon red outside, asking if you were capable of reaching its pedigree. Such naked cliquishness almost stood at odds with the attention grabbing facade. Most clubs outside of the mainstream tried to draw little attention, lest people too normal wander in and pick fights with whatever subculture hid inside.

Apparently the patrons of Evolve weren't worried about outsiders.

Shell slipped his wallet back into his pocket, a snug fit in shorts tight enough to show his build. He'd kept his coat closed over his skimpy outfit on the way to the club, avoiding the attention of the less open-minded, but once inside he shed the garment and left it at the coat check. Shell felt gorgeous in a tight halter-top with an attached collar, short enough to bare his midriff, and a pair of skin-tight shorts made from some glossy, synthetic material. Leggings and long gloves that nearly covered their respective limbs continued the theme; little fur showing but nothing hidden. Only the otter's short tail remained unadorned.

He was dressed to be flashy, and to advertise what he'd come here for: submission.

Once inside the club Shell had to shield his eyes from the burst of light and color. It was still oppressively dark but everywhere he looked the gloom was pierced with lasers swinging overhead, colored lights whipping over the crowd and sudden explosions of strobe light. Holographic screens hovered in the air, playing animatics along with the pulsing electronic music. Every now and then a projected image would dive from one holographic screen into another, like dolphins at a water show.

Once he had grown accustomed to the light Shell looked for someone to talk to. He felt unusually shy in such an unfamiliar crowd, but he refused to leave empty-handed tonight. Walking up to a pair of felines in a dark corner who stared at him blankly as he approached, Shell gave a friendly smile.

"Hey, I don't suppose either of you knows Lucid?" Shell smiled despite his nervousness; they were patently unsociable. Emotionless as robots.

One of the cats, an androgynous siamese draped in a black leather trench coat, shook his head. The other cracked a disdainful smirk, looking away from Shell as the first spoke, "Lucid isn't a popular choice here."

"Then you do know her?" Shell brightened up at how easy that was.

"No." The other cat, an equally androgynous gray furred girl, couldn't be bothered to look at him. "We mean most of us are high."

Shell moved on dejectedly, remembering the other night at the bondage club. Three Dommes he sometimes played with at a table, distracted from their usual power games with one another, trying to discourage him. He'd gone in asking about sense-hacking, a term he'd seen popping up in forum discussions; some sort of darker, harder version of BDSM born out of cybernetics and hacking.

He slumped on a wall, looking out at the crowd milling about the dance floor and examined his visible fur. It had darkened with his mood, making the e-tattoos beneath all but invisible. With some concentration he managed to lighten his fur so the dark lines could be seen beneath like circuitry. The lines carried power to devices and computing components implanted throughout his body and wired directly into his nerves, allowing the implants at the base of his skull to interact with his body's nervous system.

None of it was all that exceptional, really, but it also wasn't low end either. High enough quality that he refused to engage in any sort of play that could damage them. Electricity was right out, cutting was very dangerous and even a lot of impact play could be a problem. That was part of the reason this sense-hacking intrigued him; it was all in your head, where it couldn't damage you.

To Shell's surprise, a woman approached him. Heavy-set, canine, dressed in some sort of goth dress with a lot of tattered lace. Black make-up that didn't really compliment her well but the goth sorts never cared.

"Haven't seen you around here before." She idly swirled a cup of some oddly shimmering liquor while she spoke.

"I don't suppose you're Lucid?" Shell asked, not exactly hopefully; he could already read this girl as high maintenance.

The briefest moment of surprise crossed her face, quickly enough that Shell wasn't sure it had been there at all, and then it was gone. Instead she glanced at her cup and smiled. "I can be whatever you like, if it'll get you to keep coming back."

"No, it's a name." Shell groaned.

"I know it's a name." She snapped. Suddenly the canine seemed older, more mature, more confident. Her tone had Shell standing at attention before he realized it. He supposed her 'personality' must be an attempt to just have fun. The sort of person who switched their brain off when work ended.

The woman sighed and shook her head. "It's a name that won't help you here, though."

"Another submissive told me to come here and look for them, though." Shell heard an unwelcome whine in his own voice. "Someone here has to know how to find Lucid!"

The woman looked him over and shrugged before turning around and walking away. He'd felt so close… and then nothing! Dejected, he headed for the bar, hoping a drink would soothe his nerves.

Instead the bar just reminded him what it was like to be an outsider somewhere. He'd been going to the bondage club, and just the bondage club, for so long that he'd gotten used to being a familiar face. Now he couldn't get the bartender's attention no matter how hard he tried. There just seemed to be an endless stream of regular customers the rat would rather serve.

Then the bartender froze. Shell saw his eyes move, reading something only he could see. A private text, displayed in his HUD. The bartender looked straight at Shell and came over. With a toothy smile he slid a glass onto the bar and began pouring into it from multiple bottles, too fast for Shell to see what they were.

"On the house." He grinned at Shell, long rodent whiskers twitching. On his pupils some sort of contact displayed swirling fractals. "You seem like you could use it."

Shell accepted the drink. "Was that text about me?"

The bartender was already gone, though, off to serve other customers. Once again feeling like he'd gotten so close but falling short of an answer, Shell went to find an unattended table. He'd finish his drink and then try again… as long as he could keep up his nerves.

Examining his cup, Shell tried to guess what the faintly green mix might contain. The glass displayed an advertisement, floating just around the rim, listing the club's various theme nights. Shell pulled up the code for the advertisement. With a thought, his HUD began displaying his cloud file system. He reached up, tapping through folders, and finally pulled out a small file. He dropped it into the code for the cup and recompiled it. A tiny desert island rendered in his drink, surrounded by a sea of green liquor.

He tilted the glass back and chugged the drink. He wanted sobriety, and its requisite anxieties, to be gone as soon as possible. Normally sobriety was a must in BDSM, but if he found Lucid none of it would be real anyway.

Shell shivered and made a face. The drink was pretty strong, much too strong to take so quickly.

"Why are you looking for Lucid?" A voice behind him. Emotionally flat, raspy like a smoker's and stern like a Dom's. He couldn't determine a gender from it. Shell began to turn. "Keep still and answer me."

The otter swallowed hard. "I heard about you at a bondage club. They said to go to you to find out about sense-hacking."

"That doesn't sound like any of the bondage clubs I've been barred from." The voice sounded almost proud of that.

"Maybe it's one you haven't been thrown out of?" Shell inquired.

"I've been thrown out of all the ones I've gone to, kid."

"Well, they actually told me to keep away from you… and sense-hacking." Shell chuckled. "But they still gave me your name when I wouldn't stop asking."

The mysterious voice laughed then and came around to take the seat across from him. Casually, the mysterious hacker leaned back and put their footpaws up on the table. "I've already checked you out. You don't appear to be a cop or anything like that."

A gray squirrel, a little shorter than Shell but somehow seeming large and powerful. They had an athletic build, no make-up, and hair in a simple pony-tail. Clothed in a plain t-shirt with a baggy coat, all in black, Shell couldn't tell if Lucid had breasts or not. Their feet were bare, not an uncommon choice for species with prehensile toes. The only interesting thing about the squirrel was a pair of thick, flat visor-type sunglasses, giving them an oddly robotic appearance.

Well, that and the fact Shell still couldn't figure out if Lucid was a boy or a girl.

"Not quite what I expected," Shell admitted.

"I don't care what you expected." Lucid's voice was flat, unreadable.

"I just mean, you aren't really dressed up or anything." Shell spoke too quickly, panicked, afraid he'd already screwed up. "I mean, we're at a club, so I thought you'd be dressed up like the other folks here, you know?"

The squirrel just stared at him. He hung his head shamefully. "I'm sorry."

He felt a paw settle on the back of his head, patting gently. He raised his head but Lucid remained silent.

"So then, will you dominate me?" Shell blushed a little, not used to having to be so direct and forward.

Lucid shrugged.

"Should we negotiate our limits?" Despite the shrug Lucid was still there listening to him, so it didn't seem like a rejection.

The squirrel pulled up a window, the holographic frame hovering in the air, though the contents weren't visible to Shell; only the frame. "Feel free to talk."

"Well, I don't really know a lot about this sense-hacking yet, so I'm not sure where to put my lines there. I guess I need a safeword or something like that I can use no matter what's going on." Shell glanced down at his empty cup, feeling the need for a little more liquid courage.

"You would have one." Lucid didn't seem to be inputting any data in the window, just scanning whatever was in there.

Shell nodded, letting the specifics wait until later. "I'm not into bodily waste and nothing that could damage my implants; cutting, beating the areas they are, etcetera…"

After waiting for Lucid to respond, fruitlessly, Shell went on. "And no gender-bending. Seriously. I may be kinda twinky but I am a boy and I want to be treated like one."

Lucid's gaze swung to him, steady, finally paying attention. With a flick of two fingers their hovering window vanished. "Interesting. I guess I will dominate you after all."

Shell swallowed nervously. "Because… of that last bit?"

The squirrel nodded, standing. "You're a puzzle now. Hackers love puzzles."

"Oh… okay." Shell stood as well and followed Lucid's swishing tail, already walking away from him. He couldn't see much of Lucid past the voluminous appendage. "When do you want to do it?"

Lucid remained silent, weaving between bodies, casually silencing friends who tried to speak, and finally pushed open a door in the back of the club. After Shell entered, too, Lucid locked the door with a wave of their hand. He had to wonder if the squirrel was allowed back here, or if this was a display of expertise.

"Get undressed." Lucid flipped on a light switch, illuminating a plush but barren room. It was clean, well lit, carpeted in dark gray, but it contained nothing save for a bench next to the door.

Shell stripped off his gloves and leggings, then his shorts. "Ordering me to do things is kind of tame."

Lucid motioned to his neck and, regretfully, Shell removed the collar and the attached halter-top. Stripping bare was a common exercise for him in the bondage club, not something that even embarrassed him anymore, but being without a collar left him feeling oddly out of his element.

Dropping the collared top onto the pile of clothes he'd already made, Shell folded his arms behind his back and awaited his next order. Instead, Lucid pulled up another window and made a flinging motion with two fingers. A file transferred to Shell in a moment, a window popping up automatically in front of him: *Do you accept this file (unverified)?*

"Run that installer." The squirrel continued tapping away at the window, no doubt readying the programs this session would require.

Shell hesitated. Running a file he knew nothing about could be incredibly dangerous, even if it wasn't coming from an admitted hacker. Anything could be lurking in that code. But, then again, this was the whole reason he was here. He tapped 'accept', and then 'run'. Alerts popped up all over his body, signaled by tiny vibrations under his skin, telling him that files were being installed or altered in his implants.

"I now have backdoors into all of your systems, right down to your nerves. The systems that aid your body, the ones that transmit data, the failsafes and lockouts, everything. You'll be surprised what all is in there." As Lucid tapped a window, text popped up in Shell's HUD, warning him that another user had accessed his systems.

"I thought those systems were closed from network connections, to keep things like this from happening." Shell eyed the warning, once again wondering how good an idea this had been.

Lucid laughed. "Tricky wording. The systems don't, but they're connected to the same systems that let you get online without a ter-

minal. One back door to another… some of them left open intention-
ally. For instance, know what a federal agent would do if you resisted
arrest?"

Shell scoffed; he'd heard the conspiracy theories, as if every exploit
had to be some secret government plot. "I imagine they'd shoot me."

"Lie down." Lucid's finger hovered before the window.

Shell began lowering himself, but moments before reaching the
floor Lucid tapped at the window and suddenly his arms and legs simply shut off. He still felt them, and even felt the white-noise hum of his
data connections still working all over his body, but the signals simply
cut off. He fell the last few inches onto his ass, then slumped onto his
side on the floor.

"One command. Elegant. All those systems and e-tattoos and data
connections, they can feed a false signal into your nerves that cancels
out your natural motor control signals. Quite grand for something that
wasn't planned, huh?" Lucid started pacing around him.

Shell struggled to shift into a more comfortable position while he
watched the squirrel's feet passing through his field of vision. Their
long toes sank into the soft carpet, stopping in front of his face. He
took a deep breath and said, "That's a good point, actually."

"Call up subroutine 'safeword.'" Lucid knelt down, cocking their
head to meet his eyes. "You know how to do that? Accessing systems
with your subconscious?"

Shell nodded, closing his eyes and focusing on the OS running in
his neural implants. The command line appeared on the back of his
eyelids, and he thought the word. A prompt appeared, asking him to
enter a safeword.

"The word you enter will write into the code I gave you. It will
shut me out, return all control to you, and trigger a deinstallation of
the code I gave you. Whatever word you choose, only you will know."
He barely heard Lucid's voice beyond his eyelids, droning like elevator
music.

A safeword should be a term that will never come up in play, ever.
For this, he supposed, it didn't matter that much. He had to run it as

a command, after all, but habits are habits. Shell input his birth name. "Done."

Lucid grabbed his shoulder and rolled him onto his back, limbs flopping like dead fish. The squirrel clambered over his naked body and perched over his belly, fingers dancing over his fur. In their paths small windows popped up over his body, displaying schematics for the various implanted devices beneath his skin. Lines of holographic orange trailed from them to other devices, giving an easy path to follow from one to another.

And then Lucid's fingers stopped, hanging in the air as the hacker's eyes followed one of those lines. It trailed from his sternum down his belly and lower, vanishing into the crotch of Lucid's jeans where they straddled him. Lifting their visored sunglasses, Lucid's eyes met his curiously.

Shell's fur shifted to a deep red in embarrassment. "Please don't ask. That's a line no one crosses."

The squirrel's fingers twitched, downward, threatening at that orange line and the artificial nerves it signified. Not merely augmented nerves... artificial ones.

"I'll safeword." Shell hated saying it so early in their session. He took his resilience as a matter of pride. Holding off as long as possible, hoping not to need his word at all, hoping to impress a Dom who can't push him past his limits... but some things weren't a matter of BDSM.

Lucid pouted at him, waiting for him to change his mind, but finally shook their head. "Fine then. The other direction." Fingers flicking up along his neck, Lucid tilted his head to the side to identify the exact spots his neural implants were sunk into his skull. Different locations for different purposes, to spread out the load and limit the potential for physical damage.

"In scenes, a sub expects to be treated as less than a person." Lucid brushed their finger over a holographic window next to Shell's temple, sending the data scrolling. "A slave, a pet, a child... something like that. You aren't any of those things to me, though. You're a computer."

Lucid looked him over and scoffed. "I never would have made a computer so tacky, though. Color changing fur? Really?"

Shifting back to sit on his lap, Lucid's denim-clad ass pressed against his erection unmindfully. "There was a time that hackers were nothing but computer jockeys, you know. Then computers started creeping into the world more and more, and you know, we got more important and more powerful. We were the new business people, the new rich, the new power in the world and the computers, they just kept infiltrating more and more."

Shell grunted at the squirrel's weight, thankful they were fairly light at least, but even so the pain in his hips was growing hard to handle. "Hackers became legitimate," he wheezed.

Lucid smirked. "We were hackers because we didn't want to be legitimate. We always found a way to get back out of the system, some way to use our skills against the mainstream's desires. But you got me off topic." Leaning back against Shell's erection, the squirrel lifted one leg and pressed their foot to his muzzle. The long, prehensile toes closed around his snout, holding it closed.

"Anyway, then came the day cybernetics really took off. Not just replacement limbs and pacemakers and things that made us a little less broken anymore. No, things that made us better! The computers became a part of us. Now a programmer isn't just powerful, they're a god! And a hacker, well…" Lucid gave him a vicious, predatory smile. "A hacker is the boogieman."

The squirrel's toes unraveled from his muzzle. Shell cracked his jaws. "Is there any reason you're giving me this little history lesson?"

"It was a bad idea putting yourself in my hands." Lucid collapsed all of the windows hovering around his body, rising from his crotch. "And now I've got all the data on you I need. What you can take, where you can take it, and so much more."

Shell let out a long sigh. "Does that mean you'll finally start acting like a Dom?"

Lucid leveled a humorless glare at him. The hacker opened a window, tapped it, and pain crackled through Shell's body. He writhed on the floor, crying silently. And then, abruptly, the pain cut off.

He sobbed on the carpet, longing for the lingering ache that should have been left behind. The artificial pain had felt real but it left none of the artifacts; no burning, no bruising, no dull ache. Aches that became treasures to a sub, orbs of reality and life to cling to. Memories in the flesh.

"I need more…" Shell gasped, eyes wet with tears.

"That was just sort of generic pain. I can do different kinds, though: hot, cold, cutting, impact, electric…" Lucid's fingers traced over the window, and in their wake lines of pain, nuanced just how they had said, slithered their way over his body. The intensity just kept growing until he became numb to it, the sweet depths of subspace beckoning, where the pain would be a thing to observe instead of feel.

Then the pain turned off again. "No… I was so close to subspace!"

Lucid laughed at him. "This isn't like other BDSM. You aren't going to get the same experiences. Why would I want to put my computer into subspace?"

Breath finally evening out, Shell nodded. Lucid was right. There was no point if this was just a new way to get the same experience. He had to try and embrace this new thing he was being offered.

"But it's my fault, I guess. This is just pain, yeah? What about something you can't get any other way." Lucid's window expanded, growing into a 3D space like a graph. Shell could see a wireframe of his own body in it, and Lucid's fingers entered that space, lines running from the fingertips to the wireframe.

Shell's limbs began jerking around, independent of his will, like a clumsy puppet following the hacker's whims. The squirrel wasn't especially good at it, either. His arms would swing, slam into the ground, twist around him and finally, hands splayed palm-up and with a good deal of pain, they finally managed to push him up from the floor into a sitting position. Wobbling, he bent over, legs curling under him, and with a lot of effort he rose from the ground, though only into a hunched position; standing upright would have been a risky thing to attempt.

"This whole puppet thing isn't really necessary." Lucid droned while marching him in a plodding circle, "in fact it was pretty hard to program this interface. I just find this way more fun."

After a few clumsy steps, Lucid seemed to be getting the hang of Shell's body, the movements growing more complex, and once comfortable with the controls they got inventive. Shell's arms twisted behind his back, painfully. He rose onto his tiptoes and stayed there, long after it became unbearable. Then, arms shooting over his head, he leaned backwards. With a bend of the knees, he experienced a short fall, catching himself with his arms over his head, holding himself up in an awkward crab-walking pose.

"Hah, I'm getting better at this!" Lucid cackled, "I didn't think that was going to work."

The exertion finally left the searing pain in Shell's limbs he'd been hoping for. Calm detachment washed over him. As his body crab-walked around against his will and his straining wrists promised days of delicious aches, he felt surrender stealing his will away.

Shell's body went limp, and he fell onto his back with a small wince. Craning his neck around, he looked for Lucid through his detached haze. Still in the same spot, staring at the 3D window, the squirrel gave him a meaningful look. "So you know all about artificial nerves, I guess. But that whole system is pretty exploitable, too. You have nodes that interpret the data from your nerves, real and false, but the false ones only transmit to the nodes. The nodes then transmit to your actual nervous system. So I can give you completely false nerve data."

Blinking, Shell tried to respond but there seemed to be too many steps between where his mind was now and that.

"You maybe think, 'of course, like the pain'. But oh no, this is nothing like that. Well, it is, but the results aren't. For instance…" Lucid opened another window, pulled out a bit of code, and dropped it into the matrix. What looked like an arm appeared in the wireframe and the Dom maneuvered it onto his body. And just like that, the sensation of an arm appeared growing out of his stomach, flopping around, groping and exploring its environment while a matching image, shimmering in that not-quite-real way everything projected into a HUD did, reached out from his belly.

Shell squirmed as well as he could. He felt a strange panic welling up from the back of his mind, like seeing a severe injury or mutation, but seeing it in his own body instilled a panic he'd never felt before. That arm was alien, dangerous… and he couldn't shake the feeling it was corrupting him somehow. With a struggling whimper he managed to find his voice. "I don't like this, Master."

"I don't care." Lucid was pulling out more files.

Wings then, an almost pleasant experience besides the shock of it. Then a tentacle from his shoulder, an extra tail, another arm… Lucid was just grabbing pre-coded maps of limbs, or at least the nerves, and plugging them on almost randomly. Shell groaned in the confusion of it all and began to understand the appeal; his personhood really was being stripped away. He was becoming a thing… and it was amazing. All of that panic transformed into something surreal, a whole new level of surrender.

And then there were breasts. The feeling wasn't intense, just a bit of weight and a different shape to the chest. Many subs might not have noticed them among all the other strange sensory inputs. Shell did.

"No…" he whimpered.

Then the fake limbs assaulted the breasts. Hands groped, tentacles wrapped around them, wings curled inward to brush feathers ticklishly over the nipples. The pleasure of it was undeniable, though the sensations were overwhelming and the eroticism only made his discomfort worse.

"No!" Shell growled between deep, gasping breaths. "I'll safeword!"

Immediately the phantom limbs stopped moving. Lucid's finger hovered over a button, some sort of pause, and gave him a measuring look. "Will you, though?"

Shell stared back silently, trying to look as fierce as possible. "I told you, no gender play."

With a shrug the squirrel hit another button and the fake limbs vanished. His mind railed at the sudden loss of sensation and sometimes he felt flares of those phantom limbs, as if they were still there. Lucid collapsed the 3D window and paced over to him. "Fine then. But you're going to have to make it up to me, you know?"

With a relieved sigh Shell's nerves settled. "As long as it's not gender play."

"Ever done sensory deprivation?" The squirrel knelt down next to him, bushy tail wavering behind, pulling windows up from his implants again.

"Uh, no." Shell chewed his lip nervously. "I guess a blindfold sort of counts… sort of."

Lucid smiled down at him and with a few taps Shell's sense of feeling vanished.

"Removing touch is a simpler thing than you'd think. Feedback interference, using the nodes to block the sensory data from reaching your brain at all. This would cause a sort of phantom limb effect for your body, but the nodes can also feed an interference signal to your brain, keeping that part of your mind just distracted enough not to process anything. The same scripts that let you dull pain for improved functioning can be used to just block out everything, basically."

With a little more work he suddenly realized he couldn't taste or smell anymore. "Let's get the boring ones out of the way. Those mechanical ear drums may never burst or lose hearing, but turn them off and you don't even get vibrations from your own body to hear. And your taste buds, that's just a simple interference signal sent to the right neural receptors." Lucid collapsed most of the windows scattered around his body, then did a little more work and sound vanished. He was nothing but a floating, helpless viewpoint. No body, no voice, no means of interacting with the world.

And then everything disappeared. It was like floating in darkness… only there was no floating. There was no him, no thing to float and no place for it to float. He was only a series of thoughts, some on the surface, some deep and flowing uncontrolled, while he was something that observed this swirl of ideas.

He may not have ever done sensory deprivation but Shell had read about it… and was somewhat frightened by it. He'd read you started going a bit insane pretty quickly, especially as time lost meaning and minutes felt like hours. But he'd also read one's own heartbeat and breathing and sloshing stomach became deafening sounds when nothing else was there, and he didn't even have that.

There was no him to hold his mind together.

With that startling realization Shell felt his thoughts slipping away. The deep, unbidden ones that whispered in the back of his mind started swimming further and further out. The ones so deep that they weren't even in words seemed to drift from the core, insubstantial as a cloud of gas. Even his own, active thoughts and the part of his mind that observed it all seemed to be pushing away from each other.

And as his own mind grew quieter, Shell struggled to hold onto his sense of self at all.

He was just a blip in the darkness, searching for the rest of itself.

Bare feet dragging along the ground. He felt them, clear as day. They weren't dragging on the carpet in the club, though… it felt like dirt and gravel. Then he could feel the hands under his arms, carrying him. The soreness of his back and hips came next, awkwardly supporting his weight while his body was moved roughly.

Then he could hear the slow scrape of his heels on the hard-packed dirt. He could hear Lucid's footsteps on the ground. He could hear the wind, insects, birds… and the distant sounds of a city night. Too distant.

A door opened, and he felt rough floorboards under his heels. He smelled. First his own sweat, then the musty and dank building he'd been taken to. Next came the taste of his own mouth. Normally it was unnoticeable but after so long with nothing it tasted incredible.

Then he could see. He was in a small, run down building. Clearly outside the city, on some back-road somewhere. The place was mostly empty, dirty, dark… no one seemed to be taking care of it. The sort of place one did things they didn't want anyone to ever know about.

Lucid stepped into his line of sight. "How dare you tell me what not to do? You want to be a sub but still call all the shots? This isn't a fucking game!"

One bare foot kicked him in the ribs, knocking the breath from his lungs. "All of you pathetic, whiny fakers at those stupid clubs with all your rules. A real Dom doesn't let the sub be in control! But you all hang out in your little clubs, telling each other you're the real deal. You come to a real Dom and you know what interest they have in your rules?"

The squirrel knelt down, putting their muzzle close to Shell's ear, and whispered, "I only want to know your rules so I can break them."

Shell's fur shifted to stark white as fear overcame him.

Lucid's fingers slid over his chest and a window opened. The orange line of artificial nerve data rose up again and the squirrel's fingers followed it down to his soft cock.

Limbs still disabled, Shell struggled and whimpered to get away. He wasn't sure if this was part of a dominance game or not anymore, and he didn't want to stop if it was still just fun. But… where was he? How long had it been? Why had Lucid taken him here?

Shell froze as he realized his life might actually be in danger.

A window popped up in the air over Shell's crotch. After scanning the information briefly, Lucid smiled wickedly. "I thought so. It could have been reparative surgery, but I thought not, and I was right! You had a sex change!"

Shell hissed out an angry breath. "Why won't you drop that, you fucking creep!"

The back of a paw slammed into his face, much harder than it looked like Lucid should be capable of, and Shell's ears rang. Then the hacker casually turned off the nerves to Shell's penis. One moment it was there, and then it wasn't. The pit of his stomach sank and he felt like he might throw up.

"I've only read about these. Things used to be so complicated for trannies, huh? But now, you get some vat grown organ, some cybernetic implants and artificial nerves, and it's as good as the real thing!" The squirrel's eyes turned on Shell. "But it's not real. It's as artificial as the internet. That's what black-hat hacking is all about, you know? Reminding people that their sense of security is an illusion. The places you feel safe are really just playgrounds for people like me."

"I don't want this." Even as far as things had been pushed, and Lucid had pushed things incredibly far, Shell felt sad to let this Dom down.

Opening a window, Lucid pulled out a file that unpacked into a floating nerve layout. The shape was clearly a vagina. Then out came the breasts from before. "Isn't that the point?"

Shell sighed and nodded. As rude as Lucid was being, it was mostly ignorance behind the disrespect the squirrel was showing him. Besides, the disrespect was sort of turning him on, too. Though he was still nervous about it he just didn't want this scene to end. "I'll try… if you don't push it too far."

Lucid pulled out the 3D matrix again and dropped in the false organs. Suddenly the weight of breasts were back as well as the faint, unstimulated bundle of nerves he'd hoped never to feel again.

"You really miss it, don't you?" Lucid's fingers ran over the false breasts, their shape displaying over his body. They looked like a special effect, not quite real, but he felt the touch to them like they were real. "I'm sure you like your cock but don't you deep down still long to feel what it was like to be someone's little girl again? You must miss it, right? Even just for the sake of variety."

Closing his eyes, Shell took a deep breath. He could handle this. He'd had sex before his transition, after all, and none of this was real. He didn't want that but he'd also been clear they couldn't go too far with this gender play. Besides, the fear was really turning him on. Even though he couldn't feel his cock anymore, he could see a bobbing erection that matched his own excitement. Blood flow did its job regardless of nerves.

One of Lucid's paws slipped between his legs, stroking where the labia would be. Not even a scar was left on his real body, but he felt those lips tingling under the squirrel's fingers. The feelings were intense and undeniably pleasurable, so he just tried to enjoy it.

Panic was screaming from the back of Shell's mind, though. So many years of hiding, shame and self-loathing wouldn't allow him to enjoy this. Blind, animal panic forced his body to resist, to try to escape, flopping like a worm. It was useless, though; there was no way he could escape this hateful pleasure. He just hoped the hacker would get bored of this soon.

Lucid watched his face scrunch up in concentration and repression and laughed. "I could put a fake dick on myself and fuck you. That would be interesting."

Shell shook his head as Lucid pulled out the nerve map for a penis. The squirrel laughed again. "That only makes me want to do it more, though!"

"I'll safeword." Shell tried to look as stern and confident as he could. "I still mean it. I've let you get away with too much already."

Lucid gave him a long, humorless stare. "I could just disable it, you know. I gave it to you. Did you really think you could trust it?"

Shell stared at the hacker, uncertain but uncompromising.

"Fine, we'll have a little game of it instead." The squirrel's jeans and panties dropped to the floor, revealing a softly furred vaginal mound. Lucid attached the nerve map for a penis into her own pelvis and the shape of an erect cock rendered over the mound. "I'll try to make you want it, ok? I'll only use it if you beg for it."

Having the mystery of Lucid's gender solved seemed unremarkable now that Shell knew. Perhaps because it would play no part in their interactions, or perhaps the mystery had simply been more interesting than the reality. He thought about making a comment but reconsidered, and instead nodded. "Fine, if I beg for it then you can use it."

The otter whimpered as Lucid knelt at his side, grinning down at him despite his fear. Her fingers slid over his body, and as they passed lines of fire burned. He felt them and saw the licking flames, again not quite real looking, leaving trails of pain on his flesh. Lucid wound these around his belly, up between the false breasts, and over his shoulders.

Then the squirrel's touch changed to lines of ice and traced around his arms and legs, leaving holographic frost on his fur. Another moment later and electricity crackled from those fingertips, tracing over his cheek and down the bridge of his nose.

Then the other paw tapped his cock tip, a spark arching to his urethra, traveling down the shaft and leaving his balls shivering. The nerves had been reactivated just for that and then they were gone again. He snarled at the cheap trick, not even telling him she was going to reactivate the organ.

"I'll stop if you let me fuck you, girlie." Lucid whispered in his ear, attempting to sound sweet.

At Shell's silence the sensation changed again. As the flames smoldered into lines of smoke and the frost thawed, Lucid's fingertips felt like they were cutting into his flesh, deeper than claws could reach. A line of knives, dancing like ballerinas through his skin.

Shell gritted his teeth and thought, *It isn't real.* But really… he wasn't sure anymore, was he?

A whimper rose from his lips and Lucid placed a finger there, hushing him and leaving the sensation of a split-open lip in its wake. "Are you ready yet?"

The otter shook his head again, licking his lip and feeling relieved he didn't taste blood; one part of the illusion that had not been included.

"Then let's turn this up." She gave him a broad smile.

Shell tried to ask what that meant, but as his mouth opened water flooded in. With unreal pressure it forced its way up his nostrils and down his windpipe, burning in his lungs like fire. His vision blurred as adrenaline flooded his veins, a warning popping up in the corner of his visual field, and he gasped for breath hungrily. Trying to ignore the growing ache in his chest, Shell puzzled over whether this was actually dangerous; was he breathing normally, but just thought he wasn't? Or did the belief he couldn't breathe rob him of those precious breaths? And more worrisome, did the reality of those breaths really keep him safe? He didn't know enough about this situation to really be sure, and that only made the panic more visceral.

Lucid grinned at his terrified reaction. "A bit more exciting than breath play, huh? But for some real fun, let's try something truly new."

With a tap to her window, Shell's skin burst into blinding flames and, as he watched, the fires consumed him. For several long minutes he felt the inferno devour flesh, so long he had to wonder if real flames would have destroyed his nerves by now. And yet the drowning also continued, his throat gulping in painful spasms for air. Limbs and torso scorched down to blackened remnants clinging to bones. Skin curled and flaked, then blew away. And even when he could see the empty ruins of a rib cage, through eyes that felt dried to dust yet could still see, he felt the water burning in them anyway.

The otter's mind couldn't make sense of the contrary sensations, and that bred a fear beyond anything he'd felt before now. A fear greater than the nagging thought he might actually die in this abandoned building. The terror he felt came from the animal instincts at the back of his mind, the part that could never understand illusions, and was certain the world had gone completely insane. Or else, he had.

The squirrel blew a kiss, and a smear of lipstick flew through the air like an old cartoon, and when it struck him the pain faded. Skin grew back all over his body, and the new lungs gasped in a deep breath. That stupid, animal part of his back-brain clamored praise for the magic squirrel that had saved it. Shell growled to himself, trying to find some way to argue against his own mind.

"I am your god now, boy." Lucid leaned in, smiling excitedly, and whispered, "But I don't have to be a cruel god. Are you ready to offer yourself up as sacrifice?"

Pulling in a deep breath to his hungry lungs, Shell squeaked out, "Never."

Lucid's tongue clicked in annoyance, fluffy tail whipping. "Fine. Let's try something different."

The squirrel's fingers moved to his head, just behind the ear, and pulled out a window. With a few taps his body went dead. All of a sudden he couldn't feel anything, not even the false body parts. He could see the breasts on his torso, the line where the projection met his real body, meshing clumsily, and he was almost relieved not to feel them anymore.

And as Shell watched, Lucid's paws started moving over his body again. At first it was just gentle caresses, weaving through his fur like ripples of water. The lack of feeling was disconcerting, though, and it was beginning to disturb him. He longed for feeling and, in fact, the entire practice of BDSM seemed suddenly very pointless without it.

Then Lucid slid her fingers over his penis. The organ was soft now, deflating with the lack of feeling, but with a couple of taps to a window it erected itself. That function was partially cybernetic, giving him greater conscious control over getting aroused and resisting it, which also made the process easy for the hacker.

Lucid jerked him off languidly, grinning devilishly up at him. After a while the squirrel brushed her lips against his cock, or maybe only almost touched it (he couldn't really be sure). Lucid licked along the length and, again, he was denied the pleasure of it.

He lay motionless on the ground, mind crying out to squirm and twist and thrust while he gave out a high-pitched whine. Even though he'd come here to be abused he'd much, much rather have pleasure over nothing. But he knew what it would cost… and this wasn't a game he was willing to lose.

Or so he kept telling himself. In the back of his mind, another voice was speaking. *It would be short… simple… pleasurable even. You've done it before, long ago; you can handle it again. Please your master and break out of this cycle.*

But Shell knew that once that door was opened it wouldn't close. It was like that with secrets, especially ones about sex; once someone knew there was some potential, some activity, some fetish locked away inside you, they fixated on it. They wanted it. Being denied that would drive them mad… especially if it was something they really did desire.

Besides, if Lucid could let someone keep their secrets and their security, she wouldn't have been a hacker. That realization struck Shell like a fist.

He only realized he was orgasming when Lucid's chuckle pulled his attention back, white seed spraying over the squirrel's furless fingers. She cleaned it off on his belly fur, leaving the mess for him to worry about. "Still haven't given in, huh?"

Reaching back up behind his ear, Lucid returned the feeling to his body. He still couldn't feel his cock, though, spent and dribbling on his thigh. Then he felt Lucid's fingers sliding over his taint and felt the bloom of sensation in the false labia that had been placed there.

"No!" Shell was shocked at how loud he said it. His whiskers bristled, his lips were drawn back in a snarl and he growled low; he'd won that little game, damn it, and he shouldn't have even had to!

The back of Lucid's paw slapped across his muzzle and he was actually happy to have the familiar sting; finally something like the BDSM he was used to. He suspected Lucid would be annoyed to know that.

"I keep telling you, bitch, don't tell me what to do! You want to get me really angry? You want to see what I can do when I'm pissed?" Her left paw reached out and tapped the floating window, then her right paw plunged through the false breasts. Rather than feeling the flesh press flat, like the programming had previously done, it molded around her hand like putty… and kept going, past where his real chest should be. He wondered at how she managed the illusion of that, with her real limb, but then he felt the squirrel's fingers around his heart. She squeezed the organ and his body convulsed. She pulled, and the beating lump lifted out of his skin, veins trailing back into the putty-like breasts.

"You know I can mess with this thing, too? I mean, obviously this is a projection but I could interfere with your heartbeat. It's tricky, but there's lots of backdoors in these cybernetics I could do all sorts of terrible things with. Would you enjoy having your heart stop for a few seconds?" She plunged the throbbing muscle back into his chest and he gasped in pained relief.

"Now maybe think about who you're saying 'no' to." Her paw was inside his body again, sliding down his torso where ribs should be, then his stomach, and the feeling of those bones and organs making way was sickening. As her hand finally left his body, it caressed the false vagina from the outside, stroking it like a pet. Just as her fingers exited his flesh, the tips slid over the labia from his exterior.

Shell didn't make the threat this time. He hoped Lucid wouldn't realize what he was doing in time to block his safeword. He just closed his eyes, brought up the console on his eyelids, and thought the safe-word. *Shelly.*

Suddenly he felt his spent cock against his thigh, dribbling into his fur; the dull ache of release without the euphoria that usually came with it was vexing. Worse was the sudden vanishing of the breasts and labia, the sudden shift in sensation leaving him dry heaving, curling into a ball while his limbs came back under his control. All four ached like they'd been beaten.

All of the lines of pain painted on his body were simply gone and his mind reeled at this, itching lines along their paths demanding he confirm that there really was no damage. In the mix of sensations his vision blacked out, like he'd stood up too fast.

Then he noticed the musty smell of the old shed was gone. The distant sounds of the city had been replaced by loud, thudding music. As his vision returned, he saw that he was still in the back room of the club, right where he'd collapsed when his limbs stopped working.

Never in real danger.

Well, not that kind of danger.

Lucid drew her paw back quickly when he began moving around. The hacker clicked her tongue in annoyance. "I can never find a real sub. Just you lousy fakers who can't let go of control."

The squirrel turned around, tail swishing as she stalked out the door, leaving him alone.

Shell took a few moments to calm down. Taking deep breaths, he stretched his aching limbs and gathered his clothes, redressing quickly and sloppily in his eagerness to leave the club. He just had to accept the semen in his fur and smearing inside his clothes. The fluid on his belly would show in the club's lights and he'd simply have to live with that.

Pushing the door open cautiously, he hurried out once he was sure Lucid wasn't nearby. He heard laughing, voices calling after him in mocking tones. Some of them belonged to those he'd talked with when looking for Lucid, now snickering. More than a few clearly knew exactly what had happened. For all he knew, they might have been getting a live feed of it.

Shell stopped at the coat check, foot tapping impatiently while he waited to get the garment back. As soon as it was in his hands he wrapped himself up tight, the cloth feeling like armor.

When Shell got out the door he was thankful the bouncer, this late in the evening, had gone inside. Alone, he leaned against the wall, resting his forehead against it, and just cried.

He heard a ding and his HUD notified him that his credit card had been charged for the drink he'd been given. An attached note said, *You didn't earn it.*

Shell pushed himself off the wall and shivered. He didn't know how Lucid had gotten access to his card but he had to wonder, would changing his card information be enough to stop her, or would it only make the hacker more annoyed? He'd think about that in the morning.

All he knew was that he didn't want anything to do with Lucid again, whatever that took.

As Shell turned around he found himself in the backroom again, alone and naked.

Disoriented, Shell returned to the door. Had the shock of the experience caused him to hallucinate? Was he dreaming?

He opened the door to find the club just like last time. People were still laughing at him. The coat check still seemed to take too long. The bouncer still wasn't outside. And just as Shell turned to leave…

Shell was in the room again.

This time, out in the club, he tried to approach the laughing strangers, but they sank away from him no matter how hard he tried to reach them, leaving him forever in a hollow circle, facing mockery from every side. He finally left again, and carefully kept his eyes in the distance, down the street, keeping his goal in view.

Shell's vision warped and again he was in the room. All the colors around him just swirled and dimmed until they took the shape again. He slumped down, back to the wall, and just started crying. Whatever was happening, how would he even know when it had ended? He could try to leave a hundred times and wake up here again and still not know… because surely his body was still in that room, in some sort of stupor?

Working up some courage, Shell stepped out of the room again. He screamed at the patrons. He threw chairs at people who always managed to step aside. And the mockery never stopped.

He felt the bouncer's hand on his shoulder and heard the gruff man's voice near his ear. "Hold still. Your system is rebooting, but if you keep panicking the reboot will cancel. Safety feature."

Shell held still, breathing deep, wondering if this was another part of the hallucination. But as he waited the club's image began to corrupt. The figures stopped moving. The audio skipped and froze. Then everything went dark.

Lines of code appeared behind his eyelids. A system boot, just like the bouncer had said.

After a few moments Shell could, again, see the backroom around him. He was laying naked on the carpet, a wire stuck to one of his e-tattoos like a hospital monitor. The bouncer sat beside him, tapping keys on an old fashioned computer tablet.

The bear looked over at him with clear relief as Shell let out a low groan. "Oh thank goodness… you're lucid again! I was afraid I'd have to call an ambulance."

Shell choked at the word before realizing the bouncer didn't mean it as a name. Gathering his nerves, Shell asked, "What happened? I safeworded…"

"You shouldn't have messed with hackers. What they told you was a safeword actually started a simulation. It activates the same signals a dream would so your mind doesn't question it too hard, unlike projections. The method is usually used to custom build drug trips without the actual drugs, but it's just as easy to write a bad trip. A little nightmare for those that fail them."

The bouncer gave Shell a reassuring pat on the head. "You're not the first to fall victim to one. We keep this around so no one has to directly link into the victims, lest we get attacked by the programs, too. All we can do is reboot their systems and try to scrub out the newest applications added."

"How do I know…" Shell stretched aching limbs, the pain as much from laying still so long as from the abuse. "How do I know I'm actually out?"

The bouncer just shook his head. "Can't tell you. But you've been back here a while, kid. Bar's been closed for an hour. We only found you when we came to clean up. I hate to do it to you but you need to get out of here."

Shell nodded, gathering up his clothes. He went back into the unattended coat check himself to retrieve his own and left without another word.

As Shell walked home he thought about what to say at his usual club, the next time he was there. How could he really put this into words? A flat description wouldn't do justice to how horrible the experience had been. It might even sound exciting.

It dawned on him, then, that this is probably what happened to the person who gave him Lucid's name… and if faced with another naive, pushy sub all he could do is tell them the same.

Lucid.

Out of curiosity he checked his notifications; he really had been charged for that drink. Honestly, not much of a surprise.

About the Authors

Patrick "Bahumat" Rochefort
www.rochefortwrites.com
www.twitter.com/rochefortwrites

Patrick "Bahumat" Rochefort is a professional writer with a background in occupational health and safety and education. In his scant spare time, he takes breaks from writing training programs and ad copy to write speculative fiction, science fiction, and fantasy. He finds his work inspired by grotesque and beautiful questions of "What if?", and writes about the futures he hopes his children will live to see, or about the futures he hopes they'll never have to witness. He occasionally writes erotic fiction centered around happily flawed people and their happily flawed hearts.

Dark End
www.furaffinity.net/user/darkend
www.twitter.com/darkendwrites

Dark End is the pen name of a shy and soft-spoken writer from the Midwest, who drinks a bit too much coffee and writes a few too many tragedies. His stories have appeared in *Heat* and *Hot Dish* with a few more expected to appear in upcoming Rabbit Valley anthologies. He also works as an editor and proof-reader at Sofawolf Press.

Dark's story in this volume was inspired by a simple question: how might furries react to the ways that humans fetishize aspects of animals?

Slip-Wolf
www.furaffinity.net/user/slip-wolf/
https://slip-wolf.sofurry.com/

Slip-Wolf has been active in the furry scene for over three years, and has put on performances in *Heat* Issue 11 and 12 for Sofawolf, *Dungeon Grind*, *ROAR* 6 and *FANG* 6 for FurPlanet, and *Trick or Treat 2: Historical Halloween* for Rabbit Valley. He has other narrative scenes in anthology dungeons to be performed in the following years and hopes his editorial masters will remain pleased.

While dealing with the conflict between pent-up sexual desire and the need for mutual support that keeps healthy relationships going, the story "Mustard Mulato" was primarily inspired by the games played in museum art scenes. It was a fun idea to play with how sex is turned into a commodity and the myriad ways viewers might interpret such a piece, none of which are ever wrong, as the viewer plays the role of the domineering master and the art-piece ever a leashed subordinate, begging for approval. And so this tale begs for yours.

Ocean Tigrox
ocean.sofurry.com
www.fangsandfonts.com

Ocean Tigrox is a writer and editor hailing from the Western prairies of Canada with dual citizenship in both Alberta and Saskatchewan. Never far from his headphones, he's often found shaking his stripes to his love of EDM while writing up another story. His favorite genres to write are action and adventure based: pulp, noir, or a good futuristic sci-fi. Along with storytelling, the purple Tigrox also enjoys motorcycling, travel, games of all varieties, and expressing strong opinions about his hatred for winter to all who will listen.

Ocean is the lead cat herder, editor, and co-host of the furry writing podcast Fangs and Fonts (fangsandfonts.com). He is the lead editor of *Inhuman Acts*, a collection of anthropomorphic noir stories. You can find some of his published works in such anthologies as: *ROAR 6, The Furry Future*, *Furtual Horizons, A Menagerie of Heroes*, and *PULP!* Sometimes he posts things on SoFurry (ocean.sofurry.com). To hear his random ramblings and writing updates, follow him on Twitter: @ TigroxTales and @OceanTigrox.

Laura "Munchkin" Lewis
https://twitter.com/MunchkinRambles
www.munchSized.LiveJournal.com

A munchkin cat in 'sona and a dwarf in truth, Laura "Munchkin" Lewis has learned to embrace all of life's 'shortcomings'. She was born in Hawaii, raised in SoCal, grew up in NorCal, died in Indiana, and was reborn in Washington where she finally met her better half. She also met friends there who encouraged her to finally write the stories in her mind for other people to enjoy.

Laura's works can be found in *Furtual Horizons* with the story "Tech Flesh" and *ROAR* 6 with the far shorter story "The Cat Thief". She is piecing together an anthology about the many shapes of love titled *Fragments of Life's Heart* with her coeditor Mr. Mandolino. She is also working with a small group on a non-for-profit poetry collection titled *Civilized Beasts*.

This story took on a life of its own. It grew into a love child created by the original intent of the freedom open communication can bring and the idea that home isn't a location, but the people you love.

Ava Herries

http://www.furaffinity.net/user/avaherries/

Ava got into writing in college when an English professor was kind enough to convince her it was something worth pursuing as more than just a hobby. During an independent study with him she wrote and completed her first novel. Ten years later, that novel is still trunked and Ava is now working with two separate writing groups on new and drastically better projects. She enjoys most genres but is very fond of horror and dark fantasy/scifi and always finds herself drifting back to those no matter what. Outside of writing, she does a little art when the mood strikes and has a lot of interest in webcomics.

Ava enjoys exploring the mind of a character indulging in whatever gets his or her heart pumping, especially anything that involves the complexities of powerplays. BDSM has so much possibility, and the added science fiction setting resulted in such a fun playground that she's planning another project to utilize it further.

Chastity Chatterley

Chastity Chatterley writes furry erotica and racy steampunk. Her novelette, "The Gentle Monster" appeared in *Hot Dish*. You can find more information on her blog, Lady Chatterley's Chat Parlor: http://ladychatterleyschat-parlor.blogspot.com/

Under her other author name, she has sold over 80 short stories to fantasy and science fiction markets. Her award-winning, werewolf romance novel, *Silent Moon* was published by Soulmate Publishing and is available on Amazon. More information can be found at: www.sarinadorie.com

Tarl "Voice" Hoch

A complete list of his works can be found at: https://www.goodreads.com/author/show/5759304.Tarl_Voice_Hoch

He can be found on Twitter @voicespider and on Facebook at: https://www.facebook.com/TarlWriter

Tarl "Voice" Hoch is primarily a writer of horror and erotica. From his lair in Alberta, Canada, he spends most of his time writing, reading, harassing his feline overlords (both 2 and 4 legged) or exploring the kinky side of life. The subject of BSDM is one of significant interest to him as it plays a part in his personal lifestyle. He finds it interesting due to the sheer variety and creativity one can find within the community, as well as the ability to play erotically without resorting to outright sex. It is something that you can let yourself go fully while in a safe environment with a person or people you trust. (none of this 50 Shades crap)

Tarl's works can be found in the original *Will of the Alpha, Taboo*, and *FANG* Volume 5, all published by FurPlanet. He was also head editor of the horror anthology *Abandoned Places*, also by FurPlanet.

StormKitty

https://stormkitty.sofurry.com/
http://www.furaffinity.net/user/stormkitty/

StormKitty, a furry fan from the US Midwest, first dabbled in furry erotica in 2002 when he wrote A Private Heaven. Since then he's been turning out a story now and then whenever he gets the urge to write about some kink or another. His first published work appeared in the *Taboo* anthology in 2014.

StormKitty has long been fascinated by the exchange of power that underlies BDSM play. Why would someone give up their will and their body to another, to serve or be restrained by them? What could be going through their head when engaging in such activity? It is a central theme in many of his stories, including his contribution to this anthology.

Whyte Yoté
www.furaffinity.net/user/whyteyote/
www.twitter.com/WhyteYote

Whyte Yoté has been writing erotic furry fiction since 1995 when he was probably far too young to be doing such a thing, and he has been seriously pursuing his craft since 2000. His works have appeared multiple times in *FANG, ROAR* and *Heat* magazine, as well as the anthologies *X, The Fortune Teller's Poem, Holidays, Will of the Alpha* and *Trick or Treat.* When he's not writing, he… oh wait, nevermind. He juggles personal work with anthology submissions as well as commissions and collaborations.

Kansan by birth, South Dakotan by serendipity and Californian by convenience, Whyte Yoté currently lives in Sacramento with writer/graphic designer Tym, his forever boyfriend since 2004.

Marriages carry their share of obstacles and troubles, but misunderstanding and complacency are easily-avoidable poisons often ignored, to both partners' detriment. Sometimes all it takes is a little spark to reignite that fire; sometimes not even years in therapy can heal the wounds. I wanted to illustrate a relationship in crisis, and the unorthodox solutions to which people turn when they're both desperate and stubborn to rekindle the love that brought them together in the first place. And when the therapists decide to join in… well, whatever floats your boat.

Lafitte
www.furaffinity.net/user/Lafitte
www.robur.sofurry.com

Co-editor of the very tome you now hold, Lafitte spent many years studying literature in Academia and earned a Master's Degree in English. However, his primary interest is in less traditional forms of writing: genre fiction, comics, pornography, etc. He doesn't see any reason these forms and topics aren't worth serious consideration. Lafitte also dabbles in art on occasion.

Rechan
http://www.furaffinity.net/user/rechan/
https://twitter.com/molewords

Rechan has been in his lab for the last year working on this book and the one before it, *Will of the Alpha 2*. The mole has organized a plethora of bondage and eroticism for your reading pleasure, and now that it's done, he can nap.

In between engaging in the mad science of editing, the mole writes erotica, fantasy and horror. You can find his creations in *Taboo, Dungeon Grind, ROAR 6, Abandoned Places*, and Sofawolf's *Heat* magazine. In addition, he has stories on his SoFurry and FurAffinity accounts.

The first *Will of the Alpha* was started because Rechan wanted to see a publication exploring the many facets of the kink community and the stories that could be told from it. The enthusiasm shown to the first volume encouraged him to open the door for more. He is most intrigued by the power exchange and mental elements of D/s, humiliation and objectification, and many smaller aspects and kinks. This interest is all due to a wonderful accident during a Theatre Arts class, but that's a story for another time.